Liverpool-born **Abbey Clancy** is one of the UK's most in demand models. She successfully combines being a wife and mother with her career as a presenter and model. She is a UK brand ambassador for many top brands including Matalan, Reebok and Avon. Abbey is married to Premiership footballer Peter Crouch and has two small daughters.

Remember My Name is her debut novel.

D1621401

with Debbie Johnson

REMEMBER
MY NAME

Harlequin MIRA is a registered trademark of Harlequin Enterprises Limited, used under licence.

First Published in Great Britain 2016
By Harlequin Mira, an imprint of HarperCollins*Publishers*
1 London Bridge Street, London, SE1 9GF

Remember My Name © 2016 Abbey Clancy

With thanks to Debbie Johnson

ISBN: HB: 978-1-848-45454-5
C: 978-1-848-45538-2

58-0516

Our policy is to use papers that are natural, renewable and recyclable products and made from wood grown in sustainable forests.
The logging and manufacturing processes conform to the legal environmental regulations of the country of origin.

Printed and bound by
CPI Group (UK) Ltd, Croydon, CR0 4YY

For Neale – gone but never forgotten.
I love you.

Prologue

Liverpool, a few years ago...

Jess could feel the heat of the spotlight; the glare of the multi-coloured strobe flitting over her face as it criss-crossed the stage. She could feel the sweat oozing its way through her make-up, the strain on her lungs as she recovered from that last note. She was blinded by the dazzling glow, deafened by the sound of applause hammering in time to her own frenzied heart. Her legs were weak from dancing, her throat was sore from singing, her stomach was cramping with effort and nausea, and she felt like she might collapse at any second.

It was, quite frankly, the best moment of her entire life.

She blinked her eyelids a few times to try and get rid of the droplets of sweat that had gathered on her long lashes, and stared out at the audience. She knew they were there—she could hear them, feel them, and, thanks to the hot dogs that had been served at the interval, even smell them—but the spotlight turned them into a mass of dark blobs. Dark blobs that were all standing up, shouting and cheering and clapping. Even people that weren't related to her by blood were joining in—although she could definitely hear her dad yelling louder than everyone else. All she could see was the dark outline of bodies, silhouetted hands waving in the air.

All those people. Cheering. For her.

Panting, exhausted, on the biggest high she'd ever known, a wide smile cracked her face in two. She'd done it. She'd played the lead role in the biggest show of the school year, and she'd played it well. So well that the whole place was on its feet.

So what if she passed out afterwards? And who cared if the fright wig she was wearing tore her own hair out in clumps when it was removed? And what did it matter that she might have broken her big toe during that last routine? It was all worth it.

All the hours of rehearsal; the time away from her friends and family; the pain and the dehydration and the frustration of getting it wrong time after time. It was just…worth it. This was where she was born to be, and she'd never been happier.

Jess sensed the rest of the cast running out to be with her; grinned as Ruby grabbed one of her hands and Adam grabbed her other, and raised them up in victory before they performed their bow. The others were there too: the dancers and singers from the chorus; and the girl who'd worked on the costumes; the woodwork team who'd built the set; and Mr Carlisle, the teacher who'd produced it.

Everyone apart from Daniel Wells, that is. Daniel, who'd not only written the story, but also scored the songs, designed the stage, and organised the lighting—he, Jess knew, would still be tucked away in his tech booth where he seemed to live. Daniel hated the spotlight as much as she loved it.

Finally, eventually, after several more bows, the curtains swished closed in front of them. The lights dimmed. The roar of the crowd subsided.

It was over—and Jess felt a momentary burst of panic as she wondered what she'd do now. Now she was no longer playing a role—now she was back to being plain old Jess Malone, instead of the spunky, sparky heroine of Daniel's show. Now she had to go back to reality. It was going to be a huge downer, she knew.

She didn't have time for the thoughts to settle, which was probably a good thing. Ruby shook her out of it by hugging her so hard she thought her lungs might pop out of her mouth.

'Come on, Jess!' she said, finally letting her go; laughing with sheer joy. 'We've got a party to go to! All back to mine… my mum's been the offie and got the drinks in, your lot are coming as well. They said the whole street is going to party like it's 1999.'

Ruby's lipstick had smeared, leaving a bright red slug-trail across her cheek, and one eyelash was falling off, spider-legging its way down her face. Jess reached out and used her finger to wipe away the lippie, and stuck the lash back into place. She was always doing repair jobs on Ruby—not just for the make-up, but for the broken hearts, the hangovers, and the dog-ate-my-homework disasters that seemed to make up the whole of her best mate's life.

'There,' she said. 'Now you're perfect. Give me a minute. I'll get my stuff and see you outside.'

'Yeah, right. You're off to see Danny McDumbass, aren't you?'

'Don't call him that—he wrote this whole thing. And he's not dumb.'

'Maybe he's not dumb. But he *is* an ass…anyway, catch ya later!'

Ruby ran away, heading to the back of the stage. Jess heard her screeching as she went, and laughed at her antics. So Ruby didn't appreciate Daniel—that didn't exactly put her in the minority.

She sighed, smoothed down the curls of her fright wig, and took one more quiet moment to recall exactly how she'd felt when she heard that applause. It had been…perfect.

Jess could hear the sounds of the others celebrating, and the shuffling feet of the audience leaving the college auditorium, and knew it was time for her to leave too, even if she didn't want to. Maybe she could just get a sleeping bag and curl up in a corner…except, no. She couldn't. It was time to party—and her mum and dad would be first up on the table doing the Macarena, which was always a sight to see.

First, though, she needed to say goodbye to Daniel, and try and persuade him to come to the party with them. She knew he wouldn't, but she had to try. It was part of their relationship—her constant battle to drag him into the real world, and his constant refusal to come along. Strange as it seemed, he preferred playing '*World of Warcraft*' and building computers from scratch to getting hammered on vodka and Red Bull and copping off with people.

Daniel lived next door to her on their quiet terraced street—

his was the blue door and hers was the red, which reflected the footballing loyalties of the inhabitants. It was always good natured until derby day, when the two families diplomatically avoided each other as much as they could until the result came through. Then all bets were off. The walls were thin enough that as each team scored, you could hear the other family cheering next door.

She'd known him since they were three, and they'd gone all the way through primary school and junior school and high school together, ending up at the same college. He was what her little brother Luke called 'a bit of a weirdo', and what her mum Michelle called 'an intellectual'. To Jess, he was just Daniel—the kid that nobody seemed to quite get except her.

She made her way to the tech booth and found him hiding away there, as she knew she would. They were eighteen now and, whereas Jess had blossomed—losing the cute baby fat that her mum loved showing off in embarrassing photos, gaining curves in all the right places, and blooming from gap-toothed schoolgirl into a young woman—Daniel hadn't. He was still on the short side, smaller than Jess's five eight at least, which would have been fine if not for the fact that he also had the body weight of a six footer.

He took up most of the space in the booth, his too-long dark blond hair tucked behind his ears, his blue eyes serious and intent as he flicked switches and stashed discs. He always looked serious, Jess thought, even at moments like this, when he should be walking on the same cloud of happiness as the rest of them.

He looked up as she approached, and gave her a small smile.

'No,' he said, straight away.

'What do you mean, no?' she replied. 'I haven't even asked you anything yet!'

'No, I'm not coming to the party at Ruby's.'

'Oh. So you're just going to go home and listen to suicide songs and be a miserable get on your own, are you?' she asked.

'Yes, that's exactly the plan, so don't try and persuade me. Anyway—you were great tonight. I knew you would be, Jessy.'

Warmth spread through her at his words, and she couldn't help but grin like an idiot.

'I was, wasn't I? But it's all down to you, writing that part for me.'

'Well, who else would I write it for?' he asked. 'A cheer-leader who saves the world from alien invasion?' Daniel was packing cables and sockets into a bag as he spoke. 'You were the only one who could pull it off.'

'You just wanted to laugh at me in this costume,' she said, gesturing to the neon-pink outfit that had been threatening to bring her out in a rash ever since she first wore it.

Daniel looked her up and down, then quickly turned away. It was hard to tell in the dim lights, but Jess could have sworn he was blushing for some reason.

'I only laugh at you when you're funny—which is most of the time, whether you mean to be or not. But seriously—your voice was amazing. You're going to be a big star one day, Jessy.'

She watched him as he bustled around, confused by her emotions. On the one hand she was sad that she couldn't reach him—drag him out of his shell long enough for everyone else to see what she saw—but on the other hand…a *star*. Even the word made her go a bit cross-eyed with excitement.

Daniel thought she'd be a star. That she could do this— every night of her life if she wanted to—sing and dance and entertain and drive round in a limo and drink Cristal. Buy her mum and dad a posh house in Formby, have enough money so he could stop driving taxis, and Mum could say farewell to her job in Tesco…a *star*.

'You really think so?' she asked, suddenly not feeling quite so sure of herself. Now she was here, out of the spotlight, away from the crowd, it didn't seem entirely possible.

Daniel stopped what he was doing and turned to face her, his expression firm and insistent.

'Yes. You, Jess Malone, have more X factor than there is on every talent show on TV. You sing like an angel, you dance like a pro, and you're…well, you're not ugly. Some might even say you're beautiful. The world's your stage, Jess—and you're the star of the show.'

Chapter 1

Cheshire—a few years later…

'And here she is—the star of the show! Give her a big hand, ladies and gents, boys and girls…it's Elsa from *Frozen*!'

I stood behind the Princess Mobile, shivering from the cold, cringing at Ruby's over-the-top announcement. There was static on the microphone as she spoke, and every word came out distorted and fuzzy and painful to the ears. It was yet another thing we had to get fixed.

The Princess Mobile itself was looking as if it needed a day at a spa, the lettering peeling off and one wing mirror held on entirely by tape. Pink tape, though—we had a brand to protect. It was meant to look like a beautiful fairy-tale carriage on wheels—but it looked more like a clapped-out van designed to carry drunk women round Mathew Street on their hen night.

My costume was in need of some TLC as well. It was our most popular range—the kids still couldn't get enough of Elsa—and I practically lived in this disgusting blue polyester nightmare. One of Ruby's mates had run up all our costumes for us, and, like the Princess Mobile, they'd been all right to start off with.

Now, after two solid years of bringing Disney-fied joy into the lives of kids all across the north west of England (and occasionally, North Wales, which made us practically global), it was a bit frayed around the edges.

Much like myself, I thought, as I tottered forward to greet the crowds. I'd have preferred not to totter, but the grass was really soggy after three solid days of rain, and my white high heels kept sinking into the mud as I walked. It wasn't raining right then, but it was probably only a matter of time before it started lashing it down—it was one of those brilliant British summers that make you fantasise about winning the Euromillions and buying a villa in the Bahamas.

I emerged from behind the Princess Mobile as elegantly as I could, bearing in mind the wind was blowing my blonde Elsa wig so hard the plait kept whacking me in the face. It was pretty heavy as well—I could end up with a broken nose at any moment. I kept my smile in place and my mouth firmly shut—it would be bad for business if Elsa suddenly started effing and blinding in front of the munchkins.

There were about thirty kids at this party, which was being held in the garden of a very nice house in what the telly always calls 'leafy Cheshire'. The posh bit—not Warrington. The bit where footballers and business tycoons lived, in homes with cinema rooms and security gates and stables for their ponies. Which meant that I probably shouldn't call it a garden—I should call it 'the grounds', as you could fit the whole of Bootle into it if you tried.

The kids obviously didn't realise they were supposed to be posh, and were behaving like absolute little shits. They'd fought during the party games, stolen each other's pass-the-parcel prizes, and pushed each other off their seats in musical chairs so hard that one of them had already been taken to A&E.

The birthday girl herself was called Jocelyn. She was five years old, and already a total diva nightmare. Don't get me wrong, I don't believe in hitting kids—usually—but I'd make an exception for Jocelyn. She was wearing an Elsa costume herself, though hers looked a lot more classy than mine to be honest—more velvet and satin than polyester and rayon. And her hair was real—a gorgeous, thick, blonde fishtail plait that draped over her tiny shoulders oh so perfectly.

That was where the perfection ended. She'd been glaring at me and Ruby ever since we arrived, following us around as we set up, telling us we were doing everything wrong, demanding she won every party game, and generally being a miniature bitch. Her parents just smiled and laughed, as though she was being especially cute or entertaining. Obviously, money didn't buy parenting skills—my mum and dad would have killed me if I'd been that rude to anyone.

The grown-ups were all sitting around at white-clothed tables, sipping expensive-looking wine, and wrapped up in Barbour jackets and posh pashminas. The women were perfectly made up and a bit Botox-y, and the men were tanned and fit and looked like they went skiing every winter.

It was very different from the world I usually lived in—a tiny two-bedroomed flat 'near the city centre' (that was what the letting agent said—in reality it was Dingle) that I shared with Ruby. Ruby and, more and more often, her boyfriend Keith. Keith was fifteen years older than Ruby, carried a selfie stick around wherever he went, and, in my opinion, was a huge sleazebag—but that was one of those opinions you have to keep to yourself. Until she dumped him, and then I could really let rip.

Still, at least our flat wasn't inhabited by Jocelyn, who was staring at me with really evil eyes as I made my way—heels sinking into the mud—towards the central area we'd designated as our performance spot.

I tried to ignore her as I smiled and took my position, feeling the first drops of rain land on my face as I did. She made it pretty hard, though, by pointing at me and yelling: 'That's not the *real* Elsa! That's just the silly woman who gave out the jelly!'

Big laughs from the mums and dads at that one. Screeches from the other kids. And torrential rain now pouring down on my head as if God was emptying a bucket all over me.

It was all right for them. They were all sheltered beneath a huge gazebo, and even though it was billowing in the wind, it was keeping them dry, the rain draining off in rivulets down the side and onto the soggy grass.

Ruby was under there as well, and I felt a moment of pure hatred for her as she gave me a thumbs up, and a huge fake grin. At least I thought it was fake—maybe she was just really happy to see me out there on my own, soaking wet, blue polyester frock clinging to my skin, being heckled by a group of five-year-old sadists as my Elsa braid repeatedly thumped me across the forehead.

I switched on the handheld microphone and waited until Ruby flicked on the backing track. She'd pulled the equipment under the gazebo with her as well, which was a pretty sensible idea. Otherwise she might get electrocuted. This way, I thought, looking at the snow machine and the wires stretching out to an extension plug, at least only one of us would get electrocuted. Me.

I glanced up at the heavens as the now intensely familiar opening chords of 'Let It Go' kicked in. The sky was completely black now, almost as though there'd been a total eclipse of the sun. I said a quick prayer to the Patron Saint of Children's Party Entertainers—and if there isn't one, there really should be—and asked very nicely if any lightning that was planned could hold off for the next ten minutes at least. I wasn't at all keen on that electrocution thing.

I closed my eyes, took a deep breath, and…let it go. However wet I was, however tired I was, however itchy that dress was, I loved to sing. Even this, which I'd done over and over and over again for so long, still had the power to lift my spirits.

It was a beautiful song, and an absolute dream to perform. I tried to avoid Jocelyn's gaze—I suspected her eyes were glowing red like an evil child from a horror film by now—and threw myself into it heart and soul. That's what I was paid to do, and, more importantly, that's what I loved doing.

Things might not have worked out quite the way I'd hoped when I was eighteen, but at least I had managed to make a living from singing—assuming by 'living', you meant a steady diet of Ramen noodles, no landline, and sneaking vodka into pubs in my handbag to add to my coke on nights out.

Still, I was doing what I loved. What I still thought I was born to do—and at the ripe old age of twenty-two, I wasn't quite ready to give up on my dreams just yet.

Plus, if I kept my eyes screwed closed, and ignored the rain, and blocked out the sounds of the kids screaming at each other, I could still lose myself in the music; lose myself in the joy of the song…and imagine everything was very different. That I wasn't standing here being mocked by a group of mini-psychos and their boozed-up parents. That I was on my own stage, doing my own concert, for my own adoring audience…

As I sang out the last few lines, my fantasy was rudely interrupted by what felt like a giant blast of washing-up liquid to the face. It sloshed up my nose, choked my mouth, and stung my eyeballs. I yelled and tried to back away from the liquid punch in the gob; sadly, my heels were still firmly embedded in the muddy ground and, although the rest of me backed away, my feet didn't.

As a result, I landed on my blue-polyester-clad backside, squelching around in an ever-expanding puddle of dirt, grass, and rainwater. I'd dropped the mike, and was now screaming as the snow machine continued to spew at me.

It was supposed to create a beautiful fairy-tale effect as I finished the song—one that the children usually loved. We filled the special tank with what was mysteriously called Snow Fluid, and when Ruby pressed the button, it gently showered me with foamy snowflakes. It got oohs and aahs every time we used it.

This time, though, something had gone badly wrong. I don't know whether it had malfunctioned, or Ruby had pressed

20

some magical and previously unused setting, but the stuff had blasted me full in the face like one of those water cannons police use in riots.

As I lay there, drenched to the skin, unable to get up again because the mud was now of a level that hippos would enjoy wallowing in, I finally heard it. The sound that usually made me happy.

Bloody applause.

Chapter 2

I craned my neck up at such a weird angle I knew I'd have a crick in it later. Yep, I was getting a standing ovation—not for my majestic performance of 'Let It Go', but for falling on my arse in a load of mud. What a knob!

I could hear the kids screeching and cackling and whooping, and the deeper tones of the parents joining in. So much for being the grown-ups. I peeked up again, and saw that even Ruby had tears of laughter rolling down her cheeks. Her slightly too chubby cheeks, I thought, with a spike in my usually low bitchiness levels. Being stuck in a trough of dirt in a fake Disney Princess costume will do that to a girl.

Everyone was so busy laughing it up at my expense that nobody bothered to come and help me. Ruby hadn't even turned the snow machine off, so the foamy water was still shooting out of it, making my predicament even harder to escape from.

I was pondering whether to just give up—maybe turn face down in the mud and drown myself—when someone reached down and grabbed hold of my flailing hands. I gripped on, not caring who it was, and I was pulled up so hard I slammed right into the body of my rescuer.

A body that was tall and strong and very, very male. I gazed up, and looked into a pair of deep, dark, chocolate-drop eyes. Okay, they were a bit crinkled up from laughing, but at least he'd bothered to help.

The eyes were gorgeous—and the rest of the package wasn't to be sniffed at either. Even if he did smell so nice I was quite tempted. He was about six foot, broad-shouldered but lean, and had dark hair that was done in one of those really super-expensive cuts that looks super-casual, a bit of fringe flopping over his forehead in the wind and the rain.

He was getting drenched by the snow machine and, I realised, covered in mud from me—the Disney Princess who'd spent the last thirty seconds resting in his arms and looking at him like he was a hot chocolate fudge cake. With squirty cream.

'Oh God!' I said, jumping away from him and almost falling over again. 'I've got you all dirty!'

He reached out and took a solid hold of my arm, ignoring the mud and holding me steady. He gave me a huge grin—one of those infectious ones that makes you see the funny side in everything.

'I don't mind,' he said, with a cheeky sideways smile, 'I like being dirty.'

There were so many responses to that one, I didn't know where to start. So for once in my life—and anyone who knows me will agree this was a once-in-a-blue-moon occurrence—I kept my mouth shut. This guy was handsome and dashing and probably rich. He was giving me the once over in a way that let me know the princess dress was now extremely wet and extremely clingy, and he was still holding on to me.

It was one of those situations that should come with a
DANGER! HIGH VOLTAGE! sign, and maybe a little cartoon of
a woman with a broken heart. I'd just come through a nasty
break-up with my ex, a window cleaner called Evan, who I'd
discovered was whipping out more than his chamois leather
on his rounds. I'd decided to become a born-again virgin—and
this man looked like he ate born-again virgins for breakfast.
In a good way.

I kept one hand on his arm to steady myself, leaned down,
and pulled my white heels off. It meant I'd have to squelch
barefoot in the mud, but at least I wasn't trapped any more.
Ruby had finally recovered enough from her laughing-gas
attack to turn off the snow machine, and I could hear the
sound of her leading the kids in a rousing rendition of 'Happy
Birthday'. I usually did that—in character as Elsa—but all
things considered, it was probably best to move on without me.

'Thank you, so much,' I said, staggering off to one side,
being led by him to the shelter of the gazebo. 'I honestly
thought I was going to pop my clogs then.'

'If you'd been wearing clogs,' he said, grabbing up a navy
blue gilet from the back of a chair, 'you might not have had
that problem in the first place.'

I tried to shrug him away—the gilet looked as expensive
as him—but he draped it around my shoulders and gave my
wet, chilly arms a good rub.

'Yeah,' I replied, grateful for the warmth. 'But until they
come up with a Dutch Disney Princess, I'm screwed. I'm so
sorry, I've messed up all your clothes…'

His once-white shirt was now splattered with mud, and his

black jeans were smudged all across the waist, crotch, and thighs. He glanced down at himself and his face broke out into that grin again. He must have been quite a bit older than me—early thirties or something, I'd have guessed—but that grin made him look like a naughty schoolboy.

'Yes. It looks a bit like I've been having sex with a pig, doesn't it? From behind.'

'I suppose it would have to be,' I answered, finding myself giving the idea some serious thought, 'you'd get squashed otherwise.'

'What a way to go, though, eh?' he asked, those gorgeous brown eyes crinkling up in amusement. As he spoke, he picked up a full glass of red wine and passed it to me. I looked at it as though it was the Holy Grail—I don't think I'd ever wanted a drink more in my life.

'Uh, no,' I said. 'Ta very much, though. But princesses are like the police—we never drink on duty.'

'Nobody will ever know,' he said, gesturing to the back of the gazebo, where Evil Jocelyn was sitting on what looked like a throne, surveying her minions as they finished up their birthday song and started on three cheers. I couldn't help it—I stuck my tongue out at her. And that was without the wine.

'Did you just blow a raspberry at the birthday girl?' he asked, sounding shocked. I thought he was faking it, but I wasn't sure, and I felt myself blush under the mud on my face. My Elsa plait was now completely covered in dirt, and draped over my chest like a big brown turd.

I grabbed the wine and downed it in one. He was right, nobody would notice.

'Yes, I did,' I said. 'She's…a bit strong spirited?' I ventured, trying for diplomatic—which was never my strong suit. He definitely wasn't Jocelyn's dad—I'd already met him—but he must be connected to the family somehow to even be here. Though the fact that he was necking wine with me in the naughty corner rather than passing a gift to the Golden Child suggested they weren't that close.

'Strong spirited. I like that one. I suspect what you wanted to say, though, was "evil little bitch from hell", wasn't it?'

'Maybe,' I said, wiping my lips so I didn't end up with tell-tale red wine stains. 'But that wouldn't be professional.'

He glanced back at the present parade behind us. Everyone was handing over a beautifully wrapped parcel or an elegant gift bag, and Jocelyn was throwing them all to one side like Henry VIII with chomped-up chicken legs. Ugggh! She was enough to put you off having kids for life.

'Jocelyn is my niece,' he said, calmly. 'My only niece.'

I froze for a moment, wondering if he was secretly pissed off at me for almost (but not quite) slagging off his flesh and blood. His face stayed serious for a second, but then the grin was back, and I was able to let go of the breath I didn't know I'd been holding.

I punched him on the arm—which is a sign of affection where I come from—and smiled back.

'You had me going then,' I said. 'I was a bit worried you might report me to the Princess Police for being a bit of a cow about the birthday girl.'

'Never. I've known Jocelyn her whole life and, believe me, she brings out the cow in every sane person. Anyway…now we've been mud-wrestling together, how about you tell me your name? Assuming it's not Elsa.'

'Ha ha. No. I'm Jess. Or Jessy to my family. And Jessica when I've been naughty.'

He held out his hand to shake, and kept his fingers wrapped around mine for far longer than was decent.

'And are you naughty often, Jessica?'

His eyes met mine, and I suddenly felt very, very warm, despite the rain and the soaking wet costume and the soggy plait.

'Er… I'm trying very hard not to be,' I replied quietly, pulling my fingers away from his.

Everything about this bloke screamed money and success and class. He was one of those men who was clearly used to getting his own way—and unless the mud had infiltrated my brain, at the moment he looked like 'his own way' might involve me. In the same position as the pig.

Much as that appealed to the lusty part of me—and the part that had just downed that red wine—the timing just wasn't right. I'm not ashamed of my roots, of my accent, of my home town. And I'm proud as anything of my family—they're the best. But me and this guy? We came from different worlds. If he was interested in me it would be as a bit of rough (not that I'm rough, but you know what I mean), and it wouldn't last. And after Evan, I wasn't ready for another man whose brain was located next to his dangly bits.

I busied myself over by the snow machine, unplugging the bastard thing, winding up the wires, and stowing the plug in the back. He followed me over, which I somehow knew he would.

'I'm Jack,' he said, leaning over the machine and making me look up at him. 'Jack Duncan. And I was planning on coming to talk to you after the party anyway, Jess. Even if you hadn't needed pulling out of your early grave.'

'Oh!' I said, standing up tall and tilting my head to one side. 'Why's that?' I asked. This, I thought, should be good. He'll come up with a load of old codswallop about how he thought we'd met before; or how I looked like a Cancer and he was a Taurus; or did I have any cards so he could pass them round to his friends with children...

'Because of your voice. That performance—before the Unpleasant Incident—completely bowled me over. If you can do that with an overworked Disney song, I'd be interested to know what you can do with original material.'

Well. That one was new. And...maybe he meant it? He certainly looked sincere enough. The naughty schoolboy had gone, and his tone of voice wasn't at all flirtatious. In fact it was just business-like, and genuine. In all honesty, nobody had shown any interest in my singing for such a long time, I'd started to assume I might be a bit crap at it. I did the odd gig at the pubs round town, and won a few karaoke competitions, but it wasn't like I had a fan club or anything. Talent scouts weren't exactly camped outside my front door in Dingle, and the only bidding wars I was ever involved with were on eBay.

I might possibly have looked like I was fishing for flies; my mouth was hanging open so wide.

'Are you okay?' he asked. 'You look like you might be about to have some kind of seizure...'

I clamped my jaws together and wiped the frown off my brow. That was no way to react to a compliment.

'I'm sorry,' I said. 'I'm just a bit…surprised. Nobody usually notices. Especially today.'

'Well, I did,' he said, 'and I was really impressed. There's just a unique quality to your voice that I found so refreshing—and even though I suspect you've done that song thousands of times, you still put so much feeling into it. It was…authentic. Do you sing professionally—outside the princess community, I mean?'

I almost laughed out loud, but just about managed to retain my dignity enough to make it all sound a bit better than it actually was.

'I have a few regular venues,' I said, not adding that those venues were usually populated by old men with no teeth, so drunk on happy-hour-lager that they barely noticed I was there—and the ones that did, asked me when I was going to take my clothes off.

He nodded, possibly guessing all of that anyway.

'And have you done any auditions? Have you got any demos?'

Now I was really puzzled. Why was he asking all of this? What was it to him?

'You're a bit of a nosy so-and-so, aren't you?' I said, looking him right in the eyes. If he thought praising my singing might help him get in my knickers, well…he might be right, actually. But I tried to look tough anyway. A useless effort, really, as I'm about as tough as blancmange.

'I am indeed,' he replied, looking amused. 'But I'm also

serious. I work for a record company down in London, and I'm always looking for fresh talent. And you—even when you're covered in mud—are as fresh as it gets. I have a partner—let's just call him Simon—and I know he'd be interested as well. Obviously, we've just met, and you don't know me at all, so I don't expect an answer right now—but I'd love for you to come down and meet him. Maybe get involved in the label. Get to know the business—find your feet a little. There's always studio time available, young producers keen to make a name for themselves. It could be a great way for you to take your next steps in the music industry.'

As he spoke, he pulled out a leather wallet from his back jeans pocket, and handed me a card. It was plain black and white, but made of thick card—not the stuff we used for ours, which was like tracing paper—and all the lettering was embossed. I ran my finger over it, reading the words, 'Jack Duncan—Head of Talent Engagement—Starmaker Records.'

Starmaker Records. I'd actually heard of them—it was the label that Vogue was signed to, among others. Vogue was one of my all-time favourites—a diva in the Whitney Houston vibe, but who could also crack out a really sassy rap section, and mixed dubstep with power ballads in a way that shouldn't work but kinda did. I'd downloaded all her tracks, and—though this must be something I never, ever told Jack Duncan—sometimes sang them in front of the mirror, using the traditional hairbrush-as-fake-microphone technique.

Wow. I might be the most mud-encrusted Disney Princess of all time—but maybe something good had actually just come out of it all. Maybe I'd just got a break—and not the kind that results in a trip to the Royal and four weeks in a plaster cast.

By this time the kids were all running back towards us, screaming and yelling and heading for the section of the garden that had several fancy bouncy castles planted in it. They'd all be covered in rain, but that probably made it even more fun for them. They streamed past us, so loud I couldn't have said anything to Jack even if I'd known what to say. I was completely stumped. Gobsmacked, as my dad would have said.

Jack got caught up with the flow as they went—Jocelyn grabbing hold of his hand and hissing. 'Come *on*, Uncle Jack!' as she dragged him with her. He disappeared off into the distance, massively tall among the sea of bobbing young heads, and waved at me as he went.

'Call me!' he shouted, before he turned and ran. Maybe he wanted to be the first on the bouncy slide.

I stared at the back of his body as he jogged away. Looked at the card in my now-shaking hands. Shivered as a particularly strong gust of wind reminded me that I was wearing soaking-wet-clothes.

What the Elsa had just happened?

Chapter 3

The smell of roast yumminess hit me as soon as I opened the front door. I stood still and sniffed like a Bisto kid, picking up traces of chicken and spuds and gravy. My mouth watered in response—between the party games and the singing and the mud and the potentially life-changing encounter with Jack Duncan, I'd completely forgotten to eat all day.

My empty tummy was rumbling in a very un-ladylike way, and I sighed with happiness. Asking Ruby to drop me off at my mum and dad's was definitely a very sensible decision.

It hadn't been just for the food—although my mum was a boss cook and that was a definite bonus—it had been for the company. After such a weird day, I needed comfort. I needed to be with people who I knew loved me, and appreciated me, and cared about me. I needed to be with my family.

The door to the living room opened and my little brother Luke popped his head around the frame.

'What's up, fart face?' he said, before rugby tackling me to the floor.

I kicked him in the head with one bare, muddy foot, and managed to escape from his grip. Luke is eighteen, and already over six-foot tall. He'd inherited some sporty gene that had completely skipped me, and played football, rugby, and took part in swimming contests. He also did mixed martial arts, and had a black belt in being an irritating knob head.

I staggered upright, not exactly feeling the warm glow of family love I was hoping for, and gave him another kick in the ribs. He made pretend 'oof' noises and rolled around on the hallway carpet like he was having a heart attack.

'I'm going for a shower!' I yelled, loud enough for my mum to hear me. She'd be in the kitchen, elbow deep in potato peel and surrounded by steam. I heard her shout back: 'Okay, love! Tea will be ready in ten!'

Leaving Luke in a heap of fake pain, I ran up the stairs, and into the familiar bedroom that had been mine and my sister Becky's until a year ago, when I'd decided—for some reason I can't quite remember now—to move out.

The house was one of those Tardis homes: it looked small on the outside, but it was big on the inside. There were three bedrooms—the biggest was Mum and Dad's, Luke had the box room, and me and Becky had the medium-sized one. As I closed the door behind me, I felt swamped with relief. Everything here felt so…safe. The smells—plug-in air fresheners, cooking, Dad's Old Spice—all meant 'home' to me.

Luke had been campaigning to get the bigger room since I'd left and Becky had moved in with her boyfriend Sean. She probably wouldn't be coming back, as she was three months pregnant with her first baby, but Mum and Dad had kept it just the way it used to be. I climbed up onto the top bunk—that was always hers, and we used to fight like cat and dog over it when we were kids. For some reason I still always felt like I'd scored a win when I managed to lie on it without her attacking me. Childish but true.

I stared at the ceiling for a few minutes, listening to the voice of Michael Bublé floating up the stairs. My mum Michelle bloody loved Michael Bublé. We'd bought her tickets to see him in concert for her fiftieth, and she practically passed out with excitement. Still, it could be worse. My nan was obsessed with Daniel O'Donnell ('such a *nice* young man!').

The noises coming from my stomach told me it was time for food, so I dragged myself out of my pit and headed for the bathroom. As I got in the shower, I mentally prepared myself for the torture that was washing in a house that contained both dodgy plumbing and my evil brother Luke. This weird thing happened where if you flushed the downstairs loo, the shower water went freezing cold.

I stepped under the spray and sure enough, straight away, heard the sound of the flush. I jumped back to avoid the chill factor, waiting a few seconds before I continued. It carried on like this for the whole event, but somehow I managed to wash my hair, clean up, and dress myself in some comfy tracky bottoms and one of my old T-shirts.

By the time I got downstairs, everyone was ready, sitting around the old dining table at the back of the through lounge.

'You little shit,' I said, whacking Luke on the head as I walked past him to my chair.

'What do you mean? I just had a floater!' he said, smirking at me. Like I said, evil.

My sister Becky was there, and I gave her a quick hug

before I sat down. I hadn't seen her for a week, which in our family was practically reason to file a missing person's report. She looked a bit peaky, and only had a few slices of chicken breast on her plate, which she was pushing around with her fork. Not exactly glowing, but hopefully, it would get better.

'So,' said my mum, looking across the table at us all and smiling. 'The whole clan is here.'

'Better call the paramedics and put them on standby,' added my dad Phil, pouring gravy over his mash.

My dad is fifty-two, but looks a lot older—mainly because he lost all his hair when he was in his thirties. It never seemed to bother him, and he calls himself the Bald Eagle to make it all sound a bit more macho. He's tall—everyone in our family is apart from my mum, who is technically some kind of midget—and carries his beer belly with as much pride as his lack of hair. He calls it his 'Guinness Six Pack'.

My mum is fifty-one, and tiny. She has dyed-black hair, and looks a bit like an energetic garden gnome. She's always busy, my mum—with work, with us lot, with her own mum. I swear if she sat still for five minutes we'd all think she was ill. She couldn't wait for Becky's baby to arrive, just to give her even more to do.

'So, how are you, Sis?' I asked Becky, a bit worried about her.

'Fat. Knackered. Puking up all day.'

Ah. The joys of motherhood.

Becky shut up after that, but I noticed my mum sneaking glances at her as we ate. She'd been through it all three times, obviously, but she was like Superwoman—she probably just gave birth to us in the middle of doing the laundry and carried right on with a hot wash.

I was so busy stuffing my face that I didn't hear when my dad asked me about the 'gig'. He always called them 'gigs'. I think it made him feel young and hip.

'Earth to Jessy!' said Luke, poking me in the side with the prongs of his gravy-covered fork. I yelped and looked at everyone, almost choking on my cabbage.

'You seem a bit distracted, love,' said Dad. 'Anything up?'

'What he means is, you look like a mental patient with that cabbage hanging out of your gob,' said Luke.

'Shut UP, you little fuck!' I replied, kindly.

'Language!' said Mum and Dad at exactly the same time. Tea time with the Malones—it was always X-rated, no matter how much they tried. Served them right for having too many kids.

I debated whether to tell them about Jack Duncan. I needed to talk to someone about it, but I wasn't sure who. Ruby was distracted with the disgusting Keith. Becky was distracted with her morning sickness. Luke was distracted by being a complete tit.

I had a sudden flash of yearning for Daniel, the boy who used to live next door. He'd moved away with his family not long after our concert, heading 'down south' (which could mean anything from Birmingham to Berkshire) with his parents, who'd inherited a small B&B by the seaside. We'd stayed in touch for a while, but that had faded when he went off to uni—studying something techy I never quite understood. I'd tried to find him since, usually when I was a bit pissed and feeling nostalgic, but he was untraceable—possibly the only twenty-two-year-old on the planet to not be on Facebook. New neighbours had moved in, and every time I saw their front door that they'd painted cream, I felt a bit sad about it. So, I had to work with what I had—my family.

'I met this man,' I said quietly, not sure what their reaction would be, putting down my knife and fork when I realised my hands were shaking. 'Who works in the music business.'

'Let me guess,' jumped in Luke straight away, 'he wanted to take you away from it all? Make you a star? As long as you gave him a blow job first?'

'Luke!' said Mum, in her don't-mess-with-me voice. The voice that could make any one of her kids freeze in the middle of whatever they were doing. Sure enough, Luke looked terrified, and suddenly became very interested in his chicken leg.

Becky was staring at me over the table, frowning. Her skin looked slightly green, as if she was a space alien.

'He does have a point, though, Mum,' Becky said. 'Let's face it, Jessy is so gullible she'd believe anything.'

I wanted to argue, but I couldn't. There had been a few… incidents. Like the bloke who claimed to be a talent scout for a modelling agency, and asked me to take my top off as soon as I walked through the door of his studio. Like the 'audition' I'd gone to where all the star-struck girls were expected to perform while dressed up as Playboy bunnies. And my personal favourite, the guy I'd met at a kids' party who'd booked me to sing at his wife's fortieth—except the wife hadn't been there. In fact, nobody had been there, apart from me, him, and a very brassy lady of the night who'd obviously been brought in to join the performance.

Each time, they'd seemed genuine. Each time, I'd believed them. Mainly because I wanted to—I wanted to be respected, admired, discovered. I wanted to be a star—but unfortunately, the road to stardom was paved with perverts.

I stayed quiet. It was depressing, really. Even my own family didn't believe that someone could be genuinely interested in my talent. And they were probably right. I'd be a Disney Princess until I was too old, then I'd have to join an Abba tribute band.

'Well,' said my mum, realising that an uncomfortable silence had settled over the room, and that I was possibly on the verge of tears. 'Jessy, you know how much we love you—and nobody knows better than us how hard you've worked at this. You're beautiful, you're talented, and you deserve a break. We all want that for you, hon. We just want you to be…careful, as well. We don't want anyone to take advantage.'

'What's his name?' asked Luke, whipping out his iPhone. I told him, almost scared to find out the truth. It would all just be another fairy tale bust to pieces if Jack hadn't been what he said he was. I tried to stay positive—but sometimes even princesses get down in the dumps.

We all waited while he Googled him, and looked on as he frowned and swiped over different pages on the screen. Eventually, he looked up and gave us all a big grin.

'Bloody hell,' he said, 'looks like she's hit the jackpot this time, folks. Jack Duncan, Starmaker Records. Thirty-three years old, and one of the rising stars of the music industry. He discovered Vogue—and now he's interested in our Jessy!'

Everyone was quiet for a moment, weighing up what he'd said. Considering the fact that it might not all be bullshit after all—that something could finally be happening for me.

'Still,' added Luke—his confidence back—just to spoil the moment, 'it doesn't mean he's not after a blow job as well…'

Chapter 4

My dad gave me a lift home after dinner. Part of me had wanted to stay the night, but I needed to do some thinking. And it was always hard to think with my family around—they were just too noisy, bless 'em. Everyone had an opinion, and everyone wanted you to listen to it at the same time. Even the lure of sleeping in the top bunk wasn't quite enough to tempt me.

So I'd climbed in the back of Dad's black cab, and we'd lumped and bumped our way across the city centre, which was all lit up and looking gorgeous, milling with glamorous women and tipsy tourists and people of all ages out for a good time.

We drove past the Albert Dock and up towards my end of town—which was slightly less glamorous, but a bit more affordable for a pair of struggling children's entertainers. Plus, it was on the same road as a Lidl, which was quite a selling point.

He pulled up outside the flat, and made his usual joke: 'That'll be twelve pounds fifty, please, queen.'

He'd tried to charge me for lifts since I was twelve, and he never seemed to get tired of the gag. Instead, I climbed out, grabbed hold of my bag, and gave him his usual tip when he wound the window down—a big kiss on the cheek.

'Bye, love!' he shouted cheerily, waving me goodbye as he stopped traffic in both directions with a very anti-social three-point turn. Cabbies, eh?

*

When I walked back into the flat I shared with Ruby, I immediately knew that her boyfriend Keith was round. And I immediately knew they were getting jiggy with it in the bedroom.

None of that makes me Sherlock Holmes—I could actually hear the headboard banging against the wall, and Ruby screaming her head off as Keith performed his manly duties. Uggh.

I shuddered, and slammed the living room door as hard as I could to let them know I was home. There was a pause in the headboard banging, a few giggles, and then it started again. Charming.

Our living room was open plan with our kitchen. And our dining room. And the utility room. In fact, there was just one quite small room, with a couch in front of the TV (one of the old ones with the fat backs), and the cooker and sink and fridge right behind. I was lying about the dining room—there isn't one. We eat our noodles off trays on our laps, usually while we're watching crap reality shows and slagging everyone off. It's a very glitzy lifestyle.

I threw my bag on the couch and put the kettle on to make a coffee. Opening the fridge, I found that Ruby had not only used the last of the milk, she'd put the empty carton back on the shelf. It sat there, mocking me, next to a piece of mouldy cheese and some eye drops I'd used for conjunctivitis two weeks ago.

So much for the comforts of home, I thought, deciding that I should have stayed at Mum and Dad's after all.

The only other item in there was a bottle of Prosecco—one that Jocelyn's mum had given us as thanks after the party. And possibly to stop us suing her for emotional trauma. I was amazed that Ruby and Keith hadn't nabbed it and taken it into their love shack with them, and I grabbed hold of it quickly, just in case they remembered and appeared naked to claim it back.

I opened the cupboard to get a glass, then remembered they were all in the dishwasher—the dishwasher that had broken last week, and we were still waiting for the landlord to get repaired. I didn't dare look in there. It'd be like a scene from a sci-fi special, complete with new lifeforms. Instead, I popped the bottle open and retreated to my own room.

It was only small, but I'd done my best with it. I'd repainted the crappy box-built furniture in a pretty pastel shade of light green, and the walls were plain and white to make it feel bigger. There wasn't space for much, but I had a wardrobe, a dresser filled with all my make-up and hair stuff, the mirror spotted with Blu-tacked photos of friends and family. One of Mum and Dad, outside the Michael Bublé concert. One of Luke when he was six and still cute. One of me and Daniel, the night of the school concert…which seemed about a million years ago.

My queen-sized bed was decorated with fairy lights draped

around the wrought-iron headboard that made it look like there was a party going on when they were illuminated. Not that it had seen much action recently, I thought, not since Evan, and, despite having a couple of hot flushes when I was crushed up against Jack earlier that day, I intended to keep it that way. Life was simpler without men in it, even if a bed was a lot less fun without a man in it.

I pulled off my clothes, suddenly exhausted, and climbed under the duvet naked. My mum had washed all my bedding for me the day before (like I said, she never stops), and the smell of the fabric softener she'd always used wafted into my nostrils in a way that comforted me far more than the few mouthfuls of chilled booze I'd just swallowed.

Still, I decided to persevere and see just how comforting a whole bottle of Prosecco could be… I thought I deserved it after the day I'd had. And maybe it would give me some inspiration; help me answer a few of the dilemmas I was facing.

I had some decisions to make. On the one hand, the chance to work with Jack Duncan—the chance to be part of Star-maker—was a dream come true. I had a work ethic as well-developed as my mum's when it came to my music, although I lagged behind a bit on the hoovering front.

I was willing to work—to slog my guts out, in fact. I'd always wanted to be a singer—I'd never entirely given up, no matter how many knock-backs I'd had. No matter how many people had told me I wasn't quite right: not blonde enough, not cute enough, not sexy enough, not…*something* enough. All those auditions and meetings that ended in the same conversation: 'You have a strong voice, but we're looking for XXX'—and then it was just a matter of filling in the blanks. They were looking for someone older. Or younger. Or Korean. Or, on one occasion, someone fatter—they were going for a plus-sized girl-group vibe. There was always something missing, something not right.

Jack Duncan hadn't said I wasn't right, though. He'd said I was fresh, and talented, and *authentic*, which I knew from watching *The X Factor* was a good thing. He wanted me to come to London, to meet his mysterious music-biz friend Simon (my heart wished for Cowell, but my head said don't be so gullible). He was offering me the chance I'd been waiting for—and if it worked out, not only could I be a success, but I could share that success with my family. Pay off their mortgage. Send my mum and dad on that cruise they were always talking about. Make sure that Becky's baby wanted for nothing. Get Luke a personality transplant.

It wouldn't just change my life—it would change theirs as well.

But on the other hand—although both my hands were a bit shaky now as I was halfway through that bottle of Prosecco, chugging from the bottle like the pure class I was—I'd have to go to London. I'd have to leave my friends, my home, my family. I loved the bones of my family, and I'd only ever been away from them for a few weeks at a time for shameful holidays to Malia and Ibiza. If I was gone for too long I'd miss Becky's baby being born, wouldn't be around to welcome the next generation of Malones set to terrorise the world.

I'd have to leave Ruby, and my other friends, most of

whom I'd known since I was a little kid. I'd have to leave Liverpool—a place I'd never dreamed of escaping from.

I'd have to leave my flat. My bed. My Lidl…how could I ever leave my Lidl, I thought, as I felt my eyelids droop shut and found just about enough conscious thought to put the bottle down before I crashed out into snoozeland. Once I was there, I was plunged into a very nice dream involving Jack Duncan, an igloo, a roaring log fire (I wasn't sure how that would work in an igloo, but hey, it was dream so I was going with the flow), and bearskin blankets that smelled of my mum's fabric softener…

'Jess!' Jack shouted, shaking me by the shoulders. I rolled over on the bearskins, sniffing the fragrance, and sighing.

He shook me again—a bit harder this time—and I decided I might go off him. Shaking a girl like this wasn't very romantic.

I swatted his hands away, mumbling at him to bugger off and do the dishes, and he yelled again: 'Jess! Wake up!'

Uggh. I opened one eye, and that was enough to tell me it hurt, and that I should definitely keep the other one shut. I lashed out, and realised that it wasn't Jack shaking me at all—it was Ruby, her face so close to mine I was tempted to bite her nose off.

I glared at her instead, and pulled the duvet up over my boobs. I was glad I did, as I noticed right then that Keith was lurking in the doorway—his belly, so big he looked like he was about to give birth to miracle triplets, hanging over the waistband of his saggy boxers. He had one hand shoved down the front as well, which made him even more attractive.

'Good morning, gorgeous,' he said, leering at me, still

poking around in his pants. I felt a bit sick in my mouth, and wished I had a lock on my door.

'What do you want?' I said to Ruby, glancing at the bedside clock and seeing it was only six a.m. I hadn't voluntarily seen six a.m. since I did my Duke of Edinburgh Award and, even then, 'voluntarily' was stretching it. Nobody booked party princesses any earlier than ten.

'Have you got any condoms?' she asked, as though it was entirely normal. 'We had one of those multi-packs but we've used them all up…'

'It's been all aboard the love train,' added Keith, pulling an imaginary whistle and making 'wooh wooh!' noises. Seriously, if I'd had a shotgun, I'd have blasted his head off like one of the zombies on *The Walking Dead*.

'No. Now fuck off…' I muttered, pushing her away. 'Try the Lidl. And close my door on your way out. And…go and get some bloody milk!'

Ruby backed off, a daft grin on her round face, bundling her almost-naked boyfriend out of the door as she did.

'All right, Sleeping Beauty,' she said, 'I was only asking… no need to bite my head off…'

They giggled their way out of my room, slamming the door shut behind them. Oh. My. God. I was soooo tired. And so hungover. And so bloody fed up of my life.

I sat up, rubbed my eyes clear of the crusty stuff that had magically appeared overnight, and looked at myself in the dresser mirror. My long, highlighted hair was clumpy and tangled and the roots needed doing. My skin was pale and dry from too much party make-up. My blue eyes were exhausted, red-rimmed, and missing the sparkle that even I knew used to live in them.

I was only twenty-two, but I felt like everything was closing in around me. No matter how much I loved my family, no matter how much I loved Liverpool, I needed to make a change. I needed hope. I needed a total life make-over. I needed that chance that Jack Duncan was offering me.

I reached for my phone, his card lying tucked beneath it. It was too early to call, I decided. I suspected people in the music industry slept in even later than princesses. But I could still contact him on the email address.

'Hi, it's Jess,' I typed, as quickly as I could with a hangover and long nails painted candyfloss pink, 'we met at Jocelyn's party yesterday. Give me a call when you can.'

I had a small debate about adding some kisses—I mean, everyone does that, don't they? Ruby even puts kisses on the end of messages to her credit-card company. But no, I thought, let's keep it professional.

That decided, I pressed send before I could change my mind, and sat very still for a few seconds, wondering if I'd done the right thing or not.

Well, it was too late to worry about that now—I'd already Let It Go.

Chapter 5

Every single member of my family was wearing matching T-shirts. They all had a photo of my face on them—a nice one at least, the Cinderella we used on the party website—and the words Team Jessy emblazoned in red capital letters.

Becky's was stretched over her now just-about-visible baby bump, and Mum's was so big it hung down to her legging-clad knees. I suspected my dad had ordered them all in the same size—large enough to fit over his Guinness Six Pack—so everyone else was just having to make do.

We were all crowded on the platform at Lime Street Station, waiting for the London train to arrive. We gathered a few curious stares—which takes a lot in Liverpool, believe me—and a few 'go on, girl' type comments from men who were already on their third can of Special Brew.

They'd picked me up from the flat in Dad's taxi, and I was allowed to ride in the front as a special treat. Ruby and Keith had waved me off, and that had started a wave of tears that I had a feeling wasn't going to stop any time soon. Ruby and I had had our ups and downs, but I'd known her forever, and I was going to miss her.

I was going to miss everyone. Even Luke, and his rugby tackles. If someone rugby tackled me in London, I'd probably emerge without my handbag and my front teeth.

If I was being honest, I was a bit scared. I mean, I'd been to London before, obviously. On school trips. For auditions. To see *Mamma Mia* in the West End. But living there was a whole different kettle of fish—especially when I was heading to a flat I'd never seen in person, and to a job I didn't really understand.

Jack had called me back the same day I emailed him.

'So,' he'd said, once we'd exchanged small talk. 'Can I tempt you down to the big city, Jess Malone? Are you ready for the challenge?'

Something in the way he'd said it sounded flirtatious—like he wasn't just challenging me to come and work at Starmaker. Like he was challenging me was a woman as well. It prompted two reactions. One was horror, in case he just wanted me down there so he could, to put it bluntly, get his leg over. The other was a tingle of excitement that floated around in my tummy like tiny, sex-starved butterflies. He was gorgeous, and I'd been a good girl for a very long time. Maybe I wouldn't object quite as much as I should if he did want to get his leg over.

The call had been short, and he said he'd get back to me with some details. And now, four weeks later, I was off. Leaving my home, leaving my family, leaving my friends—for my next big adventure. My first big adventure, really. Ruby had already found someone else to take my seat in the Princess Mobile—which didn't exactly make me feel useful—and Mum and Dad had been absolute saints.

Jack had explained that I'd be joining as a kind of paid intern—I'd do some practical work that would help me get to grips with the way the business worked; get enough money to live on (barely), and he and Simon would work out a mentoring programme for me that would involve singing coaches and studio time and laying down some tracks with one of Starmaker's producers.

I'd tried to explain it to the folks, to put their minds at rest that I wasn't moving all the way to London to work as a high-class call girl, but they hadn't really understood it. Which was fair enough, as I didn't either—I just had to take the chance.

'So,' Luke had said, frowning, 'it's a bit like *The Apprentice* crossed with *The X Factor*. Are you sure you can't come up with a really good business idea as well so we can get *Dragon's Den* in there too?'

My dad had perked up at that one. He always had some great invention he'd come up with—it was the way he kept his mind busy in a job that involved lots of sitting around. His latest concept was the 'Mini Ciggie'—literally a half-sized cigarette for people who were trying to give up and just wanted a few puffs, or for drunk people on a night out who were too hammered to smoke a whole one without falling over. He based the psychology of this on the many interesting sights he'd seen in Liverpool while looking for fares on a Saturday night, and had even taken a photo on his phone of all the almost-unsmoked discarded butts outside the smoking spots.

He'd never make it happen—but it kept him 'out of trouble', as my mum always said.

The two of them had helped me pay for the deposit on my

new flat in Kentish Town, as well as booking my train for me—and paying the extra so I could go first class.

'Start as you mean to go on, love,' Dad had said, when I protested that it would cost too much. 'Nothing but the best for my girl.'

'Plus, it was only ten quid extra,' Mum had piped up as she did the dishes.

So now, finally, the big day had come. I was packed. I was ready. I was willing and able to take on the world. And Team Jessy was a blubbering wreck around me.

As the train pulled in and we waited until the queue had cleared, all four of them huddled round, hugging me and kissing me and giving me words of encouragement. By the time I had to leave them, and drag my wheelie cases down the platform, we were all messed up with snot and tears. Even Luke had a few drops in his eyes, but that could have been misplaced hair gel from his perfect combover.

I watched them as the train slowly chugged away, waving and jumping around in their daft T-shirts, knowing I was leaving behind much more than Liverpool. I was leaving behind the very best family a girl could ask for.

I swiped away my own tears—they were going to make my mascara run, and panda eyes was not the look I was going for—and waved until they disappeared from view. As soon as they'd gone, I heard a text land on my phone—from Dad.

'Knock 'em dead, girl,' it said.

They had so much faith in me. So much belief. I couldn't let them down.

I settled into my very comfy chair, looking around me.

First Class was a bit posh, and so were the people in it. Lots of sun tans and expensive-looking clothes, and fit-looking businessmen who already had their laptops on the go.

I felt a bit out of place, and a bit knocked for six emotionally by the farewell scene at the platform. I fought an urge to get off at Runcorn and run all the way home, and gave myself a good talking to.

I was taking a leap of faith. It was time to believe in myself as much as my family did, and make them proud. If this all worked out, I'd be travelling first class everywhere I went—and so would they. Dad would be chauffeured around rather than driving other people. Mum could get a cleaner instead of doing it herself. I could make this work—I could change everything for the better.

A lady in a smart red uniform came round and offered me one of those little bottles of wine. Obviously, I took it—Dad had paid an extra tenner after all, it'd be rude to say no. I poured my drink, and made myself relax.

I was going to London. I was finally going to get the break I'd been waiting for. I had to believe that it would work—that my voice would finally be heard by the world, and that I'd manage to fight my way to a first-class life.

First Class trains. First Class flights. First-class clothes, and food, and a gorgeous place to live where nobody dropped their old kebab wrappers in the street.

I knew I'd have to work for it, but that was fine. I'd work my arse off if I needed to.

As I sipped my wine, I visualised my new world. The gigs and the studio time and the fans. The interviews. The TV appearances. The stylists and make-up artistes. The holidays I could afford; the fantasies I could live out. The islands in the Caribbean I could visit. I could almost feel the sun on my skin, it was that vivid.

I leaned back, starting to feel a bit snoozy. I willed myself into a light sleep, urging my own brain to be positive while I rested—to see those images coming true. To give me the encouragement I needed to overcome the fact that I was practically pooing my pants with fear at leaving home.

Before I drifted off, I tucked my clutch bag tightly between my thigh and the window, just in case. I was sure nobody in first class was going to rob my purse—and if they did, they'd be very disappointed—but old habits die hard.

I conjured up a picture of the beautiful house in London that I'd buy. It'd be like something from one of those lovely films—*Notting Hill* or *Bridget Jones* or *Love Actually*—all whitewashed, with steps up to the door, and columns either side of it. There'd be a courtyard garden, and cobblestone streets, and all the cars parked there would be Jags and Bentleys…and I'd have my own PA, and my own stylist, and my own chef…my own songwriting team, my own publicist, my own manager…it was going to work, I thought, as I fell asleep, a big daft grin on my face.

It was going to work. It had to.

Chapter 6

'It's not working!' Patty screeched at me, throwing a pen at my head. It bounced off my cheek, leaving a faint dent, and landed on the plush cream-coloured carpet.

'I'm sorry,' I mumbled, rubbing at my face. It had hit me with the pointy end and felt a bit sore. Much like the rest of me.

'Don't stand there gawping—just get me another one! And get me some coffee while you're at it!' said Patty, fixing me with that glare she had. The one she'd stolen from Cruella de Vil. Patty was about the same age as me, but had clearly been taking Bitch Lessons for the whole of her life. She was part of the Starmaker PR department, but the way she behaved, you'd think she was the Mayoress of London. Possibly the universe.

As far as I could see, she spent the whole day tweeting on behalf of the company, drafting crap press releases, and schmoozing with tabloid journalists. Her idea of a scoop was getting a picture of Vogue on the celeb gossip pages as she bought sexy underwear, or did her weekly shop in Tesco, to show she was 'just like the rest of us'. Half the time the pictures were a complete set up as well—something I'd not realised before I started my dream job.

Patty called the paparazzi and told them what the day's activities were for Starmaker's biggest acts, and they did the rest, turning up 'unexpectedly' with their cameras. I suppose it was a deal that worked for everyone—the celebs had warning, so they could make sure they had their slap on and were wearing knickers (or not) as they climbed out of their limos, and the photographers got their 'exclusive' shots. And Patty? She just got more annoying every time she pulled it off.

It was a whole new world—which, even as I thought it, I realised I was still singing in my head as the Disney song from *Aladdin*. This whole new world, though, was a lot less princess and a lot more pain in the arse.

I'd been here for a month. A whole month of effort and hope and hard work—and I was still getting pens lobbed at my head and I was still making coffee for the PR team.

I ambled off to the stationery cupboard to get Patty a new biro, then made my way to the break room to get her coffee. I fought the urge to spit in it, and looked around at my alleged work colleagues.

There were a few of the other ladies from the PR team, all having high level meetings that seemed to involved sharing the crumbs of one chocolate croissant between three of them as they slagged off everyone else they worked with. There was Dale, the Starmaker dance teacher and choreographer—who did at least give me a smile and a cheery thumbs up as he pranced past in his tights, swigging a blue Powerade. There were a couple of suits from what was always mysteriously known as Legal. And there was Heidi, Jack Duncan's assistant. She was the best of a bad bunch, and walked over to chat to me as I waited for the coffee to brew. Patty was very particular about her coffee. No instant. Nothing from the coffee pot. It had to be made with her very own cafétière, using her own poncy blend she paid a fortune for and tasted exactly the same as Nescafé.

'Hey,' said Heidi, staring at me from behind her trendy red-framed glasses. 'You've got a bit of a smudge...'

She pointed at my face, and I licked my thumb and rubbed at it. Ha. The pen *had* been working, after all.

'Thanks,' I said. 'She threw a pen at me. Apparently, it was my fault it ran out.'

Heidi pulled a sympathetic face and leaned back against the counter, her larger-than-average bottom spreading out over the cupboard doors.

'Chin up, chuck,' she said, in the fake Scouse voice she always threw into our conversations. I got that a lot—people telling me to 'calm down, calm down', making jokes about me stealing their hub caps, and generally behaving as though people from Liverpool were some exotic foreign animal they'd never encountered before. I'd never even been aware of how strong my accent was until I lived in London. Now, it seemed to be the only thing about me that people remembered. That and the fact that I made the coffee.

Heidi, at least, didn't mean any harm by it, so I just smiled. I was having to do that a lot lately. Just take a deep breath, and smile, and try not to swear or punch anyone. It didn't come naturally.

'Jack says are you okay with your schedule this week, by the way,' she added, getting a packet of chocolate Hobnobs out of the cupboard. One of the few perks of working at Starmaker was the free snacks and drinks. Unfortunately, I'd already been told I had to make sure I didn't put any weight on, so even that was off limits for me. I'm a size ten, but that was considered a bit on the plus side, so the joys of living above the best kebab shop in North London, and the cupboard choc-full of biscuits, were lost on me.

To be honest, the joy of pretty much everything was lost on me right then.

I nodded to let Heidi know I was okay with my schedule, and she trotted off, stuffing a Hobnob in her mouth as she went.

My schedule was…knackering. I'd never been so tired in my entire life. Jack had held true to his part of the bargain, but it wasn't quite the dream lifestyle I'd imagined. More of a living nightmare, in fact. I got into the office at half nine, and spent the whole day being treated like something the PR team would scrape off their shoe after a walk on Hampstead Heath. I made their coffee, fetched their lunch, did their photocopying, collected their press cuttings, made their hair appointments, and provided target practice for their pen-throwing workshops.

I wasn't allowed to answer their phones, or meet their guests at reception, or deal with the public in any way—because, as Patty had put it, 'Nobody will understand a word you say—you practically speak a foreign language.'

If I was lucky, I got to shadow them in meetings, which allowed me to at least get to know a few people in the rest of the business, and get an idea of how things worked. And the way things worked was…badly.

I'd never come across so many egos and divas and prima

donnas in my life—and that wasn't even the performers. Everyone here thought they were a star, or at least thought they should be treated like one. Even the cleaners had a habit of singing while they emptied the bins, presumably hoping that someone would hear them warbling Whitney Houston tracks, and say 'Now, that's what I call music…'

The only genuine star I'd met was Vogue, and ironically she was adorable—probably the least up-her-own-bum of everyone I worked with. She certainly couldn't beat Patty for being a rude cow, she always remembered my name, and she never threw anything at my head. She'd even complimented me on my singing when she'd heard me one night.

The singing that I would get to do after a full day's work in the office. I usually finished at about six—when the others would go off to wine bars and parties and glitzy functions, and I'd stay behind, like Cinderella being banned from the ball. Maybe I was too fat and too Scouse to be allowed on the guest list.

After that, the rest of my work schedule would start—and from six until nine I'd get to do the stuff I'd come all this way for. The stuff I'd left my family for. The stuff that the dreams really were made of.

I'd see Dale in the dance studio and learn steps to the routines he was choreographing for Vogue and the other A-listers on the label. I'd see Frankie, the vocal coach, and spend an hour gasping for air and doing freaky voice exercises and perfecting my runs and pretending I was Mariah Carey. I'd see Neale, the junior make-up guy, who seemed to be as low down the ladder as I was, and 'we'd gossip as danced around to R.Kelly's She's Got That Vibe, Neale showing off the moves he still had from his time as professional dancer. And maybe—when there was time available—I'd get to go into one of the studios and work with a producer. That didn't happen too often, but when it did, it was absolutely the best bit of all.

Standing there, alone, in that darkened booth, headphones on and singing my heart out, was what made it all worthwhile. It was the same feeling I used to get when I sang the princess routines—I could shut everything else out, and lose myself in the song. Go to my happy place.

So far, I'd only done Vogue songs and a few covers—nobody was writing new tunes for the PR slave, let's face it. But it still made it all worthwhile—it gave me a delicious taste of what it might all be like, one day. One day that I had to hope—had to believe—would arrive soon.

If it didn't, I might just shrivel up and die, and they'd find me in the stationery cupboard one morning, like a slug that had been sprinkled with salt.

After all of that, at the end of my typical day at Starmaker, I'd trail my poor, exhausted body back out through the office. Down the plush corridors lined with framed platinum discs. Past the dark studio booths. Through to reception, with its vases full of lilies and spotlessly clean mirrored furniture, to the glamorous chrome spiral staircase, its curving walls decorated with enormous blown-up pictures of the talent on the label's roster. When that mysterious 'one day' arrived, I'd be up there too—I had to believe that. I had to believe that Annie was right, and tomorrow was only a day away.

Most nights, I'd walk as quickly as I could to the Tube station, hunch down, and push my way onto the Northern Line. It had taken me a while to get used to the fact that nobody spoke to each other—in fact people looked at you as if you had a screw loose if you even made eye contact with them. It was a lot different in Liverpool, where you could get someone's whole life story over a burger on the night bus. Here, I'd learned to hide behind a magazine, or spend the whole journey checking my phone while I listened to music on ear phones—which was about as much fun as it sounds.

It was only a few stops to Kentish Town at least, where I lived in an extremely glamorous studio apartment. Or, if you wanted to be more accurate, a one-room bedsit above a kebab shop, where the most exciting thing to happen was the mouldy pattern on the ceiling slowly changing shape because of the leak in the roof.

Once I was home—and once I'd managed to get past Yusuf, the shop owner and landlord, who talked so much he made up for the rest of London—I'd collapse. I'd watch telly, or read, or stand in front of my fridge, staring into it, wishing there was more food and that I was allowed to eat it if there was.

I'd be in bed by eleven, going over the high points of the day and trying to stuff the low points to the back of my mind, where they belonged. Between seeing Yusuf and getting into work the next morning, I wouldn't speak to a single living soul—and then it would just be Patty screaming at me because her tights had laddered, and it was all my fault.

Other nights, though, it would be different. Very different.

So different, in fact, that it was a bit like I had a foxier twin sister who'd been stolen at birth, and lived a completely opposite life to mine.

Because on those other nights, Jack Duncan would message me, and arrange to meet me nearby. He'd have his flashy little Audi, and he'd be wearing beautifully crisp white shirts, and his hair would be artfully flopping across his handsome face, and he'd smell completely fantastic, not like a kebab at all.

On those nights, my life would be very different. They'd involve romantic dinners and long chats over expensive wine and lingering kisses that made my toes curl up in excitement.

Because, yes—Jack Duncan did, in fact, seem interested in getting his leg over. And he was starting to make me think it was a really excellent idea.

Chapter 7

I know, I know.

It sounds bad, doesn't it? Sleeping with the boss? It sounds like a complete stereotype, in fact—the bright-eyed young wannabe shagging her way to stardom. The older, more experienced record exec taking advantage of her desperation to get a roll in the hay.

Except…it wasn't like that at all. It really wasn't. For a start, we hadn't even done it.

And—although I might sound like I'm trying to convince myself here—everything that *had* happened had felt very natural, and very real. It wasn't as though I'd arrived in London, been chucked on a casting couch, and ordered to get jiggy with it. If that had happened, I'd have told him where to get off, and caught the next train back to Lime Street. Team Jessy just didn't roll that way, thank you very much.

In fact, though, it had all started with a cappuccino. On my first day at the office, Jack had taken me for a coffee at this trendy place around the corner where a cuppa cost as much as a crate of ale. He'd explained my schedule, he'd asked about my flat, and he'd told me what I needed to hear—that I'd done the right thing.

'Life's all about taking chances,' he'd said, sipping his drink and gazing at me with those dreamy dark eyes of his. 'And that's what you've done. Bravo. How do you feel now you're actually here?'

I still felt on the nervous side around him, so I wasn't completely truthful. That would have involved words like 'petrified', 'terrified', and other things that ended in 'ied'. Instead, I settled for 'a bit anxious'.

'That's understandable,' he'd said, leaning back in his chair and smiling at me. He was so calm. So charming. So completely comfortable in his own skin, and in this over-priced café full of beautiful people. 'And I get it. But you need to know that I'm here for you, even if you fall on your backside in a pile of mud. Metaphorically speaking.'

'Well, you've seen me do it before,' I replied, 'and it might well happen again. Although so far I've not even seen any grass, never mind mud.'

'I can fix that. One day, when you've settled in, I'll have to take you out and show you the sights. It's a beautiful city, and there is plenty of mud to roll round in if you know where to look. And if you're that way inclined. Maybe if the mood takes me I'll roll round in it with you—get in touch with my inner druid.'

He was so well turned out in his tailored shirt and posh jeans, he looked like he was more likely to have an inner male model than an inner druid. I tried to picture him dressed in a white toga and prancing round Stonehenge chanting, but that just made me giggle.

Giggling is never a good idea when you've just chugged your posh coffee, and I choked on my cappuccino—spluttering it up, and spraying the whole table, his face, and the front of my top with frothy foam. Of course.

I blushed bright red, having one of those you-can-take-the-girl-out-of-Liverpool moments as I felt like every hipster in the place turned to stare at me. Even the girl chalking up the specials on the blackboard stopped to have a gander.

Jack just wiped his face and laughed along with me—putting me completely at ease again, just like he had at Jocelyn's party. This was starting to become a theme: me messing up, everyone else being amused/horrified by me, and Jack just... not caring. Just keeping calm, and carrying on.

'I'm so sorry,' I said, swiping at the table top with the sleeve of my best Karen Millen jacket. 'Every time I see, you I seem to be doing something stupid. I'm not normally like this, honest to God. Usually, I can go whole days without a cock up.'

He raised one eyebrow at me, and gave me a very direct look in response to what I'd just said. Um. Maybe I could have phrased that one a bit better. As usual. At home, Luke or Becky would have poked me and said: 'A cock up where?' or something equally rude. Here, I realised I was treading on foreign soil.

'Sorry, *again*,' I muttered. 'I've got to learn to think before I speak...'

'It's all right,' he replied, grinning. 'It's cute. And anyway, I'm here to help. It'll be like in *My Fair Lady*—I can be Professor Higgins to your Eliza Doolittle.'

'Well, I'm definitely common enough, I'm starting to realise,' I answered, looking around me.

It was funny, but I'd never felt common in Liverpool. I'd felt normal. But here, people already seemed more precise; more driven. More capable of drinking a cup of coffee without spitting it everywhere.

'You're not common,' he said quickly. 'And don't ever feel like you're not good enough. Didn't I read somewhere that Liverpool was the pop music capital of the world? You come from a place that's produced a lot of talent, a lot of stars. Must be something you all breathe in from the Mersey. So don't ever be ashamed of what you are—just be yourself.'

'That's not what Professor Higgins says to Eliza,' I replied. And I should know—it was one of my favourite musicals, and I'd watched it maybe a hundred times.

'Fair point…okay, be a *better* version of yourself. One you feel comfortable with, but also one where you don't feel embarrassed when you realise what you've said or what you've done. If this thing works out—and I really hope it will—you'll need to be aware of how you come across in interviews, on stage, on camera. You can still be you—but maybe save the real you for your people who don't mind getting covered in mud or drenched with cappuccino.'

'Like you?' I asked, not quite able to stop myself sounding a tiny bit flirty. He was too old for me, I told myself. He was my boss. And anyway—he was out of my league, and probably just being kind. A man as hot as him, working in the industry he did, probably had seventeen supermodel girlfriends on speed dial. Why would he be interested in a slightly tattered blonde former princess from Liverpool?

'*Exactly* like me,' he answered, his voice slow and drawling and the sheen in his eyes making my tummy do little loop-the-loops. *Oooh*, I thought. He was interested—which made the whole thing a lot harder to ignore. It was possible I was reading too much into his tone—but I definitely wasn't reading too much into the way he'd reached out, and covered my hand with his on the table top.

He gave my trembling fingers a little squeeze, stroking my palm with his thumb in a way that promised all kinds of interesting skills, and gave me the super-smile again.

'Just don't worry. I'm here. I'll help you any way I can. You need to put the work in—but you need to play as well.'

'Play?' I mumbled, losing my ability to think straight—not that I seemed to have much of that particular ability anyway—and staring at him like a brain-dead muppet.

'Play,' he confirmed. 'Have fun. Relax. Let go. And I don't want to sound like I'm bragging, Jess, but one thing I'm really good at is playing…'

It turned out he wasn't bragging at all. That first trip out for coffee had been repeated the week after. Then it had turned into a drink after work a few days later. Then it had evolved into dinner. Our hugs at the end of the night had evolved too—into gentle kisses, slow and sensual and oh-so-yummy.

Jack Duncan wasn't like any other men I'd met. He certainly wasn't like any of the men I'd been out with. For a start, he didn't stick his tongue down my throat the minute we started snogging. He didn't shove his hand up my top and root around for my bra strap. He didn't point to his hard-on and say, 'Come and get it, you lucky bitch'—which admittedly had only happened to me once, but still tops my least-romantic-quote-of-all-time list.

He was…slow. Teasing. Tempting. He kissed me as though I was precious, as if I was some wonderful delicacy he wanted to savour and enjoy. Like he wanted to make it last, instead of racing towards the next hurdle. And he didn't just kiss my lips. He kissed my neck, my earlobes, my collarbone, my wrists, all in such a gentle and tantalising way that I was begging for more. Hoping for more.

But it hadn't, as yet, gone beyond that. Even though I really, really wanted it to—at least I did at the time it was happening. In the cold light of day, I could recognise that it was a bad idea. In the warm light of night, though, in the shadow of streetlamps and under the gaze of the moon and stars, it always seemed like a very, very good idea indeed.

It wasn't just the way he touched me—it was the way he treated me. We had fun together. We enjoyed each other's company. He told great stories about the music business, and he laughed at my not-so-great stories about the Princess business, and he listened to my hopes and dreams and never mocked them. He understood how hard it was getting through my days, but he never let me feel sorry for myself—he was sympathetic, but tough, telling me it was just a stage, just a step. That one day, I'd look back and be grateful for the fact that I had real insider knowledge of how the industry worked…

Somehow, he made it all make sense. Somehow, he made my hellish days with Patty and her cronies feel worthwhile, part of my work ethic. Somehow, he made all my fears and doubts and insecurities disappear—at least for a few hours. A few hours of great conversation that would be followed up with one of those delicious, heart-rate-bumping kisses.

Those nights with Jack were the absolute highlights of my London life—not that they had much competition.

And, I reminded myself as I trekked back to Patty with her miraculously un-spat-in coffee, tonight was going to be one of those nights. We'd already arranged it, and I couldn't wait.

I just needed to keep my head down, get through the day without killing anyone (including myself), and look forward to spending time with Jack. We were going for dinner at Chico's, a little Italian place tucked away in the cutest mews street I'd ever seen, and then, if I was lucky, I'd get some of those gourmet kisses for pudding.

At least that was the kind of pudding that didn't add inches to my apparently ginormous hips.

Chapter 8

I half expected someone to spot the difference in me the next day. I thought Patty would notice the glow, and declare I was looking radiant. Instead, she just narrowed her eyes at me and suggested I should start getting more beauty sleep—'like twenty-four hours a day'.

Huh. So much for my radiant glow, I thought, as I arranged their organic artisanal macadamia nut cookies on a plate. Not that they'd eat them—the whole PR department was on a permanent diet. They just kind of inhaled them, and then spent the rest of the day talking about how guilty it made them feel. If one of them chewed on a chia seed they'd declare themselves full.

I nipped to the loo while I waited for the coffee to perc, and glanced at myself in the mirror. Hmm. Maybe she had a point—I did look a bit rough round the edges. My hair had a tangle in the back of it the size of Dubai, and my liner had done an unintentional zigzag beneath my left eye. I wasn't wearing the same clothes as the day before—Jack had booked me a cab home at the crack of dawn to avoid any Walk of Shame scenarios—but I could definitely do with some quality time in the shower.

Somehow, though, I just couldn't find it in me to care. I was happy—I was walking on sunshine, as Katrina and her Waves might have said. I was even happier than I'd have been if I'd scoffed all those organic macadamia nut biscuits.

It had finally happened. After what felt like a month of foreplay, it had finally happened...and boy, had it had been worth the wait.

Dinner was lovely, even if I did skip the tiramisu—something that would normally have had my mum feeling my forehead with the back of her hand in case I was running a temperature. And after that, we'd gone to this little place in a backstreet in Chelsea that was all dark wood panelling and smelled of brandy and whisky and cigars, even though nobody seemed to be smoking one.

We'd spent ages talking; just talking and talking and talking—about music, about life, about family and friends and our hopes for the future. Okay, I will admit that he didn't reveal too much—but it was a nice change to be with a man who wanted to listen as much as he wanted to bang on about himself. He was genuinely interested in me, which took me a while to get used to—I mean, I'm not that interesting, to be honest. At least I don't usually think I am.

I'm all right—I'm not so boring someone would fall asleep while they're having a conversation with me or anything—but I'm not likely to be signed up as a guest on *Newsnight* any time soon either. And I'm okay looking—I know I'm not a minger, and I scrub up well, but I'm nothing special. Nobody's going to trip over themselves staring at me on the street.

But with Jack, I felt different. He made me feel like I was a sexy supermodel, not just someone who scrubbed up well. He made me feel like my stories were brilliant, my views were important, that everything about me was fascinating. We laughed and we chatted and we flirted and we drank—and it was all totally dazzling. It was like being exposed to a completely new species of manhood—one I'd never encountered before.

Maybe I was a bit star struck, I don't know. Maybe I was also a bit grateful, that Jack had seen something in me that so many others had missed. Maybe I was just sex-starved and he was gorgeous. Whatever the reasons, though, the end result was the same—I was hooked.

When we'd emerged from the bar and climbed into his Audi I'd been merry and giggly and high on life. He was nowhere near as merry—he was driving, after all—but he did seem happy.

'I've had a wonderful night, Jess,' he said, turning towards me and laying one hand on my knee. I don't know whether he'd planned it that way, but he'd parked right under one of those old-fashioned streetlights that's made of curved wrought iron and looks all olde worldy, like something from a Dickens film. The glow from it was cast over his face, shining from his dark eyes, glinting on the deep brown waves of his hair. To use an intellectual term, it was pretty hot.

'Me too,' I said, then straight away burped like a frog with some serious digestive issues. It was a good, strong burp—

deep and croaky. Luke would probably have given it an eight out of ten for comedy effect.

I quickly covered my mouth with my hand, and realised I was too tipsy to be as horrified as I should be. Instead, I started laughing—because, you know, noises that come from your body are naturally funny. At least they are where I come from—we never get fed up of fart jokes in our house.

He joined in, and we both laughed for a few minutes, until I was able to speak again.

'I'd say I'm sorry, but I'm not really,' I said. 'It's your fault for getting me drunk. And at least it was only one burp—my sister Becky can do them on demand. She can even make tunes out of them.'

'Really?' he asked, raising one eyebrow and grinning. 'How fantastic. Has she considered going on *Britain's Got Talent*?'

'Not yet, but I might suggest it to her… Anyway, I really did have a great night, Jack. I suppose I'd better get home and sleep this off.'

He nodded, and looked at me seriously, his eyes never moving from mine. Unlike his hand, which was definitely moving—in little circular motions on my thigh that should have tickled, but instead just made me feel a bit gooey inside.

'Is that what you want?' he said simply, all traces of laughter gone from his voice. 'To go home? Because of course, I'll take you if you do. But… I was wondering… if you'd like to take this to the next level? Come back to mine for a coffee?'

Something in my expression must have changed—and maybe he interpreted it as something negative—because straight away he continued: 'And by coffee, I do mean coffee—no strings attached.'

'Oh,' I said, leaning back in the plush leather seat in a way I hoped was sexy, but probably just made me look like I needed a wee. 'Just for a coffee? I can get coffee at my flat.'

'Mine's better,' he replied, instantly, smiling at me in a way that I can only describe as Pure Sexy. 'It's hotter and it's smoother and it'll definitely keep you up all night. If that's what you want.'

It *was* what I wanted. In fact—and I'm so glad I didn't actually say this out loud—I was gagging for it. I'd always tried to have good intentions about Jack; no matter how good-looking or charming he was, I'd tried to avoid thinking about it becoming anything more. Because he was my boss. Because I didn't want to behave like an idiot and get the knock back if he wasn't interested, beyond a few casual kisses. Because I knew I was vulnerable—my glamorous life was taking its toll on me, with the long hours and all the hard work for so little return. I wasn't at my strongest, and didn't want to make it all even worse by getting my knickers in a twist about a man.

But, well… I'm only flesh and blood, you know? And it's not like I jumped into bed with him. We'd taken the time to get to know each other. We'd had coffee dates and dinner dates and drinks dates. We'd had kisses and cuddles and long, lingering moments where things could have moved quicker—but they hadn't. We'd taken it slow. Or—if I was being really honest with myself—Jack had taken it slow.

So, cutting a long story short, I'd spent the night at his flat. His penthouse apartment on the top of a modern building with views over the Thames—a place that I'd have to call a bachelor pad. It was ultra-sleek and ultra-stylish and it had an ultra-big bed—which is where we spent most of the night. A lady doesn't kiss and tell—and neither do I—but it had been fantastic. I was a bit drunk, which helped—I worry less about the way my body looks when I'm a bit drunk, which makes it all a lot better. It's no fun when you're too busy holding your tummy in to enjoy yourself, is it? Plus, there was the Jack factor—the way he made me feel, during our dates: as if I was the centre of his world, and he was lucky to be spending time with me. Well, he was like that in the bedroom as well.

I'm not that experienced when it comes to sex—I've not had very many boyfriends, and the only time I ever had a one-night stand, I didn't know it was going to be one until the next morning. But I was experienced enough to understand that Jack was good at it—and that he could become addictive.

That was the only thing that was worrying me, as I scuttled around the office carrying the tray of drinks and cookies back to the PR pillocks. That I'd be too into him. That I'd do that girl thing and mix up good sex and good company with something more, and blow it all out of proportion. That even if I didn't intend to, I'd find myself doodling Jess Duncan on scrap paper to see what my new signature would look like.

We'd had a bit of a talk about it, afterwards. When we were lying tangled up in his silk sheets, listening to softly playing soul music, the candles he'd lit around the bed burning low and filling the room with the scent of something spicy and musky. We agreed that whatever happened next, we'd need to keep it a secret—for both our sakes.

He didn't want to be seen as the Starmaker lech, taking advantage of the talent. And I didn't want to be seen as a slapper, understandably enough.

'Let's just go with the flow, Jess,' he'd said, stroking my hair and leaning forward to gently kiss me. 'See where this takes us—letting other people in on it will only complicate matters. I want to have you all to myself for a while, anyway. I'm selfish like that.'

The way he'd said that had sounded so romantic—wanting me all to himself. Like I was a chocolate fudge cake or something. And last night, I'd been happy with that. This morning, as I scooted around my flat trying to find clean underwear and wondering if all that energetic bonking had earned me a bacon buttie for breakfast, I'd still been happy with that.

Now, as I tried to work and found myself constantly finding excuses to walk past Jack's office, I wasn't so sure. I'd checked my phone about three million times. I'd casually chatted to Heidi at her desk only a few times less. And all I got from it was a crick in my neck from trying to stare through his glass door from behind one of the potted palm trees. I don't know why I bothered—the glass was frosted, and all I could see were vague shapes moving around. It could have been my uncle Brian in there for all I could tell.

I knew I was behaving badly—stupidly—but I couldn't quite stop myself.

I'd been here before. All women have, I think. At that stage where you feel brilliant and crap all at the same time. That stage where everything could happen—or nothing at all.

That stage where I'd normally have Ruby to talk to, or Becky—and now, here in London, I had nobody.

Unless you counted Patty—and as she was currently taking off her platform boots so I could go and polish them for her, I really, really didn't.

Chapter 9

'You have kebab,' said Yusuf, thrusting a wrapped paper package at my sister's hands. He pointed to her belly, which was now noticeably carrying a passenger, and added, 'Make big strong baby for you.'

Becky took hold of the parcel and grinned at him, saying 'thank you' over her shoulder as we walked up the stairs to my flat.

'I think I'm in love,' she said, glancing back down the steps as Yusuf waved at her. 'I might leave Sean and move in with you, just to be near him. He can be my new baby daddy.'

'Yusuf is sixty-four, he's married with seven kids, and that belly of his won't go away in a few months' time like yours will,' I replied, shoving the key into the door and turning it.

'I know. But who can resist a man who gives you free food? And he seems so nice…'

'He is,' I said, as I led us back inside. 'He's a love. If he didn't come free with the flat, I'd pay extra for him. I always know he's looking out for me, and it never matters if I lose my keys.'

'Plus, you know, free kebabs?' she said, walking to the

kitchen counter and unwrapping her food. I grabbed two plates down from the cupboard, and she sighed with contentment as she plonked her mega-meal down onto hers.

I did what I usually do when Yusuf gives me a freebie—pulled the meat off the pitta, and threw the bread in the bin, leaving just the lamb and the salad.

Becky pulled a face at me as we collapsed down onto the sofa.

'What's up with that?' she said, through a mouthful of meat and lettuce. 'Is the bread minging, or something?'

'No... I'm just, you know, off carbs,' I said, looking regretfully at her pitta, which was dripping with juices and sauce. I'd not eaten bread for six weeks now, and it was starting to bite. I sometimes went into a trance-like state, and when I came to, found myself standing outside the French bakery on the corner, my nose pressed up to the window, making a pig face and sniffing deliriously. One day I'd get stuck and they'd have to peel me off.

'Off carbs?' she said, looking confused. 'Are you going to Marbs?'

'I wish!' I answered, making the most of the kebab I did have left. 'I'm just trying to stay in shape—I have dance classes, and they're pretty hard. The last thing I need is to be dragging a lard arse around with me.'

'You don't have a lard arse,' replied Becky. 'And you never have had, much as Luke would like you to think different. You don't need to lose any more weight—you look fantastic. Apart from, well...'

'What?' I snapped, my eyes wide open. I was on a bit of

a roller coaster with my self-esteem these days, and seemed to have lost all balance and control. If someone—okay, Jack—said something nice to me about the way I looked, my confidence would sky rocket. If someone—okay, Jack—said something less nice, I'd plummet into misery.

It was kind of pathetic, but I didn't really know what to do to change it. I mean, Jack rarely ever said anything critical—on the whole, he was lovely. He was attentive and flattering and charming and usually made me feel brilliant about myself. When he was around, at least. Which wasn't all that often.

After we'd spent our first night together, I hadn't seen him properly for another five days. He'd texted me, something cute and slightly rude that tided me over and stopped me taking a detour into crazy town, but we'd not actually got together again for what felt like a lifetime.

By the time we did—a walk along the river, drinks, back to his place—I'd given myself a good talking to. I was taking it all too seriously—I was clinging on to what might happen with Jack because the rest of my life was so empty and depressing. And that wasn't fair to either of us—it put too much pressure on him, and it made me feel like a great big loser, with a capital L.

I didn't want to be the kind of woman who sat around all day mooning over some bloke. The kind of woman who was constantly checking if her phone had run out of charge because she hadn't heard from a man. I wanted to be the kind of woman who treated it all as fun, who was carefree and light-hearted and good to be around.

In the end, I kind of became both. When I was with him,

I managed the carefree and light-hearted—and he was such good company, he made that easy. It was hard to be miserable with Jack around, and even if I was, he could whisk me off to bed and make me forget all about it. He could even make me forget about bread, it was that good.

But when I was on my own? Trekking back from the office after a long, exhausting day, hungry and tired and lonely? After not seeing him or hearing from him and wondering what he was up to and who he was up to it with? That's when I took out my L plate, and stuck that loser sign on my forehead, and wallowed in it.

It was one of the reasons I'd been so made up when Becky said she was coming to stay for a couple of nights—seeing her would distract me, and take my mind off everything I was worried about. Now, though, I felt suddenly self-conscious.

'Well…you just look a bit tired, Jessy,' she said tactfully, picking up on how sensitive I was feeling. 'And a bit like you need to eat some doughnuts.'

'I'm fine,' I said quickly, standing up and throwing the rest of the kebab in the bin, where it joined its long-lost bread family.

'I don't think you are,' Becky answered, looking around at the flat as I sat back down next to her. I'd spent days scrubbing and tidying before she came, and bought fresh flowers that I'd arranged around the place in old wine bottles, and one of those floral plug-ins to try to mask the eau de kebab that pretty much always wafted up from the shop downstairs. But looking at it through her eyes, I saw it for what it was: small, shabby, and a little bit sad.

'You seem a bit lonely, love. And those cows you work with don't seem to be helping.'

I'd taken Becky into the Starmaker offices that day to intro-duce her to people, hoping, I suppose, to impress her with my glamorous new life. Patty had just looked her up and down, listened to her talk, and said: 'I'm sorry, I don't understand a word you're saying,' before flouncing off to meet someone from the *Star* for brunch.

After that, it had just got worse—the whole PR department seemed to have chosen that day to have some communal meltdown, and Becky had to sit in reception waiting for me, while I did emergency photocopying and made vats of coffee and generally ran round like a blue-arsed fly.

The only highlight had been bumping into Vogue in the lifts. Vogue was a megastar—and came across as a total diva on stage. But in the flesh, she couldn't be nicer. She was about six-foot tall and looked a bit like Naomi Campbell, and she should have been scary. I'd seen her in interviews, and sometimes she definitely seemed scary.

In real life, though, she was a babe. She'd remembered my name—pretty much a first at Starmaker—and asked when Becky's baby was due, and even asked her where she'd got her shoes from (Kirkby Market, so I can't imagine Vogue would be dashing out to get her own pair any time soon). The whole conversation lasted about two minutes, but it had made my day—and Becky's. At least now she had a good story to tell when she got home.

Of course, one of the reasons I'd taken her into the office was the hope that Jack would be there. That he'd see us, and come over, and I'd get to feel that thrill of having such a gorgeous boyfriend and showing him off to my big sister.

Except, you know, he wasn't my boyfriend. He was my... well, I had no idea what he was. And he wasn't in the office anyway—even though I'd told him Becky was coming. Apparently, according to Heidi, he was at a meeting in Brussels. He did things like that—had meetings in Brussels, or lunch in Paris, or a gig in Barcelona. He was a VIP, and his schedule was just a little bit different to mine.

It was one of the aspects of Jack's life that made him feel like an unattainable mega-being from another planet. My reaction varied from 'this will never work' to 'why is a man like that interested in a girl like me?' to 'I'm never letting him go, and I want to have his babies', depending on what mood I was in. Even thinking about him then, with Becky sitting right there, I wondered if he was back yet—wondered if he'd message me, wondered when we'd meet up again.

I snapped myself back to reality, and met Becky's probing gaze. She—unlike me, apparently—was looking great. The morning sickness had obviously passed, her fair hair was glossy, her skin was clear, and she'd obviously hit that 'glowing' stage that preggers women are supposed to get.

I gave her a big, bright smile, and said, 'No, I'm good—honest. I work hard, but I always expected that. And it's all worth it.'

'Are you sure?' she replied, with a look on her face that was very similar to our mum's when she thought you were hiding something—like the fact that you'd secretly drunk her bottle of Baileys with your mates; or snuck out to go to a party when you were grounded, or put your red T-shirt in the whites wash and made it all pink. It was frightening—Becky hadn't even had her baby yet, and she was already developing scary Mum-like telepathic powers. It must be hereditary.

I nodded, gesturing for her to get up as I pulled the sofa-bed out into its bed form. I grabbed the pile of sheets and pillows from the chair where I'd dumped them earlier, and started making it up to sleep on. Becky was having the bed—although not the bed*room*, as there wasn't one. We'd be kipping together again, just like when we were kids.

'I'm sure,' I said, 'and I'm knackered. Let's crash out and talk crap before we go to sleep, like we used to.'

'Yeah,' she answered, pulling on her pyjamas and laughing. 'All right. As long as we can talk about boys. Because I know there's a man on the scene, Jessy.'

I ignored her, and climbed under the covers, pulling the fleecy blanket up to my chin. Obviously, she was right. But I just couldn't talk about it to her—because I had no idea what to tell her. It was all very hard to describe, especially to someone who didn't know Jack, and didn't know the music business, and didn't know the way this weird London world worked.

When I stayed quiet, she took that as her cue to carry on. I'd hoped she'd think I was asleep—I should probably have manufactured some fake snoring.

'I know there's a man because you've checked your phone about three hundred times today. And because there are con-doms in your bathroom cabinet, and—'

'What?' I spluttered at her, outraged, and obviously not asleep.

'Of course I looked! Have you ever met me? It's my sisterly duty to snoop as much as humanly possible. So, tell me all about him.'

'There's nothing to tell,' I said, reaching out and switching the lamp off. 'It's nothing special.'

I was so scared that that statement was actually true, I felt tears stinging the back of my eyes, and hoped Becky's new maternal superpowers didn't extend as far as having non-goggle night vision. Or the same eyes in the back of her head that Mum always claimed to have.

'All right, keep your big secret, Little Miss Superstar. But look after yourself, okay? And please tell me it's not *him*.'

'Who?' I asked, knowing full well who she meant.

'That Jack Duncan one. He's the one who brought you down here, and he's the reason you seem to be living in a shitty flat, working with bitches, and starving yourself. I know you're doing the other stuff as well—the singing and the dancing and the recording—and that's all brilliant. But the rest isn't. And I'm worried about you. So tell me it's not him.'

'It's not him,' I said quietly, fingers crossed on both hands as the lie slipped out, along with a few random tears that I'd not managed to completely squish away. I felt them trickle away down my cheeks and disappear, along with my self-respect.

I told myself the lie was for her sake. That she was pregnant, and her life was changing fast; that she'd just bought a house and was in the process of moving and that her plate was full. That the last thing she needed was to be worried about me.

I told myself that, but that was a lie, too. Or at least it

wasn't a hundred-per-cent truthful. I was also embarrassed, and ashamed, and miserable. When I was with Jack, it all felt right. But when I was away from him, I started to feel like some dirty little secret, hidden away from the real world he lived in. And now—just when I'd thought it couldn't get any worse—I'd fibbed to my sister. My pregnant sister—which had to be bad karma.

'*Good*,' she said, firmly, rolling around on the bed, trying to get comfy. 'Now I've got that off my chest, I feel relaxed enough to do this…'

She paused, then let out a giant, rip-roaring fart that seemed to echo around the tiny flat, before it came to settle fragrantly in my nostrils. I tried not to inhale—I'd suffered those sisterly gifts many times over the years and knew they were lethal— but I was laughing so much I couldn't help it.

'Jesus, Becky! I think I need a gas mask!'

'It's my hormones. I can't help it.'

'It's the kebab, and you are loving it!' I said, pinching my nose together to try and block out the smell, still laughing.

'That's good to hear,' she said, fidgeting around. I suppose it was hard to settle when you had an alien being growing inside your stomach. 'You laughing again.'

She finally seemed to find a position that agreed with both her and the baby, and I made out her face in the moonlight seeping through the curtains that never seemed to quite close properly. She was smiling at me, and reached out to hold my hand.

We touched fingers, and I smiled back. Nothing was perfect

in my life—but I still had Becky, and the rest of my family. No matter what.

'You can always come home, you know,' she said. 'Nobody would think any the worse of you. Nobody would think you'd failed.'

Nobody apart from me, I thought, but didn't say it. When I didn't respond, she carried on.

'Because home,' she said, screwing up her eyes in effort, warning me what was coming next, 'is where the fart is.'

The sound of that one—along with the sound of us both giggling like the little kids we were not so very long ago—was the last thing I remembered before I fell asleep.

Chapter 10

When the text first landed, I thought I'd finally made it into the inner circle. How wrong could I have been?

'Get to the Panache Club by 8 p.m.—urgent! Make sure you're clean!' it read. Typically, Patty hadn't bothered with any internal debate about whether to add kisses or not, and was presumably labouring under the illusion that Scousers didn't wash. I had no idea where she got that concept from, but I spent a good twenty minutes standing under the lukewarm jets of the shower before I left for the club. Just in case she checked behind my ears or something.

The Panache Club was in central London, and was currently considered the Cool Place to Be. It was the kind of club where Rihanna would go for a boogie if she was in town; the kind of club where supermodels would ignore canapés and look moody. The kind of club I was never, ever invited to.

I knew there was a big event there—Patty and her pals had been having orgasms about the tabloid opportunities for weeks now—but, as usual, I wasn't asked along. It was a Saturday, and I was supposed to be in my broom cupboard, polishing my glass slippers and wishing for a Fairy Godmother. Instead, I thought excitedly, I was maybe—just maybe—going to make my first public Starmaker appearance.

Maybe Jack would be there, and we'd snog on the dance-floor. Maybe Rihanna would be there, and we'd down some tequilas together. Maybe the tabloid snappers who turned up would be wowed by my awesome beauty and stunning star quality, and I'd be papped as I arrived.

Maybe, I thought, rubbing myself dry and feeling the chill of a flat that simply never warmed up until the kebab shop did, I would finally be accepted.

I heard the phone beeping again, and dashed over to check it out, hoping it would be from Jack—saying he'd pick me up, or meet me beforehand, or that we'd spend the night together after the party. Also hoping—if I was entirely honest—that he'd magically arranged for a beautiful dress to be delivered, so I could make some grand entrance in modern-day *Pretty Woman* style. Without the prostitution angle, obviously.

Shivering, I swiped on the phone to check my messages. Huh. No such luck—it was from Patty again.

'Black skirt and white blouse. No stains.'

As the words and all that they implied slowly sunk in, I fell backwards onto the sofa, deflated and disappointed and damp. Black skirt, white blouse—I knew what that meant. It meant they needed an extra pair of hands for the waiting-on staff, and I was their very first draft pick.

So much for downing tequila with Rihanna—I'd be the one serving it to her. Not that she'd be there, of course—this was my fictional Rihanna.

I did a grumpy face for a few minutes, and considered

texting Patty back to say I couldn't make it—that I had a hot date at a cage fight with Tom Hardy that night, or I was busy strolling down the Ramblas on a city break in Barcelona with Orlando Bloom. It would serve her right for the 'no stains' comment—I mean, as if! My mother was the queen of laundry, and some of it had been passed on by genetics.

I toyed with the idea of refusing for a while, and started to mentally compose the message, before I turned off the phone and placed it well out of reach on the mantelpiece. I gave myself a good talking to, recalling all of Jack's words about playing for the Starmaker team, about learning my craft, about understanding the industry from the inside out. Starting at the bottom, soaring to the top.

I wasn't entitled to anything—and I needed to keep my feet on the ground, and not give in to the depression.

But truth be told, since Becky had left, I'd been struggling. We'd spent her last morning here wandering around Camden Market, where she'd bought an entire set of baby clothes decorated with tiny skulls, before I saw her off at Euston. As I waved her away with tears in my eyes, part of me just wanted to jump on that train with her. To give up, to abandon it all, and head for home. Liverpool was only two hours away on the train—but a whole world away on the lifestyle scale.

At home, I could sleep in my own bed, get annoyed with my baby brother, and be fed huge plates full of bacon and eggs the next morning. Without any guilt whatsoever. Mum and Dad would welcome me back, and I could pick up right where I left off.

Except…where I left off wasn't exactly brilliant, was it? I

was sharing a flat that was almost as crappy as the one I lived in now, with Ruby and her perverted geriatric boyfriend, singing princess songs to spoiled brats every weekend. I might not have any spare cash now—but I didn't have any then, either.

I realised, as Becky's face in the window dwindled to a tiny blob heading into the tunnel, that I didn't care about the flat, or the money. Or even the bacon and eggs, that much.

What I really missed was the people. The casual conversations that could start any time and any place in Liverpool. The way you could bond with someone at the fish counter in Tesco, or in the queue at the chippie, or at a lock-in at the pub. I missed that—and I missed my family. My family, who thought I was worth something, that I was special. Who loved me and consoled me and made me laugh all the time.

That had been replaced with Patty, who clearly thought I was worth bugger all, and Jack, who thought…well, who knows what he thought? He certainly wasn't telling. It felt perfect when I was with him—but shaky as the rope bridge in *I'm A Celebrity…* when we were separated. I was only a tiny part of his life—but he was fast becoming the most important part of mine. With Yusuf the Kebab Man as a close second, which tells you everything you need to know about my social life.

Still, I knew I had to stick with it for a little while longer—that I wouldn't forgive myself if I packed it all in too soon, before I'd given it my very best shot. If I wussed out, and spent the rest of my life wondering about what *could* have been.

So, I'd let that train go, wiped my eyes, and fought my way through the refugee camp that Euston at rush hour always felt like, getting my feet run over by suitcases on wheels and getting jostled as I walked towards the escalator into the Tube. It was literally all downhill from there. And now, here I was, reaping my reward. Wet. Cold. Alone. And planning an excitingly glamorous night out as hired help who probably wouldn't even get paid.

But, I told myself as I rooted suitable clothing out of my wardrobe, it was better than what I had had planned for the night—sitting at home watching crap telly, listening to my tummy rumble and wondering what Jack was up to. Anything, in fact, would have been better than that.

I needed to stop feeling sorry for myself—millions of people in London would be working that night. Millions of people would be getting ready for a long shift at a pub or a restaurant or driving a bus or being a cabbie, like my dad. Hard work never killed anyone—and at least I was here pursuing a dream. At least I had hopes. At least there was light at the end of the tunnel.

Admittedly, it felt more like a train about to splatter me into squelchy pieces, but it was something. I could sing. I could dance. I could make it—and I needed to view every event like this as an opportunity, not purgatory. I'd been raised with a work ethic, and now was not the time to give up on it.

I'd wear a black skirt and a white blouse. There would be no stains. I would be clean. I would be cheerful. I would smile like a clown on Ecstasy as I waltzed round the Panache Club serving appetisers. I would be the best waitress ever.

Chapter 11

'You,' said Patty, pointing one long shellac-ed nail at me, 'are the worst waitress ever. You've had that tray of smoked salmon twists for the last hour. You must be putting people off somehow—you haven't been *speaking* to them, have you?'

I laid the offensively full tray down on the table, and plastered a tolerant smile on my face. What I really wanted to do was slam the whole tray at her head, and watch the cream cheese slither down the front of her D&G frock. But, no, that would be bad. Satisfying, but bad.

'The problem is, Patty,' I said, speaking slowly and clearly and in my poshest voice, 'that this isn't exactly a crowd that eats a lot. There are actresses and supermodels and singers, and all of them are probably on some kind of weird macrobiotic fasting diet. They just don't want food—they only want alcohol. If you give me a tray of champagne instead, I'm sure it'll be gone in a flash.'

She stared at me, the make-up lines where her eyebrows should have been screwed up in a frown, and replied, 'Oh, it's no use! I give up—I need a bloody translator! Go and take another break, will you? Get out of my sight for a while!'

She whirled around, and I saw the transformation as she did it—from a pouty-mouthed gargoyle to smiling PR professional as she faced the rest of the crowd. I was obviously so special, she saved her True Form for me and me alone.

I stuck my tongue out at her back as she tottered away on her super stupid high heels, and grabbed a handful of the cheesy salmon twists, shoving them into my mouth in defiance. Hah—take 'another' break, she'd said, as though I'd even had one at all.

I'd been working non-stop for the last three hours. I'd been smiling and happy and professional, offering the canapés to everybody in the room, even the ones who looked like they only ate via intravenous drip. The place was packed, but it was so dark it was hard to make out where everybody was—the club was hazy and black, striped across with flashing neon lighting, dance music pumping out so loud that even the smoked salmon probably had a headache.

There were booths all around the dancefloor, black leather seats and gold-topped tables overflowing with expensive booze. Each little booth had a red velvet curtain at the side of it, like in an old-fashioned cinema, tied with thick gold cord. Lilies that had been spray-painted gold and red were arranged on the tables, filling the place with that prickly pollen smell that always made me think something was on fire.

I'd already seen several famous faces, well-known names from the soaps and music and film. The first time it happened, I even said 'Hiya' to an actress from *EastEnders*, my brain somehow convincing me I knew her on a personal level.

Even if I was only there as a waitress, it had all felt pretty exciting to start off with. I mean, who doesn't like seeing famous people getting hammered?

The answer to that question, by the time I'd been on my poor feet for a while, was: Me. I'd stopped being interested in their outfits after about an hour, and lost all notion of them being remotely special when a vaguely famous weather presenter belched in my face as he stared at my boobs. Yuck. The rich and famous, I was rapidly deciding, were just as capable of being twats as the rest of the world—maybe even more so, as nobody ever dared pull them up on it.

Jack was there, looking tastier than the party food in his Tom Ford suit and white shirt with the top three buttons undone, but we'd hardly spoken. He hadn't ignored me—he'd given me a flash of that terrific smile, and waved at me as he chatted up the hot-shot new producer I knew he was keen to woo into the Starmaker stable, but it hadn't exactly been a date night either.

Only once did our paths properly cross—when he saw me carrying my tray of unwanted food towards a booth that turned out to be empty (you had to be really up close to see that, in my defence), and hurriedly followed me in there, pulling the red velvet curtains firmly closed behind us to create a secret den.

'You look hot as hell in that get-up,' he'd said, pushing me backwards into the black leather, leaning in for a kiss and letting his hand drift slowly and deliciously up beneath my pencil skirt.

I'd wrapped my fingers into the dark waves of his hair and smiled into the kiss, knowing exactly how he'd react to the rest of the outfit, and counting down the seconds until he got there.

'Aaah! Stockings! You're killing me…' he said, his fingers exploring the skin he had easy access to, leaving me hot and bothered and with my skirt as ruffled as my pulse.

Almost as soon as he'd started, though, he pulled away, standing up tall and grinning at me as he straightened his hair and adjusted his trousers.

'You're a very bad man,' I said in my best fake-sex-kitten voice. 'Don't you know I'm just a humble waitress, trying to get through the night without being molested by passing VIPs?'

'You loved it, you slut,' he said, peeking out of the red curtains. 'And we'll definitely be following up this naughty-maid theme later, I promise you.'

'Later?' I asked, tidying myself up and hating the way I managed to pack a whole world of neediness into just one little word.

'Later…this week. Not tonight. After Vogue does her spot, I'll be tied up—all work and no play for me tonight, sweet-heart. You understand, don't you? I'd much rather be seeing what you could serve up in the privacy of my bedroom than schmoozing with this lot, but it's all part of the job.'

'Of course I understand,' I said firmly, giving him a quick kiss on the cheek and picking up my tray again. 'And now you must excuse me, Mr Duncan, while I take my hot-as-hell outfit back into the club. You're not the only one with work to do.'

I'd sashayed away, giving my bum a bit of an extra swish as I did, knowing that his eyes would be glued to it. I might feel secretly devastated that we wouldn't be getting together tonight—but at least I could leave him feeling uncomfortable about it. In a world where I was largely powerless, the ability to provoke a hard-on in the man I suspected I was falling for was something to be celebrated.

Since then, I'd only seen him in passing—he was indeed schmoozing for Britain—and I occasionally stopped to admire his tall, dark and handsome-ness as I paused with my tray. I scanned the crowds to look for him before going on my break, then realised I still had a mouthful of salmon twists and probably shouldn't be allowed out in public.

I made my way to the side door behind the stage area, which led to the staff break rooms, dressing rooms, and the corridor that connected to the kitchens. It was a lot less glamorous once you passed through the magic door—no red velvet, no golden lilies, no celebs. But, I realised as I kicked off my shoes and carried them towards the staff room, also no noise—which was an absolute blessing. I hadn't realised how loud it had been until the thumping sounds echoing around my brain stopped. Or at least reduced—now it just sounded like a gentle rhythmic tap instead of someone whacking me across the ear-holes with a sledgehammer.

I was walking towards the break room—looking forward to ten minutes with my feet in an elevated position while I digested way too much smoked salmon—when the door to the dressing room burst open, catching me on the shoulder as I passed it and flinging me back to bang up against the corridor wall.

Well, I thought, as I unstuck my lip gloss from the plaster-work, at least I hadn't been carrying a tray of canapés when that happened. Things were looking up.

I rubbed my face to make sure it was all still in one piece, and turned round to see what all the commotion was about.

I came face to face with Neale, the trainee make-up artist. His shaved head was glistening with sweat, and there were actual tears running down his cheeks. His hands flew up into the air in panic, and he looked at major risk of hyperventilating.

'Neale!' I said, reaching out to take hold of his hands. I thought he might float up to the ceiling like a helium balloon if somebody didn't pull him back down to earth.

'What's up? Calm down, for goodness' sake—What's happened?'

He grasped on to me for dear life, his slim skinny-jean-clad body slumping towards me in desperation.

'Jess! Help! It's Vogue! She's…she's…'

'She's what?' I asked, peering past him into the dressing room, trying to see what was going on.

'She's puking her guts up!' came a gravelly voice from inside, shortly followed by an unpleasant retching sound that left very little to the imagination.

I stepped inside, dropping my shoes to the floor, and walked towards the megastar—who was currently burying her head in a vase that had, I guessed from the damp patch and the crushed lilies lying on the carpet, until recently been full of fresh flowers.

She was wearing what I recognised as one of her stage outfits—I'd watched her rehearsing in it enough times to know it—made of thin leather straps and sultry dark fishnet. She normally looked amazing in it—all Amazonian sex appeal;

a kind of black-dominatrix-Madonna look that I could never pull off in a million years.

But just then, she looked anything but sexy. She looked absolutely terrible, her body hunched in over the vase, shaking and shuddering as she vomited. She finally looked up, wiping her face clear of drool and smearing vivid red lipstick all across her mouth as she did it.

Her wig had come loose and slipped to one side, so her natural close-cropped curls were peeking out, and her false eyelashes were barely weathering the storm of puke, sticking together in clumps as tears streamed from her eyes, drizzling mascara over her cheekbones.

'Oh, my God!' I said, kneeling down in front of her and gazing up at the disaster zone that was Vogue's usually beautiful face. I grabbed a handful of tissues from the box on the dressing table and started dabbing at her, trying to rescue some of the work that had been done to get her stage-ready.

I glanced at my watch. She was due on at ten thirty—which, horrendously, was only thirty minutes away. Either Vogue was going to start a whole new trend of zombie-faced vomit-chic, or the show was going to be very, very late.

Her shoulders were still shaking, and the tears were still flowing, and she smelled, frankly, like sick—which is an aroma that not even the very glamorous can successfully pull off. She pushed me away with her trembling hand, which, as she immediately started throwing up again, I was very grateful for.

'How long has she been like this?' I asked, looking up at Neale, who appeared pretty nauseous himself.

'It started about fifteen minutes ago,' he answered, hands

flapping and voice racing upwards to the kind of note that could shatter lightbulbs. 'At first she just thought it was nerves—she says it sometimes happens before shows—but…it just won't stop! I'm only here to help out—she arrived half an hour ago, already done by Suzi, her stylist. I was hanging around in case she needed a touch up, or there was a wardrobe malfunction, or…well, I was just hanging around, really!'

I nodded, letting him know I got it. He was looking for his big break at Starmaker, just like I was—which seemed to involve an awful lot of hanging around, just in case.

I stroked Vogue's back as she puked, holding the strands of her black wig away from the sides of her face and making what I hoped were reassuring noises until the latest bout finally came to a throat-wrenching halt.

With a final shuddering moan she leaned back in her chair and tore off the wig completely, throwing it away from her so hard it got caught on the lampshade, hanging there dangling down from the middle of the ceiling like some hideous Halloween decoration.

She held her face in both hands, using her shaking palms to smear away snot and tears and spit and make-up, turning her look into something Picasso might have dreamed up while he was on an acid trip.

'I can't go on,' she finally said in her thick south London accent—the one that Patty never objected to, even though it was twice as strong as my Scouse one. 'I just can't fucking do it. Not tonight. You'll have to go find Jack, Neale. Tell him I'm almost dead. Tell him I've got cholera.'

'I don't think you've actually got cholera, Vogue…' started

Neale, then abruptly shut up when she snapped her eyes wide open at him, her watery green glare so vicious he decided to whimper instead.

'Cholera. Right. Got it. I'll be right back.'

He fled from the room in a blur of black, and I heard him squeaking to himself in horror as he ran back along the corridor.

I stood up, feeling my knees crack after squatting down for so long, and walked to the dressing table. I found a packet of baby wipes—make-up artists never leave home without them—and handed them to Vogue, keeping a safe distance just in case she started chucking up again. I unscrewed the lid to a fresh bottle of water from the mini-fridge, and passed that to her as well.

She nodded gratefully and took a few sips, before using the baby wipes to start cleaning herself up. I looked on, fascinated, as the layers came away. The make-up and the lashes and the fake beauty spot and the now-smeared lippie. The wig was long gone, and she was snapping open the fasteners at the back of her tight leather bustier so she could breathe better. She tugged out her earrings and lashed them down on the dresser. She used one finger to poke out her intense green contact lenses, revealing her own huge brown eyes. Her thigh-length patent leather stiletto boots followed, slung across the room, where they settled into a shiny, creaking heap.

By the time she'd finished, she looked…well, still gorgeous, in all honesty. But gorgeous in a way that wouldn't have looked out of place down the market on a Saturday morning. Gorgeous in a way that you could look if you were doing the shopping, or going to church, or picking the kids up from school. Gorgeous like a normal, genetically blessed young woman—who'd just endured a major vomiting fit.

Underneath the slap and the bling she emerged like a different person—one who looked very much like she needed to go and crawl under a duvet for a few weeks to recover.

'Are you all right?' I asked, holding forward the waste-paper bin so she could throw her crumpled up wipes away. 'Can I do anything else for you, Vogue?'

I could, of course, have offered her a smoked-salmon twist—but somehow I didn't think that was a cure for cholera. Or whatever it was that Vogue actually had.

She took a deep breath, and another long drag on the water, before looking up at me. She gave me a sad, tired smile.

'Nah,' she said. 'Thanks, though, sweetie, you've been awesome. Sorry if I caught you with any splash back. I don't know what's happening…my little sis had a tummy bug earlier this week, as did half the other kids at her birthday party. I probably should have stayed away, but, well, you know—it's family. I don't see enough of them as it is, and it was her tenth. I couldn't skip that, could I? They'd have killed me, apart from anything else.'

'I understand,' I answered. And I did. Family was family—and it had to come first, even if it made you quite literally throw up as a result of spending time with them. 'But are you feeling any better now?'

I looked nervously at the door, wondering when Neale would finally be able to find Jack and bring him back here so he could sort everything out. Jack would know what to do—he was that kind of guy. He'd have a masterplan, I was sure. He was probably a qualified doctor as well as a music-industry guru.

'A little bit,' she said, voice wobbling and cracking, 'but I don't think I can go on stage tonight. Even if I didn't look like the Joker after he's been in a sauna, I couldn't sing. Not the way my throat is hurting right now. Plus, I couldn't dance—I know this is probably TMI, Jess, but I have my suspicions the puking was just the start... I think it'll be both ends soon, if you get my drift.'

I pulled an 'eek' face that hopefully conveyed both my confirmation of the fact that yes, I definitely got her drift, and also my sympathy. We've all been there, let's face it—nobody is immune from the levelling power of Having the Shits. Not even really classy people, like the Queen of England, or George Clooney's wife.

I had no idea what they'd do about it. The party was a Starmaker celebration—a shindig to raise its profile, gather the great, the good, and the gossip-worthy under one roof and get the flash bulbs popping. Not that people really used flash bulbs that much any more.

There were plenty of well-known faces here already; there'd been masses of alcohol consumed, masses of food left to rot, and masses of cocaine had entirely possibly been snorted in the toilets. That was only a guess, mind—I didn't go in for that kind of thing myself. But I had noticed, during my time on the outer fringes of the celeb world in London, how strange it was that these people could be obsessed with looks and health—eating juiced kale for lunch, going to the gym every day, taking every vitamin supplement known to man—and still bugger it all up by going on class-A binges at parties. A puzzling paradox.

This party was probably no different, if the high-energy, high-octane atmosphere in the club was anything to go by. As well as the celebs, there were all sorts of important people from the record industry—the execs, the big bosses, the true VIPs. The people with levels of wealth that would make them contenders for hosting the Judges' Houses section of *The X Factor*. Not just from Starmaker either, but from the company that owned it—and the distributors, the digital-music-movers, and media from TV, print, and online.

It was, to give it its correct term, a Big Deal—and the star of the show, the diva who was supposed to be providing the highlight of the evening, was slowly turning as grey as out-of-date pigs' liver and rooting in her bag for an Imodium so she could get a cab home with her dignity intact.

I felt sorry for all the people who'd organised it, who'd put so much effort into making the night a success. Apart from Patty, of course, who evoked about as much sympathy as a velociraptor where I was concerned.

'Shit,' said Vogue, throwing her handbag to the floor and kicking it with her bare foot. 'I was sure I had some there. God, I'm dreading the drive home—and I'm dreading reading the papers tomorrow. They'll have made up all kinds of stories about why I was a no-show.'

'Maybe they'll have you pregnant,' I suggested, probably not very helpfully.

'Ha! You're not wrong, kid. Or they'll give me an eating disorder.'

'Or they'll have you booked into rehab.'

'Or,' she said, looking at me with the first signs of laughter in her tired eyes, 'maybe they'll give me cholera!'

'Don't be daft—who'd come up with an idea like that?' I replied, grinning.

We both laughed, briefly, and then both stopped just as quickly, as Vogue doubled up in sudden agony, rolling over into a foetal position and clutching at her stomach with her arms. She moaned and groaned, and was obviously in a lot of pain.

When she eventually straightened up, still wrapping her arms across her belly, her face was drawn and haggard and her eyes were screwed up against the spasms that I could actually hear rippling through her.

'No,' she said, more definitely than she had before. 'I actually really can't do it. I thought maybe I could once the vomming had passed, but now we're heading for round two, and nobody wants to see that live on stage, no matter how drunk they are. Shit, I don't care what the tabloids say, but I really hate letting people down. I try so hard to be professional and good to work with, and they'll all be so pissed off and think I'm just throwing some kind of diva fit—but, look at me! I just can't do this!'

I stepped towards her, and put my arm around her shoulder, giving her a quick squeeze and hoping nothing popped out as a result.

'Don't be stupid,' I said, copying the no-nonsense tone I'd heard my mum use with us when we were being down on ourselves. 'Nobody will think that. We all know how professional you are—it's just one of those things. I know they always say the show must go on, but unless you can do it from the bogs, I don't think it's going to happen this time, is it?'

Vogue leaned into me, and I could feel the clammy, cold sweat on her forehead, poor thing. She really wasn't very well at all. She was quiet for a few minutes, and I genuinely started to wonder whether she'd fallen asleep on me, and how I was going to move her so I could get back to work.

I glanced at our reflection in the mirror, and saw that far from being asleep, she was looking at me through slightly narrowed—but suddenly more alert—eyes. She was chewing one corner of her lip, as though she was wrangling with a big philosophical issue, or an especially hard question on *Pointless*. I raised my eyebrows at her, my expression asking her what she was thinking.

'Jess,' she said, finally.

'Yes,' I replied, feeling a little bit freaked out by her change of mood.

'I have an idea.'

'Okay?' I said, not willing to commit any further until I knew what it involved.

'You're right—the show must go on. And I think I know exactly how we can make that happen…'

Chapter 12

It was very difficult to speak with someone else's fingers poking around in your mouth, I was discovering—but I was trying desperately hard to do it anyway.

'I aaan't oo it!' I mumbled, tempted to bite Neale's hand as he smoothed the Crest whitening strips down onto my gnashers.

'Of course you can do it,' he said back, smoothly, refusing to be distracted by my wriggling or my distorted words. 'And you're going to look fab-u-lous while you're doing it.'

He finally finished, and I clenched my mouth shut in relief. He'd already scoured the existing make-up off my face with a touch as gentle as a WWF wrestler, and had sprinkled drops into my eyes to 'give them a little oomph'.

He'd slathered a quick facemask all over my skin, and when I looked in the mirror I saw that not only was I wearing plastic strips across my teeth, but my whole face was green. I'd gone Hulk within the few minutes it had taken for Neale to realise that this was his big chance to prove himself—whether I was willing or not.

Vogue's great idea had been so ridiculous, I'd actually

laughed out loud when she suggested it. It was only when I saw her still-serious expression that the true horror of it all sunk in.

'You go on instead of me,' she had said, not even cracking a hint of a smile. I fought the urge to look round for the hidden cameras, before coming to the conclusion that she actually meant it.

'What?' I'd replied. 'I can't do that. I'm just here to hand out the food that nobody wants. I can't… I'm not… I couldn't…'

'You are, and you can,' she'd said briskly, real steel coming into her voice. She stood up, still clutching her tummy, and I suddenly felt a bit scared. Even without her heels she had a good six inches on me.

'I've heard you rehearsing, Jess. I've seen you practising the routines in the dance studio. I know—I one hundred per cent know—that you are capable of pulling this off.'

'That's different,' I bleated, pathetically. 'That's just rehearsing. That's just in private. That's…no. I can't do this.'

'I thought you were here because you want to be a star?' she said, tilting her head and staring at me.

'I do…but I'm not ready for this, Vogue.'

'Nobody is ever ready, Jess. It's like having a baby—you might not be ready, but you won't ever regret it.'

I wondered briefly, amid all the panic that was flooding my senses, how she'd know about having a baby—but it was definitely not the right time to ask. It was the right time to flee for my life, and I found myself eyeing the door, wondering if I could make it out alive before she rugby tackled me to the floor.

'This,' she said, walking so close to me our noses were almost touching and I could smell the sour note of her breath, 'is a once in a lifetime opportunity. You've been putting the work in. You've got the talent. And that room is jam packed with some of the most important people in the music world— are you going to be the one who jumps in and takes her chance to shine, or are you going to be a waitress for the rest of your life? You have to ask yourself which of those paths you want to follow—because right now, you're at a crossroads. If you want to stay on the road to nowhere, that's your choice.'

Ouch. She'd hit a nerve just about as effectively as a trainee dentist with a hangover—and I felt the jolt of what she was saying flow through my mind. I *had* come to Starmaker to make a name for myself. Whether that name was going to be 'Jess Malone—star' or 'Jess Malone—waitress to the stars' was still debatable.

This was the opportunity I'd been waiting for—and if anybody had told me it would arrive like this, in a cloud of vomit and panic, I wouldn't have believed them. I also wouldn't have believed them if they'd said I'd be so scared—terrified, in fact.

Because suddenly, now that the opportunity was here, standing in front of me in the form of a hugely tall diva with an upset stomach, I was petrified. Singing at children's parties was one thing—it was easy to shine when you could hide behind a flouncy polyester princess dress and nobody was that interested in you anyway. But doing it here, in front of this hand-picked super-important audience? The very thought of that made me feel like I could be following Vogue into puke-town any minute now.

'You know the songs,' she said, continuing to beat all my spluttering objections down.

'But—' I said, before she cut me off with an imperious wave of her hand.

'And you know the dance steps. Jack can sell this, Jess— you know what he's like. He'll persuade everyone out there that they're lucky to be seeing you and not me. He'll convince them that they've chosen this time to reveal Starmaker's latest talent—and then, when you pull it off, that will become true. Everything you've ever dreamed of will come true.'

I gazed up at her, wondering if she had any idea about what I dreamed of—she'd been famous since she was seventeen, practically a child herself.

'You'll be able to look after your family,' she added. 'Sort out all their financial problems. Look after the people who've looked after you. And you'll be able to sing and record and tour, and get your voice heard by all those people who rejected you in the past—you'll show them what they've missed out on, what you're really made of. And those people who believed in you, who encouraged you? You'll be proving them right. It'll be making their dreams come true as well.'

Uhh, I thought. Okay. So she *did* understand what I'd dreamed of—and she was offering me a chance to make it all happen.

I stayed silent, turning it all over in my mind, my trembling hands absentmindedly tidying up the make-up scattered across the counter just to give themselves something to do.

Before I could answer her, the door to the dressing room burst open, and Neale almost fell through it—just about recovering his balance enough to stay upright. He was followed by Jack, who was frowning at Vogue in concern, and—horrendously—by Patty, who strutted into the room like a demented peacock.

Jack glanced at me briefly before striding over to Vogue and taking her in his arms. I was close enough to hear the quiet sigh that escaped from her lips as she collapsed into his embrace, and see the way her clammy hands clutched at his expensive suit.

'It's okay, darling,' he murmured, stroking the back of her head and making soothing sounds. It looked like Vogue and Jack were closer than I'd thought. Even though I knew he'd mentored her in the early days, I'd never seen them together much at the office. I had to assume that those early days had left them with a bond of friendship that had lasted for all these years.

Vogue pulled away from him, and looked into his eyes. I could hear Patty tapping her talons impatiently against the clipboard she was carrying as she watched.

'I can't go on, Jack,' she said, simply. 'The details are too disgusting to reveal, but I can't. I don't want to let you down, but there are limits. I have an idea, though. A good one.'

'Okay, sweetheart, I'm all ears,' he replied, running his hands through his hair until he left furrows. He was worried— I could see it in his frown, in his body language, in the tone of his voice. I'd never seen him worried before—and I knew that there was something I could do to help him. If I could pull this off, if I could turn this disaster into a victory for Starmaker and for him, it would change the balance of everything. It

would make me feel less like the poor relation, and more
like the star he said he'd spotted all that time ago in a soggy
summer garden in the Cheshire countryside. It could be a
way to repay him for all the belief he'd had in me, just like
Vogue had said.

'Put Jess on instead,' she said, simply, as though it made all
the sense in the world. I saw Jack's eyes flicker over me in my
waitressing costume, and felt his hesitation as he formulated a
response—probably he was trying to find a polite way to say
no, a way to nix the idea without hurting my feelings.

'No, listen,' said Vogue, sensing the same reaction. 'She's
been working on my songs—she knows them all, including the
new single we were going to do tonight. She knows the routines. She's got talent, Jack, you know that—or you wouldn't
have brought her here, would you? I trust your instincts, and
I've seen what she can do. Go and sell her as your next big
star—she can do it.'

I felt my eyes mist over as Vogue's impassioned speech
drew to an end—impossibly touched by how much faith she
had in me. It was a real Hallmark moment, right up until the
second that Vogue clutched her stomach and ran to the toilets,
yelling: 'Just do it! I'm about to shit myself!'

We all stayed silent as we heard the door slam behind her,
and then the horrendously large groan as our diva positioned
her famous derriere onto the loo. The rest of the sounds were
pretty evil, so we all started talking at once to try to drown
them out.

'Can you do this?' said Jack, looking at me with something
akin to wonder.

'She can't do this,' said Patty, looking at me with something akin to hatred.

'She can look fabulous while she does this,' said Neale, already rooting in his make-up kit, and cuing up R. Kelly on his iPhone.

'I can do this,' I said, looking around at everyone, with as much determination in my gaze as I could pull together.

Chapter 13

Now, though, as everyone around me burst into a bubble of hyperactivity, I was starting to doubt myself. To think that I couldn't do it, after all. To bottle it, as my dad might have said.

Neale had leapt into super-stylist mode the moment Jack had agreed to let me go on.

'Have you got your kit with you?' he'd asked him, and Neale had immediately nodded like the Churchill dog, even replying with an 'Oh, yes!'

'I always have it with me,' he'd said proudly, 'in case there's a cosmetics emergency.'

Apparently, I counted as a cosmetics emergency, and Neale was currently scraping off the green goo and standing back to survey my face the same way a builder might before he demolished something.

'You'll need to sell her up, Jack,' said Patty, staring at me with more interest than I'd ever seen from her before. I wasn't sure I liked it—it felt a bit like her eyes might actually laser holes into my skin, and leave me smouldering and sore.

'The advantage is she's been useless so far, so nobody will know anything about her. Big up the Liverpool thing, people like the common touch. Emphasise the way you plucked her from the shithole she was living in to make her a star.'

'I did *not* live in a shithole,' I snapped, pushing Neale's hand away to object.

'You shut up,' said Patty, 'and concentrate on looking good and remembering the words. This part of the business has nothing to do with you.'

Funny how she'd suddenly started to understand every word I said—and even funnier how she'd suddenly decided that 'the Liverpool thing' could be an advantage, instead of the kiss of death she'd always regarded it as before.

Still, I did as she said, and shut up—I didn't have much choice, as Neale was back at my teeth, checking the whitening strips.

'I get it,' said Jack, nodding at Patty. 'I'll sell the story—a star is born, yeah?'

Patty twisted her face up as though she'd just accidentally eaten a dog turd, and reluctantly agreed.

'It's the only way, I think,' she replied. 'We need to distract them from the fact that our *real* star is inconvenienced, and make them think this is a better alternative. I'll go back out and talk to a few of the journos, get the buzz started. By the time she's on stage, they'll be excited about it, not disappointed. At least until she opens her mouth.'

She cast me a final scathing glare, and added: 'You need to sort out costume. The dancing waitress look just won't cut it, even if it is her natural calling in life.'

Neale looked up as she said it, doing his Churchill-dog impression again. Boy, was he keen to please.

'I'll sort it,' he said, sounding thrilled at the opportunity. 'I'll create something…magnificent!'

I cringed a little inside—partly at his words, and the sense of terror at what Neale's idea of 'magnificent' might involve, and partly because he was currently yanking my hair around at all angles while he heaped on dry-shampoo powder to 'volumise' it.

He rubbed it all in vigorously, and I looked at myself in horror as I saw my blonde hair was now lifted a good three inches from its roots, sticking out as if I'd been electrocuted.

'Don't worry,' he said, patting my hand reassuringly, 'I'll finish that when I'm back.'

With that, he followed Patty out of the room, his Converse squeaking on the lino in the hallway, presumably to go and find me a costume from thin air.

That left me—channelling Medusa—and Jack. Plus, every now and then, a very vocal reminder that Vogue was still locked in the toilets, earning her PhD in pooing. Poor thing.

Jack walked over and crouched down in front of me. He smiled and, as usual, I felt better—his smile was like the equivalent of heroin for me, I was starting to realise. He reached out and cupped my face—now thankfully back to its usual colour—and kissed me once, very gently.

His brown eyes met mine, and I felt a tremble run through my body. I was so completely, utterly scared—at exactly the time I needed to be confident.

'Now then, Princess,' he said, holding on to my shaking hands and squeezing them softly. 'This is it. This is your moment. This is your chance to show everyone what you've got. This is what you came here for, isn't it?'

I nodded, still incapable of speech, and feeling embarrassing tears welling up in my eyes.

'You can do this,' he said, firmly. 'I know you can. Vogue is right to trust my instincts. I spotted her at a youth dance festival in Peckham, and I spotted you at a garden party in Cheshire. I don't back losers, Jess. I back winners. And you're a winner. Let me hear you say it.'

I gazed at him, wishing we could just go back to his flat and eat pizza. Or go to the pub. Or have a bare-knuckle fist-fight with Godzilla—anything but this. God, I told myself, you're not a winner—you're a whiner.

I squeezed his hands back, took a big breath, and muttered: 'I'm a winner,' with as much convictions as I could find. Which, in all honesty, wasn't very much.

Jack nodded, and stood up to leave.

'I'm going out there now to tell everyone about you, Jess— and I believe every word of it. You were born to do this—so just believe in yourself as much as I believe in you, okay?'

My lower lip was wobbling, my heart was racing, and I kind of had the feeling I might just cling on to his trouser leg and hope he didn't notice me dragging along on the floor behind him when he left.

Luckily for any shred of self-esteem I had left, Neale chose that moment to come barrelling back into the room, clutching a pile of random cloth and what looked like two of the spray-painted-lily table decorations perched on top. I could barely see his glasses peeking over the heap, and he dumped the lot at my feet, grinning insanely.

Jack gave us both a mock-military salute, and left us to it. I stared at his back as he went, wondering how I was going to get through this.

'Right,' said Neale, oblivious to my mood, rummaging around in his kit and coming up with a pair of vicious looking shears, 'here we go!'

I recoiled in horror, genuinely convinced for a moment that he was going to start hacking away at my hair, or trimming my nose or something.

'No, silly!' he said, laughing at my expression. 'This is for the costume! Now, take all your clothes off and let's get a look at you…'

I stared at him, wondering if he'd lost his mind. There was no way I was going to strip in front of a deranged make-up artist wielding a pair of scissors. Or any other man I didn't know who wasn't a qualified medical professional.

'Believe me, girlfriend,' he said, 'you ain't got nothing I'm interested in.'

He delivered it in such an overdone 'strong independent Beyoncé' kind of way that it made me laugh. That alone came as a relief—to be able to breathe again, never mind laugh. I stood up and removed my skirt and blouse as instructed, feeling ridiculously exposed, even if Neale's gaze was purely professional and not in the slightest bit sexual.

He inspected my black panties and bra—matching, and lacy, thank you very much, just in case it *had* turned into a date night with Jack—and my pattern-topped stockings and suspenders. Never had I been happier not to be wearing those washed-out greying knick-knacks that had been through the washer a million times.

'Okay…could be worse. Now, let's make the magic happen!' he said, disappearing head first into the pile at his feet and emerging with a red velvet curtain, which he'd clearly filched from one of the booths outside.

Somebody would be missing their privacy tonight—probably me, I thought, catching a glimpse of myself almost naked in the mirror. At least avoiding those carbs had paid off—I was definitely a sleeker version of my former self, and all the dance rehearsals meant I was a lot more toned as well.

That, of course, ruled out using any of Vogue's costume—as she was a foot taller, had curves in all the right places, and then some more on top. I was also relieved that Neale seemed to have ruled out using her discarded wig, as it was still dangling from the ceiling, and had vomit crusted into one side of it. Not a good look for anyone.

'So,' he said, as he draped the velvet over me, looked at it, nodded, hummed, and then nodded again, 'what's your name?'

'You know my name…don't you?' I said, frowning in confusion. At least I'd thought he knew my name—I could have sworn he'd used it several times, but maybe I just had delusions of grandeur. I mean, nobody else at Starmaker had bothered to learn it; why should Neale be any different?

'I *mean*,' he replied, giving me a look that told me how retarded I was being, 'what are you going to be called on stage? I don't suppose Vogue's her real name, is it?'

He gestured towards the toilets with his shoulder, then bellowed out: 'Vogue, love! What's your real name?'

'Paulette!' she yelled back, the last bit drowned out by the sound of the loo flushing. Hopefully, she'd peaked.

'See?' said Neale, closing one eye and peering through a needle as he threaded it. 'You need a name. Usually, there are meetings about it—you know, head of marketing, head of brand, head of blah-di-blah, all having these top-level debates about being bang on-trend and capturing the key demographics. You're not getting that, sweetheart, so you need to come up with one on your own.'

I ouched as the needle accidentally poked into the flesh of my side, and Neale gave me a little 'oops!' apology before he carried on tacking away.

A name… God, I'd never even thought about it before. I felt like a superhero who needed a new secret identity, fast.

'Well,' I said, breathing in hard as he tugged the red fabric so tight around my waist I thought my boobs might pop out of my mouth, 'I was always Jess at school. And Jessy to my family.'

'Maybe you could use Jessy, but just add your initial after it?' he suggested, standing back to survey his handiwork.

'Erm… I think that's already been done,' I answered, trying not to cringe as he knelt down in front of me, chopping away at the velvet until he made a skirt so short it revealed the lacy black stocking tops. 'And Jessie J sounds a lot better than Jessy M, anyway.'

'What about Jessica, then? Is that your naughty name? My parents always use my full name—middle name included—when I've been bad, which seems to be a lot of the time.'

I giggled—looked like it was the same the world over. But… Jessica. It *did* sound classy. A bit more mature than Jessy, and more 'take-me-seriously-goddamn-you' than Jess on its own sounded. I ran through a few scenarios in my mind: 'And now, live on stage, it's JESSICA!'; and, 'For the first time on the *One Show*, all the way from Liverpool, it's JESSICA!'; finishing with, 'And at number one in the UK charts this week, it's JESSICA!'

Hmmm. It kind of worked. Especially if I said it in capitals. Admittedly, I was more used to hearing it in terms of Mum saying things like, 'I asked you to do the dishes, Jessica!' and 'Jessica, how many times do I have to tell you, empty the bath when you're finished with it?'—but it worked. And bearing in mind that Neale and I were having to hold this particular top-level meeting without the benefit of the head of brand, or even the head of blah-di-blah, it would have to do.

'Yeah,' I said, eventually. 'Jessica. I like it.'

'Well that's that sorted then—we make an amazing team! We came up with that without even using PowerPoint! I'll run over and tell Jack as soon as I'm done here, okay?'

He was still kneeling down, and was using the edge of the scissors to create a deliberately frayed, ragged look at the end of the red velvet mini skirt. The waist was cinched in tight, and he'd used one of the gold cord tie-backs as a belt. He'd looped the other one around my neck, tying it in a knot and letting the ends dangle down into my cleavage, which was covered in the black fishnet he'd pulled loose from Vogue's abandoned outfit. Luckily, I decided after a quick sniff, it had escaped the worst of the vom-a-thon.

Neale reached up one hand to grab an eye liner gel from his kit, then mysteriously crawled around on the floor until he was crouched behind me.

'What are you doing back there?' I said, twisting my head back over my shoulder and trying to see.

'Drawing seams onto your stockings to make them even more fierce,' he replied. 'My nan says the women used to draw lines onto bare legs covered in gravy browning during the war—at least we're not that desperate!'

Once he was done, he stood up and faced me, looking at my hair and face critically. I realised then how short he was—barely an inch or so taller than me, and even slimmer.

'How do you cope when you need to work on really tall people, like Vogue?' I asked, realising as the words tumbled out of my mouth that they should probably have stayed as part of an internal dialogue instead. I'd basically just called him a midget, which could be considered rude—especially when he was doing his very best to turn me into a megastar. The phrase 'silk purse from a sow's ear' sprung to mind.

He fixed me with a look as he started to mess with my hair, pulling it this way and that in a solid mass.

'Well, darling, they're usually sitting down—and not wearing an impromptu hand-crafted artisan bespoke one-of-a-kind couture garment that could, very easily, fall to pieces at any moment. Or sometimes,' he said, sweeping my hair up and giving me a super-cheeky grin, 'I just wear white stilettos.'

He'd done the impossible, I thought—made me giggle yet again.

'You're very naughty,' I said as he moulded the roots of my hair into an upsweep. 'I can see I'm going to have to call you Benjamin all the time.'

He pouffed up the parts of my hair that hadn't turned to putty with the dry shampoo powder, letting the loose blonde strands flow down over my back and shoulders in a kind of explosive waterfall, before getting out a can of industrial strength hairspray and almost choking me with it.

Through the haze, I saw him messing around with his powders and creams and glosses, and endured his prodding and rubbing and blending while he turned me into a painted lady. We'd done this bit together before, so I felt a bit more relaxed about it—he already knew what colours suited me, and what my skin was like, and how to make my eyes pop and my cheekbones shimmer. He finished off with a vibrant red lipstick, and then sprayed my face—hopefully not with the same stuff as he'd used on my hair, but you never can tell.

'Am I done yet?' I asked, glancing at the clock hanging on the opposite wall. Ten minutes until…show time. Yikes, bugger, and OMG!

'Almost,' he said, starting to dismantle the golden-spray-painted lilies he'd nicked from the booth tables. He peeled one off the base, and wove the steam through the gunk in my hair, repeating it all around my hairline with different blooms.

When he'd finished, he stood back, gave me a thorough once-over, then a big grin.

'Ta-da!' he said, standing back so I could see myself completely in the mirror. 'The princess shall go to the ball!'

It wasn't quite the same 'holy cow' moment as the big

reveal on one of those Gok Wan make-over shows, as I'd been half watching the transformation all the way through the very hurried process. But Neale had, I have to say, created a very powerful look when it was all taken together.

I stared at myself, turned around, and craned my neck to see as much of the back view as I could, and blinked rapidly to see if anything had changed. No. I still looked nothing at all like my real self. I mean, I'd been made up before. I'd worn sexy clothes before. I'd had my hair done before. But never quite like this.

As I was coming to terms with the new me, there was yet another flush from the toilet, and the sound of running water as Vogue washed her hands. She emerged unsteadily from the door, her face wet where she'd splashed herself down, and stopped dead still as she saw me.

Her face gave nothing away—other than the fact that she was feeling like crap—and I had a moment of complete horror where I thought she didn't like it.

Then, eventually, she grinned—or she grinned as much as she was capable, under the circumstances.

'I love it,' she said, walking around me slowly so she could see me from all angles. 'It's kind of a sexy slave girl vibe, a bit like Katy Perry went straight from the set of the Roar video to a Roman orgy...excellent work, Neale! I think, looking at this, you can even get away with doing it barefoot, too. The radio pack will tag onto the belt, and you'll have an in-ear monitor that will be covered up by all your hair. It's brilliant.

'Just be careful on that high C in 'Midnight'—you'll have

come straight out of the dance steps, and you need to buy yourself a bit of time to breathe before you go for it, all right? I've heard you sing it. You can do it. You're going to kill this, *Jessica*.'

God, I thought, I hope so.

Chapter 14

I'd like to give a detailed account of that first performance—the one that changed everything—but I can't. The truth is, I don't even remember most of it—it's like I was drunk or high or having some kind of out-of-body experience. Singing and dancing on the astral plane.

I remember the walk back down the corridor, out of the dressing room—the room I'd entered as a tired waitress, and emerged from as a dolled-up superbabe from outer space. I remember Jack glancing down at me from the stage, where he stood with a microphone in his hands, and him giving me a huge grin that felt like an energy drink whooshing through my body.

I remember Neale rubbing my shoulders, whispering encouraging words, and the tech guy checking my radio pack and mic. And I remember Jack announcing me to the crowd, managing to make it sound like the event of the decade: 'And here she is, ladies and gentlemen, the star we've all been waiting for… Jessica!'

After that, it's all a blank—apart from occasional spots of clarity, like the moment I managed to nail that high C. The moment I realised I'd changed up the dance moves and still didn't fall over. The moment I finished 'Midnight', Vogue's new single, and stood there, exhausted and panting and sweating so much I thought my whole face might fall off.

Mainly, I remember the moment after that—the moment when the whole room burst into stunned applause, the sound of the cheers ringing around the club, crashing into my ears as I froze there, the spotlight still shining vividly into my eyes, blinding me.

As I looked out at the audience, I couldn't make out a single individual face in the pulsing sea of humanity there before me, but I could feel their energy—their appreciation, their pleasure, their approval.

I felt it so clearly, that moment—and it reminded me so much of that time at the end of the college show, all those years ago. When I'd been dressed no less ridiculously as a cheerleader who'd saved the planet from an alien invasion. It might have been a different world, a different life back then—but it was the same feeling. The sense of utter exhilaration, the same high I realised I'd been chasing ever since—and, unsurprisingly, not finding at kids' parties and in bingo halls in Liverpool.

I knew I might crash and burn immediately—discover that they'd all been paid to cheer like that, or turn around and see that Vogue had been behind me, doing the performance all along. That I might be plunged back into my normal world again—but for that one magical moment, standing there in the spotlight, my chest heaving from the effort of singing and dancing my heart out, everything felt...perfect. I never wanted to it to end, which possibly explains why I didn't move from that stage—I just took my bows, grinned like an idiot, and tried to make it last forever.

Eventually, Jack jumped up onto the stage with me, giving me a big hug before holding my hand and leading me in one final bow—before he edged me firmly away to the steps at the side. It was the Jack equivalent of yanking me off with a crooked stick around my neck.

I wanted to stay there, in the dim recesses, hidden away in the darkness with Jack, to enjoy my moment—to see how proud he was of me, to hear his words of praise, to let it all flow over me. But the world had other ideas—and my job clearly wasn't done.

Jack smiled down at me, his brown eyes shining with happiness, which gave me almost as much of a high as the performance had.

'I knew you could do it,' he said, gazing at me as if I was a precious jewel. I gaped, still too tired to actually formulate words, and clung onto his hand. Without that, I thought I might actually float away, off into the distance, never to be seen again. Still, if I was going to go, what a way it would be.

Neale ran over, his mouth spasming with a grin that could only be described as inane, his glasses bouncing up and down on the bridge of his nose.

'Perfect,' he said, holding my face up to the light and inspecting it for cracks. 'And now…just a quick touch up before you go and meet your adoring public, sweetheart!'

He immediately started dabbing at me with sponges and brushes, and sprayed me with a bottle of perfume, wafting it around my hair and face and every part of my exposed flesh. It was probably a good idea, as eau de sweat was never attractive, even in a nightclub.

'Good as new!' he proclaimed, as I coughed in the middle of the toxic mushroom cloud of fragrance. I looked behind me, towards the magic door that led backstage.

'Did Vogue see it? What did she think? I hope I didn't let her down...' I muttered.

'She had to go, honey,' replied Neale. 'There was a brief pause in the shitstorm, so she made the most of it and dashed off home. But don't worry—she'll be able to watch it tomorrow, and there is no *way* you'll have let her down. That was amazing.'

'No,' added Jack, still holding my hand but looking around, distracted, obviously thinking about what happened next. It's a good job one of us was. 'You were magnificent, Jess. But now it's time to get back to work...'

For one startled, unreal moment, my brain short-circuited and I genuinely thought he meant I had to get back to work as a waitress. That I needed to run back to the dressing room, take off this ridiculous outfit, and sneak back out here in my stain-free black and whites, hoisting a tray of smoked salmon twists on my shoulder. I wondered if anybody would recognise me if I did, or if I'd be like Clark Kent, and nobody would know who I was with a costume change...

Luckily, I was prevented from making a huge tit of myself, by actually asking out loud if that was what he meant, by the arrival of Patty, in a cloud of sulphur. Or Dior Poison, which amounted to the same thing when she was wearing it.

'Right!' she said, staring at me with narrowed eyes. 'Now you've done the easy bit, it's time to come out there and meet the press. This is where the hard work starts. I've primed the pump, they're all excited to meet you, for some reason—so don't screw it up, all right?'

I gulped in air and realised I was so dehydrated I might shrivel up like an Egyptian mummy. It was partly the physical effort of the show, and partly the new wave of terror that Patty's precise words had brought on. My God—the performance was the *easy* part? What the hell would this be like? I glanced out at the darkened club, and tried to stave off paralysis.

There were hundreds of people out there. Famous people. Important people. People who would shape my public image, dictate how the world saw me. People who, I knew, could make or break a young singer just taking her first steps on the road to success. It was even more terrifying a prospect than getting up on stage had been—I mean, I knew I could sing. It was one of the few things in life I was truly confident about. But could I perform just as well on a one-to-one basis? What if I said something stupid, like I usually did? Or used a swear word by accident? Or my costume exploded while I was talking to Piers Morgan? Not that he was there, but the theory was the same.

Patty unscrewed the top of the bottle of water she was wielding, and thrust it into my shaking hands.

'Drink this. Take some deep breaths. Stay calm. You can do this.'

I looked at her, feeling pathetically grateful as I accepted both the water and the words, which were just about the most supportive ones she'd ever tried out on me. Predictably enough, the détente didn't last.

'I would normally tell people to just relax and be themselves in circumstances like this,' she added, looking me up and down. 'But in your case, I'd say smile a lot, laugh at everything they say, and try not to look like any more of an idiot than you absolutely have to. Understood?'

I nodded, finished the water, and gave Jack one final glance before I entered the main room. I suspected it looked pleading—something along the lines of 'Please don't make me do this,' but he just smiled encouragingly, and used the hand he had on my back to propel me forward through the gates of hell.

The next hour was possibly the longest and most bewildering of my entire life. Coming off stage, I felt like was underwater, and could hear a frenzy of voices talking to me. Everyone seemed to want a photo of me, and my smile became fixed to my face, liked a demented ventriloquist's dummy. I posed and I grinned and I looked, I realised the next day when I saw the photos, like someone who'd just been hit by a bus and survived to tell the tale.

All the celebs who'd ignored me—in some cases politely, in some cases aggressively—while I was trying to offload the smoked salmon twists were suddenly interested. The journalists wanted to get quotes from me, the bloggers wanted to record video chats, and the record execs from Starmaker were staring at me like those cartoon characters that have dollar signs flashing in their eyes.

It was utterly chaotic. Part of me recognised it for what it was: shallow, fickle, superficial, and on some level sickening.

I mean—I was still me. I was still the girl they'd all looked straight through as though I didn't exist an hour ago. Except now I was me to infinity—I'd suddenly become a commodity, an option, a product. I'd become the Talent.

The other part of me, though…well, the other part of me absolutely loved it. I loved the attention and the focus and the flattering comments and the way that people were muscling in to chat to me; people who hadn't got a clue who I was half an hour earlier. That quickly, it had changed—and I lapped it all up.

It was, after all, what I'd been fighting for all these years—recognition. The acknowledgement of the fact that I could sing, that I could make it in this messed-up industry, that I had something to offer as more than a waitress or a children's entertainer.

Jack snapped me out of that underwater feeling and stayed glued to my side all night, a protective hand on my elbow or the small of my back, always ready to steer me away to the next crowd that had gathered; always ready to jump in with a cool soundbite when my not exactly PR-ready brain failed to kick start into action. Always ready to protect me from anybody who was being too intrusive, too pushy, too touchy-feely.

That—and the fact that Patty was hovering behind me like a hungry bird of prey—was probably the only thing that got me through it. I'd been well and truly thrown in at the deep end, and Jack was my rubber ring.

We moved around the room together, me and Patty and Jack, with Neale lurking on the edges ready to dive in if I had a wardrobe malfunction or a life-threatening mascara emergency or my hair fell off. I was introduced to each new group by either Patty or Jack, depending on who it was—both of them so utterly smooth and effortless and charming with everyone we spoke to. I wasn't surprised at Jack pulling that off—but I must admit I saw a whole new side to Patty, one that I grudgingly had to respect.

I knew from working with her that she had a spreadsheet of media and online contacts who she rated out of ten in terms of their usefulness—and that was reflected perfectly in the way she co-ordinated the interviews; ten minutes to someone on the upper levels, just a quick photo or video for those lower down her PR stratosphere. But somehow, she did it all so well that nobody seemed insulted or rejected when she swept me away from their clutches. She did it with a smile and a joke and a promise of 'catching up over a Mojito some time very soon'.

It was also astonishing to see how easily she'd switched into 'Jessica is Awesome' mode—bigging up my vocal abilities, my work ethic, my determination, the dazzling career that was ahead of me, thanks to Starmaker's amazing talent machine. She even did a gag where she produced sunglasses from her handbag, popped them on her face, and pronounced, 'Jessica's future is so bright, I have to wear shades.'

As Patty had spent most—well, all—of the time since I'd met her in 'Jess is Shit' mode, it was really quite confusing. She'd almost have had me fooled if not for the fact that every now and then, when I wasn't performing properly or I was starting to say something she disapproved of, she pinched me, really hard, on the side. The real Patty was still in there—she'd just been taken over temporarily by her nicer twin sister.

Everything was going well until one of the journalists looked at his notes, presumably based on what Patty had told him earlier, and asked me how it felt to escape my deprived childhood and make it in the big city.

I gaped a bit at that one, and frowned as I tried to come up with an answer that would both defend my childhood and my home town without provoking a pinch from Patty. I had enough bruises already.

'Well,' I said, eventually. 'Like all big cities, Liverpool has its share of problems—but to be honest, I had a really happy childhood.'

'But didn't you suffer because of poverty, and drug use in the family, and going to a school that's since been closed down because of gang-related shootings?'

I stared at him, and the phone he was using to record my replies on, and felt a real sense of anger starting to rise within me. Not aimed at him—he was just doing his job— but at Patty. Patty for coming up with this bullshit; *and* at Jack for presumably signing off on it. I mean, I thought my story was strong enough on its own—couldn't they just have sold me as a real-life princess-whose-dreams-came-true? A fighter who never gave up? An ordinary girl who believed in an extraordinary dream? The girl who was plucked from obscurity at a garden party and catapulted to almost-fame? The waitress who dumped her tray and picked up a career?

Surely, any of those lines would have done the trick—and again, I realised as I processed it all, that in some ways Jack had been right. I had been learning the industry from the inside out, and I knew from the PR team's activities that all of those stories were sellable.

Instead, they'd chosen to portray me as some street urchin from a crack house who dodged bullets on my way to PE lessons. That, I decided, was going too far—none of it was true (apart from the school closing down), and my mum and dad would be horrified if they read all that in the papers. I couldn't go along with that kind of betrayal, even if Patty did think it was the best way for me to grab headlines.

'The short answer is, no,' I said—or yelled, to be precise, as the noise levels in the club were still set to brain-splitting. 'None of that is true. My mum works in Tesco, and my dad's a cab driver. The closest they've ever come to doing drugs is taking some Alka-Seltzer after a big night out in town. We weren't rich, but I wasn't ever deprived. The school didn't close down, it was merged with another one because there weren't enough pupils—and as far as I know, they were never any gang shootings. Not there, at least.'

'But there were elsewhere? Were you involved? Were you ever in a gang?'

I laughed out loud at that one—as if my parents would ever put up with any of that nonsense.

'The closest I ever got to being in a gang,' I said, trying to keep my voice pleasant and not show how annoyed I was, 'was being in the netball team. Admittedly, it could get a bit rowdy, but the only things we shot were goals. Liverpool isn't some third world country, you know.'

I could feel Patty incessantly pinching my side as I spoke,

and could practically feel the heat of her scowl, and Jack's persistent tug on my elbow as he tried to draw matters to a close.

I shook Jack off with a twist, and slapped Patty's hand away as subtly as I could; much as I didn't like this particular interview, neither did I want to hit the headlines for assaulting a PR manager in public, even if she did deserve it.

'I'm proud of where I come from,' I said to the reporter, ignoring the fact that Jack was staring at me with a 'shut-the-fuck-up' expression. 'I'm proud of my family. And Liverpool is *not* a shithole.'

I don't know why I even said that. The guy hadn't said it was a shithole—but Patty's comments earlier in the night were still bugging me, and the fact that she was trying to make people believe I was a character from some Scouse-based Girlz n The Hood style drama was starting to really piss me off.

I was willing to do a lot of things to achieve my goals—but this was a fiction too far.

Unfortunately for me, the one single, solitary pause in the ear-numbing music chose that exact moment to present itself. After a whole night of non-stop thumping, there was a perfectly timed break before the next tune was pumped out. It might have been a DJ error. It might have been a moment of serenity at the end of a fast and furious dance track. It might have been God's way of agreeing with Jack, and telling me to STFU—whatever it was, it meant that anyone within listening range heard that last word of mine.

To make matters worse, my voice had done that thing that Liverpool girls' voices do when they're upset or over-excited, and gone up a couple of octaves at the end—so it ended up not as a good old-fashioned, run-of-the-mill 'shithole', but a long, high-pitched 'shithoooooole'. I felt immediately embarrassed and ashamed of myself—not for the intentions, which were good, but for the delivery, which wasn't exactly classy. Calling myself Jessica hadn't, apparently, been enough to turn me into a proper lady. My very own Henry Higgins, standing by my side, was trying not to look horrified.

The journalist, luckily, was made of sterner stuff. He took it in his stride and laughed.

'I know that,' he said. 'It's just that I'm from Manchester. I was winding you up a bit. Anyway…congrats, Jessica. That was a great night. I'm sure we'll being seeing a lot more of you.'

I nodded and smiled and looked around me, feeling a bit sheepish, and insanely glad that the music was now back up to its usual levels. I purposely avoided meeting Jack's eyes, and accidentally on purpose trod on Patty's foot as I walked away. It didn't have much effect as I wasn't wearing shoes, but it's the thought that counts.

I decided that I'd talked enough. I'd given enough quotes. I'd smiled enough smiles, and posed for enough pictures. I'd handled enough bullshit, frankly—and I was fast realising that this particular aspect of stardom wasn't as fun or exciting as I'd always thought it would be.

I needed to rehydrate, go home, and sleep. This whole fame thing was a minefield, and I was too exhausted to stay ahead of the game. Without asking Patty or Jack their opinion, I strode off, aiming to head back to the dressing room and deglamorise myself before setting off for my flat. I might even treat myself to a taxi, I decided. I'd earned a bit of luxury, and sitting in the back of a black cab would remind me of my dad and calm me down.

I was pretty sure, beneath the tiredness and the stress, that I'd probably cave in if Jack invited me back to his place instead—but for five glorious minutes, I decided I just wasn't going to care one way or the other. It had been a mental night, and my head was mashed. I didn't want to be a diva—but I really needed to put my feet up for a bit. Not many pop stars, after all, do a full shift of waitressing before their stage shows, do they? I can't imagine Madonna or Gaga have to hand out the snacks before they strut their stuff, anyway.

I started to politely push my way through the crowds, making my excuses, telling anyone who asked it had been a fantastic night, thank you for coming, and smiling so hard I genuinely doubted my mouth would ever feel the same again.

As I neared the Promised Land—that door to the backstage area that I'd walked through as a waitress not so very long ago—I was stopped by a firm hand on my shoulder.

I wasn't delighted about that for a few reasons—mainly, I really needed ten minutes to myself. But also, there was every possibility that a firm hand on my shoulder could make my whole curtain dress drop off, and there were way too many cameras on the go in here for that to be a cool thing.

I glanced behind me, trying to keep my polite smile in place even though I felt a bit like stabbing someone, and saw a tall, beautifully built blond man towering above me. The lights from the strobes were casting his face in shadow, but I could make out white teeth and a huge grin and golden hair, a bit too long, a bit too floppy. He looked vaguely familiar. Or, no, to be precise, he *felt* vaguely familiar—something about the smile, I think.

'Jessy?' he said, raising his voice to be heard over the racket. 'Is that actually you underneath all that war paint? I wasn't certain, until I heard that magnificent "shithole" echoing through the place…'

I turned around to face him, screwed up my eyes against the flashing lights, and squinted in what was probably a super-attractive way as I tried to figure out who this person was. This person who seemed to know me—well enough to call me Jessy, at least, which narrowed it down to very close family and friends. None of which, I'd assumed, had been here tonight.

'Jessy?' he said again, starting to look a bit confused now. 'It's me.'

'Erm—who is "me"?' I said, still unable to either see his face properly, or put a name to the voice that was nagging away at me as belonging to someone I knew. Someone I'd be glad to see under normal circumstances.

'Daniel,' he said. 'Daniel Wells, the Evertonian from next door. Don't tell me you've forgotten me already?'

Chapter 15

I was so shocked I didn't know how to react for a moment. My whole day—my whole life these past weeks—had been insane. I'd managed to draw a line between my London world and my Liverpool world, and now Daniel was here, right in front of me, crashing down the walls between the two.

After staring at him, befuddled, for a few seconds, I threw my arms around him, crushing him to me in a hug.

It was Daniel. My neighbour, my friend, my ally in life. And somehow, he was here—in London, in the Panache Club, in my arms.

He was also, I couldn't help but notice, a lot…more. He was taller, and bigger, and firmer. He felt like a man, instead of the pudgy boy I remembered. Somehow, I'd frozen Daniel in time, and done him a disservice by freezing him at a time when he was overweight and awkward. We'd both changed since we last saw each other, I knew—but my brain hadn't compensated for those changes, and was still in shock at this new Daniel. Daniel version two.

'Oh, my God!' I said, pulling away from him, breathless

and overwhelmed. 'I can't believe you're here! I can't believe you still exist!'

'What,' he replied, that familiar laughter in his voice, 'did you think had happened to me? That I moved to the South and disappeared from the face of the planet? Brighton's not that far away, you know!'

He was mocking me—but in that quiet, fond way he always had. Like I was the funniest thing ever, and he loved me for it. There was never any viciousness to his mocking—it was just teasing, his way of showing he 'got me', and that even though I was pretty daft, he was down with it.

'Well, it felt like that,' I answered, standing back and trying to get a better look at him. That proved impossible in the dim lighting of the club, so I tugged at his arm, and pulled him through the magical door with me.

Even as I did it, a tiny part of me—the part that was probably dehydrated and on the verge of hallucinating—wondered if we'd go through the magical door and emerge back home, in Liverpool, tumbling out into our quiet terraced street. Years ago, and miles away, at a time and place when everything seemed so simple, so possible. When the world was at our feet, and anything we wanted was there for the taking.

My performance tonight might—just might—have changed my life; but it hadn't exactly been an overnight success, no matter how much Patty and Jack tried to spin it that way. There'd been knock-backs and knock-outs and so many times when I'd had to dredge up the energy to get back up and fight another day. All of that—every single rejection, every Princess party in the rain, every time I had to go back to my excited parents and explain why the latest stage of the Make Jessy a Star plan had failed—had left its mark on me. Every cheating boyfriend and every packet of noodles and every time I'd had to borrow money from my dad had left scars.

I knew—because I wasn't completely stupid—that things must have happened to him as well, to Daniel. There'd have been years' worth of experiences we hadn't shared; years' worth of stories to exchange. There'd have been friends and relationships and jobs and highs and lows. I knew that he must have changed too, and not just physically.

I'd thought about him a lot over the years, but in a way that made him unreal. A way that left him firmly rooted in the past, as a distant and comforting memory.

As I dragged him towards the dressing room, I felt the excitement of having him back in my life—of this unexpected appearance—bubble up inside me. It was weird, considering everything what had happened to me that day, but somehow seeing Daniel again felt like the highlight of it all.

I pushed open the door, still clutching his hand, and pulled him inside with me. I stood there, just staring at him, for what felt like ages. He was *so* tall now—and so perfectly balanced, with wide shoulders and narrow hips, a bit like a swimmer. His hair was still blond and still a bit too long, but it was clean, and shining, and framed those familiar blue eyes that were sparkling down at me.

He was, quite frankly, gorgeous—in a way I could never have imagined back then, even if I did love him to bits. I'd loved him to bits in a purely platonic way; the way I'd have loved him if he was my brother. But he'd blossomed so much, he brought The Ugly Duckling fairy tale to life. He'd morphed into this super-tall, super-built, super-hot man—and I really wished all those girls who'd been mean to him at school could see him now.

'Why does it smell of sick in here?' he asked, wrinkling up his nose and looking around cautiously.

'Oh! Well, that's because someone was being sick—Vogue to be precise. She had to pull out of the gig at the last minute, and they replaced her with…well, me! Did you see it? Did you see the show?'

'Yes, I did, Jessy. And I can't believe that was a last-minute change of plans—you were brilliant. I've always wondered, over the last few years, when I was going to turn on the TV and see you smiling out at me…and I guess that time is now. You've finally made it.'

'Maybe,' I said, sweeping aside my doubts and focusing on the here and now, 'but I took a long time getting here. A lot's happened. And a lot hasn't happened. And… God, I have, like, a million questions for you! What are you doing here, anyway? We've not spoken for so long, and you just seemed to fall off the radar—I did try and find you online, but for a techy nerd, you seem to have avoided it. Last I heard, you went off to uni, doing something that probably involved nano-secs and things that make robotic beeping noises…'

He laughed and pulled a face—it was amazing how quickly we were falling back into our familiar routines.

'Not quite,' he said. 'I studied music production. You weren't the only one bitten with the bug after the school show, you know. And after that…well, I tried working for a

few labels, doing internships, that kind of thing. It just didn't
stick. As you know, my amazing social skills, together with
my male-model-like appearance back then, always made it
hard for me to get on with people. You were pretty much
the only person I ever spoke to at school, and that was only
because our parents made us have baths together when we
were two. The London life…all the people, the parties, the
crap that went with it…well, it wasn't for me. So I went my
own way—started my own production team. Well, I called it
a team, but to start off with it was just me: Wellsy.'

'Wellsy?' I said, frowning at him, trying to figure out
where I'd heard that name before. Within a few moments, I
had it—Jack had mentioned him. At the time I'd stalled on
thinking it sounded like Banksy, and wondering if he was an
anonymous graffiti artist slash music producer, not giving it
a second thought—and certainly not connecting it to my old
pal Daniel.

Wellsy was the hot-shot producer that Jack had been hoping
to woo to Starmaker—his aim had been to get him to sign an
exclusive contract to work with his acts, something that Wellsy
had never done before.

'He's one of those self-styled lone-wolf characters,' Jack
had said, rolling his eyes. 'But he's good—brilliant, in fact.
He's become this mysterious recluse—never gives interviews,
no social media profile, doesn't do meetings. Doesn't do the
scene. Lives holed up in some country house on the coast,
and all the artists have to travel to him. Everything he touches
seems to turn to gold, though—and he'd be a perfect match
for us.'

I tried to make all of that fit with Daniel Wells, the shy, spotty teenager who'd lived next door to us for so long, and found that I simply couldn't. I don't know why—I always knew he was talented, and if anyone was going to grow up to be a lone wolf, it was Daniel. He hadn't even 'done the scene' when the scene in question involved nothing more hard core than swigging cider from plastic bottles on the local playground.

'Jack invited you,' I finally added, realising that I hadn't spoken for minutes. I needed to work on my thinking-and-talking-at-the-same-time skills.

'Yeah,' replied Daniel, shrugging, and looking slightly uncomfortable. 'Jack Duncan. He's trying to talk me into a deal with Starmaker. I don't even know why I agreed to come—I usually avoid these things as much as I used to avoid all those parties at Ruby's house. But…well, I suppose it must have been fate, mustn't it? Because now here we are—back together again.'

He grinned at me, and I felt a very strange tingling sensation in my tummy. I mean, Daniel had grinned at me many times. And, like he'd said, we'd even had baths together when we were kids—and there are still the embarrassing photos around to prove it, stuck in albums back at Mum and Dad's. But this was different…he was different. This was a very grown-up, very good-looking Daniel. He still talked like the old one—but he looked like the kind of bloke I'd stop and stare at on the street.

It all felt too weird. For a start, I was with Jack. Kind of. And also, this was Daniel. I could never fancy Daniel, surely?

Probably I just needed to go home and eat a kebab. I also needed, I realised, to get changed—me standing here in stockings and seventeen layers of sex make-up probably felt weird for him as well.

'Well, I'm glad you did come, anyway,' I replied. 'It's brilliant to see you again. Listen, I'm just going to go and get changed, all right? Be back in a tick.'

I scooted to the toilets, and tried not to inhale—Vogue's stomach problems had definitely made their mark—as I climbed out of my makeshift costume. Unfortunately, the whole thing fell to pieces as I did so, but at least it had held together long enough to preserve my dignity on stage.

I dressed in my waitressing clothes again, and glanced at myself in the mirror before I went back out. I looked utterly ridiculous—normal clothes, and the most abnormal hair and face possible. I knew all the layers of slap would have worked while I was performing, or on the photos and videos afterwards, but in the real world I could have scared young children. The hair was lacquered completely stiff, and I wasn't sure I'd ever be able to get those spray-painted lilies out again. I'd spend my whole life sniffing, wondering where the fire was.

Still, it was the best I could do until I got home and bleached myself.

When I came back out into the main room, Daniel was perched on the edge of the dresser, long denim-clad legs stretched out in front of him, crossed at the ankles.

'Nice boots,' I said, pointing at his Timberlands. They were pretty much exactly the same ones as he'd worn all through his teenage years—just newer and less scuffed.

'Yeah. Thanks. Nice…lilies?' he said, pointing at my head and looking confused.

'Long story.'

'Did you have to use the table decorations as stage costume?'

'Erm…yeah. Apparently not that long a story. Anyway, tell me all—how are your mum and dad doing?'

'Great,' he answered, a wide grin cracking open his face. 'Still running their B&B. They don't need to. I've…well, they don't need to. But they want to, so that's good. Keeps 'em out of trouble. Dad's managed to find a few ex-pat Scousers down there, watches the derby match with them on the big screen in the hotel lounge.'

'That must be fun for the other guests,' I replied, imagining the scene. Daniel's dad wasn't the quietest of men when the footie was on. I'd also filled in the rest of the sentence that he'd broken away from—that he'd done well enough that his parents didn't have to work. But Daniel, being Daniel, wouldn't want to appear as though he was bragging, or drawing attention to himself in any way. Some things never changed.

'What about your lot?' he said. 'Are they here? Did they come down and see you?'

'Well, I started this particular day on a waitressing shift, as you might be able to tell from the outfit. And I didn't think it was worth dragging them all the way to London just to see me hand out canapés, so, no. I suppose someone will have video of it, I can send it to them tomorrow. But they're all good. Luke's still an annoying shitbag, and Becky's having a baby.'

'Wow! You're going to be an auntie? That's brilliant! Bet

you'll be the best auntie ever…and, duh, yeah, I think someone
might have video of it, Jess. I might keep a low profile, but I'm
not dead—pretty much all the biggest names in the showbiz
media were out there tonight, and most of them interviewed
you afterwards.'

'Including that one I screamed "shithole" at.' I asked, cringing a little bit inside. Daniel burst out laughing, and the sound
of it had the same effect on me as climbing into a time machine
and zooming all the way back to when I was seventeen.

It was a great laugh—loud, genuine, infectious. It had also
been pretty exclusive—only his family and me ever seemed
to hear it. My friends had always wondered why I'd bothered
with him, because they never knew what he was really like.
Teenagers are quick to judge people by the way they look,
and I count myself among them—it's not like I was especially
deep or perceptive. I just knew him—and how much fun he
could be, when he wasn't wandering around looking like the
cover of a Smiths album.

'Yeah, including him…but I'm sure he's had worse yelled
at him. It'll be fine. I have every faith that the entire world
of music will fall in love with you overnight, Jess Malone.'

'Really?' I asked, trying to wipe off my eye make-up but
only succeeding in making myself look like a panda. My ego
was horribly, embarrassingly fragile—and my big break could
just as easily end up in disaster as far as I was concerned.

'Really,' he said, firmly. 'You always were irresistible. And
you will be a star—if that's still what you want.'

I gazed at him; seeing the new, improved Daniel, but
listening to the old one. It was strange how life had delivered

him here, to my doorstep, at exactly the time I needed him. Still, I needed to get a grip and not go all needy-weedy on him. He did have a life outside giving me pep talks—and I was looking forward to hearing all about it. Ideally, back at my flat, over two kebabs—with the bread—and a beer. We had a lot of catching up to do.

'It is still what I want,' I replied, smiling at him. 'But at the moment, I'm just made up that you're here, Daniel. Or should I call you Wellsy?'

'Oh God, please don't,' he said, reaching out and unpicking one of the lilies from my hair. 'That's my music name. It's not my real life name—and strange as it might seem as we've just met each other again here, you're part of my *real* life. You were always one of the best parts of it, in fact.'

His fingers lingered on the side of my face, touching my cheek gently, looking at me as if he still couldn't believe I was actually there, in front of him.

I felt exactly the same, and we both started to grin like idiots—idiots behaving like easily amused teenagers. Because when we were together, that was still what we were—it was like the intervening years hadn't even taken place. It was the most relaxed, the most happy, I'd felt for…well, years. Having Daniel back felt like a missing puzzle piece was slotting into place, and that everything in the world would be much better with him in it.

We might have changed—he certainly had, which I hoped I'd stop noticing very soon—but at heart, we were still the same. Still friends. And boy, did I need a friend.

'Listen,' I said, breaking the moment, 'I'm completely

knackered, but do you want to come to mine for a bit? Because guess what—I live above a kebab shop, and I get free donners whenever I want them!'

He opened his eyes in fake amazement, and let out a slow whistle of appreciation.

'Well, looks like you've really lucked out there, Jessy—and yeah, I'd love to…you know I could never resist a free kebab.'

'Brilliant!' I said. 'I'll just nip to the staff room and get my bag. It's been a confusing night—I'm all over the place. Give me a sec.'

I dashed to the door, keen to grab my gear and run. I wasn't sure if I was Jess the Waitress, or Jessica the Singer, but I did know one thing—I was definitely just Jessy with Daniel, and that would be good enough for me. At least for the next few hours.

Before I could leave, the door was pulled open in front of me. I did a rapid hop, skip, and a jump to avoid falling over as my hands grasped in thin air for a handle that was no longer there, and possibly uttered a few of the kinds of words I must definitely never, ever use with reporters around.

I steadied myself, and looked up to see Jack smiling down at me. Jack. My kind-of boyfriend. My definite lover. My potential career-maker. The man who I knew I owed everything to.

Just then, though, I realised that I wasn't happy to see him. The usual rush of affection and excitement I got when he walked into a room was missing in action; and the grin that would normally be making me weak at the knees right about now wasn't hitting its mark tonight.

In fact, it felt wrong, him being there at all—I just wanted to climb in that time machine with Daniel, and enjoy a ride all the way from our shared past back to the future. Plus, I was a bit worried he was here to give me a tongue lashing about my last interview, and that Patty might follow him in with a cat o' nine tails to give me an actual lashing.

'Jess!' he said, scooping me up into a hug. 'Well done! Patty's just been chatting up the room, and we can expect some great coverage tomorrow. You did a superb job, and…'

His voice trailed off, and I felt his hold on me slacken. I knew exactly what had happened—he'd noticed Daniel standing behind me.

Which must have been weird for him. I mean, there's this mysterious big shot record producer you've invited down to London to chat up. And there's your kind-of girlfriend, definite lover, who's just given an impromptu show in front of some of the most influential people in the music industry. And the two of them—who, as far as you know, have never met—are having a chinwag in the backstage dressing room.

'Wellsy, hello again,' he said, pulling away from me and walking instead towards Daniel. I waited, wondering if Daniel would ask him to use his proper name—his 'real world' name.

He didn't. Jack was obviously firmly marked off as being from his fake world.

He stood up and shook Jack's hand, suddenly looking a lot less relaxed than he had moments ago, when we were on our own.

'I see you two have met?' Jack said, glancing between us, eyes trying to assess the situation and its weirdness levels.

'Yeah,' I replied, walking over and poking Daniel in the stomach. 'We met when we were one, and his parents moved in next door to us. We lost touch years ago, and tonight was…'

'Your big reunion?' asked Jack, giving us both an easy smile, full of charm. 'That's fantastic. Jess, I think you're going to wake up to a very different life tomorrow—and maybe Wellsy, if he agrees to join us, will even be able to work with you. It'd obviously be the perfect match.'

And, I silently added, knowing he would be thinking it, a fantastic media story: high-school friends back together to conquer the music world.

I cast my eyes at Daniel, who now had his hands shoved in his jeans pockets and had adopted that slightly awkward stance I always associated with him. The one that said 'leave me alone' just as clearly as it would if it was printed up on a T-shirt. It was his retreat position—the one he used most of the time as a kid, protecting himself from the pressure of the social life going on around him, from people he didn't like and didn't trust.

I'd never been part of that group of people—and I desperately didn't want to be now.

'Maybe that's something you can talk to Da—I mean, Wellsy, about tomorrow, Jack. I'm pretty wiped out, and was planning on going home. Is there anything else you need me to do?'

He turned back to me, and reached out to hold my hand. He raised it to his lips and gave it a kiss, and I must confess to feeling a tiny bit of a jiggle down below. Jack knew exactly what buttons to press, and much as I wanted to head out to Kebabsville with Daniel, I found myself staring into the deep brown of Jack's eyes, trying to read the signals. That certain look he always gave me—a half-smile, a raised eyebrow, a wicked gleam of very white teeth—that, translated, said, 'Hey, babe, would you like to be reduced to orgasmic rubble tonight?'

It was there. The quirk of the lips, the slight pressure of his fingers holding mine. It was there, and it was hard to resist.

I was still trying to resist it—trying very hard—when Daniel walked towards the door.

'Jessy,' he said, giving me a little salute. 'It's been awesome, as usual. And we will catch up, soon, I promise.'

'But, what about the kebab?' I spluttered, trying to pull my hand away from Jack's and finding that he was holding on to it, just a little bit too tightly.

'Tempting, but not tonight. I'm sure you're exhausted, anyway. Huge congrats, though—looks like you might save the planet after all, Jess. I'll give you a call, okay?'

'You don't have my number! And I don't have yours! I might not see you again for another five years!' I bleated, knowing that I sounded pathetic.

I was trapped—physically and emotionally—between the two of them. In other circumstances, being sandwiched between the smooth, chocolate-drop sexiness of Jack and the brand-new, movie-star-hot Daniel would have had its appeal—but just then I wasn't feeling it.

'Don't worry,' said Jack, finally letting go of my hand,

'I've got both numbers, and I'll pass them on. As long as you promise to tell me all the gossip about Jess as a teenager, Wellsy.'

Daniel gave him a small smile, nodded, and left.

Chapter 16

I woke up the next morning with a throat like sandpaper, and hair that closely resembled something you might enter for the Turner Prize.

It had been near to four by the time I'd made it back to my flat, dozing away in the back of the cab I'd ordered from Jack's place. He had, indeed, reduced me to orgasmic rubble that night—even more energetically than usual.

We'd both been wired, and high on the adrenalin, and had channelled it all into the wildest sex we'd ever had. As soon as we walked through the door to his place, he had me pinned up against a wall, kissing my neck and murmuring delicious filth about what he wanted to do to me into my ear.

One hand was tugging my blouse out of my skirt, and the other was sliding to the tops of my stockings, probing and stroking and edging ever upwards until I was incapable of doing much more than sigh and squeal.

By the time he carried me into the bedroom with my legs wrapped around his waist, he was minus his T-shirt and my blouse was minus its buttons. My bra was hanging off the light fittings, and any inhibitions I may have ever had were completely blown away by the urgent way we made love to each other.

We both seemed more desperate than usual; more savage— as though all that energy had to go somewhere. It has been near to four by the time I'd made it back to my flat, dozing away in the back of the cab I'd ordered from Jack's place. He had, indeed, reduced me to orgasmic rubble that night—even more energentically than usual. And I'd been glad of it—despite my exhaustion, there was still so much adrenalin running through my veins, I was completely pumped up. I suddenly understood how performers could go on from a show and party all night—it was so hard to switch off after a high like that. I could also understand—though I promised myself it was a route I would never go down—why a lot of them ended up doing drugs.

Drugs to keep them up, drugs to bring them down, drugs to keep them steady—I got it, I really did. I felt like I was trapped on an everlasting roller coaster—reliving the insanity of the night, the show, the interviews, seeing Daniel again, over and over.

Going back to Jack's penthouse was probably my equiva-lent of doing the drugs, if I'm honest—but hopefully with fewer side effects, and no need to worry about my nostrils exploding.

He'd been as hyped up as I had, thrilled with my triumph, zooming along at a hundred miles an hour with plans for my future. He'd always believed in me—but now it was all stepping up to a brand new level. It was all becoming real. He was talking about getting me in to do some extra vocals on

Vogue's new single, 'Midnight', so it could be released as a 'Vogue featuring Jessica' deal, capitalising on my new-found fame until they could find me my own songs, and get my own tracks recorded.

I'd felt a moment of discomfort at that idea, wondering if it would piss Vogue off, and knowing that that was the last thing I wanted to do—because much as Jack had believed in me, she was the one who had believed in me enough to make it happen. I didn't know her well, but I liked her, and trusted her, and didn't want to do anything that would damage her. Still, I let him go on about it, knowing that it was a conversation for another day.

As, it seemed, was the conversation about our entire relationship. We'd been lying together, tangled in his silk sheets, both coated in sweat, when the most tragically needy part of me had decided to emerge. I should have felt like a goddess just then—but instead, I felt a tiny bit melancholy. A bit hollow. Possibly it was just because I hadn't eaten since scoffing a handful of salmon twists hours earlier, and my body was running on empty. Possibly it was just part of the natural comedown after a night of crazy highs—that roller coaster ride had to come to an end at some point.

Possibly, I had to admit to myself, it was because of Daniel. Seeing him again had been so utterly, unexpectedly brilliant— but instead of spending the night with him, catching up and reminiscing and getting to know each other again, I'd ended up here, in Jack's gym-muscled arms.

That wasn't a bad place to be for any red-blooded female— but once the sex glow started to fade, my mind had begun to drift. To wonder what Daniel was doing; if he was still in London or if he'd disappeared back off to his mysterious countryside castle. To wonder if he'd just fade away again, and the next time I saw him would be at some showbiz party, where he'd be Wellsy and I'd be Jessica, and Daniel and Jessy would be buried under the reality of our current lives.

I could feel everything shifting, changing—and although it was what I'd always wanted, I wasn't sure I was ready for my new life.

All of which might possibly explain why, as we were lying there, Jack stroking my shoulders and looking as content as a kitten who'd just disappeared head first into a vat of cream, I asked him what was going to happen with 'us'.

In fact, what I actually said was: 'So—can we go public now, Jack? Now nobody will think you're taking advantage of the hired help, can we stop all this sneaking around?'

He didn't reply straight away, but I felt a sudden jolt in his breathing, and the effort he made to calm it back down. Fairly typical male reaction to anything verging on the 'where is this going?' talk, in my experience, and I screwed up my eyes and forced myself to stay quiet for a moment instead of gabbing on and embarrassing myself even more.

'There's nothing I'd love more, Jess,' he eventually said. 'But I still don't think the timing is right. If this thing takes off like I think it will, you're going to wake up famous tomorrow. Everyone will be interested in you—and saddling yourself with an old git like me won't do anything good for your image. I'm sure Patty has plans for you, and they'll probably include you being single—at least in public. I'd just get in the way.

So…for now, let's keep it our own, delicious secret, okay, sweetheart?'

I snorted at the very thought of anyone describing Jack as an 'old git', and felt a tremble of fear at what Patty's plans for me might include. But part of me got it—understood what he was saying, and why he was saying it. He was seeing the bigger picture—and the ability to do that was one of the reasons he'd made it as far as he had in this industry. I sighed, and snuggled into him—a bit disappointed, but accepting it. As ever, I just had to trust him—and that had worked out all right for me so far.

After a few more minutes of hazy conversation, Jack had fallen asleep, softly puffing out cute little snores as he drifted off into dreamland. I, however, still felt horribly awake—my eyes popping so wide, it was like they'd been propped open. My body was completely knackered—but my brain just wouldn't shut up. It yammered on and on and on, leaping from one subject to another, refusing to rest.

Eventually, I gave up on even trying to sleep, and wriggled out of his arms as quietly as I could, not wanting to disturb him. I glanced back down at him, his usually perfect hair skewed over his forehead, his very appealing torso bare and glistening, chugging away like a snoozy pig. Like I said, cute.

I decided to make my way home—I'd only wake him up if I stayed here, tossing and turning and thinking out loud, and anyway, I suddenly felt like I needed a bit of time on my own. Time in my own territory, even if it was a crappy bedsit above a kebab shop. I needed to try to relax, switch off, get a bit of shut-eye—tomorrow, I knew, was going to be a weird one. And I needed to call my parents and tell them everything as well—not just about the show, but about seeing Daniel again. They'd be as made up about that as they would about my tentative steps into stardom, I suspected. Mum in particular had always adored him, and not-so-secretly always hoped we'd end up together.

I gathered up my clothes from where they'd ended up randomly scattered around the bedroom, and made my through into the lounge. Wearily, I pulled on my waitressing skirt yet again—I'd been in and out of it all night—and, as I did it, noticed Jack's phone and keys lying on the coffee table next to the wine glasses we'd used earlier to celebrate our victories. We'd drunk quite a lot of wine, enough for two bottles to be sitting there next to the glasses.

I bit my lip slightly as I stared at the phone, knowing I was considering doing something I really shouldn't do, and attempting to mentally talk myself out of it. After a few minutes of mouth-gnawing while devils and angels danced on my tired shoulders, I reached out and picked it up.

I wasn't going to turn into one of those crazy women who checked their boyfriend's text messages—because, let's face it, we've all been there and it never leads anywhere good—but I really, really wanted to talk to Daniel again. Jack had said he'd swap our numbers, but when I'd asked for it earlier, he'd brushed it aside with a vague 'Yeah, I'll do it in a minute…' type comment, before pouring more wine.

I flicked on to Jack's contact list and was faced with a sea of names, some of them so mind-bogglingly famous that I was half tempted to jot them down as well—I mean, who wouldn't want to call Cheryl Cole for a late night chat about the latest *X Factor* contestants?

I restrained myself though, and scrolled down to 'D'. I felt a momentary swipe of disappointment when it wasn't there, before I had to give myself a slap around the head and a great big Homer Simpson 'D'oh!'—of course it wasn't filed under 'D', which in my case would have stood for 'Dumbass'. It was under 'W' for Wellsy—both a mobile number and an email address. I quickly tapped the details into my own phone, and noticed that Vogue's was just above it—so, while I was already violating the sleeping prince's privacy, decided I might as well be hung for a sheep as a lamb and typed that one in as well. I most definitely owed her a great big thank-you message.

After that, I felt so guilty I called a cab straight away—leaving Jack a note scrawled on the back of a Thai takeaway menu, explaining that I'd gone home to try and decontaminate my hair.

Once I finally made it back to the flat in Kentish Town, after a dream-like drive through the dark London streets, I didn't even have the energy for that. I dragged myself up the stairs, inhaling the familiar smells of stale kebab, and collapsed straight into bed, just about managing to get changed into a reindeer onesie that Ruby had given me last Christmas.

*

That, I realised as soon as I looked in the mirror when I woke up, had been a big mistake. I hadn't even taken my make-up off and, after a night of energetic bonking, it was sprawling all over my face in a post-coital stupor. Seriously, my make-up was so relaxed, it wanted to light up a cigarette. My mascara was streaked over my cheeks, and the layers of caked foundation were flaking off. My hair was completely glued into a shape that looked like something from a science-fiction film, and at least one of the lilies had hung on for the whole of the night. I pulled the hood of the reindeer onesie up over it, watching the little felt antlers bounce around.

I also had a wicked hangover from drinking way too much wine back at Jack's place, on what was essentially an empty stomach. My head was thumping, and all I could do was stagger to the fridge, and get to work on a large bottle of water.

I was rooting through the drawer in the kitchen, searching for paracetamol, when I heard my phone buzzing. I didn't have a landline, and it took me a couple of frantic seconds to locate my mobile, skittering away on my bedside cabinet. My first thought was, 'I wonder if this is Daniel?' and my second thought was, 'Don't be so bloody stupid, he doesn't even have your number.'

I glanced at the caller ID and saw that it was Becky, my sister. I quickly answered it, mumbled a hello, then paused to swig down the painkillers. My body would thank me for it later. I didn't hear the first few sentences that she squawked at me, and had to ask her to repeat herself.

'I said,' she drawled, sarcastically, 'what the fuck has been going on with you? Luke woke us all up this morning, saying there was loads of stuff about you on his Google alert.'

I could hear the sounds of screaming toddlers and hyped-up kids in the background, which told me she was at work, at the soft play centre she managed.

'This morning?' I mumbled, confused. 'Isn't it still morning? And Luke has a Google alert set up on me—why, so he can take the piss?'

'It's almost one in the afternoon, sleeping beauty. And I'm sure Luke would like to take the piss, but he's too excited right now. I've just been over there, and everyone is buzzing about it. That show you did last night is all over the internet…the YouTube clip already has, like, a million hits, and your Twitter account's gone insane. Since when did you have two hundred thousand followers?'

Uhh. Since, never. I barely even used my Twitter account—it was something I'd set up to promote the Princess-party business, and I cringed as I realised there was still a profile picture on there of me as Cinderella. Yet another thing I needed to get fixed, before Patty skinned me alive.

'Wow, that's weird…' I muttered, feeling as though my whole life was suddenly making no sense at all. 'I mean, I know there were a lot of media people there, but I didn't think it would all happen quite this quickly. I was planning to call you lot this morning and tell you about it, just in case.'

'Well, you didn't!' she snapped, sounding a bit huffy. I didn't really know why—I mean, I know I should have texted her last night, and let her know, but it had all been so hectic. Crazily hectic.

'And,' she carried on, still sounding frosty, 'we're also wondering why you've changed your name to Jessica with a K?'

'Ummm…what do you mean? Like, Kessika?'

'Oh God—you're hungover as well, aren't you?'

'No!' I said, a bit too loudly. It made my non-existent hangover hurt just that little bit more.

'Yes, you are, I know the signs. Anyway, no, not *Kessika*, you idiot, Jessika—with a K where the C should be. That's how it's spelled, everywhere. Not just on one website, which could have been a mistake, but everywhere. It looks daft—like that hairdresser's at the top of the road called Krazy Kutz.'

I took a few more sips of water, and tried to wipe some of the mascara crust out of my eyes. This was all a bit too much. Plus, it was the afternoon—I should have been in the office hours ago.

'Well, I don't know anything about that, honest, Becky. I didn't choose it—and if they'd asked me, I'd have said no. It's just…it all happened so fast, Sis. I'll tell you all about it later, but the short story is, I went there to work as a waitress for the night, and Vogue got sick, and—'

'She's in rehab, apparently,' Becky cut in.

'No, she's not! At the worst she's got cholera. Anyway, I ended up going on in her place, and it was all bonkers, and I had to do interviews afterwards, and then Daniel turned up, except he's not Daniel any more, and…'

'Stop! Daniel turned up? Daniel who? Daniel from next *door*? And what do you mean, he's not Daniel any more? Are you on some kind of acid trip?'

'No, but it's starting to feel like it. Becky. Yeah, Daniel from next door. He works in the music business now, he's some famous producer called Wellsy, and anyway, he was there. Which was…brilliant.'

'I bet. You two were always close. Does he still look like Leonardo di Caprio's fat little brother?'

I paused, recalling the way the new Daniel had looked. All long limbs and soft blond hair and sparkling blue eyes.

'Erm, no. He doesn't. He looks like Leonardo di Caprio's taller, better-looking brother. He's really changed, Beck, you just wouldn't believe it.'

'Well, there's a lot I wouldn't have believed this time yesterday, Jessika with a K. And you're going to have to tell me all about it later—Mum and Dad have been trying to get hold of you as well, so you need to call them as soon as you can. They're dead pleased, but a bit worried as well—so make sure you let them know you're all right, will you? I'm on my break so I've got to go. There's a fourth birthday party due in any minute.'

'Okay. And, yeah, I'll call them as soon as I can, I promise—but tell them I'm doing fine. And tell them I'm sorry about my name getting changed. And tell them about Daniel.'

'Tell them yourself, superstar—assuming you're not too famous to bother any more. Listen, before I go, are you still coming home for Nan's eighty-fifth? Mum's booking a table at the Harvester and she needs to know how many for.'

Shit. I'd completely forgotten about my nan's eighty-fifth, even before I'd become an overnight Jessika with a K—I couldn't even blame that. I'd just lost track of time, between my work in the office and my work on my music and, well, my work on Jack. I knew how excited my nan would be too. The Harvester was her favourite restaurant because they let you take as many turns at the carvery as you like.

'Course I am,' I said, lamely, wondering if there was still enough time to book one of the cheapo train tickets back to Liverpool.

'Good,' replied Becky, sounding relieved. 'It wouldn't be the same without you, even if you do spell your name like Krazy Kutz, you soft mare.'

As she disconnected, I put the phone back down on the cabinet, and put my head back down on the pillow, desperately wanting to go to sleep. I didn't even want to look at how many missed calls I had—at least some of them would probably be from the office, wondering where I was and what the hell I was playing at. I mean, in the normal world, what I'd done last night would have been enough to earn me a lie-in—but with Starmaker, and with Patty in particular, I had no idea.

I didn't know if I'd be going back in as Jess the PR slave, or be able to make a grand entrance as Jessika with a K—or what the reaction there was going to be. I needed to see Neale, and thank him for his help, and call Vogue, and see how she was, and, mainly, call my mum and dad. At some point, I also needed to go online and see what all the fuss was about.

But just then, all I really wanted to do was sleep for seven hours straight, then wake up to find the Bacon Butty Fairy had magically visited my flat and left me a stash of goodies at the side of the bed.

I lay there, hiding my eyes with my fleecy arm, and tried to ignore the pounding in my head. And the buzzing in my ears. And the doorbell that wouldn't stop ringing…

I sat up, so sharply I thought I might puke, and frowned as I listened properly. Yes. It was definitely the doorbell. I hadn't recognised it at first as nobody ever visited me—the only time it had been rung before was when some drunk mistakenly staggered from the kebab shop to the door at the side and tried to get in because he'd forgotten to ask for salt and vinegar on his chips.

I groaned, and dragged myself to my feet. It didn't seem like they were going to stop, whoever it was, and I stood no chance at all of getting back to sleep with that racket going on. I grabbed a pack of baby wipes from the rickety old table I used as a dresser, and scrunched off what I hoped was the worst of the leftover make-up, before heading down the stairs.

It might, after all, be the Bacon Butty Fairy—and I didn't want to scare her away.

I was still giggling at my own nonsensical non-joke—in that way you do when you're basically still a bit drunk the morning after—by the time I reached the downstairs hallway and pulled open the door.

Chapter 17

It wasn't the Bacon Butty Fairy. It was a whole squadron of Photographer Fairies, complete with flashing lights and shouted instructions and recording devices being shoved under my chin.

'Jessika! How does it feel to wake up famous?' one of them yelled.

'Jessika! Tell us all about it!' banged another.

'Look this way, Jessika!' screeched another.

'Is that a reindeer?' asked yet another, in a delighted tone of voice.

I grasped hold of the doorframe for balance, trying not to reel back in shock as the barrage continued. I was terrified—and suddenly very conscious of my bleary eyes, smeared make-up, and less than glamorous ensemble. I mean, it was all well and good in Notting Hill—but I was no Julia Roberts. I wasn't even a Rhys Ifans, looking like this. I was just a hungover Scouse girl dressed as a reindeer, wondering what the hell was going on.

I could see Yusuf and his sons lurking in the doorway to

the kebab shop, looking just about as confused as I was, but definitely more stylish in their striped aprons and hairnets.

Even at my best, I probably wouldn't have been able to handle this—the shouting, the questions, the constant and annoying flashing as I was captured in all my glory. And this really wasn't my best, by any stretch of the imagination.

I realised that the mass of bodies was lurching closer and closer towards me, and if I didn't do something soon, my stairway would be invaded by the ladies and gentlemen of the press. Once they'd breached the barricades, I'd have no choice but to run back up the steps, and then they'd have photos of my arsing retreating, with its little reindeer tail bobbing away.

I slammed the door shut, and leaned back against it, still able to hear the commotion from outside. I stood there for a moment, learning how to breathe again, until I felt someone open the flap the postman used to deliver junk mail, and leapt away.

I pounded up the stairs as fast as I could, back into my flat, closing and locking the door. I felt sick and scared and trapped—plus the doorbell was still ringing.

I held my face in my hands, not having a clue what to do—I couldn't get away, unless I did a Batman over the fire escapes, and I had no clue how to handle the hordes outside. It was like being under siege by a zombie invasion, and I wondered how long my water supplies would last.

I forced myself to take some deep breaths, and walked back over to the bed, all dreams of a few more hours' sleep well and truly kyboshed. I picked up my phone, having no idea who I was going to call. As I didn't have the Ghosbusters on speed dial, I was faced with few choices: Jack or Patty.

Much as I hated to admit it, Patty was the sensible option. This was her world. These were her colleagues and contacts. This was probably, if I analysed the situation without panic, entirely her doing anyway—I mean, how did they know where I lived in the first place? Only Jack and people at Starmaker and my family had my London address. I'd spoken to Becky minutes earlier, and she didn't mention anybody getting in touch with them about it—not that they'd have told them anyway.

And Jack…well, Jack might have told them, but he'd have warned me first. Patty—it had to be Patty.

I looked at my phone and finally forced myself to check all the missed calls and messages. Sure enough, as well as the ones from Mum and Dad's landline, there were three missed calls from Patty's mobile, and one text from her: 'Expect media after lunch. Make sure you're out of bed and looking good.'

Aaaagh. She *had* warned me—I'd just been too out of it to notice. But still—she should have tried harder. She should have come herself, or cancelled the whole thing when I didn't reply. She should have…oh God, I couldn't even properly blame Patty, much as I wanted to. Yes, she could have prepared me better. She could have mentioned these evil plans the night before. She could have taken me to one side and told me to go home and get a good night's sleep because the world's media (okay, that might be an exaggeration—but at least London's) would be camping out on my doorstep the next day.

But really, I should have been ready. I'd worked with her long enough to know this kind of thing was her bread and butter—and I'd even had that chat with Becky about the Twitter and the YouTube and the Google alerts... I was an idiot. I was a hungover, exhausted, unprofessional idiot. Dressed as a bloody reindeer.

I hit Redial with shaking hands, praying to all that was holy that she answered; that she wasn't getting a mani-pedi or doing her shopping or worshipping at whatever Church of Satan she attended—it was a Sunday, after all.

'Yes?' she screeched, her voice high-pitched and already annoyed with me. Bizarrely, I'd never been so glad to hear anything in my whole life.

'Patty! I need help! The world and his wife are outside my flat, and they all have cameras, and...and... I'm wearing a reindeer onesie!'

There was a pause, and a sound that reminded me of long fingernails being dragged across a chalk board. I thought maybe it was Patty breathing fire.

'I'll be there in twenty minutes. Get ready, and make sure you look like a star. Life as you know it is about to change, and you'd better get used to it, you idiot—I won't always be around to hold your hand and coddle you.'

She hung up, and I physically shivered at the thought of Patty's 'coddling'—if this was coddling, I'd hate to see her when she was being deliberately unpleasant. Still, I did feel an immediate sense of relief that she was on her way—as well as a sense of underlying anxiety about the rest of that sentence.

The part that had included the words 'life as you know it is about to change'.

I'd come to London looking for change. I'd desperately wanted change. I'd hungered for it, and worked for it, and fought for it.

And now it was here, ringing my doorbell, and I was suddenly worried that I wouldn't know how to deal with it at all.

Chapter 18

To say that the rest of the day was strange would be a vast understatement. It was a day unlike any other I'd ever experienced—and it ran from the good, to the bad, to the downright ugly.

The ugly part would be me, when I got off the phone to Patty, and burst into tears. Big, fat, over-emotional morning-after tears that I knew I hadn't earned, but I couldn't keep back anyway. I felt so very, very alone—especially after I called Jack and it went straight to voicemail. I considered phoning my mum and dad, but I was too upset. It would break their hearts to hear me sobbing, hundreds of miles away, and knowing Dad he'd just load them both up in the cab and head down south.

Much as seeing them again was a comforting idea, I knew it wasn't a good one—they wouldn't be able to help me with this, and they'd just end up getting dragged into the madness with me. I needed to talk to them, but I needed to have a better grip on my senses before I did it. I reminded myself that everything that was happening right now was good—it was what I wanted. And by the time I spoke to my parents, hopefully that would feel more real, and the conversation would go a whole lot better.

So I let the floodgates open, until there were no tears left. I drank more water. I jumped into the shower for a very quick and very much needed wash. Then I wrapped myself in a towel, and stared at my wardrobe, wondering what I should wear—what would meet Patty's concept of 'looking good' without the assistance of Neale to get me professionally ready for my big media meet and greet.

In the end, after standing there shivering for five minutes, dripping onto the carpet, I pulled out a pair of brand-new super-skinny Topshop jeans that I'd picked up in the sale in town. They looked a lot more expensive than they were, and now fit me even better than they had when I'd bought them. I pulled out a pair of Kurt Geiger platforms that I'd never worn, and settled on a silver shimmery Reiss top I'd used a few times for nights out.

I gave it a quick sniff test, and came up with nothing worse than deodorant, so we were good to go. Once I'd decided on my outfit, I got to work on the rest of the transformation—giving my hair a good backcomb, Bridget Bardot-style. I really needed to get my highlights touched up, but money and time had been scarce, so this would have to do. I still looked mainly blonde—and maybe they'd think I was starting a dip-dye. After that, I put on my make-up as well as I could with very nervous hands.

As I did it, I tried to remember everything I'd picked up by osmosis from working with Patty, recalling the way she'd stage-managed various star's 'impromptu' appearances. I didn't want to be too showbiz, but I couldn't be too girl-next-door either—I was supposed to be a new-found star, and needed to find the balance between being glamorous and being approachable. Someone you could aspire to be like—but still root for. Like Katniss in *The Hunger Games*, but without the death and the bow and arrows.

Luckily, you can't grow up female in Liverpool without learning a few make-up tricks—or without learning how to survive nights out in sub-zero temperatures wearing a mini and no coat. The weather was much cooler now, but I'd be fine—it was in my DNA.

By the time I was almost done, a beep from my phone told me there was a message—and having well and truly learned my lesson about ignoring them, I looked at it straight away. Patty. Telling me she'd spoken to Yusuf, and that he was going to sneak her in through the back door. ETA two minutes.

I wondered if Yusuf had offered her a free kebab, and wondered what she'd say if he did. It wasn't a natural match, Patty and kebabs. Or Patty and food, for that matter.

I hooked in some dangly feather earrings, sprayed on some Marc Jacobs perfume, and sat nervously on the bed, tapping my fingers against my knees and not daring to look in the mirror again. The first time I'd been fairly pleased with my emergency efforts—the second time I might feel differently. It wasn't worth the risk, so I kept my eyes carefully averted.

When the short, sharp knock finally came at the door, I leapt up again, practically flying across the room to let Patty in. It was a crazy, messed-up world when I was looking forward to seeing her, that's for sure. I was even willingly inviting her into my own home, which I might live to regret if she turned out to be a vampire.

She pushed past me and immediately threw a paper-wrapped package into the bin in the kitchen. I could tell from the delicious smell that Yusuf had, indeed, given her a free kebab—but at least she'd accepted it, and not been rude to him. Being rude to me was one thing, but I'd have been peeved if she'd lashed out at my lovely landlord.

'Kebab?' I said, lamely, pointing at the steaming parcel.

'No, my firstborn child,' she snapped back, standing hands on narrow hips to look me up and down. She was dressed elegantly and smartly, in a sleek black dress that managed to be both business-like and vaguely hot. I had no idea if she'd also had to put together her look for the day, or if she always dressed like that. In fact, I realised, I actually knew nothing at all about her—and now I was putting my life, or at least my mental health and my career, in her hands.

She nodded once, very briskly, and said, 'That's not too bad. Slutty but wholesome. Appeals to all markets. Now, are you ready?'

'For what?' I asked nervously, running my hands over my hair, not really that happy with the 'slutty' part of her comment. I mean, nobody ever called Katniss slutty, did they?

'To go out there,' she replied, sounding completely exasperated with me. 'Honestly, Jess, you've worked with my team for long enough now—I expected you to be able to handle this better. I left a message, I warned you—I didn't throw you to the lions, tempting as it was. I have to admit there are more of them out there than I anticipated, but that's not a bad thing.

That's the whole point, in fact. What you did last night was adequate—the rest starts now, and you need to pull yourself together.'

I stared at her for a moment, fighting down the urge to cry like a big fat baby again, and nodded in agreement. Because I did agree, unlikely as it seemed. This might not have all happened in the way I'd anticipated, but it was happening—and I needed to stop feeling sorry for myself, and start seeing it as the fantastic opportunity I'd been hoping for.

'Okay. But what about the reindeer photos?'

'Don't worry about that now. They'll use them—of course they will—but it could have been a lot worse. At least you didn't answer the door in S&M gear, or even worse, in a Liverpool kit…although we might get some mileage out of that at a later date. Reindeers are cute. Everyone loves reindeers. And onesies are both common and adored by the unwashed masses, so that works. Anyway, it's too late to change it—now we have to go out there and do some damage control.'

'And…erm…how do I do that?' I asked, amazed at my sudden and total lack of ability to think for myself. Maybe this was part of the process of becoming famous.

'You smile. You laugh. You simper pathetically. You talk about how grateful you are to be in this position. You talk about Vogue as though she's your hero, and you stay completely and utterly vague about what happens next. Can you manage that, do you think?'

'Yes,' I said, firmly, trying to put some self-belief into my voice. Because, in all honesty, all of that was completely true—so I should be able to sell it.

She turned away from me, whipping her phone out, and I heard her talking to someone about bringing a car around. Once she'd finished issuing orders, she snapped her gaze back at me.

'Sorted. Grab what you need for the next few days—you might not be coming back to this place for a while. Which,' she said, glancing around her in complete disgust, 'must come as a huge relief.'

I wasn't quite so sure about that, and muttered back at her: 'It's not that bad…' as I scurried around throwing underwear and make-up into the only bag I could find, which happened to be a stylish little number that was plastic and said Superdrug on the front.

'Maybe, if you're an Albanian refugee,' she replied, grabbing the bag out of my hands as soon as I was done. 'Or from Liverpool,' she added, giving me one of those pointed stares that made me realise all over again how much I hated her. 'Now come on—they won't wait forever, and you haven't earned the right to be a diva just yet.'

The experience itself was short, sharp, and scary. Patty went out first, hiding the carrier bag behind her, and did a little announcement, making a reindeer joke before she let me walk past her. For a few moments, I just stood there on the step, smiling, and doing my best to respond to what felt like a million separate commands. Look this way, look that way, give us a wave, turn round and look at us over your shoulder… the list was endless.

All the time, people also shouted questions at me, and I answered them as well as I could. They were all about the show, and about Vogue, and about when I'd be releasing a single and, on one occasion, about my love life.

'Are you single, Jessika? Are you looking for love?' I heard, yelled over the din by a short, round man with a beard that Yusuf would have been proud of. I froze for a second as soon as the question was asked, my mind whipping me back in time to the night before—to everything that Jack had said.

'Yes,' I replied, grinning on demand. 'I'm still one of the single ladies!'

The worst thing was, I had no idea if it was a lie or not—I wanted to believe that what Jack and I had was special, was going to last, but we'd never discussed it. Never defined it, or set out terms and conditions. But I did know that I'd given the right answer—at least from his perspective. And admitting I'd been sleeping with the boss of Starmaker for all this time wasn't exactly going to play well with the public, was it? People would immediately assume that was why I'd been given my big break, no matter how far from the truth it was.

Luckily, nobody had the chance to quiz me any further in that particular direction, as the car arrived. It was a big car, and it was black, and it wasn't a cab; beyond that I can't describe it, other than to say I was bloody relieved to see it turn up. I waved goodbye to the journalists and the photographers, and sank into the comfort of the dark leather seats, delighted beyond belief that it was finally done with. I'd not tripped over my own feet, said 'fuck', or vomited—all of which I was counting as a massive victory.

I glanced at Patty as she climbed in next to me, waiting to hear her verdict—but she ignored me, and immediately got to work, tapping away on her iPhone as though I wasn't there. As the car started up and we pulled away, I saw Yusuf out of the window. He was watching me, a confused smile on his face, as we drove past.

I waved at him and kept my head turned in his direction until he disappeared out of sight. I had no idea when I'd see him again, and felt a bit sad about it.

The car took us straight to the Starmaker offices, where there were also a few members of the paparazzi hanging around. Despite what I'd just been through, and despite what Becky had told me on the phone, I still automatically assumed they were there for Vogue, or Beckett, one of the other Starmaker acts. It wasn't unusual to see photographers there, looking for a shot—but this time, bizarrely, they were there for me.

We got out of the car, and after Patty hissed 'stop looking like you're here to clean the bloody toilets' in my ear, I realised that was the case. I slipped back into the 'pose and smile' routine, and hoped I wasn't pouting too much, like a bad selfie, before Patty shooed them off and I was ushered into the lobby.

The same lobby I'd walked through, exhausted, on so many nights since coming to London. The one with the chrome and the flowers and the platinum discs and the huge, blown-up shots of the label's biggest stars. The one I usually snuck through, slouching, feeling tired and out of place and vaguely anxious, scared that the security guards might pull me up and ask me what I was doing in the building.

This time, though, it was all different. As soon as I walked in, I saw Heidi, Jack's assistant, waiting for us. She was dressed, as usual, in a business suit that looked slightly too small, and she was wearing a big, dazzling smile that told me very clearly that she was up to speed on the strange twists and turns my life had taken.

I wanted to go and give her a hug—she was one of the few people at Starmaker who'd treated me like a human being since the day I got there—but she immediately flipped open her notepad, tapped it with her pen, and announced, 'They're waiting for you in the Mash Up room, Jess. How do you take your coffee?'

I paused, completely taken aback by this new development. I'd handled the show last night. I'd handled the media this morning—sort of. I'd handled the fact that my name had magically changed its spelling, although there would be words about that at some point. I'd been driven here in a luxury car by a chauffeur, and been greeted at the door by paparazzi.

But what truly amazed me the most was this: I was no longer the one *making* the coffee. I was the one who had the coffee made for me. It was, utterly and truly, an astounding moment—and the one that finally made me start to realise that this was all real. It was actually happening. I was going to be a star!

'Erm…could I maybe have…would it be possible to have a cappuccino?' I mumbled, still a bit gobsmacked by the whole thing.

'Sure,' said Heidi, 'I'll get the new intern to make it—we seem to be one down all of a sudden. Now, come on, they'll start scribbling on the walls if I leave them alone for too long.'

She gave me a cheeky wink, and walked away.

'Who will?' I asked, scurrying to catch up with her as

she headed to the lifts. Patty, I noted, had traipsed off up the stairs without so much as a goodbye. I suppose she was busy plotting world domination and changing innocent people's names behind their backs.

'Oh, you know—the creatives. The execs. The *team*. Honestly, they have the combined attention span of a six-year-old child.'

I just nodded as she pressed the button for the top floor. The floor I'd only ever visited once before when, in fact, I was delivering coffee, funnily enough. Jack's own office was on the same level as the PR team and the admin offices. The make-up people and stylists and dance and vocal coaches all tended to stay in their own gangs, around the studios and rehearsal rooms. There was another enclave for people who worked on cover design and things I didn't really understand like digital distribution and international sales.

And the top floor was where the mysteriously titled Finance and Legal lived, along with the Proper Big Wigs, and the meeting rooms. These were the posh, boardroom style places where important visitors were brought when Starmaker needed to assemble their avengers, or really impress someone.

In an accountancy firm or a law firm, they would probably just be called the boardrooms. But here—because this was the music industry, thank you very much—they had funky names that presumably matched the image of the business. There was the Mash Up room, where we were heading, and the Mixing Deck, which I'd never even seen the inside of.

I felt nervous as the lift progressed upwards, anxious about what was going to happen next, and too scared to ask. I think part of me was worried that if I asked, it might break the spell, and I'd suddenly find myself back in Kansas. I thought I was hiding it well until Heidi stared at me from over the top of her glasses, and said, 'You look terrified. Do you want me to press the emergency stop button, so we can wait here until the men from the lift company come and rescue us?'

I laughed and puffed out some air, pathetically grateful for her attempt to put me at ease.

'I'd say, yes,' I replied, 'except I really need a wee. Please tell me there'll be time for that at least?'

'Only if you make it quick,' she said, just as the doors pinged open.

I followed her out and headed for the Ladies', which were luckily at exactly the same point on every floor. A piece of architectural design genius, I thought, doing my business with supersonic efficiency.

When I came out of the cubicle and started to wash my hands, I stared at my reflection in the mirror, and gave myself a Very Stern Talking To.

I needed to get a grip of the situation. Control my nerves. Stop feeling so worried. Relax enough to enjoy this whole crazy ride. I looked good. I'd performed well the night before. I'd certainly attracted Starmaker a lot of attention, hopefully for all the right reasons. The team that was waiting for me in the Mash Up room was doing exactly that—waiting for *me*. Not the other way round. Much as I was grateful for this opportunity, I wasn't naive enough to think that any of this was happening out of the kindness of their own hearts—it was happening because I was a viable talent. Someone who could sell records, boost the label, add yet more platinum discs to the walls.

Odd as it seemed, I was a product—and that should, by all rights, make me feel better. Or at least put me in a position of strength. So I needed to stop my knees from knocking together, and put on my game face. I didn't exactly know what was next on the agenda, but the fact that there was an agenda at all—other than fetching Patty's lunch from the sushi place over the road—was definitely an improvement.

I fluffed up my hair, stood up straight, and walked out of there ready to fight monsters, slay dragons, and drink coffee that somebody else had made for me.

Chapter 19

Two hours later, I emerged from the Mash Up room as Starmaker's latest signing. Or at least, I would be as soon as the paperwork was sorted.

The meeting had involved me, Jack, his partner Simon (not Cowell), and various other people who represented the record label's interests. There were songwriters, and a producer, and Evelyn, Patty's boss, as well as Heidi, who had been taking notes on everything quietly in the corner.

It had felt overwhelming, partly at least because they were all so damn nice to me. People who hadn't given me a second glance as I walked through the staffroom with a tray of biscuits were suddenly incredibly attentive—and I can't deny it felt good.

I tried to take it all with good grace—to be the person I'd been raised to be—but hey, I'm only human. I'd been so flattened by the exhausting anonymity of my time so far at Starmaker that finally getting some attention felt sensational. It was like lying on a beach in the Caribbean sunshine after living in an igloo at the North Pole for months on end.

Despite the temptation to bask in it, I listened hard to what they had to say; I tried to stay alert, and I made a huge effort not to jump up and down with excitement when they started talking about plans for a single, an album, and eventually a tour. I heard bizarre sentences like 'Our next step is to build you as a brand', and 'We'll work as a team to find the sound that makes Jessika unique', and words I didn't really understand, like 'synergy', and 'USP', and 'global push strategy'.

Every time someone used one of the mystery words, I felt a little internal 'eek', and found myself looking at Jack, who was sitting next to me, in utter confusion. After this had happened a couple of times, he wrote a message on the notepad he was using, and pushed it towards me under the table. 'Will explain all later,' he'd scrawled, with a kiss at the end.

The fact that I had Jack as my own personal translator—the fact that Jack was so much more on my side than anybody in the room even knew—instantly made me feel better, made me feel less swamped by it all.

And even though I might not have understood the specific terms of this foreign language they were speaking, I understood what they were saying—all I had to do was sign on the dotted line, and the Starmaker machine would leap into action. I could leave my failures and insecurities behind, and start all over again—with one of the biggest record companies in the world behind me. I could forget that I'd ever been a fake Disney Princess and that I was on first name terms with Patty's dry cleaner and that I'd only been deemed good enough to serve food at last night's party. This was a completely fresh start.

I perked up even more once they started to talk about the

music. I was mainly interested in what the songwriting and producing team had in mind, and was more than happy to let the business and marketing aspects go over my head.

I knew all of that was important but, for me, it was all about the music—and if I got that right, the rest would follow. At the moment, I'd become famous for one impromptu show, singing someone else's tracks, doing someone else's dance moves, and wearing someone else's curtains. What I was thrilled about was the fact that they were keen to find new material, just for me.

'You could be the new Adele,' said Darren, one of the in-house songwriters.

'Or the new Katy Perry,' added his partner, James.

'Or a bit of both,' replied Darren, at which point I realised this could go on all day. They threw out names and styles—Beyoncé, Ellie Goulding, Rihanna, Rita Ora, Sia, Taylor Swift, and more—and paused after each one to ask if I liked them, if I could sing their kinds of songs, what direction I saw my vocal style going in.

In the end, a bit flummoxed by it all and not really sure what they wanted me to say, I just replied, 'I love all of them. They're all great. But I don't want to be them—I don't want to be the new Katy Perry or the new Lady Gaga or the new Vogue. I just want to be the new *me*.'

Darren and James had nodded and 'oohed' and 'aahed' at that, as though I'd just said something incredibly profound. I don't know, maybe I had—completely by accident. Maybe, if I'd been on *The X Factor*, one of the judges would have said I knew who I was as an artist.

The meeting wound on and, grateful as I was to be there, to be in that totally unreal position in the first place, I did fight two battles. It ended up as a one–one draw.

The first was about my name, which I thought was fair enough, as it was *my* name. Or at least it used to be.

'I don't like the K in the Jessica,' I said. 'Nobody asked me about it, and the first I knew of it even happening was when my sister called to tell me. It's upset my family, and I don't even understand why you did it.'

There was a momentary silence, while everyone sat there with fixed grins on their faces, wondering how to reply. I wasn't being rude, or being a diva, or being pushy—but I was being awkward, from their perspective, and maybe that was something they hadn't expected.

'I think,' said Evelyn, after a few seconds pause, 'that the decision had to be made very, very quickly. From what Patty tells me, there was literally less than half an hour between you agreeing to perform last night, and actually going up on stage?'

I nodded. That was indisputably true.

'Well, you see, Jessica,' she continued, the very picture of polite respect, 'usually, we'd spend months before launching an artiste to prepare. We'd look at image and brand and the target demographic audience, and we'd have meetings with all the lead creatives, possibly even a few sample members of the media. We'd test out names, looks, sounds, until we came up with a good fit. With Vogue, for example, we had six months of intensive training before we even released her first single.

'With you, we missed all of that—and although you obviously did a brilliant job last night, Patty had to essentially

cram months' worth of marketing and planning into thirty
minutes. She went with the new spelling because she thought
it gave you a little extra edge. Made you a bit more current.
Made you stand out—and Jack agreed.'

Jack, to be fair, at least had the nerve to meet my eyes, face
me head on, and nod.

'It's true,' he said. 'She did mention it to me before she
went out there and started talking to the media.'

'Well, why didn't you tell me last night back at... I mean
after the show?' I said, quickly correcting myself and hoping
nobody else noticed. I felt miffed that he hadn't seen fit to
mention it at all—at least then I'd have been better prepared
for waking up as a different person.

'I'm sorry, I should have,' he agreed, his tone placatory and
smooth. 'But it was all so hectic—all I can do is apologise,
Jess. You're right—we should have asked your opinion before
we adjusted the spelling.'

It's hard to stay angry with someone when they're
apologising—and especially hard to stay angry with that
person when he's running his fingers up and down your inner
thigh under the table while you try and keep a straight face in
front of a room full of strangers.

'Is there any way we can... I don't know, change it back?'
I asked, clamping my legs shut and trapping his hand. I let
him squirm for a moment, then let him go.

'Sadly not,' said Evelyn, firmly. 'From a media perspective,
last night was a huge smash—the YouTube hits, the Twitter
trending, the online and print coverage, it's all been
spectacular. You did a great job—but you did it as Jessika,

and I think it would be counter-productive now to try and change that.'

Even her brief mention of the word 'Twitter' made me cringe—I really, really needed to get that Cinderella photo taken down, and have it replaced with something more show-biz—maybe me in my reindeer suit. Not.

I had to accept that everything they said made sense, and move on—I wasn't happy about it, but there was no point becoming a harpy, either. It was only one letter, I told myself, and anyway, K was good. Maybe K could kick ass in a way C couldn't.

The next battle I fought, though, ended a lot more happily for me. They'd started to talk about style and image and my 'look', and how important it was.

'We all had a chat about this before you arrived, Jess, and we're all agreed that you are currently our top priority—and that we'll ask Lucas to work with you on this,' said Jack, referring to one of Starmaker's top stylists.

I knew he was meant to be fabulous—the PR team spoke his name in hushed and reverent tones, as though he was the Virgin Mary. He was legendarily good at putting together ensembles and styles that got attention—regularly placed in the fashion mags, featured on those 'who looks good in what' pages, almost famous in his own right for his relationship with all the big designer labels.

I also knew, from everyone's expectant glances, that they thought I'd be over the moon to hear that my image was going to be sculpted by one of their best—but my loyalties lay elsewhere.

'Ta very much,' I said, 'but I want Neale.'

'Neale... Neale who?' Evelyn asked, as he was obviously so low down on the hierarchy that she'd never even met him. And even if she had, she'd definitely not remembered.

'Neale who did me last night. He only had half an hour as well—and he created an outfit and hair and make-up from thin air. He was brilliant.'

'I agree that Neale really stepped up last night, Jess,' said Jack, taking over the debate. 'But this is too big a deal to jeopardise by giving the job to a junior. With Lucas, you'll be in safe hands, and you'll be—'

'Look,' I said, cutting in and placing my hand down on the table firmly enough to make a little noise and rattle the coffee cups, 'I'm not an idiot. I know what you're saying, and as someone who opened the front door in a onesie this morning, I know I need the help. But I worked well with Neale, and I like him—he gets me. He might be a junior, but until last night, I was an intern and a waitress. The fact that I'm sitting here now, that we're even having this conversation, is at least partly down to Neale, and how good a job he did. So. I want Neale.'

They all looked at me as if I was a potentially explosive device that needed careful handling, and I noticed Heidi leaning forward, an engrossed expression on her face as though she was watching a particularly dramatic episode of *EastEnders*.

Eventually, Jack smiled at me, and gave my ankle a little kick.

'Okay, Jess. You get Neale.'

Yay for me. That K was kicking already.

Chapter 20

It's quite scary how quickly life can change. One minute, I was slobbing around my flat inhaling second-hand kebab fumes and dreaming of stardom, and the next, I was installed in my luxury apartment block trying to figure out how to make the Jacuzzi jets work properly.

Well, obviously it took more than a minute—but the speed of everything was mind-boggling. I've heard people using the phrase 'it all passed in a blur' before, and always thought, well, you should've gone to Specsavers, then.

But that first week of my life, after that initial meeting, was crazy—a blur, but a multi-coloured one swathed in unicorns and sequins and that glittery stringy stuff you throw at Christmas trees. So much happened, but the overwhelming change was this: people very suddenly knew who I was. They knew who I was, and they wanted a piece of me. In fact, so many people wanted a piece of me, I wondered if there'd be anything left by the time they'd all finished taking their little nibbles.

Some of it was complete and utter fun. Telling Neale that he was now on Team Jessy, and had essentially bagged himself an A-list Starmaker client, was fun. Being swamped in

Neale's hugs for ten minutes straight was fun. Going on a massive shopping trip with him—all official and paid for by the Starmaker company credit card—was fun to the max. I mean, what more could a girl want? Her own personal stylist, gay best friend, and unlimited cash to spend on new clothes? Of course, a girl with any depth to her would add 'world peace' and 'an end to global poverty' to that list, but that wasn't where my head was at. Plus, you know, I wasn't sure that a pop star could manage all that—not even Bob Geldof.

Also fun were the photoshoots. Patty had taken one look at my Twitter account and frozen solid, as if she'd been spray-painted in ice. Not even her mouth twitched, she was so horrified. As soon as she emerged from her shocked funk, she gave me a glare that made me turn to stone myself, tapped her long fingernails on the desk so hard she left marks, and immediately organised a photographer.

It was Neale's first official job, and he did me proud—managing somehow to do hair, make-up, and clothes that reflected Patty's brief of 'make her gorgeous, but not so gorgeous that everyone will hate her'. I had a ball prancing around against various backdrops, pouting and giggling and generally playing the fool, and the other big plus was that the photographer never once asked me to take my top off—which had happened before.

Once the photos were done, Patty completely overhauled my social-media presence—which had, in all honesty, been pretty pathetic beforehand. There was a princess-led Twitter account and a princess-led Facebook page, plus my own personal Facebook page, which I'd neglected in recent years.

I mean, I didn't have much to say—and while my old school and college friends all seemed to be making announcements about career and relationships and babies and new puppies and what they'd had for dinner, I stayed quiet. There's only so many times you can post a picture of a steaming plate of noodles and not feel like a big, fat failure.

Even after I'd moved down to London, I stayed quiet—I'd made the mistake before of shouting out loud before I had any idea what I was getting myself into, and didn't want to look like a knob who was counting her chickens before anything came close to hatching.

By the end of that first day, though, I had it all—one of those official Twitter accounts with the little blue tick by them to show I wasn't an imposter (though why anybody would want to pretend to be me was still a conundrum); my own section on the Starmaker website; a revamped Facebook, and an Instagram that was suddenly and mysteriously filled with photos—from the photoshoot, from the gig at Panache, and from outside my flat in a reindeer onesie. None of it was anything to do with me—Patty did it all.

She also set me up with a day of 'phoners'—media interviews that I could do on the phone. I got a little thrill realising this was my first real 'PR'. I mean, I still didn't have much to talk about—I'd been told to keep it vague in terms of future recording plans, which didn't leave much apart from me. How I'd felt on the night of the gig; how I felt the day after; what it was like to be Starmaker's newest hope, which still made me fizz with happiness inside. This was it. I'd finally 'made it', a thought which made me beam from ear to ear.

I talked about Liverpool, about my family, about my hopes and dreams and ambitions; about Vogue and about music, and about my favourite food, fashion labels, and colours. I even got asked my star sign (Taurus), my clothes size, and my all-time best pizza topping. Luckily, it seemed nobody else was interested in my views on world peace and ending global poverty either.

In the end, I completely lost track of who I was talking to—and only Patty's military style schedule kept me on target.

There were bigger changes as well. Like the fact that I was moved into a Starmaker apartment not too far from Jack's, which might have had a security guard, swish lifts, and the Jacuzzi I could never work properly, but didn't have Yusuf. Or, for a couple of days at least, any of my stuff. Not that my stuff was any great shakes—and the shopping trip with Neale had stocked my wardrobe. But it was still my stuff, and I felt restless and unsettled until it all finally landed, boxed up and packed for me, without me ever even needing to go back for it. I suspected some poor intern had been landed with that job, and decided to find out who and thank them.

Even though it had saved me the effort, I was still a lot more sad than I expected to be at leaving the flat. It might have been crap, but it was mine—and at the very least, I'd wanted to say goodbye to Yusuf and his sons, and thank them for taking such good care of me. Maybe I could send them a note, I thought, as I unpacked my family photos and cuddly toys and half-empty bottles of nail varnish.

Once I'd done that, the new flat felt a bit more like home— admittedly a home that also came with a lot of chrome fittings and glass-topped surfaces that would drive Mum mad with the amount of dust they'd gather. Not that I had to worry about that—for a start, I was hardly ever there, and then, the Starmaker apartment also came with a Starmaker cleaner. The fridge was already stocked with water, salad, and lean and healthy things like salmon and tropical fruit, and the cupboards already contained herbal teas and brown rice cakes and other things that made me want a kebab more than ever. It looked as though I wasn't expected to do my own shopping either.

Eventually, I told myself, it would all feel normal—and anyway, it was only temporary. I was being stashed here, like some person in a witness protection programme, to escape the media attention and to allow me to concentrate on 'reaching the next level'.

I snapped a few pictures of the place, did a selfie of me on the balcony looking down over the city lights with a huge daft grin plastered on my face, and sent them to Becky and Luke and my parents. After three solid days of work—the photo shoots, the interviews, more dance training, vocal coaching, meetings, media training—I still hadn't managed to have a proper conversation with any of them. Just texts, a lot of smiley faces, and now the photos. Every time I sat down to call them for a long chat, I was grabbed up and taken away to do something else—and by night time, I was either too exhausted, or still busy, or with Jack.

Jack had been round to help me 'christen' the new flat, bearing a bottle of champagne and a cheeky plan to christen every room in the apartment in his own very special way as well. True to his word, he'd translated all the stuff I didn't understand in the meeting, and tolerated all of my stupid questions with the patience of a saint.

He explained that until my contract was fully sorted, and money started coming in from the music, appearances, and other revenue streams (I tried not to pull a face at that one—revenue streams—I could at least figure it out using the few brain cells I had left by that stage), they'd also set me up with a regular allowance that was paid into my bank account direct.

There was a little voice, squeaking away in the back of my mind, that told me I shouldn't be leaving all of this to Jack—not because I didn't trust him, but because I should keep finances and contracts separate from my love life. I should, I knew, have an agent or a manager who was nothing at all to do with Starmaker—who was independent from it all. But I told that little voice to shut up, until I could get some advice from Vogue, or pluck up the courage to raise it with Jack at all.

Having money for the first time in my life helped me ignore those nagging doubts—it felt brilliant, even though I didn't feel as though I'd done anything to earn it. Not yet, at least. That bothered me—the work ethic I'd been raised with was hard to shake off—but at the end of the day it didn't bother me enough for me to give the money back. Being able to buy something without worrying about whether the card would get declined was an awesome treat—even if I didn't really have anything I needed to buy.

Normally, I'd be food shopping, or treating myself to some new make-up or lovely smellies, but that was all done for me. And not just by Starmaker—as soon as the publicity machine really started to roll, the gifts began arriving.

Bouquets of flowers—so many I couldn't have them in the flat—from people I'd never met, or heard of, or even knew existed, all with little cards congratulating me. Fruit baskets, which I just left in the staff room for everyone else to help themselves to. Boxes of chocolates and cakes and other tasty treats, which I also left in the staff room—it was too dangerous to have them at home in case I accidentally ate them all and died of a sugar rush.

There were perfumes and toiletries and make-up and accessories and clothes and jewellery, even a small array of shiny techno gadgets like phones and music players. One package contained ten different onesies in a variety of animal forms, which was definitely a keeper.

I had no idea why anybody would want to send these things to me—until Patty explained that it was just another type of PR. If I was photographed wearing their product, or made a comment about it, it was a big win for the company concerned, and might well end up used in a magazine or on a blog. That did make sense, after all those phone interviews, it would have been really easy to slip one of them in there.

Patty, as ever, took control—but on this occasion, I was grateful. She told me to pick what I wanted to keep, and if I liked it, to let her know. Then she would make the decision about whether it was 'brand appropriate' for me to mention it in future interviews. I had no idea what brand appropriate really meant, but took a wild guess that she wouldn't want me praising the pink package of mildly S&M sex toys that had landed for me in the office. I did, however, sneak them home—you never know when you might need some fluffy handcuffs and a bottle of baby oil.

The rest I gave away. Two new interns had arrived—one to take my place as Patty's slave, and one specifically to help me. She was called Tilly, and was about nineteen, and I had no idea what to do with her. So I gave her some free body lotions and asked if she could help me carry the rest of the packages through to the break room, where I left them scattered around, beneath a cardboard sign that said FREE TO A GOOD HOME!

The other major change that had taken place in my life was the fact that 'going to parties' now seemed to be included in my job description. I'd been to four events in the last five nights, and was absolutely exhausted.

Never in a million years would I have believed that I'd prefer a night at home in one of my many animal onesies to bopping away with soap stars—but I was starting to believe that it could be true. I'd been photographed outside clubs on my way in; inside clubs with celebs; outside clubs on my way out—I'd even been offered a line of cocaine in the Ladies' by someone I'd once seen on *Big Brother*, which I politely declined.

Nights out in Liverpool need a lot of stamina—but these were getting crazy. 'We'd have a glass of wine, put on some R. Kelly and run through my dance moves together before he tarted me up. Then we'd have a chat and Neale would sneak in a cheeky Marlborough Light whilst we waited for my car to pick me up' I was starting to realise that I looked forward to talking to Neale and getting ready more than I looked forward to the party itself.

It wasn't like I could let myself go and enjoy them anyway—Patty had drummed that into me so hard, I could never forget it. It was work—not pleasure. Her set of rules was staggering: don't drink too much; don't fall over; don't flash your knickers getting into a cab (unless it's been pre-arranged, of course); don't get photographed stuffing your face with food; don't dance suggestively with anyone; don't vomit in the street; don't smoke; don't do drugs in public; don't criticise anyone for anything, even in a casual conversation. These were all, I'd been told, classic pitfalls that I could be expected to clomp my way into—and they didn't leave much room for spontaneity or, you know, actually enjoying myself. I had a tendency to disconnect my brain from my mouth at the best of times, so I lived these nights out in a constant state of near terror.

Staying out until the early hours with Ruby, or my sister before she was preggers, was easy—I'd be so hammered by the end, I often had no idea how I'd managed to get home from town. But this was a lesson in control, and I was on a steep learning curve.

Still, I reminded myself that it was a huge step in the right direction. That I was big girl, and I could handle it. That it wouldn't always feel this confusing—that one day, I'd get it all right, and the rewards would be so worth it.

One of the reasons I'd not called my parents was because of the sheer physical demands of my schedule. I was busy—and usually, by the time I got a moment to myself, it was four a.m. and they'd both be fast asleep. But the other reason was that I needed to get more of a handle on it all before I spoke to them—I wanted them to be happy for me, and proud of me, and excited about my future, the way I was. I didn't want them sitting round the kitchen table at breakfast time worrying about whether I was eating properly or whether my shoes were too high or whether I really, honestly, truly knew what I was doing.

Jack and Neale were at opposite ends of the spectrum, and were both brilliant people to have around. Jack could take a strategic global overview of my digital presence—and could explain what the hell that meant, as well. And Neale could make me laugh and make me relax and make me look gorgeous while he did it. But I still felt a bit discombobulated, as Nan used to say—and the only other person I could think of talking to was Vogue.

I'd tried calling her, using the number I'd sneakily filched from Jack's phone the night of the first gig, but something really weird happened when I did. I dialled the number, and she immediately answered, saying, 'Well, hello there, sexy,' in an amazingly sultry voice.

Now, not to do myself a disservice or anything, but I was pretty sure she wasn't expecting that call to be from me, and equally sure she didn't find me that sexy. Not unless she was hiding a very big secret indeed. So I just spluttered something along the lines of, 'Erm, um, aaagh, this is Jess?', in an apologetic tone.

There was a long pause, and eventually, Vogue's voice, saying, 'Oh! Hi, Jess…sorry about that, babe. I thought it was someone else.'

'Yeah. I guessed that. Have I called at a bad time?'

'Nah, don't worry about it—how's things?'

'I… I just wanted to thank you. For the other night. And to see if you're okay.'

'Doing good, kiddo. All is well in the land of Vogue's arse, you'll be relieved to hear. Look, I've got to go—stuff going on, you know how it is—but we'll catch up soon, okay? You're coming in to do some vocals with me next week, aren't you?'

Ah, yes. That was the other thing I'd wanted to discuss with her. The fact that the Starmaker team had decided that the best way to capitalise on my new-found fame was for me to be featured on Vogue's new single—adding in some vocals, and filming some new scenes for her video. I'd still be very much the 'featuring', rather than the star, but I'd be there. And I had been a bit worried about how she'd respond to that—the Vogue I'd always known in person was kind and funny and down to earth, but the Vogue I'd read about in the papers was a legendary diva who might get pissed off at the new kid on the block necking in on her fame.

'Think so, yes,' I answered, nervously. 'As long as that's all right with you?'

'The more the merrier, babe,' she replied. 'No worries. It'll be all fun and games. See you next week—try not to get snapped in your PJs between now and then.'

I'd been disappointed that I'd not been able to arrange to see her—but that was hugely presumptuous of me, anyway. She'd been good to me, and we were going to work together, but that didn't automatically make her my new BFF. Plus, she was clearly busy enough without having to listen to me bleating on.

But at the very least, she'd sounded genuinely all right about the single, and me essentially hitching a ride on the back of all her hard work. She was a superstar but, instead of being resentful, she seemed happy to share her time in the spotlight. I could only hope I'd be that nice if I ever got to her level.

As in that moment I was determined that I would. I was just going to have to toughen up if I was planning on making this my lifestyle permanently.

Especially as there were so many benefits. Like dreams coming true. Like cash. Like my new pad, which I was sure I'd get used to. Like fame and recording and touring and finally, finally making it in the life I'd always wanted. I just needed to relax and take it all in, to enjoy finally getting everything I've been working for.

I was sending my parents selfies of my new lifestyle partly to make up for the fact that I hadn't called them—and partly because, well, let's face it, this was everything I'd ever dreamed of.

After I'd sent them the one of me on the balcony, with the river lit up beneath me, I'd added Daniel's number on a whim and sent it to him as well. Yet another person I'd not managed to catch up with—and we had years' worth of catching up to do.

He'd texted me straight back, which meant that he must have been up at four in the morning as well.

'Welcome to the crazy train,' he said. 'Just remember you can stop it if you want to get off.'

Two kisses at the end. Nice.

Chapter 21

'The selfies are all well and good, Jessy,' said Mum, 'but we already know what you look like.'

She might have been hundreds of miles away in Liverpool, but I could picture her perfectly: she'd be sitting at the kitchen table, wearing her work uniform, and already be getting the family dinner ready to cook later. She would also, I knew, be frowning—because I could hear the irritation in her words.

'I'm sorry, Mum,' I said, trying to sound more sincere than I felt. 'But I've just been so busy.'.

There was a pause, and the sound of saucepans clattering—something going onto the stove, while she held the phone in the crook of her neck. It was such a familiar sound, such a familiar image, but it felt like one that belonged to a different life. A different world.

It was ten a.m. I was sitting in the rehearsal studio getting ready to rehearse some steps with Vogue and the other dancers for a scene we were adding to the video for 'Midnight'. The main video was not only already made, but had been playing on the music channels and streamed on Vogue's own YouTube account for weeks. Just like the song, the original recording had nothing to do with me. But the vocals had now been added—at least to the download version—and we'd be filming a few moody scenes of me in some moonlit back alley to cut into the vid. It was yet another thing I needed to get very, very right.

I hadn't even made it back to the flat at all the night before—I'd been at an album launch for Beckett, one of the other Starmaker signings, and had ended up crashing at Jack's, partially tipsy and completely exhausted. I'd thought my old schedule was tiring—but at least it usually ended up with me in bed by eleven. These days I was lucky if I saw sunlight at all. I was living life at a breakneck speed, and sometimes I barely had the energy to put one foot in front of the other.

None of which my mother knew, of course. Because I hadn't told her. I'd hoped the pictures and texts would keep them happy, reassure them—keep them off my back, if I'm entirely honest, which made me cringe a bit inside, but was true. I had a lot going on—and I just didn't need the extra pressure. I was trying to be a perfect pop star—and apparently failing spectacularly at being the perfect daughter while I did it.

'Yes, well,' she replied, banging a pan lid on with way too much force. 'We're all busy. I'm working and looking after your nan and your dad and your brother. Your dad's doing all hours. Becky's got enough on her plate. But how long does it take for a quick phone call?'

Oh God, I thought. Too bloody long, that's what. I could see Vogue warming up in the corner, and the dance teacher looking expectantly at the big clock that was hanging on the white wall over the door. I could see myself, reflected in the full length mirror, my face all scrunched up, biting my lips.

'Okay. I said I'm sorry. I'll try harder, all right? But I've got to go now. People are waiting for me—important people.'

Again, there was a pause, which gave me the chance to reflect on what I'd just said—no matter how unintentionally—and take a deep breath while I waited for what would come next.

'So we're *not* important?' she asked. 'We don't matter, then, now you've got your new showbiz friends?'

'Of course you are, Mum! All of you! But… I'm doing my best. You don't understand…'

'No!' she snapped back, in her very best you-are-in-such-deep-shit-my-girl voice. 'I don't understand, because you don't tell me anything. All I know is what I read in the magazines, and what Luke finds online, and whatever daft photo you choose to send us to try and replace actually bothering to call. But what I do know is that you are still my daughter, Jessica, whether you like it or not—you might have changed the way you spell your name, but you can't dump us as easily. I'm sorry if we're pains in the backside, but we love you, and we won't be shutting up any time soon. Are you even listening?'

No. I wasn't really. I was looking at Vogue, and Dale, the choreographer, and wondering when I'd next be able to sleep, and wondering where Tilly had got to with the chilled water I'd asked for, and wondering when my mother would just *shut up*…

'Yeah. Message received and understood, Mum. Now, I've really got to go.'

I didn't give her the chance to reply—I just hung up. I'd

never hung up on my mother in my life, and I didn't quite believe I was doing it then. But, somehow, she was much harder to handle now my own life was so hectic. The sensible part of me knew that it was the flip side of how much she cared—that she and my dad had been there for me through all the tough times, supporting me and believing in me and funding me in my crazy escapades. They'd even paid the deposit on Yusuf's flat, for goodness' sake. If it wasn't for them, I'd have had to have given up on this dream yonks ago.

But now it was all happening, I couldn't quite figure out what to do with all that concern—somehow it felt less like love, and more like an added burden. I'd already repaid them the money for the flat deposit, and was saving more to send home to them. I hadn't dropped off the face of the earth—I'd stayed in touch the best way I knew how. But asking me for more felt like too much—it seemed impossible to be both Jessika and Jessy at the same time, and I was sick of tearing myself into pieces trying to clone myself. Something had to give—and just then it felt like it might be my sanity.

By the time Tilly finally arrived, bearing bottles of water, I was too annoyed and stressed to even say thank you. I just grabbed them from her, gave her a nod, and drank half a litre down as I walked over to Vogue and Dale.

'I'm so sorry,' I said, screwing the lid back on the water and lobbing it onto the floor in the corner. 'I didn't mean to keep you waiting…'

'Trouble in paradise, babe?' asked Vogue, taking in my bitten lips and pale skin. I looked like boiled shite—which was appropriate, as that was exactly how I felt.

'Oh, no, you know—it was my mum. I always seem to be in trouble these days.'

She nodded, and gave me a sympathetic smile.

'Yeah. I know. It's hard fitting it all in—everyone wants a piece of you. There aren't enough hours in the day. I've been there. Just remember who you are, and where you came from—believe me, I learned the hard way how much you have to give up to make it in this business, and I'm still not convinced it was a good deal.'

I stared at her—looking majestic even without make-up, and dressed in leggings and a baggy sweatshirt—and wondered how she could possibly even say that. She'd sold millions of records all over the world; toured to sell-out crowds in arenas in every corner of the globe, and presumably made enough money to make her own future and her family's future completely secure and comfortable. She was a megastar—and one who never seemed down about it, either. I didn't know her that well, but I knew enough to admire her and respect her, and basically want to be her. She seemed to have it all sorted—but hey, maybe I was wrong. It had happened before.

Dale broke our bonding moment by clapping his hands and switching on the music. There was no more time for chatting, or thinking, or doing anything at all but sweat and work. And bearing in mind the conversation I'd just had with one of my nearest and dearest, that was more than welcome.

Chapter 22

Two weeks later, I was seeing my nearest and dearest in the flesh again for the first time in months. They'd all come down on the train—and this time it was me shelling out for the First Class tickets—and arrived at Starmaker in a tumble of noise, Scouse accents, and confusion. Not to mention the ever-present camcorder that Dad had been using since we were kids. It wasn't even digital, and he hefted it around like he was a bald Scouse Steven Spielberg.

Luke was excited beyond himself; Becky looked large and uncomfortable, and Mum and Dad, well... they just looked out of their depth. It's hard to explain how much of a shock to the system that was. My parents had always seemed so big, so solid—completely larger than life, always full of energy, and always totally at home in their own skins. If they'd ever suffered from nerves or self-doubt, I'd certainly never seen it—and it was one of the things that made our home life so secure when we were growing up. They always greeted the world with complete conviction that they held a place in it, and it rubbed off.

But I realised, as I watched them shaking hands with strangers in a world they didn't understand, that I'd only ever seen them in environments that were natural to them—at home in Liverpool, or on family holidays where we were always surrounded by other people just like us: working class folk blowing off a bit of steam and downing a few beers around the pool in the Costa Whatever.

As I saw my dad tugging at the too-tight collar of his new shirt, bright lights reflecting off the sweat of his bald head, and my mum tucking her freshly dyed hair behind her ears nervously, I knew that they were both off balance, both having a wobble. They were here, in a glitzy office in London, surrounded by Bright Young Things with what, to them, were posh accents—and they looked about as at ease as a pair of extra-terrestrials being invited into a government laboratory.

Unfortunately, Dad tried to cover up his nerves by being as loud and outrageous as possible. He made a few jokes that nobody got, and asked one of the male backing dancers where he got his tights, and constantly had the video camera on the go—he even took it into the toilets with him, as though he'd never seen a loo before in his life.

I was giving them the guided tour, much as I had with Becky when she came down—but this time, everything was different. Everywhere I went in the building, people reacted— they said hi, looked eager to talk to me, asked if there was anything they could do for me. This time round, I was doing the Starmaker tour as one of their big names—not one of their tiny interns. And that sprinkling of magic stardust was reflected in the way they greeted my parents, treating them like royalty—or at least the family of royalty. If anything, that seemed to freak Mum and Dad out even more.

Mum was quieter than usual, having the opposite reaction to Dad, and she seemed to shrivel into herself. The only time she really came to life was in the break room—where she insisted on doing all the dishes that had been left by the sink, and gave all the surfaces a good going over with some Jif.

I'd hoped they'd be proud of me—and I'm sure they were—but they also looked stiff and tense and uncertain, and no amount of chatter on my part seemed able to put them at their ease. I know it was a different world to theirs—and maybe I'd felt exactly the same when I was first plunged in at the deep end—but by the end of the walkabout I was starting to feel stiff and tense myself.

Which—a day before our single launch party—was exactly what I didn't need.

Part of the bad atmos was totally my fault. I can only confess to this, hold my hands up, and admit I was wrong—but I had missed Nan's birthday meal. I had no real excuse; Becky had reminded me the week before and, even as I read her message, I knew I wouldn't be able to go. It was the same day we were filming the new sections of the *Midnight* video, and there was just no way I could miss that.

I could, I knew, have asked for it to be rescheduled. I could have explained the situation to Jack, and hoped he would understand. I could even have talked to Vogue about it, after her comments relating to family.

But in reality, I did none of those things. It was like a train crash heading in my direction—and I was so frozen in its headlights, I couldn't get myself off the tracks. I just didn't feel confident enough to rock the boat—I had to make a choice, and I made the one I felt was right at the time. I'd had many birthday meals with my nan, and would be able to make it up to her—but this was my first and best shot at making it in the music industry.

So in the end I'd asked my mum if they could reschedule the meal instead—which I genuinely didn't think was that big a deal. I was working hard, I was trying to make them proud, and I was earning what felt like a ton of money, by my standards. Literally every hour of my day felt boxed in and accounted for, with Tilly and Patty managing my schedule like sergeant majors, and Jack managing my time off in ways I couldn't complain about.

From the moment I woke up—usually after three hours of patchy sleep following the latest party I was shown at, like a prize dog at Crufts—until the moment I got back into bed, I was busy: the rehearsals, the recording, the interviews, the parties.

I knew things were slipping—despite my mum's sharp words, I hadn't been calling them. I hadn't been to see Yusuf, or even written him a note. I hadn't found the intern who'd boxed all my stuff up and thanked them, like I'd vowed I would do. I hadn't even found time to speak to Daniel again—which I desperately wanted to do.

Everything was so hectic, so frenzied—and every time I remembered something else I was supposed to do, I put it off as to be handled 'After the Launch'. In fact, my whole life started to be put off until 'After the Launch'—in the end, I

was so busy, I even started reducing it to ATL. I didn't even
have time to say three whole words.

Build bridges with worried family? ATL. Catch up with
much-missed childhood friend? ATL. Show basic human
decency to the little people—and yes, I was starting to think
in terms like that—who'd helped me on the way up? ATL.
Get some sleep and drink something other than Red Bull?
ATL.

Another one I had now added to the ATL list was contacting
Ruby—who had left me about a gazillion messages since all
this began. I know we hadn't exactly been living together
harmoniously for those last few weeks, due to the arrival of
the lovely Keith, but I'd known her since I was four—I'd
built a business with her, moved in with her, shared boxes
of tampons with her, and spent countless nights both in and
out with her. And yet, I still hadn't found the time to get in
touch—Ruby was very much ATL.

And, as we emerged from the Starmaker offices and out
onto the bustling London streets, looking at their faces in the
late autumn sunshine, I was really starting to wish that seeing
my family again had also been put off until ATL.

Except that was the whole reason my family was there. To
come to the launch, to see me perform, to find a place in my
new life. To understand what my days looked like. To show
their support. I knew all of that—but I still didn't, in my heart
of hearts, want them there. I owed them a lot—but I didn't
have time to start repaying that debt just then. In fact, I didn't
even have time to spend with them—and instead was handing
them off to Tilly, who was going to take them on the London

Eye and show them the sights. It should have been me doing that—I wasn't so far up my own backside that I didn't realise. I realised, but I didn't care enough to make things change. There were dozens of last minute things to check, to practise, to get my head around. So I said my goodbyes, gave them all hugs, and slipped Tilly a bundle of cash so she could look after them for the day.

As I watched them all trundle off towards the Tube station, Luke waving over his shoulder, my mum and dad grasping each other's hands, the only thing I really felt was relief.

I walked back into the building and immediately put them out of my mind because I had things to do. It shouldn't have been that easy—but I'm ashamed to say it was.

I didn't see them again until the evening, when Jack had organised a dinner for us all at a restaurant near to their hotel. They hadn't wanted to stay at a hotel; despite the fact that my flat only had one bedroom, they offered to bring sleeping bags and the inflatable mattresses we used when we went camping, and 'make do'. But, I'd reasoned with them, what was the point of me working so hard to make money, to build a better life for us all, if we just ended up 'making do'? I wanted them to stay in a nice hotel, with room service and champagne in the mini-bar and fresh flowers in the windows—I wanted them to have the best, and I was now in a position to give them the best. At least for a couple of nights. I just wasn't in a position to give them my time—which is what they seemed to want most of all.

'Your nan sent you this,' said Mum after we were all shown to our seats. Jack was talking to my dad—playing the role of

Starmaker main man, rather than my boyfriend—and Luke
was busy snapping photos of the place on his phone, which
I fully expected to show up on his Facebook timeline within
minutes. Becky was staring at the menu, practically salivat-
ing, and Neale had also come along. I wanted them to meet
Neale—he was playing a big part in my life, and I knew they'd
like him. Plus, the uncomfortable truth was I wanted him there
as an extra buffer zone between me and the demands of my
own family.

'What is it?' I asked, taking the envelope from her hands.

'Try opening it and looking, Jessy—or do you need Tilly
to do that for you?'

I bit down the sharp retort I could feel brewing, and ripped
open the envelope. Inside was a note from my eighty-five-
year-old grandmother: 'Treat yourself to something special,
girl—lots of love your Nan xxx.' Wrapped up in the paper
was a twenty-pound Matalan gift card.

It was silly, but I immediately felt tears start to sting the
back of my eyes, and clenched them down before they could
mess up my make-up. This was a popular restaurant, and there
was always the chance I could get photographed—there was
no room for crying in public any more. Or for being anything
less than perfect in public any more.

The flip side of that pressure was that the days when I
needed a Matalan gift card were hopefully well and truly
behind me—but God, it was so sweet of Nan to think of
me, especially after me knocking her birthday party back. I
promised myself that I would go up to Liverpool and pay her
a visit—ATL, of course.

'Looks like she's forgiven me at least, Mum,' I said, tucking the gift card and the note away in the very swish handbag I'd been sent for free.

'Well, she's eighty-five and lived through the war, love— I'm sure worse things have happened to her. But you just remember that she won't live forever, and you'll regret it if don't come home and see her soon.'

'I know,' I said, pouring us both a glass of wine; I suddenly felt like I was going to need it, and wished I'd sat between Neale and Luke instead. That was definitely the easiest part of the table. 'And I will—it's all crazy at the moment, but good crazy.'

'Good crazy?' piped in Becky, staring at my wine with the undisguised envy of the pregnant woman. 'Just crazy, I'd say. I mean, Tilly's a lovely girl—but we didn't come all the way down to London just to see her, you know? Or for Dad to talk to *him*...'

She cast a glare in the direction of Jack—for some reason, she'd always taken against him. I'd always denied there was anything going on between us but I think she secretly suspected, despite that. Plus, he was the man who ultimately took me away from home...something I think my family were starting to see as a bad thing now, no matter how successful I was.

I could feel the mood declining, and just didn't have the energy to get into a debate with them—from their point of view, they were right. From my point of view, I was right—I was a big girl living my own life, and doing the very best I could. I had a hugely stressful and important night ahead of me in twenty-four hours' time, and I needed to put off the show-down I could feel was brewing. ATL, I told myself—ATL.

Luckily, Neale chose that exact same moment to screech like a banshee at something undoubtedly hilarious Luke had just whispered in his ear—and the whole table turned to them instead. For once, I was grateful not to be the centre of atten-tion—and didn't even object to the fact that my darling brother was now entertaining everyone with a story about the time he waited under my bed on Halloween night, then climbed on top of me wearing a Scream mask while I was asleep. Even I had to laugh—and it had been pretty funny, right up until the point where I tried to stab him with my nail scissors.

After that, everything seemed to relax down a notch or two—Jack chipped in with some funny anecdotes about his early career; my dad told some stories that all started with 'One night, I had this fella in the back of my cab…', and my mum and Becky focused on eating, drinking, and, in Becky's case, repeatedly going to the loo.

I caught Jack's eye at the end of the meal, when we were all on coffee and our final dregs of alcohol. He gave me a smile so wide, so charming, so outright gorgeous, that I thought I might actually melt and slide off my chair, landing on the floor where Becky could kick me in the ribs.

He stood up, and held his glass high as everyone looked at him.

'And now, ladies, gents, Neale, a toast. To Jessika—one of the most talented women I've ever met, and one of the nicest people I've been privileged to work with. Jessika!'

As the others joined in, raising their glasses and chinking

them against each other so hard the waiters looked a bit worried, my dad stood up next to Jack.

He still looked a bit uncomfortable in yet another new shirt, and was wearing a tie—which I'd only ever seen at weddings, christenings, and funerals before. His bald head was shining with sweat under the lights, and he clinked the side of his spoon against the glass before he spoke.

'To our Jessy,' he said. 'My favourite ever middle child.'

Everyone started laughing, and I rolled my eyes—that's my dad for you. Some things never change.

Chapter 23

'You look gorgeous, darling,' Neale said, standing back to admire his handiwork. 'And if I was on that particular bus, I'd be tempted to ask you for a ride.'

I giggled, far more loudly than his lame joke merited. It was the nerves; I was so terrified, every cell in my body seemed to be vibrating with fear. I hadn't eaten all day, and was surviving on coffee and Red Bull, so pumped up on adrenalin and caffeine that my hands kept shaking and my mouth was constantly dry. I'd even considered joining Neale for a cigarette break earlier, even though I didn't smoke.

It probably wasn't the ideal condition to be in when I was about to perform—but there wasn't much I could do about it. My mental state dictated that I couldn't eat, couldn't relax, could barely breathe. Although part of that was down to the hideously tight leather corset affair that Neale had me strung into—it was either made for a dwarf, or for alien beings who had no need for oxygen.

I stood up and looked at myself in the dressing room mirror. I was barely recognisable as the girl who'd been serving smoked salmon twists just a few weeks ago—Neale, plus the work I'd been putting in myself, had transformed me into some kind of borderline kinky sex goddess. My hair was sleeked smooth with some industrial strength serum, a fake pony tail shimmering down over my back all the way to my now tiny waist. My eyes took smoky to a whole new level, and my legs were encased in black fishnet tights that somehow made them look a lot longer than they actually were. Although part of that illusion might also have been down to the thigh-length boots as well.

I pulled a face like a horse at my reflection, admiring the dazzling shine of my newly whitened teeth—sleeping with plastic mouth guards on had so been worth it for the end result.

'Neale, you are a genius!' I said, grinning at him. 'Thank you so much.'

My nerves about the single launch weren't completely soothed by looking this good—but it definitely helped. I knew Vogue was in the room next door, and that she'd be looking like a squillion dollars, so my confidence had needed the boost. I wasn't in competition with her—but neither did I want to feel like her dowdy little sister, or the plain one all the boys would want to avoid at a party.

'I know,' said Neale, doing a theatrical fake sigh as he packed away his brushes and picked up the hairspray for a final toxic waft. 'I'm like the Van Gogh of make-up—except with both my ears.'

I knew the score now, and shielded my eyes with my hands as he sprayed me, making sure I didn't breathe in before the fumes had dissipated.

Althea, the stage manager at the club, popped her head

through the door, radio in one hand and all miked up like an aircraft controller.

'Ready, Jessika?' she said.

Two words. Two very simple words—both of which struck horror into my heart. Was I ready? Well, I certainly looked ready. The outfit was perfect—if a little out of character from my usual clobber. The make-up was done. The hair was amazing. The teeth would probably be visible to passing satellites, they were so white.

I'd rehearsed this song with Vogue over and over again. I knew my notes, I knew my words, I knew my key changes. I knew my dance steps, I knew the other guys' dance steps, I knew the lighting, I knew my marks. We'd done it several times on this stage throughout the day, we'd ironed out any wrinkles, and we'd nailed it. Technically, I was ready.

Except… I was still petrified. The shaking hands and rumbling tummy were now accompanied by their good friend nausea, and my whole body felt like a big, wobbly jelly. Or at least it would have done, if most of it hadn't been strapped into a too-tight corset.

My parents were out there. Becky and Luke were out there. Pretty much everyone who worked at Starmaker was out there, including Jack, his bosses, and possibly the cleaners and the bloke who came round to water the corporate plants with a spray bottle once a week. There were reporters and bloggers and columnists, not just from the UK but from all around the world. The single was available for download the next day—and this was our way of shouting about it. And of shouting about me—Jessika.

Jessika, I knew, should be thrilled. She should be ready to take on the world, and think the world was lucky to have her. But Jessy—who was still alive somewhere, under the products and the costume and the slap—was feeling like an absolute pussy.

Neale took one look at my face, and grabbed hold of my shoulders, shaking me so hard I thought my head might rattle off and roll across the dressing room floor.

'Get it together, superstar!' he said, pinching my arm really hard. 'Don't you dare fall to pieces now—there's not time to fix that make-up!'

It snapped me back to reality just enough to do exactly as he said—get it together. I couldn't let him down—or my parents, or Jack, or Vogue. Or—let's not forget—myself.

''Kay,' I mumbled, rubbing my arm where he'd pinched it. 'Ta for that. I'm ready now.'

I strode out, glad I'd spent the whole of the day wearing the scary boots to get used to them, and met Vogue, as she emerged from her dressing room looking predictably stunning. The dancers were already on stage. The live backing band were ready to go. The audience was waiting.

Vogue gave me a huge grin, her teeth even whiter than mine, and held up her hand for a high-five.

'Come on, babes,' she said, as I slapped her palm. 'Let's nail this.'

Chapter 24

We did nail it—and it was euphoric. The launch was finally the culmination of everything I had wanted, and felt like fireworks and confetti cannons and a celestial choir singing all at once. Of course I was exhausted too.

I suppose it was understandable—I'd hardly eaten, and I'd been running on fumes for so long, I had very little left to give. Everything had been building up to this night, this performance, this show—and now it was actually ATL, I felt like one of those people you see staggering over the finishing line at the end of a marathon, who immediately gets wrapped in a foil blanket and eats a Mars bar. Except there was no foil blanket, and instead of curling up in a foetal ball on the floor with some chocolate, I was going to Go Forth and Dazzle—more interviews, more videos, more posing for photos, more talking to VIPs, and more wondering if my family were doing all right. Just…more everything.

The first gig I'd done—the one that changed my whole life in ways I'd not been at all prepared for—had been kind of accidental. If it wasn't for Vogue's cholera/tummy bug, I would never have been on stage—and while that had been terrifying in its own way, I'd also only had half an hour to be terrified for. This one—this one had been a slow build of not only terror, but of pressure and expectation and sheer bloody hard work. Doing a gig as a waitress-slash-intern, with no advance warning and wearing a curtain, was tough—but I'd had nothing to lose.

If I'd messed up, nobody would have been surprised. But this one…this was completely different. I was established. I was featured on a single by one of the world's biggest divas. My parents were there. I was being well paid. I had a K in my name. I had a lot to prove—and I don't think I realised quite how much pressure I'd been under until I stepped off stage at the end of it, drenched in sweat, high-fiving the dancers as they swarmed off behind me. I was too tired to even admire the view of glistening, perfect torsos going past me, which is a definite sign of chronic fatigue.

Vogue gave me a big grin and a thumbs up as she unhitched her ear piece and mic, and Neale immediately appeared and led me back to the dressing room. I had about ten minutes to change—this time, at least, I wasn't expected to walk around and schmooze people still wearing my stage costume.

I chugged water as he unhooked the corset thing, and was so relieved when it was finally undone that I spluttered a whole mouthful out of my lips in a ladylike display of pure elegance and class.

I pulled a face and wiped my hand across my damp chin, admiring the way Neale had jumped out of splatter reach so nimbly.

'Good reactions,' I said, laughing, as I peeled myself out of the now dripping black leather.

'I've been around you long enough now to have the reflexes of a fashion ninja, Jess,' he replied, helping me climb into my next outfit. This was much less revealing, but in a way quite a lot sexier—a black catsuit with a gold belt that looked like links of chain tightly cinching in my waist, and a plunging neckline that was held together with prayer and tape. I wasn't wearing a bra underneath, which made me very nervous— we've all seen wardrobe malfunctions, and I really wasn't keen on the idea of my boob popping out in front of my dad and brother.

Neale, though, worked his magic, and stood back to look me up and down. He stared at my chest so intently I was starting to wonder if he was straight after all and the campness had all been a ruse, especially as he then stepped forward and started to physically poke, prod, and push my breasts around, frowning as he did it.

'Don't worry, sweetheart,' he said, once he'd finally finished his inspection, 'you're safe as houses. You could go upside-down pole dancing and those titties would still stay in place. Talking of dancing, do you fancy coming out later? Once all this is done? I'm meeting some friends at a…well, a place where you'd be safe, even if your boobs did fall out!'

'You mean a gay club?' I asked, shielding my face as yet more hairspray clouded around my head.

'Yes, darling, but I didn't want to be so blunt. I might have shocked you!'

'I don't think so, Neale. There's a big gay scene in Liverpool, you know—I did backing vocals to an all-male burlesque night once. Bloody hilarious, watching a six-foot-two-inch drag queen try and squeeze himself into one of those giant plastic Martini glasses... I'll have to take you some time. But as far as tonight goes, I think I'm probably going to get this over with, see my family, and head back to the flat as soon as I can. To be honest, I want nothing more than a mug of hot chocolate with some squirty cream and a flake.'

'You decadent bitch,' replied Neale, wafting me with a quick spritz of perfume.

'I know,' I replied, 'I might even watch old episodes of *Sex and the City* while I'm in bed. Okay. Round two. Ding ding!'

I flicked my fake pony, did an equally fake boxing pose, and strode back out into the venue.

I was immediately met by Patty, who was glowering at me and pointing at her watch as though I'd kept her waiting for hours instead of minutes. I glowered back—some of the boxing pose must have worked—and strutted towards her with as much confidence as stiletto-heeled dominatrix boots can give a girl.

'All right, all right,' I said, before she had a chance to open her skinny lips, 'don't get your knickers in a twist, I'm here. Just tell me who I need to talk to, what you'd like me to say, and how long for.'

She narrowed her eyes at me, then quirked one corner of her mouth in a vaguely upward direction. For Patty, it qualified as a delighted grin—at least when pointed in my direction. She normally viewed me with as much enthusiasm as she would a fungal nail infection.

'At last,' she said, beckoning for me to follow her, 'you seem to be getting the hang of it. I'd say I was surprised, but I suppose you could even train a chimp to make a cappuccino if you tried hard enough.'

I rolled my eyes and trailed along behind her, desperate to accompany the eye rolls with a few choice finger gestures but knowing I could be snapped at any stage—and a shot of me flicking the Vs to the back of my PR manager might not be the ideal photo opp. Anybody who'd ever met Patty would understand, but the millions who hadn't would think I was just being rude.

The next hour and a half was spent in the company of various journalists, bloggers, YouTubers, music writers and other assorted people classified as important by Patty. It was similar to the first time we did the meet-and-greets after the Panache gig, except this time, I was a bit better at it. By better, I mean I didn't yell at anyone, swear, or otherwise embarrass myself or Starmaker. In fact, to be truthful, I'd even got to the stage where I kind of enjoyed it—I mean, I'd wanted to be a pop star the whole of my life. I'd always imagined being interviewed, and even practised my awards speeches in front of the bathroom mirror with a hairbrush in my hand.

I knew—because I'd done it—that if the media stuff went on all day, it became not only tiring, but mentally confusing. After more than a few hours answering inane questions about yourself, your brains begin to dribble out of your eyes, and you start to fantasise about climbing out of the toilet windows like a kidnap victim when you're on a break.

But this—an hour after a gig—was fine. It was more than

fine—it was part of my job, and another chance for me to cement the progress I'd made so far. I'd had a great and unexpected start—but it was just a start. There was a lot of hard work ahead of me before I reached anywhere near the levels Vogue was at, and doing the rounds like this was all part of the process.

So I smiled and laughed and chatted and tried very, very hard to come across as fresh and exciting to every single person who asked me exactly the same set of questions over and over again. I tried to give them all something a bit different, a bit personal, and I tried to be both myself and somehow more than myself—I was aiming to find the 'special' that came with my 'K'.

I briefly saw Jack and Vogue at separate times as we did our choreographed waltz around the room, received encouraging smiles from both, and finally—finally—got the nod from Patty. The nod, followed by her abruptly turning her back on me and stalking off in the opposite direction, that meant I was done for the evening.

She hadn't slapped me or called me a cretin, so I assumed I'd done all right, and immediately started to dream about the luxuries of food, drink, and sleep. I would have loved to have snuck out the back and jumped a taxi home, but even thinking about escaping—especially in a black cab—made me feel guilty. My parents had come all the way down from Liverpool for this, and now I needed to find that extra little bit of energy and enthusiasm to go and show them that I appreciated it. Because I did, even if I wasn't feeling very energetic or enthused right then.

I decided to nip off to the Ladies' first, just to give my brain a few minutes' breathing space. Then, I told myself, I'd take a deep breath, and head straight back out—all smiles, all laughter, all excitement. The living embodiment of Pharrell's 'Happy'.

I headed into one of the cubicles to do my business, and only realised exactly how tired I was when I almost fell asleep sitting on the loo. You know when you're drifting off to snoozeland, and suddenly your muscles give a little jerk, and you're suddenly awake again and a bit surprised by it all? Well, that happened—but instead of being tucked up in bed when it did, I was leaning against the toilet wall, and jerked upright so hard I clanged my head on it. It was seriously a very glamorous moment.

I screwed my eyes open and shut a few times as I emerged back into the fancy little bathroom, and wished I could splash my face with water—except Neale would kill me for ruining his masterwork.

The lighting in the ladies' was low, and the walls were painted red. There were huge mirrors on the wall all framed with heavy gold ornamental designs, and the dresser area was fringed with red tassels. It looked a bit like a whorehouse in a movie set in the Wild West.

I stared at my own reflection, pulling various faces, trying to figure out if I looked as bad as I felt, when one of the women who'd just interviewed me walked in. I'd be lying if I said I could remember exactly who she was, or her name, or who she worked for. But I did remember that she'd asked me if I'd be going home for Christmas, which had felt like a daft question until I realised it was only actually weeks away. My life had been moving so quickly—taking the plunge and coming to London, my internship, the gig, everything since, my romance with Jack—that I'd barely registered the months flying by.

'Hi!' she said brightly, meeting my eyes in the mirror. She had one of those very straight, very thick, black Cleopatra bobs that may or may not have been a wig, and was wearing vivid red lipstick. She could have stepped straight out of a manga cartoon.

I tried to switch right back into Media Barbie mode, but my brain was lagging a little behind my face and in the end I gave her a huge grin but said nothing. I just washed my hands, still grinning, then fumbled for a few minutes trying to complete the next Mission Impossible—turning the tap off.

'Are you all right, Jessika?' she asked, frowning at me.

'What?' I stuttered, giving myself an imaginary slap across the face. 'Yes! Yes, I'm fine—just a bit…'

'Knackered?' she asked, in such a sympathetic tone of voice that I almost buried my head in her chest and started sobbing.

I nodded, not trusting myself to speak. The grin was still on my face, though, apparently stuck there—the wind must have changed. I could feel the muscles in my cheek and jaw starting to aching, but didn't seem capable of shutting it down. Patty had trained this particular chimp a bit too well.

She nodded, and started to root in her handbag, black bob bouncing around her face as she did it.

'I can only imagine—those routines must be exhausting, and I bet you've not had a minute to yourself for days. Look, would a bit of this help?'

She held out her hand, and I saw a small, square wrap of white paper. I knew what was inside it. I hadn't led a sheltered life, and I've seen my fair share of people using drugs—in the street, in clubs, in toilets exactly like these. And I'd never, ever given in to the temptation—I was quite happy getting high on traditional drugs like alcohol and tiramisu, thank you very much.

But just then, I have to admit, for fleeting moment, I was. Tempted, that is. Very tempted. I was so tired—physically and mentally strung out. I still had to face my parents, the rest of the night, Jack, and entirely possibly some of the Starmaker VIPs who'd come to the launch. My hands even trembled a little bit as I looked on, so wanting to reach out and take the little bit of pharmaceutical assistance that was on offer.

'It's all right,' said the woman—Holly, I belatedly remembered was her name; she was a writer for one of the big teen mags—'I'm not looking to stitch you up. It's not going to turn into one of those "my drug-fuelled-night-with-pop-starlet" type stories, honest. You just look like you need a bit of a boost.'

Even as she said it, I realised how naive—or possibly how fatigued—I really was. I mean, I was in the public lavatories of a nightclub where I'd just performed, giving some serious (if very temporary) consideration to accepting cocaine from a random journalist I'd only just met. I didn't need Patty around to tell me that that was a situation potentially fraught with danger—and yet, I'd forgotten. For a few moments, I'd forgotten that I NEVER do drugs; I'd forgotten that I was a celeb and she was a reporter, and I'd forgotten that I had to go back out there and see my bloody parents! I really was very close to falling over the edge into major league stupidity.

'Aaah, that's really kind of you,' I said, adjusting my grin from worryingly bright to something that was hopefully a bit more genuine. 'But not for me, thanks. I think I'll go and grab a Mojito, and maybe…erm…a bag of crisps!'

Holly smiled back, and started to unfold the paper. Looked like she was going to indulge anyway, and who was I to judge?

'All right,' she replied, as I prepared to leave. 'Be careful with those crisps though—they can be more addictive than this stuff!'

'You're probably right!' I shouted over my shoulder, as I wandered back into the main room, relieved to have escaped without doing any more damage to myself other than making a little dent in my own self-respect.

The noise levels were high—a backdrop of thumping music, and the huge, thrumming hum of hundreds of people trying to make themselves heard above it—and the lights were low. My hands were still trembling, and I felt like I might keel over if I didn't get something decent to eat or drink very soon. Then everyone would take photos of me lying on the floor—probably with my boobs hanging out, despite what Neale promised—and assume I'd taken the drugs anyway. Huh. Life wasn't fair sometimes.

I blinked against the strobe lighting and tried to pick out my family. I'd loosely arranged to meet them near a fire escape after the show—my mum was a bit freaked out by the number of people crammed into the club, and had insisted on standing by the emergency door 'just in case', which was such a *Mum* thing to say.

After a few seconds, I spotted them, and started to make my way across the room in their direction, politely excuse me-ing all the way. A few people tried to stop me to chat, but I was deffo getting better at the smooth and diplomatic brush off, I discovered.

By the time I reached them, I wanted nothing more than to dash out of the fire escape myself—and maybe take them all back to Yusuf's for a delicious kebab together. We still had another couple of weeks paid up on the rent, and he'd love it if I just turned up with the whole family in tow. I couldn't quite believe I was daydreaming about going back to my grotty flat when I had my brand new gorgeous one these days. Maybe it was just human nature to always want what you didn't have.

My dad, massively tall and bald as an egg, was easy to find—and at least he'd got rid of the new shirts and ties for this one. He was wearing his favourite Eagles T-shirt, which he probably thought of as cutting-edge rock, and Mum was in her one and only little black dress. It was from Matalan, and she'd got a discount because my aunt worked there, but she still looked great. Becky had somehow found a stool, which she was presumably sitting on—though it was hard to tell, as her arse was now so big, her whole body was draped around her chair, and it looked a bit like she was floating. There was a plate on her lap and the remains of some tasty looking snacks that made me drool.

Luke was leaning back against the wall, gazing out at the crowds in utter amazement. I tried to see it through the eyes of a horny teenaged boy: a whole room crammed full of the famous, the semi-famous, and the hundred per cent glamorous. There was more toned female flesh on show here than at a Victoria's Secret fashion show, and the poor lad looked completely dazzled by it. He'd probably taken about a million selfies already, and would be the envy of all his mates. Hah, I thought as I walked in their direction, at least I was good for something.

As I approached them, I felt a hand on my shoulder, and turned round with my fake 'thanks-but-no-thanks' smile at the ready. Instead, I realised I didn't need it—and there was nothing fake about the smile that immediately cracked open my whole face when I saw who it was.

'Daniel!' I said, throwing myself into his arms, snuggling into his chest, and wondering if he'd mind if I fell asleep there. I felt his hands on my back, slightly tentative, as though he wasn't quite sure where to put them, and grinned into his T-shirt. He might be tall, fair, and handsome these days, but he still got nervous around girls, bless him.

I pulled away, and stood on tiptoes to give him a kiss on the cheek. I left a big red lippie mark, which I decided kind of suited him.

'What are you doing here?' I asked. 'Not that I'm not pleased to see you!'

'Well, I was invited, duh! You told me about it, and Jack asked me as well.'

'I know I told you, but you didn't say you were coming, so I assumed you were busy producing or recording or milking your prize dairy cows or whatever it is you people do in the countryside.'

'I do have a cow, actually,' he said, grinning at me, hair flopping over his forehead. 'She's called Ruby. Something about her enormous backside just reminded me of her…'

'Oh, that's mean,' I replied, biting back a giggle. I really, really needed to contact Ruby—I should have invited her to the launch, I should. We'd been through so much together, and she must feel like I'd brushed her off. It wasn't intentional—everything had just piled up on me, and even having my parents down had been a strain. Talking of which…

'Come and see my lot—they'll be made up that you're here. They'll probably be happier to see you than me, the way things have been going.'

Daniel glanced over, and smiled as he saw the Malone gang.

'Look at your dad…can't believe he's still wearing that Eagles top after all these years. Bit tighter round the beer belly though. They don't look very relaxed, apart from Luke—have you been having problems?'

'Oh, I don't know…not really. It's all just, well, a bit crazy. My life has changed so much even I don't recognise it myself, and theirs hasn't changed at all—other than being here, at an event like this, surrounded by people they just don't feel comfy with. I've not had much time to spend with them—you *know* how busy this world is—and… I just want them to be proud of me.'

Even I noticed how pathetic those last few words sounded, and I squeezed my eyelids shut tight as I felt tears stinging their way out. I'd been working so hard, for them as much as for me, and now I was finally on the verge of success, I felt more distant from them than ever. I'd always been so very close to my family, they'd always been my anchors, and now I didn't feel like we were even on the same planet. It made me feel a bit disorientated, cut loose, as if I was floating around in outer space.

Daniel reached out and stroked my hair—which was a mistake, as it was frozen solid with spray. He laughed when he realised, and wiped his fingers on his jeans.

'I do know, Jessy. I've been working in this business for a while now, and that's one of the reasons I keep such a low profile, and prefer to spend time with the dairy cows on the farm than here in London. The pace of life was too fast; the relationships were too fake—it's hard to keep your feet steady when the world's rushing around you like a flash-forward scene in a movie. It's hard for people who haven't lived it to understand—but I do know how much they love you. And I do know how proud they will be—you were brilliant tonight, absolutely amazing. So forgive them if they don't get your new life, or if they seem a bit off, or if they feel clingy—and never doubt that they're proud of you. That, Jess, would just be deliberately daft.'

'Yeah. That makes sense. Is this a new thing, Daniel, or have you always been the voice of reason?'

'Always,' he said, putting his arm over my shoulders and leading me towards my family. 'You were just too deliberately daft to listen before now.'

My dad started waving as soon as he noticed us, and Becky looked as though she was considering standing up, but then thought better of it. Luke, who didn't remember Daniel as well as the rest of us, gave him a polite nod before turning his attention back to a barely-dressed reality-TV-show star who was gyrating away on the dancefloor. Mum, I noticed, had immediately clocked on to the fact that Daniel had his arm around me, and gave me a sly smile.

'Bloody hell, lad,' said Dad, shaking Daniel's hand so hard I thought he might pull his arm off. 'Where's all that weight gone? You used to be a right porker, and now you look like a bloody male model!'

I cringed inside, even though Dad was only saying what I'd been thinking since I saw Daniel again. My mum poked him in the ribs, and Becky was staring at my old pal with undisguised amazement. I'd told her what he looked like now, but seeing really was believing.

'I discovered exercise, Mr Malone,' replied Daniel, apparently not at all bothered by the conversation—he'd probably expected nothing less from a bunch of gobshite Scousers he knew and loved. 'And I moved out of my parents' house, so I wasn't always getting a fry up for breakfast. That definitely helped.'

'Well, you look wonderful,' answered my mum, leaning in for a kiss and leaving another lipstick mark on the other side of his poor face. 'What do you think of our Jessy, then, Daniel? Wasn't she amazing?'

'I always thought she was amazing, Mrs M, you know that—but tonight was perfect. I'm sure she's going to be a huge star, and do you all proud.'

I felt a warm and fuzzy sensation begin to build up inside me, and realised again how lucky I was and that maybe it was going to be all right after all. Of course my parents loved me. Of course they were proud of me. We were just hitting a few bumps in the road because everything was moving so fast—and we *would* get through it. It would all settle down, once we all adapted. Nothing was so broken we couldn't fix it.

I don't think I'd realised how stressed out about them I'd been until then. For some bizarre reason, I'd been subconsciously worried that choosing my career would mean leaving them behind—but just then, hearing my mum's words and seeing my dad's proud grin, all those worries floated away. My family were proud of me, my oldest friend in the world was by my side, and I'd just been featured on a single that was likely to be a huge international hit. I shouldn't be worrying—I should be feeling frigging fantastic.

Relieved as I was, my body was still exhausted and felt like quitting on me. Seeing Daniel had given me a momentary boost, but I still couldn't stop my hands from trembling, and I felt unsteady on my stupidly high heels. I felt myself sway and wobble, and leaned in to Daniel for support. Part of my brain registered how very nice and firm his body felt next to mine, and part of it started to crackle and fuzz like an old radio.

I was so tired my eyes were blurring. I needed to sit down, get some food, and rest. If I didn't, I had the sneaking suspicion that I was going to throw a whitey, without even having had the drugs.

'Are you all right, hon?' my dad asked immediately, stepping forward to hold my shoulders and stare at my face. Whatever he saw there didn't seem to please him a great deal, and I watched his expression change from pride and pleasure to something like horror.

'You've not taken anything, have you, love?' he asked, and I felt my mum's gaze sharpen in response.

'No!' I said, a bit too loudly. 'Of course I haven't!'

'Just tell me if you have,' Dad said, not at all bothered by the fact that I was annoyed with him, 'because I can see that most of the tossers in this place have. You don't drive a cab round Liverpool on a Saturday night for as many years as me without knowing the signs.'

I shook him off, stood up straight, and prayed I stayed upright. The anger helped. Anger not just with him for doubting me, but with myself—because only a few minutes ago I had been tempted. I had almost given in. But, well, like a good girl, in the end, I'd Just Said No. That had been hard, and now my reward was getting quizzed by my own Doubting Thomas of a father. The first words out of his mouth hadn't been about how proud he was, but to ask me if I was drugged up.

'I. Am. Not. On. Drugs. But I might as well be, for all the good saying no seems to do! I'm just knackered Dad—knackered and now a bit disappointed. I need to…go. I need some food. I need some air. I need a break…'

I don't think I've ever managed a good storming off before—I'm the sort of person who trips over their own feet as they try, or walks into a lamp post—but I must admit I managed it that time. I turned my back on my own family and stormed back into the mass of bodies and the hive of noise and the swell of strangers. I didn't really know where I was going, and I didn't really care—something inside me had snapped.

Maybe it was seeing Daniel, and believing his little pep talk. Maybe it was the contrast between my short-lived hope that everything was going to be all right and realising just how tired and stressed I was. I couldn't do it any more—stand there with them, pretending everything was great, when it really wasn't great at all.

'Jess!' said Daniel, grabbing hold of my shoulder as I strode away. I whirled around to face him, and realised that I'd lost the battle against the tears. The anger had finally pushed them over the edge, and I swiped at my own face, irritated with my own weakness.

'*What?*' I snapped, unfairly. None of this was his fault— Daniel had never been anything but a force for good in my life—and I immediately regretted my waspish tone.

'Sorry!' I said, straight away, reaching out and patting his arm in apology. 'Nothing to do with you—I'm just sick of it. I'm working my backside off, and I'm finally on the verge of making all my dreams come true. But I'm so tired I just snapped. It wasn't about what my dad said about the drugs. It's just they're always nagging me about visiting and phoning, and nothing I do seems to be enough. I've worked for this—I deserve it, Daniel! I'm doing it as much for them as me, and they're treating me like a naughty little girl who needs to fall into line!'

'I know. It's hard. But Jess—to them, you are still a little girl. And they're worried about you. If they weren't, they wouldn't say those things. They're more concerned with you as a person than you as a cash cow and—believe me—you'll see some vile things in this business, and eventually, you'll realise how lucky you are that your family don't care how much money you make.'

I let out a huge breath, and stayed silent for a moment, letting his words sink in and trying to calm myself down.

'Yeah. Okay. I know you're probably right—you usually are. And maybe we can get through all of this. But right now? I just can't do it any more. I need to get away from here. Just... tell them I'm leaving, will you? Tell them I'm all right, but I'm leaving, and I'll speak to them tomorrow.'

He nodded, and I stretched up to kiss him goodbye. On the lips this time, as we'd run out of places to leave make-up marks. An unexpected tingle surged through me as I did it, and the contact lasted longer than I'd planned. I felt his hands on the small of my back, pulling me closer, and for a second I wondered what the hell was about to happen, but just as quickly he broke away, running his fingers through his hair and looking slightly flustered.

We stared at each other for a few more seconds, the music and the chatter and the haze of the party seeming to retreat into somebody else's reality as we did. Had I imagined it, or had we just had a 'moment'?

Before I could wonder any further, he mumbled, 'Take care of yourself, Jess,' turned around, and left—heading right back towards my parents.

I stood there for a bit, arms dangling by my sides, probably looking as vacant as your average shop window mannequin, before shrugging and walking away. Men. They were a complete mystery to me, and I was never very good at puzzles.

I scanned the crowd and spotted Jack, deep in conversation with Vogue next to the bar. I'd had this crazy idea that I'd find him, persuade him to take me away from all this, and go back to his flat for a takeaway and sex. That would have been the perfect distraction from my familial woes, and the perfect antidote to what had just almost happened with Daniel—that thing that might have almost happened with Daniel, but I might also have just completely imagined. I wasn't exactly stable just then.

The problem was, I couldn't think of a way to make my intentions known to Jack without revealing our super-secret relationship to Vogue. They showed no signs of slowing up or walking away from each other, and I couldn't hang around there all night.

My phone was with the rest of my stuff back in the dressing room, so I headed in that direction. I decided I could get my bag, indulge in a bit of textual intercourse with Jack, and if I was lucky scrounge up a few snacks from the backstage staff while I was at it. Win win.

I made my way through the crowd, stopping to chat, smile, and pose for photos—eyes and teeth darling, eyes and teeth—all the way. Eventually, I burst through the door into the dressing room, and lay down on the floor.

The venue itself was very posh, very glam, and very perfect for a single launch. The floor of the dressing room, though, I have to say, was not very posh or very glam or very perfect for anything at all—unless your thing was snorting dirty carpet fibres through one nostril.

Still, it was flat, and it allowed the whole of my body to stretch out, without having to fight gravity and my own physical exhaustion in a losing battle to stay standing. I reached up with one boot and managed to nudge my bag off the chair, happy to see it crash land right by my hand. I'd have been gutted if I'd had to move and crawl across the minging carpet to get at it.

I scooped out my phone, and a two-bar KitKat I'd stashed in there earlier for emergencies. I decided this qualified as an emergency, and slit open the foil wrapper, biting a big chunk off both fingers at once. The chocolate hit my tastebuds so hard I thought my mouth was going to explode, and I rolled around on the floor for a moment, moaning in ecstasy as I chewed. Good, that was good.

Once I'd climaxed and all the KitKat was gone, I messaged Jack: 'Back to yours for a curry and a shag?' it said. I'll admit it wasn't subtle, but as chat up lines went, it had worked for me before. I stayed there on the ground, holding my phone up above my head as though I was taking the world's grungiest selfie—lying on a grotty rug covered in KitKat smears.

I heard the door slam open again, and Neale walked through it, stopping dead in his tracks when he saw me, and looking on in horror.

'Don't do it!' he shouted. 'Don't take a picture—one of your boobs has made a break for freedom!'

I glanced down and, sure enough, all that chocolate-based orgasming and rolling round on the floor had dismantled one half of Neale's tit-tape masterpiece. I held the phone in one hand, and shoved the booby back in with the other. At least it hadn't happened while I'd been talking with Daniel—that whole scene had been confusing enough as it was without accidentally flashing him.

'I wasn't going to take a picture,' I said, dragging myself

into a seating position. I was aiming for standing, but stalled halfway. 'I'm waiting for a text…but it doesn't look like it's coming. Are you still going out tonight?'

'Yes! Me and some of the dancers and a few of my friends from beauty school. Do you want to come? Have you found your second wind? Do you want me to wrangle your bosoms again?'

I thought through all his questions, and wondered what I did want to do. Not that long ago, I'd wanted to go home, alone, and drink hot chocolate. Then I'd almost snorted drugs with a journalist in a nightclub toilet. Then I'd fallen out with my parents, and come very close to shagging my oldest childhood friend. Jack wasn't replying to my message, and a gang of attractive gay male dancers wanted to go clubbing with me. My life had become a very strange place.

'Yes to all of it,' I said, hauling myself up. 'But only if you promise me one thing.'

'What's that, my treasure?' Neale said, immediately going to work with the magic tape.

'We get to call at a McDonald's on the way. There are some problems that only a Big Mac meal will cure.'

Chapter 25

The next morning, I felt so ill I suspected the only thing that would cure me would be decapitation. I'd drunk so much I couldn't even remember getting home, but as I was in my own bed, I clearly had done. Neale and the boys could really put it away and, for some reason, once we'd arrived at the club, I'd decided that tequila slammers were my friend.

I was wrong, I realised, rolling around under the duvet, holding my head in my hands and wondering if I could physically tear it off. Tequila was nobody's friend. Tequila had persuaded me it would be a great idea to go stage-diving into the waiting arms of a few hundred of my closest strangers; tequila had convinced me that recreating the bar-dancing scenes from *Coyote Ugly* was an even better idea; and tequila had somehow fooled me into thinking that snogging the one non-gay man I could find working behind that bar was equally desirable.

After that, it was all a blank. Like all those bitchy non-friends we've all had, tequila had abandoned me and left me to get home on my own, not caring if I fell down a manhole or got abducted by aliens on the way. Tequila was rubbish at sticking to the Girls Look After Each Other When They're Drunk Code.

At least, though, I was on my own, I thought, kicking my toes around the bed a bit just to make sure there wasn't someone really small in there with me. I'd been so bladdered, anything could have happened—which was stupid for any woman at the best of times, but especially stupid for someone in my position.

Neale had assured me that the club was 'safe'—that celebs went there all the time, even some of the closeted ones, and nobody ever posted pics of them on Instagram or tweeted about seeing them. 'You're free to make as much of a twat of yourself as you like, my little petal,' he'd said, kissing me on the cheek before he dragged me off into a thronging mass of disco-buff bodies.

By that time I'd snaffled my Big Mac, put the blow-up with my dad to the back of my mind, and decided I was more than capable of forgetting about both Daniel and Jack for at least one evening. What better way to forget about one group of men than by spending the night with a completely different group of men? I think there may also have been a sneaky extra McDonald's afterwards as well. I was living the dolce vita and no mistake.

I eventually persuaded my body to co-operate, climbed out of bed, feeling nauseous, tired, and very, very bruised. I paused in front of the mirror, and saw big, dark blue marks forming on my left hip. Ah. Mystery Night Out Injuries. They weren't the first I'd ever had, and they probably wouldn't be the last.

I tried to avoid looking at my face, but caught a glimpse

of it by mistake. It was a disaster zone, and I ran straight for the shower to try and scrub it off. First the old make-up, but then the whole face, if necessary.

Just as I'd managed to strip naked, so hungover I got tangled up in my own legs twice as I tried to climb out of my knickers, I heard the doorbell ringing. I ignored it to start with—the building had a doorman who never let anybody up without permission, and I hoped that if I left it long enough, they'd stop pressing the buzzer. It might just be the postman or a delivery person or a bottle of tequila with arms and legs, popping round to see if I fancied some hair of the dog.

Typically enough—because these things never worked out simply—it didn't stop, and I was forced to throw on a robe, and go to the intercom panel by the door. I hit the screen button, and saw grainy black-and-white pictures of my entire family standing in the lobby of my building, accompanied by my assistant Tilly. She was the one pressing the buzzer, and looking pretty scared about it too.

I may, at that point, have said something very rude indeed, just to myself, before I buzzed them up. I had about two minutes while they were in the lift, and I used it to swill my face at the kitchen sink, and put some clean pants on. I did a quick scan of the flat for anything incriminating—used condoms, talcum powder that could be mistaken for something more sinister, drunken drag queens stashed in the wardrobe—and trained my face to smile before I opened the door.

Hungover as I was, I still remembered what Daniel had said the night before—about needing to forgive them for being clingy, and being lucky to have people in my life who cared about me, and not about my earning potential. He was right, and I needed to try and make things right with them. They were due to leave that afternoon, and whatever else I had on, I'd make sure I went with them to the station and waved them goodbye.

Becky was the first through the door, and she immediately gave me a wink and handed me a can of chilled Diet Coke. I mouthed a silent 'Thank you' to her, realising the gesture meant she'd figured out I might be a bit the worse for wear this morning. She was always the perceptive one—or possibly I was always the predictable one.

Luke ambled through, paying more attention to his phone than to me, mumbling a quick 'All right, Sis' as he entered.

Mum and Dad were the last through the door, and I tried out a smile for size. I had the urge to say I was sorry, but I didn't know quite what I had to be sorry for. All I'd done was work hard, follow the dream they'd always told me they believed in, and make a success of myself. Somewhere along the line, though, I'd cocked up.

My dad took one look at me and gave me a great big hug. The kind of massive, bear-like hug that only a dad can give.

'I'm sorry, Jessy,' he said, whispering it into my ear before he pulled away. I felt my eyes filling up again, and knew not to push it. I immediately felt guilty and wanted ask him exactly what he was sorry for; I was the one who had snapped. But that wouldn't be worth it—I needed to accept the olive branch, and try and move on.

''S'okay,' I sniffled. 'I got you back by wiping snot on your jacket.'

He glanced down at his lapel, and laughed.

'You've done worse to me in the past, love—like that time you did a projectile shit all across the room and it hit my ankles!'

Me, Becky, and Luke all simultaneously made variations on 'uggh', 'yuk', and 'eew' noises, and Mum added, 'She was only three months old at time, Phil. And you'd better get used to things like that, Becks, because you'll be the one shovelling it before long.'

'Nah,' said Becky, stroking her round belly lovingly, 'I've ordered one that doesn't poo.'

All at once, all five of us looked up and said at the same time, 'If you don't shit, you die!', and burst into laughter.

It was an old saying of my grandad's, who was obsessed with bowel movements. He used to constantly ask all of us to 'Pop down the chemist for something to make me go,' and had a whole cabinet full of various laxatives. As far as anybody could tell, he'd never had any particular problems in that area—but perhaps that was down to his daily breakfast of All Bran and prunes. He'd toddled off to the great chemist in the sky five years ago, but the saying had always stuck. It was kind of our family motto—possibly we should get it made up into some kind of personalised Malone bunch coat of arms.

'What time's your train?' I asked, realising I had absolutely no clue what time it was. 'I'll come with you to the station.'

'Erm…' said Tilly, who'd snuck in behind my dad's bulk and was hovering nervously at the rear of the group, 'in about twenty minutes? We did try calling earlier, Jessika, but there was no answer. So we decided to just pop in on our way to the station. We really need to get going now, if we're going to make it through the traffic…'

She looked terrified, as though I was likely to give her a mighty back-hander and knock her across the room for daring to suggest such a thing. I had no idea why she was so scared—we weren't best friends, and I barely knew anything about her, but I'd never approached at Patty-style levels of intern abuse. Maybe she was just always anxious.

'Oh,' I said, looking around and wondering where I'd left my coat, or if it had even made it home. 'Okay. Give me two ticks to get dressed…'

'No, it's all right love, we'll get off,' said Mum. 'Tilly's got the car waiting downstairs, our bags are all in it. We just wanted to call in and say goodbye. And, well, you know you can always come home, don't you, Jessy? You know you're always welcome with us, and you don't have to do anything you don't want to do?'

I cringed guiltily. Admittedly, I looked like death not even warmed up this morning—but it was just a hangover. They'd seen me worse before, and I supposed that was the thing. They were used to *seeing* me worse, used to having me close. Under their protection—and their control. Now I was down here, hundreds of miles away and living in a different world—one that hadn't impressed them a great deal.

I took a deep breath and tried to keep my smile in place. I didn't want us to lose the ground we'd just made up, and for it to be constantly one step forward and two steps back between us—but neither could I just pack it all up and go home because my parents were worried about me. I was a grown-up—and I needed to live my own life.

'I know, Mum. But I want to stay. I know it's not your world, but it is mine—and I'm happy here.'

I noticed her lips press closed, really tight, as though she was physically forcing the words to stay inside her mouth. She looked as if she was keeping as much held back as I was—which was undoubtedly a good thing, or this whole doorstep reunion/fond farewell would end up in a massive slanging match that even the doorman twelve floors down would be able to hear. Nobody fights like a Scouse family fights.

Instead, she just nodded, and we all shared in another round of hugs before Tilly herded them out of the door, and back into the lift. I stayed in the doorway, waving at them, until I heard the ping of the lift heading down.

Again, the main feeling running through me was absolute relief. This was getting to be a habit—watching Tilly walk away with my nearest and dearest, and being pretty damn pleased about it. It didn't feel nice—it felt a bit, I don't know, it's hard to describe, but…icky. It felt icky. I was used to my family being my world—and now they didn't seem to have a place in my world at all, other than as a bit of a head fuck. I knew they loved me, but they didn't seem to understand me—and didn't seem to be trying all that hard to understand me, either. It felt horrible.

Still, they were gone, for the time being. I could relax again. I could scrub my face off, catch up with Patty and Jack and Vogue, and check that Neale was still alive and feeling as good as I was. I could risk looking at my Twitter account and my newsfeed, even though Patty did all that for me, and see what the feedback about last night was. I could take a moment to feel…pleased with myself. Because family dramas aside, I'd done well last night—and my life was starting to resemble the dream I'd always wanted it to be. Even if, I thought, catching another scary glimpse of myself in the mirror, I was looking like more of a nightmare that morning.

I decided on a long, luxurious bath rather than a shower. I'd mastered those Jacuzzi controls now, and the whole bathroom was full of luxurious toiletries I'd been sent for free—everything from high street names through to mega-posh organic essence of everything-berry type stuff. I was going to chuck it all in, create a Smellies Stew, and hope for the best.

I did, though, at least check my phone first. I'd learned from my mistakes before with that one, and needed to be sure that Patty hadn't arranged for Radio 1 to pop round and do a live broadcast from my balcony or anything.

There were four messages from her, three relating to interview requests from people she thought I should bother with. Two had been sent the night before and one this morning—but all of them, she reckoned, could be done later in the day or even tomorrow. That was good. I knew I had to promote the single for all I was worth, and really make the most of this fame to extend it from its traditional fifteen minutes, but I could also really do with a few hours off. Plus, you know, it was Vogue's single after all—I was just the afterthought add-on.

The other said something mysterious about a story she'd declined to comment on, and not to worry about it. Under normal circumstances, that would immediately make me worry—but I didn't have the energy just then.

Jack had called a couple of times, and left a text: 'Be ready by 3 p.m. I'm coming to take you away from all this.' Mmmm. That sounded promising, and I decided to call him back after I'd wrinkled up like a prune in the bath.

Neale had sent me a photo of the two of us at the club, with him sitting on my shoulders like he was my Glastonbury girlfriend, waving a glow stick that seemed to be in the shape of a giant penis—one for the family album, for sure. I giggled and saved that one to laugh at again later.

There was also a message from Daniel, and even seeing his name pop up on the screen made something inside me feel a bit...clenched. A bit nervous. A bit weird. And a bit wriggly. These were not sensations I was used to associating with Daniel—he was safe and solid and reassuring. He was friendship and home and history, no matter how much time had passed and how much our lives had changed. If men were drinks, then Jack would be something sleek and expensive and decadent and gorgeous from the top shelf—and Daniel would be a nice mug of tea on a cold day.

Except... I wasn't totally sure about that any more. I'd always loved Daniel—as a friend. And now he was back in my life, I'd expected that to stay the same. Instead, the new Daniel was way too tall and way too built and way too good-looking for me not to notice. And that moment, last night, in the club, where we'd almost...well, I had no idea what we'd almost done, or what it meant, but I'd wanted to shag him right there and then. Which was just too bloody confusing for a girl with a hangover the size of Peru, whose boyfriend was coming over that afternoon anyway.

I pressed Play, and heard the sounds of traffic and honking horns and sirens. I pictured him outside the club last night, holding the phone up to his mouth, shielding it from the wind.

'Jessy,' he said, firmly, as though he was about to issue some important statement or manifesto. There was a pause, the sound of more traffic in the background, and then: 'See you soon.'

Hmm. That was something of an anti-climax. I knew I should call him—make sure he'd got home okay, make sure we were still cool, make sure there wouldn't be anything awkward in the air between us—but I couldn't do it then. I was too tired, and too mentally and physically drained. Instead, I texted him a thumbs-up picture with a couple of kisses after it.

It was the best I could do—and even that was enough to make me wonder what kind of signals I was sending out.

Everything felt too confusing, so I did the grown-up thing—stuck my tongue out at the phone, and got into the bath.

Chapter 26

'Wow,' said Jack, lounging around on silk sheets and looking highly amused at the online newspaper article he was reading on his phone. 'I never had you down as the threesome type, Jess—it opens up all kinds of interesting possibilities!'

As he was stark bollock naked and vulnerable in all types of places, I thought he was taking a bit of a risk winding me up even further, and lobbed a peanut at his crotch in retaliation. It was only a peanut, but he over-reacted in the time-honoured way of men and their crotches, and folded in on himself as though someone had just whacked his crown jewels with a mallet. I'd have felt some sense of satisfaction if it wasn't for the fact that he was still laughing.

I suppose, to him, it was funny. Seeing a picture of me, clearly asleep, with Ruby and Keith apparently naked in bed next to me—one on either side, and giant grins on their faces.

I had no recollection of it being taken, but it had to have been in the last few months I was in Liverpool, as it involved Keith, and presumably his bloody ever-present selfie stick. I might have found it funny as well, apart from the fact that the two of them were claiming it was taken after a 'sizzling threesome' in our 'love nest in Liverpool'.

There were other lovely phrases in there as well; the kind of tabloid-eze you read about other people all the time, but which feels ever so slightly different when it's about you. I was, according to Keith, 'Obsessed with sex—any time, any place, anywhere.' I'd apparently talked the two of them into a dirty ménage à trois after a booze-fuelled night out in town, and exhausted them both with my rampant sexual appetite.

I wasn't entirely sure the photo fitted with that story—as I was fast asleep in my now-famous reindeer onesie, oblivious to the fact that my alleged 'friend' and her perverted partner had jumped under the duvet with me.

Jack had, true to his word, arrived at the flat at three p.m., to 'take me away'. He took me away to a blissful manor house in Surrey, where we were treated like royalty, and were spending a whole ecstatic night in their biggest, poshest suite. It was the kind of place aristocrats and millionaires went for a naughty weekend away, with views over the grounds and roaring log fires and champagne on tap and in-room his and hers massages available. It was the sort of night I'd normally have loved—but this latest little revelation had somehow spoiled it for me.

Patty had sent the link through with a little note saying, 'Don't worry—obv crap—warn family but no damage done.'

I wasn't quite sure what her definition of 'no damage' was, but it was very different from mine. I felt embarrassed, humiliated, and angry. Angry that the two of them had ever taken a photo like that in the first place—and angry that they'd presumably sold it to the paper, and made up such a crock of lies about me.

I was also—underneath all those layers—really, really hurt. I'd known Ruby for so long—almost as long as I'd known Daniel—and I'd trusted her. I'd thought of her as a friend, but she'd obviously moved on and now saw me as a way to make a quick buck, no matter what fibs she told or how much it could affect me. I'd have believed it of Keith in a flash—he was always a sleazy so-and-so—but I was so disappointed in her.

'Stop fretting,' said Jack, emerging from his foetal ball once he was sure nothing else was going to get aimed at his manhood. 'And give me a peanut. I'm starving—you've completely worn me out with your rampant sexual appetite, you naughty nympho you.'

I glared at him, but passed the peanuts anyway. I supposed the fact that Jack—who had a lot of vested interest in my reputation and the way it could affect my career—was finding it all so amusing should be reassuring. If he wasn't worried, maybe I shouldn't be either.

Except it wasn't him who'd just had the world's most excruciating conversation with his father, was it? They'd just landed back at home when I called to warn him what was likely to show up on Luke's Google alert. It was awful, for both of us. I mean, no dad on the face of the planet wants to hear the word 'threesome' coming out of his daughter's mouth, does he? Especially in relation to a childhood friend he'd known since she was in nursery school.

He'd been shocked when I explained what had happened— or more accurately what hadn't happened, *ever*—but seemed to totally, one hundred per cent believe that there was no truth in it, which was a bit of a relief after the last few days. A tiny part of me had been worried he'd add 'sex maniac' to the list of fictional faults he seemed to be compiling about me. Trust had taken a bit of a battering on both sides recently, so I was relieved when he accepted my version of events without too much probing—or maybe he was just too embarrassed to pursue it further, who knew? I did know, though, that he'd be in for a lot of ribbing from his cab driver mates, and apologised for the fact that this was now part of our new reality—not that it was my fault, I thought. But it definitely wasn't his.

After we'd got the issue of group sex out of the way—sighs of relief all round—he went a bit quiet on me.

'So, have you been in touch with Ruby?' he asked, after a few seconds of awkward silence. Awkward silence—or in fact, any kind of silence—was not something I'd ever associated with my dad before. 'Since you've been in London, I mean?'

'Erm…yeah. A bit,' I said, even though what I actually meant was, 'No, but I really intended to be—does that count?' I'd been feeling twinges of guilt about ignoring Ruby myself, but I didn't want my dad getting in on the act too. I know my family had been a bit peeved at me not being in contact with them often enough—but surely I didn't have to check in with everyone I'd ever met at any stage in my life every day, did I, just to ensure they didn't lie about me in the press? If something came with that many strings attached, it wasn't friendship, surely? Wouldn't someone who cared about you give you the benefit of the doubt if you forgot to call them for, well, a few months or so?

Part of me had wanted to get straight off the phone to Dad and straight on the phone to Ruby. I'm pretty easy going and don't have much of a temper, but the diva in me was starting to emerge—and I really felt like tearing a strip off her. It all felt so unfair—not just the story, but the criticism I felt I was getting from my family. They had no idea what pressures I was under, and it felt like they were constantly questioning everything I was doing, as though I was some out of control idiot instead of their now pretty successful daughter.

Jack had talked me out of it, saying, with some justification, that Ruby already knew it was a lie—and she already knew I'd be upset. If she'd not cared enough about me being upset when she sold the story, she still wouldn't care now, and it could only make matters worse. He'd also held my hand, and said something about dignity, but as I was sitting cross-legged and naked with tears of frustrations running down my face at the time, I didn't feel I had much of that left.

'I know, I know,' I replied, swiping my eyes dry. 'You're right. It just…sucks! She even plugged the bloody Princess business in the piece—I dread to think what kind of parties she'll get asked to appear at now!'

'That, my sweet little Scouse sex bomb,' he said, grinning and squeezing my fingers, 'is part of the price of fame. I've seen it happen time and time again. People you think you can trust turn out not to be trustworthy. People you think care about you only care about themselves. Being famous doesn't automatically make everything right—sometimes quite the opposite, in fact. Things like this, though? Don't worry about them. Anyone with half a brain can see that picture is a set up, and Patty's right to tell you to ignore it. She'll set you up with some positive interviews tomorrow that will offset it, so don't worry. It's all under control—might even be good for you.'

He'd climbed out of bed by that stage, which was helping me not worry a little bit—no matter how many times I saw it, I still found the sight of Jack's bare backside parading around in front of me very distracting. I'm deep like that.

'Anyway,' he said, reaching into his leather overnight bag, 'forget about it for a while. I've got a present for you. Surely that'll make everything in Jess-world all better?'

'I'm not seven, Jack!' I bleated, defensively, but reached out and grabbed for the box anyway. He laughed as he held it out of reach for a few seconds, then gave in and let me take it. As I was naked as well, and I think he was enjoying all the jiggling.

When he finally gave in and let me win, I came away with a beautifully gift-wrapped box, diplomatically too big to inspire any embarrassing 'OMG-is-it-an-engagement-ring!' moments. It was criss-crossed with shiny silver ribbon, and was almost too pretty to open. Almost.

Within seconds, I'd torn it to pieces, and was holding in my hand an absolutely gorgeous pendant and necklace. The chain was long and fine and gold, and draping from it was a small but perfectly formed heart-shaped stone that looked like emerald. It glowed and shone as I spun it around, admiring the way it had been carved and cut, and it was just about the most gorgeous and unusual thing I'd ever seen.

'Well,' said Jack, smiling down at me. 'Do you like it? I had it made specially for you. It's an emerald.'

'That's my—'

'Birthstone,' he finished for me, reaching out and sweeping the hair off my shoulders before fastening the chain around my neck. 'I know.' He dropped a couple of slow, sensual kisses on my bare skin, making me shiver as he let my hair fall back into place.

For once in my life, I was pretty much lost for words. Not only had he bought me such a stunning present, he'd been thoughtful enough to make it something that was deeply personal to me. I'd not had a birthday since we'd met, but he'd gone to the trouble of finding out, and arranging this amazing gift for me. It was utterly, completely sweet, and I didn't know what to say.

In the end, I went with a timeless classic 'Thank you.'

'You're very welcome, Jess,' he said, holding the emerald in the palm of his hand as it dangled between my breasts. 'I wanted to show you how much you mean to me. Just don't wear it out in public—you're supposed to be single and looking for love, remember?'

I nodded. I remembered. And now I felt guilty for even having a moment's doubt about us; and even more guilty for having a moment's doubt about Daniel, and whether he could ever be more than a friend.

I leaned forward and kissed Jack with more conviction than I'd ever felt. I might have to pretend I was looking for love in public—but right at that moment, there was no one else around, and I felt like I'd already found it.

Chapter 27

'I'm just…not sure. What do you think?' I said.

'I think it could work, but I also think I want you to love it,' replied Jack, pressing the play button again.

Vogue's single—featuring little old me—was on target for hitting number one in the download charts, and as a result, I'd had shedloads of publicity. Quite literally, if you printed it all out, it could probably fill a shed. Albeit a small one, like my dad's in the back yard, which he only actually used to sneak the occasional ciggie.

I'd been doing non-stop interviews for days now, starting in the car when we were driving back from Surrey. One of them in particular had been entertaining—a journalist who'd seen some pictures of me and Neale (I guessed it was Neale once she described him, and added the immortally classy line, 'You look as though you're standing outside McDonald's unwrapping a burger'), and asked if it was my new boyfriend!

I'd explained that no, he was my stylist and very much not interested in me (or any girls) in that kind of way, although he was one of my best friends, and reiterated the company line: Pop Sensation Jessika is Still Looking for Love.

As I uttered the words—well, not those ones precisely, I hadn't been so far sucked into the crazy that I actually talked in headlines—Jack had one hand on the steering wheel, and one hand on my inner thigh, which he was stroking in a very distracting fashion. He knew exactly what he was doing, and had a big, daft, arrogant grin plastered over his face as his fingers played against my skin. Somehow I got through the interview without choking with laughter, and we ended up pulling over into a picnic area for a shag. We'd be back in London, and back pretending, before long, so we had to make the most of it.

That was four days ago, and it had been hard to find time to be together since. I was on an action-packed schedule of TV interviews, recording for podcasts, making video clips for online pop sites, radio pre-records, and photoshoots. Patty had every minute of every day tied up, and paraded me at parties and functions every night as well. It was exhausting, as usual, but at least I didn't also have to deal with a single launch, a gig, and my family as well.

What I did have to deal with was finding my own single. And my own album. And my own sound. Starmaker had decided that I needed to get something recorded, and get something out there, as soon as possible—ideally in the New Year. It made sense: they needed to capitalise on the fact that I was riding the crest of a fame-wave, and start to establish me in my own right, instead of constantly recycling my association with Vogue.

That, much as I was grateful for the opportunity, had served its purpose—and I didn't want to be 'Vogue featuring

Jessika' any longer than I needed to be. I wanted to be Just Jessika—master of my own fate, captain of my own ship, dominatrix of my own destiny…all of which sounded great. The only problem was, I was fairly sure a dominatrix of her own destiny didn't keep muttering weedy lines like, 'I'm not sure, what do you think?'

Darren and James, the in-house Starmaker songwriting team, had come up with several songs for me. One of them I rejected straight away, as it was way too steamy. I mean, I don't mind a bit of raunch, and I can bump and grind in a dance routine with the best of them—but fresh from my Ruby and Keith inspired humiliation, I didn't think anything too saucy was going to quite work for me.

'I can't sing that!' I'd said immediately, blushing.

'What? Why?' Darren had asked, looking genuinely con-fused.

'I can't sing "I want to go down, go down, go down to your love basement"! I just can't—I'm not 50 Cent! I'd never be able to look my mum and dad in the eye again, or even talk about it in interviews without going red!'

He'd taken one look at my flame-red cheeks and obviously decided I had a point.

'All right, fair enough… I'm sure we can find someone it suits. And I can almost imagine the video, can't you?'

I could—and it involved an awful lot of dry ice and low lighting and a huge, massive orgy. Not my scene.

The other two songs weren't X-rated, thank goodness, but they didn't have the X factor either. They were nice, with good choruses and big hooks and mainly nonsensical lyrics that vaguely referred to heartbreak and pain, but neither of them made me whoop with joy, and scream, 'This is the one!'

I'd recorded demo tracks of them both in the studio, though, and had spent the last hour listening to them and discussing them with Jack, while we pecked away at a Chinese takeaway and surreptitiously played footsie under the table. Jack had told me there were security cameras in most of the Starmaker studios and rehearsal rooms, so we couldn't risk anything more obvious—not unless we wanted to look like the video to that song I'd rejected, anyway.

After listening to both songs more times than either of us wanted to, they still didn't feel quite right—but I was conscious that time was running out and that, eventually, the pressure would build to the point where I'd just have to choose one and get on with it, or let the moment pass and potentially regret it for the rest of my life.

'I don't love it,' I said, pushing my food around with chopsticks, and wishing I was allowed to eat white rice. I'd had a couple of days off my eating regime, with no noticeable weight gain—it wasn't like I'd turned into the incredible twenty-five-stone woman overnight or anything. But I'd also stopped the incessant dance training and rehearsals that I'd had before the single launch, so I needed to be careful. 'I don't love it, no. But how important is that? Can't I just pretend to love it?'

'Of course you can,' replied Jack; one side of his mouth quirked up in an amused grin. 'Acting is part of the job. But with your first single, with the first songs we get together for your album, it would be better to find something you genuinely feel good about. This is important—it sets the tone for the rest of your career, Jess. I know everything's felt rushed and impromptu so far—mainly because it *has* been rushed and impromptu—and that we're now pushing you to record, and that must feel rushed as well.

'But there is a long term future for you in this industry, I have every faith in that. You're already famous—but I believe you can truly be a star.'

I leaned back in my seat and smiled at him. That sounded familiar—and I must have done something right in a past life to find two men who believed in my talents to such an extent.

'Daniel always used to say that,' I said, and wondered why he looked a bit confused. 'I mean Wellsy,' I added.

Jack just nodded, and looked momentarily distracted—as though he was now thinking about something else entirely. For a split second I thought I'd made him jealous—that something in the tone of my voice had given away the fact that my new feelings about Daniel were, to put it simply, weirding me out.

'Right. Wellsy. We've been in talks, you know,' he said. 'About him joining Starmaker. We wanted him before, but since you arrived on the scene, we want him even more. I have to be honest—I think the only reason he's even considering it is because of you, Jess. You're very much the carrot.'

'Wow. Comparing me to a vegetable—how sexy.'

I paused, pretended to be looking at my food, while I gathered my thoughts. I wasn't sure how I felt about all of this. About Daniel, and about him potentially being tempted to join Starmaker because of me. Daniel had always been independent, always avoided crowds or gangs or much social engagement at all. From what I'd seen of him, that hadn't changed—he might work in the music industry, extremely productively it seemed, but he did it on his own terms. He lived in the countryside, he had a non-existent online profile, and he worked only with clients he hand-picked. He was a silent industry megastar—succeeding by stealth.

He also seemed happy with that. Did I want to be involved in some kind of plan to persuade him out of a lifestyle that clearly suited him? Was I being arrogant to assume I even could, despite what Jack had just said? And was part of me a tiny bit concerned that being holed up in small studio spaces with my magically transformed childhood friend and now megahunk might result in me embarrassing myself by throwing him up against a wall and snogging his face off?

'Carrots,' replied Jack, obviously unaware of my internal monologue, 'are the most erotic of all the vegetables. Fabulously phallic. Anyway—it's true. I think he has almost as much faith in you as I do.'

I met his eyes, and nodded.

'Yes. He always has had. We've known each other a long time, and he wrote this school show when we were teenagers. He did everything, the story, the tunes, the lyrics, the lighting.'

'Hmmm. I'd heard on the grapevine that he also writes. None of the people he's worked with have ever publicly credited him on their songs, but there have been rumours. Rumours that he doesn't just produce—he gets stuck in on the songwriting as well. I was actually wondering if that might work for you. Clearly, this material isn't right—perhaps some time with Wellsy, I mean Daniel, might help? You have history, as you say. Perhaps we could persuade him to come up with something for you to record?'

I stared at him blankly for a moment. Of course Daniel wrote songs. At least, I assumed he still did—although to be fair, the last song he'd written for me involved a cheerleader outfit and space aliens. He'd always had a real knack for melody and words, even as a teenager. And he knew me so much better than Darren and James and, in reality, even Jack. I trusted him to come up with something I *would* love—but all of my doubts were still there, lurking in the background, no matter how perfect a solution it sounded to Jack.

'Has he said he would?' I asked, frowning.

'Well, no…not yet. In fact, I was wondering about that. I think it would really help with our negotiations if you could talk to him, personally. I could give you his number, and you could give him a call?'

I realised as he said it that he still assumed I didn't have Daniel's contact details. Because he hadn't passed them on, had he, despite saying he would? Either he'd forgotten about it, or he'd been waiting to use it strategically. Much as I was smitten with Jack, I was under no illusions that when it came to his work, he could be as devious and ruthless as he needed to be. It was hard to make it in the music business by purely being Mr Nice Guy—which is what made Daniel's rise and rise even more amazing.

'Erm…maybe?' I said, eloquently. In truth, I felt odd about all of it. I kept in contact with Daniel, but it was usually texts or emails. We hadn't actually spoken since the night of the single launch, when he'd seen me in major-league meltdown with my family, and, I suspected, looking at him like he was chocolate. I didn't think it was one sided—I think he'd felt that way too—but it was still a bit embarrassing. It still felt uncomfortable—it was a bit like suddenly fancying your step-brother or something. Not illegal, but pretty weird.

Obviously, Jack had absolutely no idea about any of that. He assumed, correctly, that there had never been anything between Daniel and I other than friendship. And he probably also assumed, not quite so correctly, that I only had eyes for him.

'Brilliant! Look, I've got to go—I've got a meeting. But will you let me know how it goes? What he says?'

I agreed, and stayed all smiles as he prepared to leave, walking with him as far as the lobby. No kisses, obviously, other than the ubiquitous showbiz peck on both cheeks, which was perfectly acceptable for a music exec and his client. For once, I didn't mind—I had a lot to think about, and a phone call to prepare for.

Chapter 28

I was back at my flat, communing with a large glass of red wine, by the time I plucked up the courage to make that phone call. I don't know why I was quite so nervous—I kept telling myself I was just calling my old pal Daniel, that it was all normal and fine, but somehow it definitely felt like a Rioja moment.

Partly it was my own changing feelings towards him, and not wanting to confront them. Partly it was the fact that calling to ask him a professional favour felt wrong. Somehow, I felt like I was doing Jack's dirty work for him—which was absolutely bonkers. There was nothing dirty about it at all—in fact, it made perfect sense, and could be a mutually beneficial arrangement for us all. None of which stopped me feeling anxious, as I swirled wine around in my glass so hard it slopped over the edge, and waited for him to answer.

It went straight to voicemail, which came as something of a relief. I left a garbled message, realising only when I ended the call that I hadn't even said who was speaking. He'd probably be able to figure it out though—he was used to me sounding insane, after all.

I put down the phone, drank some more wine, and perched myself on one of the bar stools by the kitchen island. I had a very, very rare night off—and for once, nothing to do with it. Jack was in his meeting—and night time meetings were not at all unusual in our business. Neale wasn't answering his phone. And, well, that was it, really. I hadn't exactly vastly extended my social circle since moving to London—at least not with real friends. I'd met possibly thousands of people, especially since becoming Jessika, but nobody I could call casually on a Thursday night and ask if they fancied going to the cinema or going out for a bottle of wine. I didn't mind that—I rarely had the time anyway, and people who didn't work in the industry wouldn't last five minutes as a friend these days. The gap between my life now and my old life—a normal life—was so big, I didn't think anybody could leap across it without a jet pack strapped to their back. I just didn't know quite how to behave now I was finally at a loose end.

I stared at the phone and drank some more wine. Daniel still hadn't called back—even though it had been literally *minutes* since I left the message. I did at least manage to laugh at myself as that thought crossed my mind—since when had I started mad-woman-phone-watching about Daniel? I needed to get a grip. He obviously had a life outside precious little me, and I was being a tit by assuming he would just be sitting around, waiting for me to grace him with a phone call.

Instead, on a whim, I picked up the phone and flicked through my contacts. Vogue had given me her new number the week before, and I quickly typed up a message. What did we ever use thumbs for before texting? We all use them so much now. Maybe some weird evolutionary thing will happen, and we'll all grow giant sized thumbs over the next thousand years. And maybe, I pondered, I should stop drinking so much wine.

'Are you around?' I typed. 'If so, fancy a drink? No worries if not.'

I added a few kisses, pressed Send, and then almost jumped out of my skin as the phone immediately started to ring.

I steadied myself on the counter, glad I hadn't actually fallen off my bar stool (it had happened before, and would probably happen again), and looked at the screen. Daniel. Calling back. That was good. That was fine. That was excellent. That was... probably a reason to hit Answer?

'Hi? Jessy? Did you leave me a message?' he said, the line a little crackly. Maybe he didn't have a good reception out in the middle of his cow field.

'Hi! Yes, that was me—I kind of forgot to say who it was, didn't I?'

'You did, but it wasn't hard to figure out—for a start, it sounded like you, and secondly, my missed calls came up with your name. I'm a genius like that. How are you? Is everything all right?'

'Of course everything's all right—do I need a reason to call you?'

'No, you don't *need* one. I just wondered if you *had* one. Last time I saw you was...well, you were having issues with your family.'

And we were both having issues with each other, I silently added. If I'd had even one more glass of wine, it probably wouldn't have been so silent.

'I think me and my folks are as good as we can be at the moment to be honest. Work in progress, I suppose you'd say. But…well, now I feel bad, `cause I actually do have a reason for calling. In fact, I'm calling to talk to Wellsy.'

'Oh. Right. Hang on a second,' he said. I heard the phone bumping around, and a few mysterious noises that I couldn't quite figure out.

'Okay. I'm ready now,' he said, back on the line.

'What were you doing?' I asked, unable to resist.

'I was putting my baseball cap on backwards, so I looked more street,' he replied, making me burst out laughing.

'You're a knob, Daniel.'

'True. But you're talking to Wellsy now. What can I do for you? No, actually, let me guess—Jack Duncan asked you to call me, didn't he?'

'Um…yeah. How did you know?'

'Educated guess,' he said. 'Based on the fact that we've been in talks about me joining Starmaker, and he's been using you as the—'

'Please don't say carrot!'

'As the aubergine,' he finished, again making me grin. Sometimes I forgot how silly Daniel's sense of humour was, and how much fun it could be acting as though I was seventeen again.

'Well, you're kind of right,' I said, grimacing a bit at even discussing Jack with him. As far as I knew, Daniel had no idea about me and Jack, which was the way I needed it to be for all kinds of reasons. But I still felt off for keeping secrets from him.

'Oh, you *are* an aubergine?'

'No! Look, Jack did ask me to call. But it's not just about you joining Starmaker. He, well, we, were wondering if you'd be interested in working with me on some songs.'

'Producing?' he asked.

'No. Yes. Maybe. But on songwriting. I've spent the last few days listening to crap, and recording tracks I don't even like, and now they say they want to get something out by late January and we still don't have a single. I've kind of lost my way with it all, to be honest—I'm not even objective any more about what kind of stuff I should be singing.'

'You should be singing soulful mainstream pop music that can make people feel real emotions, but can also be remixed into dance versions for clubbers.'

'Oh. Right. See? You make it all sound so simple—you always did know what was best for me.'

'That's true,' replied Daniel, and I could almost see his grin. 'I don't know how you've coped without me for the last few years.'

'Mainly by singing Disney songs and having threesomes with Ruby and her ugly boyfriend.'

'I saw that. I believed it might be an untruth.'

'Very much so. Neither of them is my type,' I said.

'And what *is* your type these days, Jess?'

There was a distinct change in the tone of his voice as he asked that question. Not quite flirtatious, but definitely… interested. Curious. I bit my lip as I tried to figure out how to answer it, not even sure what the answer was. My 'type' *should* be Jack, end of—but here I was, chatting and laughing with Daniel, and wondering just how it would go if I simply said, 'Tall, blond, handsome Daniels are my type at exactly this moment—so come up and see me some time.'

'Oh, you know,' I replied, far too much of a chicken to actually say that at all. 'The usual. Anyone who can cook, and ideally runs their own off-licence.'

'That's very practical. Let me know if you meet the bake-off booze-buster bachelor of your dreams any time soon. And as for the song writing…yes, I still write. Or I help other people with their stuff, anyway. It's been a while since I came up with something totally new. I suppose I was waiting for the inspiration to strike.'

'Maybe I could strike you with some inspiration,' I replied. 'God knows, I'm desperate enough to strike you with whatever you want, Daniel. You know I've always wanted this, and I feel like I'm on the very verge of it all working out. I just need a bit of help. And I'd love to work with you again—our last collaboration was out of this world.'

'I remember. I think, in fact, my mum still has a video of it somewhere. Look, I'd like to work with you as well Jess—I feel like fate brought us back together for a reason. I'm just not completely sure about what I've got going on, and whether Starmaker is the right fit. To be honest, the only thing I like about the deal is the aubergine.'

'What about Vogue? You'd get to work with her as well.'

'And I wouldn't mind that—I love her stuff, and I know she's treated you well. But I've never signed an exclusive deal with any label, and I need to give it some thought. Talk it through with the cows, that kind of thing.'

'You mean Ruby? How apt!'

'I know. She gave me a wink the other day. I was quite worried she was about to tell the tabloid press I'd been fiddling with her udders. Anyway—leave it with me. I know you need a decision, and I won't drag it out. I would like to do more songwriting. You always loved the limelight and I always hated it. We were the perfect team, and maybe we could be again. Give me a few days, all right?'

'All right,' I replied. 'That's the best I could have hoped for. So, now that's out of the way, what are you up to tonight? Anything exciting?'

'I've got a date actually,' he said, then waited a beat. 'With my mum and dad. They're coming over for a long weekend—the B&B's always quiet at the start of the month, and gets busier around Christmas, so they're taking a break.'

'Well that's great,' I answered, keeping my voice even, 'give them all my love and we'll speak soon.'

As we said our goodbyes and hung up, I realised my hands were trembling. Too much wine. Too much adrenalin. Too much of a pause between him saying he had a date, and explaining who with. For those few seconds, my heart felt like it literally plunged down into my stomach, where it bounced around in an alcoholic slush, feeling sad and lonely and devastated.

I had absolutely no right to feel jealous of Daniel having a date, I knew. I was seeing Jack. Daniel and I weren't involved. And why on earth wouldn't he have a date? He was a successful music producer, drop-dead gorgeous, and an all-round lovely bloke. He was a total catch and, as his friend, I should want him to be happy.

I told myself all of this over and over again, and it was about as effective as a chocolate fireguard. I was saying it, but I wasn't feeling it. Frankly, I had no idea what was going on with me—I was a mess. Normally, I'd talk about it to Ruby or Becky and let it all out. But Ruby wasn't exactly my bestie right now, and Becky had enough going on, what with creating the next generation of Malones and all. There was still no reply from Neale to the messages I'd sent, which was just plain weird—he was usually so good at getting back to me.

I glanced at my phone again and noticed that there was in fact a message waiting. I saw that it was from Vogue, and swiped it open.

'I'm bored too. Got a new Jacuzzi. Bring bikini and booze.'

After that there was a link to a street in central London and her address.

Excellent, I thought. I might not be able to pour out all my woes about Daniel, Jack, and my pathetic little love life, but I could at the very least talk to her about music—and get mightily drunk while I did.

Chapter 29

'Hey, babes!' said Vogue, opening the door to her townhouse and ushering me into the hallway. 'Welcome to my humble abode!'

I walked through the door, gave her a hug, and clinked my heavily laden carrier bag at her.

'That sounds promising,' she said, grinning. 'Come on through.'

I followed her down the hall, which was lined with her platinum discs in frames, and photos of her with everyone from Boris Johnson to Mariah Carey. The house was one of those tall, thin four-storey affairs, tucked away in a quiet side street that was lined with parked Jags, Porches, and Audis. Every home was perfectly painted white, every front courtyard displaying perfectly manicured plants and potted bushes, and every door festooned with a perfectly polished brass knocker, and, in some cases, equally perfect Christmas wreaths.

It wasn't, in short, the kind of street you wandered down at four in the morning eating a kebab and singing 'I Will Survive' with your mates. Even as my cab had dropped me off, I noted security guards parked up in a van on the corner, and knew I was being watched. Luckily, I mustn't have looked threatening. Unless you counted the carrier bag—that was a weapon of mass sobriety destruction all by itself. All it needed to go off was a couple of bored pop stars.

'Your home is gorgeous, Vogue,' I said, following her through to the kitchen and open plan dining area. I think it probably would have been called an 'entertaining space' in the estate agent's brochure—all shining marble and black leather and chrome. To be honest, not a million miles away from the sleek modern interior design of my own flat. I wondered briefly if it was, in fact, one of Starmaker's corporate holdings.

'Oh gawd,' she said, popping open one of the bottles of wine and pouring it into two enormous glasses. Looked like she meant business. 'Please call me Paulette. Vogue's my work name, and I don't want to feel like I'm working right now. I've had it with work—with interviews, appearances, the lot. I'm knackered.'

'I feel your pain,' I replied, hopping onto a stool and accepting the glass from her. 'I'm only the office junior compared to you, and I'm knackered as well. Still, looks like we could end up as…you know…'

'Number one in the hit parade? I know. And don't get me wrong—I'm grateful. I don't take anything for granted in this business. But it's not quite as exciting when you've already had over twenty number ones, which again, I know, sounds arrogant. But it's not, I don't mean it like that. I just mean that as time goes by, you start to realise how much you've given up for those wins. I'm a veteran now, by pop music standards, and I'm…tired. Not so sure I made the right choices. Apart from these big glasses, which were an excellent choice—nice wine, Jess!'

'Thanks. I can't take credit. I just picked the one with the prettiest label. And, well, you don't look like you've lost much. You have this amazing home at least.'

'This isn't my home,' she replied immediately, which I found a bit confusing. I mean, I know I'd already had a couple, but this definitely looked like it was her house. Either that or I was sitting with the world's best Vogue impersonator, surrounded by stalker photos.

'What I mean is,' she continued, 'it's my house, but it's not my home. I bought this because I needed somewhere central for work, and I was told it was a solid investment. It's good for when I need to have parties, or those "at-home-with-Vogue" photoshoots where I recline on my sofa and look sexy and stuff...but it's not my home. That's still in Peckham.'

'With your mum and dad?'

'And my little sister Simone. The one who was ten a while ago. This is her.'

She picked up her phone, and did the usual faffing around getting into her photo album, before holding up the screen to show an adorable little girl with elaborate cornrows in her hair. Her huge, dark eyes were sparkling with mischief, and she looked like an absolute bundle of the best kind of trouble.

'She's gorgeous,' I said, smiling at the picture. 'She looks so happy.'

'Yeah,' sighed Vogue—I mean Paulette—putting the phone down but still staring at the screen wistfully. 'She is. She's a really happy kid. I wanted them all to move in with me, not necessarily here—anywhere. As soon as I had the money I said come on, let's do it. Anywhere you like—London, the countryside, wherever. But my parents didn't want to move. They've lived in that same community in Peckham since I was a teenager, and they like it there. They have friends, and a church, and they both work as volunteers in a youth centre. To be honest, they have a better life than I do. All I could persuade them to do was let me buy them a bigger house, one with a nice garden for Simone to play in. I see them as much as I can but it's nowhere near enough. I miss them.'

She sounded so sad, so lonely, that I wanted to get off my stool and hug her again. I kind of understood—well, I certainly understood this life causing problems with family. But at this particular point in my journey, I wasn't really missing my family, to be honest. Not the reality of my relationship with them as it stood now, anyway. I missed the way it used to be—but not the new version of things. In the new version of things, they came tied up with a barrel load of guilt and stress that I could really do without. I loved them, I really did—but I was glad they'd gone home.

I was trying to come up with a suitable reply to Vogue's confession when she suddenly jumped to her feet and clapped her hands together. She loomed over me even when I was standing up; when I was sitting she was even more statuesque.

'Come on!' she said, clearly making a huge effort to put some jollity into her voice. 'Enough of this crap—nobody likes a maudlin drunk, do they? Let's take this wine down to the Jacuzzi in the basement and make our lives more bubbly!'

It sounded like a good plan to me and, within minutes,

we were both emerging from separate bathrooms in our bikinis ready to get soaked—in both the bath and the wine. We padded barefoot into the basement, which was kitted out with a massive Jacuzzi—like the communal type you usually see in gyms, not my little one back at the flat—and several weight training machines. They looked like medieval torture devices to me, but I supposed Vogue had to maintain looking like a warrior princess somehow.

There was old soul music playing from speakers I couldn't see; something by Percy Sledge or Marvin Gaye, I thought—perfectly smoky and sultry and a million miles away from the songs I'd been recording recently, thank God.

We eased ourselves into the bubbles, both making 'ooh'-ing and 'aah'-ing noises that made us sound like old ladies. To be fair to both of us, all the dance training we did was tough on the old muscles, and nothing felt quite as good as submerging your entire body in buoyant water. Especially if it was accompanied by alcohol.

'We're probably breaking all kinds of health and safety rules doing this, you know,' I said, leaning my head back against the padded tiles, and sipping another mouthful of wine.

'I know,' she replied, giggling, 'drunk in charge of a Jacuzzi! Guilty, m'lud!'

'I'm just glad it's in the basement—at least there's no chance of getting papped in here, and us waking up to a story about us being secret lesbian lovers!'

'True,' she said, kicking her long legs around in the water. 'I saw you've come in for a bit of stick on that front. Don't worry, nobody in their right minds would have believed that threesome photo. And you and Neale outside McDonald's isn't going to hurt anyone, is it?'

'I hope not,' I replied. 'Although I've not seen that one. I remember doing the interview—has it appeared yet?'

'Yep. It went online this afternoon. Patty will probably be busy negotiating some kind of burger-based publicity appearance as we speak…'

I shuddered involuntarily, and glanced quickly around the room.

'Don't say her name,' I whispered. 'And definitely don't say it three times in a row while looking in a mirror—it might conjure her up!'

'I know, I know, she comes across as evil—but she's good at her job. She'll get you out of more scrapes than she'll land you in, I promise. She might be a lot of things, but she is a professional. In fact, now I think of it, I have no idea what else she is. She could have six kids and live in a camper van, or be married to Batman, or be a pastor at the Church of the Poisoned Mind, for all we know.'

'You're right. I know nothing about her as a person. And I think, all things considered, that I'm happy to keep it that way. Gosh, this is nice, isn't it? Talking like this, having a drink with nobody watching?' I said.

It really, really was. And not just because of the wine or the Jacuzzi. Because of being in the company of someone I could relax around—someone who knew and understood the world I now lived in; who didn't judge me, and who didn't seem to want anything from me other than company.

'It is,' she agreed, opening her eyes and smiling at me. She looked amazing, all curves and glistening dark skin packed into a red and white polka dot bikini. I kind of wished, just for a moment, that I *was* a lesbian—being Vogue's secret lover probably wouldn't be so bad.

'It's good to be around people you feel you can trust,' she said. 'You don't get a lot of that in this business. And I think it'd be even better with a top up…'

She twisted around to get the now half-empty bottle of wine that was on the tiled floor behind her and, as she did so, the gold chain she was wearing around her neck rode up. It was a long, long chain, and had been draped so far between down her cleavage that it disappeared from sight.

She turned back around, brandishing the bottle, with the necklace now fully pulled free of her boobs.

As she poured herself a glass, and reached out to refill mine, I stared at the pendant, feeling the colour drain from my cheeks. My fingers started to tremble, and I suddenly felt ever so slightly nauseous.

No, I told myself, firmly. It's just a coincidence. It's not what your horrible, suspicious mind thinks it is. It's nothing… nothing at all.

'Babe,' said Vogue, frowning at me. 'What's wrong? You're staring at my tits and looking a bit like you're going to throw up in my new Jacuzzi. You okay?'

I met her gaze, and felt my mouth go dry. I had to talk to her, but my body didn't seem to want to co-operate with that idea. My body seemed to want to go into some sort of catatonic state while my mind pieced together what it thought it was seeing. Part of it did, anyway—the other part was busy calling that part names, and chucking the mental equivalent of rotten tomatoes at it.

'Erm. No. I'm not going to throw up. I don't think, anyway. Vogue—Paulette—that necklace…'

She glanced down at her breasts, at the gold chain, and at the stone dangling from the bottom of it. The small but perfectly formed stone that looked very much like a ruby, cut into the shape of a heart. It was gorgeous. It was unusual. But it wasn't unique. In fact, I had one very similar to it back home—but as per Jack's instructions, I'd not been wearing it in public in case it gave the correct-but-not-ideal sign that I was attached, when I was supposed to be young, free, and single.

As she looked at the pendant, Vogue wrapped her fingers around it, stroking the stone and smiling.

'Oh, yeah. I'd forgotten I had this on. It's nice, isn't it?'

'It is,' I replied, voice shaky. She didn't seem upset by me asking about it, or overly sensitive about me noticing it. Maybe I was just having one of those dumb girl panic attacks for no reason.

'Is that a ruby?' I asked.

'Yes,' she said, still stroking the glinting heart. 'It was a gift. It's my—'

'Birthstone?' I asked, almost whispering the word, and praying that I was wrong. That I was making crazy assumptions. That buying your girl a hand-crafted birthstone necklace was common—that it had been featured on some 'chick gifts made easy' style article in *FHM* or something.

'Yes again!' she said, still smiling, still looking as though there was nothing at all wrong in the world. I had the terrible suspicion that I was about to spoil illusion for her. 'How did you know?'

'Because I have one like it at home. Except it's an emerald, because my birthday's in May. It's exactly the same pendant— the same heart shape, on the same sideways angle. I was told by the person who gave it to me that it was hand-made, just for me.'

Vogue's eyes started to widen, and the smile finally began to fade from her face. She gulped the rest of the wine that was left in her glass in one huge mouthful, and put it down on the tiles. After a few moments of silence between us, where the only sounds were the bubbles in the Jacuzzi and Mr Sledge singing very inappropriately about the things a man is willing to do when he loves a woman, she eventually asked the question that neither of us really wanted to hear—but that had to be asked.

'Jess, who gave you your emerald necklace?'

'Jack,' I said simply. 'Jack Duncan gave me my necklace. I suppose I have to ask—who gave you yours?'

Chapter 30

It had been an absolute shit of a night. The answer to my question had been exactly what I'd dreaded it would be—Jack Duncan.

After the initial shock had worn off, we both decided that this was a conversation best had on dry land. We climbed out of the Jacuzzi, both of us silent as we processed the situation, and wrapped ourselves up in big, furry bathrobes. Taking the wine back upstairs—this was definitely going to be a chat that needed to be accompanied by wine—we settled in on the biggest leather couch in the lounge, and also cracked open a giant bag of Doritos. Emergency rations.

'How long?' Vogue asked, squeezing the words out from the side of her mouth that wasn't crammed with Doritos.

'A few months,' I replied. 'It didn't start straight away. Well, the flirting did, I suppose. But not the…you know, the…'

'Shagging?'

'Yes,' I said, blushing for some reason. 'The shagging. You have to believe me, Vogue—Paulette—I had absolutely no idea that he was seeing you as well. There is no way—no way—I would have got involved with him if I had. I…I just don't do stuff like that, you know? I don't shag other women's men, plain and simple. I honestly had no idea.'

'I know that, hon,' she said, reaching out to pat my robe-wrapped leg. 'I could tell from the look on your face when we both realised what was going on. And I had no idea about you, either. It's not our fault, and we need to stick together now—blaming each other won't do us any good.'

I nodded, feeling pathetically grateful for that Girl Power moment. Because if Vogue had decided it *was* my fault, she was big enough and strong enough to have drowned me in the Jacuzzi by now.

'What about you and Jack?' I asked. 'How long has that been going on?'

'Oh, not long…' she said, her voice laced with bitterness. 'Only about five bloody years. Five years of sneaking around, and secret meetings, and constantly being told it was "best for my image" if we weren't seen together. Five years' worth of various excuses and lies and, now I'm seeing it a bit more clearly, a pathetic lack of self-respect on my part. I can't believe he's done this to me. And I can't believe I let him…'

Tears started to flow down her cheeks, which was all it took for mine to join in and start a sympathy sob. I knew exactly what she meant, it felt terrible—and I hadn't wasted five years of my life on Jack like she had.

I looked back on all the times he'd bullshitted me—all the times he'd told me he was 'busy at a meeting', or come up with yet another reason why we couldn't go public. All the times he'd assured me in private that we were real, that I mattered to him. All the times he'd presumably been giving poor Paulette exactly the same lines—but for a lot longer.

'He told me I needed to be single,' I said, swiping away my own tears angrily. 'That it was better for me to be seen as single. That people might think I'd slept my way to the top if they found out about us.'

Vogue gave a tight little laugh, one that contained no real humour at all, and replied: 'Yeah. He said similar stuff to me too, to start off with—except he was worried about people thinking he was exploiting me. To be fair to Jack, I've known him since I was a teenager—he did at least wait until I was in my twenties to start up with me. And I got the same lines. I think, with hindsight, he loved all the mystery of it. Kept me on my toes, always keen to see him. It was exciting and illicit and forbidden—he even asked me to use a phone just for him. Remember that time you called me, and I answered by calling you sexy or something?'

I nodded, remembering it vividly—it was the number I'd lifted from Jack's phone without him knowing.

'That phone was one only Jack had the number to—so whenever it rang, I'd know it was him, and only him. When you were on the line, I was totally freaked out—and I should have realised right then something was off. I know he wouldn't have given that number to you, so you must have girl-snooped it from his phone, yeah?'

I nodded again, feeling a bit like the Churchill dog.

'I did,' I said. 'I was round at his flat, the night you were sick. The night of the first gig at Panache.'

Vogue was staring off into space, chewing her lip so hard I could see spots of blood appearing.

'Yeah. That night I was sick—the night I was here, on my own, puking my guts up. The night he'd told me he loved me, and that he'd be round first thing in the morning to check on me. To be fair, he was—and I was so grateful. I don't think I'd have been quite so grateful if I'd known he'd spent the night with you, Jess.'

'Oh God, Vo—I mean Paulette—I am *so* sorry…'

'No!' she said, snapping her eyes back to mine. They were big, and round, and filled with tears that spilled out as soon as she blinked. 'It's not your fault—let's not even go there. There's only person at fault here, and that's him.

'I've listened to his advice for so long, I think I was blind to what was going on. You probably weren't even the first, Jess, let's face it. I met Jack when I was seventeen. He changed my whole life—he created Vogue, if I'm honest. He shaped me and moulded me and I've always trusted him. I've made decisions based on his views, and lived my life in a way he thought was best…and now here we are. Two girls crying into their wine, and wondering where it all went wrong. Part of me is devastated and hurt—but part of me just wants to kill him. Do you know what I regret the most?'

I shook my head. I had no idea—but I suspected I was about to find out. Her pain, her anger, were so fierce and so raw, I felt I had to keep mine inside for just a little while longer.

'Simone,' she said simply. I frowned at her, confused.

'Your little sister?' I asked.

'Well, that's the thing, you see. She's not my little sister.

She's my daughter. I had her when I was sixteen. It was… God, it was one of those teenage things, you know? I was trying to be tough, trying to be cool and impress some boy, and ended up pregnant while I was still at school. I can't blame Jack for that—and I can't blame him for what we decided next. Me, my parents—we moved to Peckham from a different estate, and started over. We told all our new neighbours that the baby was my mum's—a late in life miracle—and I went back to college. It seemed to make sense at the time… I was just a kid myself.

'But college didn't work out—because I ended up leaving Paulette behind, and becoming Vogue instead. I was young enough and selfish enough back then to want that more than I wanted anything else—it was way too easy to concentrate on myself and leave Simone with my mum and dad. And I've had to forgive myself for that. But once she was two or three, I really wanted to find a way to tell her. My parents agreed, and we decided we'd do it by stealth—she was young enough for us to do it back then, without it totally freaking her out. I'd move back in, they'd move out, and gradually, I'd become Mum. And, once it was sorted at home, I'd go public. Except… well, you can probably guess the next bit.'

'Jack,' I said simply, my heart breaking for her, for Simone, for myself. For the whole bloody mess. 'Jack advised you that it would ruin your career. That it would expose Simone to the tabloid press. That your parents would start getting papped. That the best thing you could do for everyone was keep it a secret.'

'Pretty much word for word, Jess, yeah. Now I think—well, I know—he was only really thinking about Starmaker, about himself. I'd made a lot of money for them by that stage—and he didn't want anything to happen that could threaten that. He fooled me into thinking he was saying all of that crap for my sake, for the sake of my family. But he was only thinking of himself.'

I puffed out my cheeks, swigged some more wine, and chewed some more Doritos. I was hurt beyond belief. My confidence was shattered, and I also felt decidedly dirty—the thought of him jumping from my bed to Vogue's and back again made me feel sick, as if I needed to scrub myself with bleach.

Everything he'd ever said to me about our relationship had been a lie—one that I'd fallen for hook, line, and sinker. My sister Becky had always hated him—and now I realised why. She'd seen beyond the good looks and the veneer of charm, to the selfish, scheming snake that lay beneath it all. He might have given both Vogue and me our big breaks—but he'd also broken our hearts.

'So,' I said, after we were both silent for a few moments. 'I think we can both agree that he's been an absolute bastard. I suppose the question is, what are we going to do about it?'

'We're going to make him pay,' she replied, her voice quiet and determined and frankly all the more terrifying for the low volume. 'We're going to make him pay, and we're going to get whatever we want. Tomorrow, we both pretend like nothing's happened. We go to work, we do our jobs, we smile and laugh and reply to those stupid text messages he's likely to send to both of us. Then at some point—after this hangover has worn off—we get together, and we plan. We plot and we scheme and come up with a way to turn all of this to our advantage. What do you say?'

'I say,' I replied, clinking my glass against hers. 'That I'm in—a hundred per cent. He's not going to know what hit him.'

The fighting talk made us both feel better, I think. Certainly, it was a lot better than crying and wallowing and feeling sorry for ourselves—but it was a high that only lasted as long as I was actually with Vogue.

By the time we'd drunk the house dry, compared war stories, and called Jack every name under the sun, I was exhausted, and so was she. I crawled into a cab at about three in the morning and fell asleep while the driver navigated his way to my apartment building.

When he woke me up, shouting, 'Oi! Sleeping Beauty! We're here!' very loudly through the plastic partition, I was dazed and confused and a complete mess. My eyes were swollen from crying, and I was drunk to the point where I couldn't be bothered fumbling for change, and just gave the cabbie two twenty pound notes and muttered 'Keep the change' as I almost fell out of the door and onto the pavement.

Luckily, there were no enterprising photographers lying in wait in the street, or they would have had an absolute eye full of me, Jessika, staggering around like a faulty wind-up toy, bumping off walls and feeling my way to the doors with my hands, as my eyes seemed to be too blurry to function properly.

I tried to pull myself together as I made it into the lobby, doing that 'I'm-not-really-pissed-look-I-can-walk-in-a-straight-line' strut that actually just announces to the world that not only are you completely off your head drunk, but you're daft enough to think you're not. I waved at the doorman as I passed his desk, and he said something to me in reply. I couldn't completely understand the words, so I just smiled, waved again, and pressed the lift buttons. Possibly, I pressed all the lift buttons, as it seemed to stop on every single floor before it reached mine.

I was dying for a wee by that point, and desperately hoped the lift wouldn't get stuck between floors. It's the kind of thing that occurs to you when you're hammered and watching lift doors constantly open and close in front of you while you jig about on one leg.

When I finally made it to my floor I zigzagged out down the hallway to my flat, wondering how many attempts it was going to take for me to use my key. I got it out in advance, practising in the air in front of me.

It was only when I was right by my door that I realised there was something in front of it. Or, to be more precise, someone.

I frowned and stared at the small heap of black clothing, curled up in a ball on my doorstep. I poked it with one pointy-toed boot and a smooth black head emerged, like a mole coming up for air.

The face followed, along with a pair of trendy glasses knocked askew by his impromptu kip, and recognition finally kicked in.

'Neale!' I shrieked, unbelievably happy to see him. My gay best friend. My partner in wine. The man who knew my body almost as well as Jack—the bastard!—knew it. I leaned down to hug him, and almost fell over in shock when he knocked my hands away.

'How could you, Jess?' he asked, standing up and glaring at me as I tried to regain my balance. 'I thought we were friends—how could you do that to me?'

Chapter 31

Ten minutes later, I'd had a wee, which came as an enormous relief. I'd splashed my face with cold water. And I'd made both me and Neale big mugs of coffee, which it looked like we could both use.

I was still technically drunk, I was sure, but the fact that the person I thought of as one of my closest friends in London was staring at me with what I can only describe as hatred was quite the sober-up.

Neale's usually impeccable clothes were rumpled from having been collapsed outside my front door for several hours, his eyes were red-rimmed from crying, and there was a sore looking crease on the bridge of his nose where his glasses had dug in.

'I just can't believe you said that about me,' he muttered, wrapping his shaking hands around his mug.

'But…said what, Neale? I don't even know what I've done! Please, tell me, so I can make it right! I've had the worst possible day, and—'

'Well, that's bloody typical, isn't it? Here I am, looking at the scrap heap that is now my life, and it's all about you! All about the megastar that is "Jessika"!'

He used his fingers to create sarcastic apostrophes around my name, and I closed my eyes for a moment. I could actually feel my hangover starting to develop behind my forehead, and wanted to do nothing more than to take my poor, battered heart, and my poor, battered head, and climb under the duvet for a few hours. Which, I thought, forcing myself to pay attention to Neale again, was just about as selfish as he was accusing me of being.

'Neale. Please. Tell me what's wrong.'

'I can't even believe you're saying you don't know. That either means you think so little about me that you don't even remember discussing me in an interview, or you're lying. Either way, it all spells bitch. I don't know why I even waited out there for you…'

I stared at him, feeling fragments of memory bind together in the confusion soup that was my brain. Discussing him in an interview? I did discuss him in an interview—the one that Vogue had said had gone online. The one about our night out after the single launch. The one that used a picture of us outside McDonald's. Could that be it? Could that be what had upset him so much?

'Erm…do your friends think you're a vegetarian?' I asked, realising as the words tumbled from my mouth how ridiculous they sounded.

'NO!' he shouted, standing up tall and waving his hands at me. It probably would have looked a little more intimidating if he wasn't so short, but he made up for it with his absolute fury. His eyes were full of tears as well, and I guessed he suffered from the same disease as me—crying when he was angry as well as crying when he was sad.

'You said I was gay! In an interview! With a national newspaper!'

'But…you are gay, aren't you? Surely you are—you snogged about four people that night, and they were all blokes!'

He sighed, completely exasperated with me, and I felt really sorry for him. I knew I was drunk, and being dense, and making things even worse, but I didn't quite have the mental wherewithal to pull myself back together.

'Yes, Jess. I *am* gay. But my parents—my extremely religious, extremely conservative parents—don't know that. Or, they didn't know that—until they started getting calls from friends asking if they'd seen the story about their Neale. Now they do know—and they might never talk to me again! How *dare* you discuss me like that?'

I sat down heavily, feeling the horror of what he was saying seep through me bit by bit. It wouldn't be a big deal in my house if one of us was gay; but clearly, Neale's house was a different kettle of fish.

'Okay…right. But, how did they *not* know? It's so completely obvious…'

'Does that even matter, Jess? Maybe I'm less of a flaming queen when I'm at home. Maybe they don't know any gay people and aren't quite sure what the signs are. Maybe you should have just kept your big, fat mouth shut!'

'Couldn't this be, I don't know, a good thing? I mean,

my mum and dad would still love me if I told them I was a lesbian…surely they won't mind that much?'

He stared at me, as though he couldn't quite believe what he was hearing, and I suddenly wished I was recording this whole conversation on my phone so I could listen to it the next morning. I knew I was going to wake up with that horrible, vague self-worth problem, knowing I'd said loads of stupid things but not quite sure what, and having to piece it all together as the flashbacks came.

'You are unbelievable, Jess. Completely unbelievable. My relationship with my parents is absolutely none of your business—and it's certainly not your place to decide to break the news to them that their only son is gay. I might have told them, one day, when I felt it was the right time. But that would have been when *I* decided—not you, Jess! It's nothing to do with you—you've created this whole stinking drama, and now you're trying to convince me it could be a good thing? And somehow judging my parents for not being as cool as yours?'

I really wanted to say something in return, but couldn't think of a single thing that made sense and that wouldn't make the situation worse. Not a single word. Instead, I just flapped my lips like a goldfish, and tried to look contrite.

After a few seconds of me not replying, Neale threw his coffee mug at the sink. An arc of black liquid sloshed out of it and splattered all over the wall, and the mug itself shattered as it landed. We both jumped at the noise.

'You,' he said, pointing his finger at me accusingly, 'need

to learn when to keep your mouth shut. You also need to find yourself a new stylist, because I'm out.'

As he stalked towards the door, slamming it behind him as hard as he could, a single word finally came to mind. The one I should simply have said to start with.

Sorry.

Chapter 32

The next few days were among the weirdest I'd ever experienced in my entire life. I had an official number one single; I had a massive row with my parents; and I took blackmail photos of my cheating scumbag boyfriend. I also had to get to know a brand new stylist, as Neale had disappeared home for a few days, and wasn't returning my calls. No matter how many messages I left, he ignored me—and part of me didn't blame him. I'd let my big mouth run away with me again, and he was the one dealing with the consequences.

Predictably enough, the morning after the night before was hellish. I had a hangover the size of Mount Everest, coffee stains on my kitchen wall, and a massive dose of man-related misery. That thing happened where for just a few seconds, after you first wake up, you forget how sad you're feeling and everything seems normal—and then you remember and it all crashes in on you like an avalanche of pain.

I couldn't believe what Jack had done to me. What he'd done to Vogue. That we'd both fallen for it, both fallen for him. Everything I thought I'd loved about him was now soured. Even remembering the great sex made me feel a bit sick—

knowing now, as I did, that it wasn't in any way exclusive. At least not on his side—I might have cast a few curious glances in Daniel's direction, but I'd never done anything about it. I just wasn't that person.

I felt so violated and betrayed, and cursed with vivid images of Jack with me, and Jack with her, and Jack with God-knows-who. In the end, I had to try not to ponder it too deeply—I was sure, if I tried hard enough, I'd be able to pinpoint days where he went from me to her or vice versa, but I'd probably go mad in the process.

It was all just too disgusting to contemplate, and I couldn't think of a single time I'd spent with him without it being tainted. Even the innocent stuff—the walks around Hyde Park, the coffee shop dates, the Italian meals—felt ruined now. It had all been a lie—everything he'd claimed to feel about me had been a lie. Presumably he lied for sex, or for control, or just because he was a psycho bastard—I had no idea.

None of it was making me feel good about myself. My last boyfriend, Evan the window cleaner, had cheated on me as well. There was a pattern emerging. I spent hours feeling sorry for myself, thinking that maybe it was something to do with me. Maybe I was crap in bed, or ugly, or boring. There must be something wrong, if this kept happening to me—I must be defective in some way. And maybe it would keep on happening—perhaps I was just one of those women, fated never to be able to keep a man loyal.

Plus, if the situation with Neale was anything to go by, I wasn't even capable of keeping a friend either. In fact, I was an all-round loser—even my own family was pissed off with me.

I'd called home later in the afternoon the day after, following a cathartic scrubbing session where I'd cleaned the
coffee marks from the kitchen paintwork. I don't know what
I'd hoped for—perhaps to tell them something of what was
going on. Tell them my heart was broken. Tell them about
Neale. Tell them I felt sad and lonely and lost and blue.
Except it didn't quite work out like that. My mum answered,
and at first it was fine—the usual chit chat about life in general,
catching up on neighbourhood gossip that now seemed to have
no relevance to my world, discussing Becky's birth plan, Nan's
latest trip to the diabetes clinic, and a few digs about the fact
that I'd bothered to call at all.

I suppose that put me on the defensive—I knew she was
right. I hadn't called for days, hadn't even messaged them
or sent one of my traditional selfies. There had been reasons
for that, but she didn't know them. Being blatantly, horribly
honest, I'd called her because I needed a shoulder to cry on,
and I wasn't that interested in what was going on at their end.
It all sounded a bit petty and pointless compared to what I
was going through—which tells you a lot about how messed
up my head was.

'So,' she'd said, after filling me in on everything I wasn't
bothered about, 'when are you coming up for Christmas, love?
We can't wait to see you, especially your nan. She saw a
picture of you on the front page of the *Echo*, at a film premiere
or something—Becky tells me you were wearing Prada, but
your nan's convinced you bought the entire outfit with her
Matalan gift voucher.'

I laughed at that one, and promised not to tell her otherwise.

The conversation went downhill from that point on, when I had to break the news that, actually, I wouldn't be making it home for Christmas at all. I'd been booked to film a live TV broadcast from London, along with Vogue and several other big names in music. I was the newest and the least famous of all of them, and it was quite a big break to have even been invited—plus, I would be getting paid a ludicrous amount of money.

The only problem was, of course, that I'd have to be here. In London. Not in Liverpool with my family.

My mum had gone silent, and I waited for the barrage of abuse that was about to come my way—I even held the phone away from the side of my head just in case the noise levels exploded my ear drums.

Instead, she was just quiet, which was kind of even worse. Eventually, just as I thought maybe she'd passed out and I should be calling 999 and ordering an ambulance, she spoke.

'I see, love. Well, if that's what's best for your career, then that's what you'd better do. Your nan will be disappointed, though. She's not really well enough to travel down there and see you, like we are. And I don't want to be a drama queen, but she might not have those many Christmases left, you know.'

'I'll make it up to her,' I said, feeling even worse than I had when I picked up the phone. 'I'll get her a brill pressie.'

That, apparently, was the wrong thing to say. Which was fast becoming my specialist subject.

'I don't think she really needs anything, Jessy. She's eighty-five and lives in sheltered accommodation—what are you going to get her, a Mercedes mobility scooter? All she really wants from you is your time, which seems to be the one thing you're not willing to give.'

'I can't help it, Mum! It's not my fault!'

'Well, we all make our choices, love. We all do what we think is best—but I'm telling you now, living with those choices afterwards is the real challenge. Saying things weren't your fault doesn't really help when you realise how much you regret something.'

Right then, the only thing I regretted was calling my mum in the first place. Or at least calling my mum and not bursting into tears straight away. This hadn't gone the way I'd planned at all—which meant it fitted in perfectly with the rest of the disaster zone that was my life. I hadn't planned to fall in love with a man who was already in a relationship with one of my friends. I hadn't planned to alienate my family, or Ruby. And I hadn't planned to destroy Neale's entire life. Maybe, I thought, it was time to actually start planning—and not just keep stumbling along hoping everything would be all right.

'Okay, Mum. Message received and understood. I'll see you in the New Year.'

I'd hung up before the tears started. I knew they were coming, and I knew they were because I was angry as well as suffering on account of Jack. I also knew that I had to start taking some action, and I texted Vogue straight away.

We arranged to meet at her place, both of us looking and feeling like microwaved crap, and set up a battle station at her kitchen table.

She sympathised about the situation with Neale, saying that one of the biggest lessons you had to learn once you were famous was 'how to think before you open your mouth', and encouraged me to try and make up with my family. I understood where she was coming from on that one—but at the end of the day, just as Neale had said to me, my relationship with my family was my business, and nobody else's.

I was more than happy, though, to listen to her ideas about Jack Duncan—and how we could both make ourselves feel better by giving him a dose of some very nasty medicine.

Once we had all our plans in place—which happened pretty quickly, as being screwed over by your boyfriend seems to be a great motivator—we high fived each other and agreed to put the dastardly deed into action the night after.

Jack, bless him, made it all very easy for us. I spoke to him on the phone, and invited him round to the flat for a 'special night in'. After that, there was a spate of saucy messages between us all day, with the tone getting racier and racier with each one. Little did he know that far from me sitting there getting turned on, I was actually sitting there crying, and wondering if I'd ever trust a man again. It was hard to keep the façade up all day—but I managed it.

I had a lot riding on my ability to make this work—we didn't just want to pay Jack back, we wanted to make sure he couldn't ever hurt us. At the end of the day, neither Vogue nor I could simply cut him out of our lives—he existed. Starmaker existed. We needed Starmaker for our careers—so killing Jack and mincing his body up in a sausage machine wasn't going to be possible.

By the time he arrived, I was in a state of absolute madness. I'd had two glasses of wine, changed into a flimsy black baby-doll outfit that I'd bought for the occasion, and done my hair and make-up to the very best of my abilities. The negligée was all sheer net and lace, and I was wearing matching fishnet stockings and suspenders—I needed to look like a knock out. I needed to look so good, he wouldn't notice there was anything wrong with the way I was behaving.

It worked. As soon as I answered the door and he took one look at my outfit, he was all over me—there was no time for talking, no time for me to crack up and start swearing at him, and no time for me to look into those big, brown eyes of his and start sobbing. Instead, we started kissing, and I led him over to the bed and pushed him down onto it.

He lay there looking up at me as I straddled him and started to undo his buttons, clearly thrilled beyond belief at this new dominatrix side of me. Every time he started to talk, I shut him up with a kiss—not that I wanted to kiss him, or ever touch him again, but it was better than engaging in a conversation with him. I didn't trust myself that far.

Within a few minutes, he was stark naked and chained to the bedpost by the pink fluffy handcuffs I'd been sent for free after my first gig at Panache. The ones I'd swiped before Patty could veto them, and had had in my wardrobe ever since, just waiting for the right chance to use them. I hadn't imagined this would be it—but there you go. Life is full of unexpected little twists, isn't it?

Once I had the cuffs on and I'd tied his ankles snugly with black silk scarves, I leapt off him, and took a moment to tidy myself up before I called my partner in crime.

'Jess?' he said, looking confused—his boy parts still bobbing around in excitement, his hair all messed up, and his wrists starting to pull at the cuffs. Only a few days ago, I'd have been pleased as punch to see his gorgeous body stretched out on my bed; now I just felt sad. 'What are you doing? Where are you going?'

'You know that newspaper article, Jack?' I said, walking towards the bedroom door and opening it. 'The one about me having a threesome?'

He nodded, and I saw a flash of curiosity in his eyes and a smug smile curling his lips. Lips that had been on every part of my body, which now made me want to remove my skin with sandpaper. He looked so happy—he genuinely seemed to think that his wildest pervy dreams were about to come true, and I was going to bring out Ruby or some other friend, and all three of us would have wild, S&M-flavoured group sex.

He was partly right—I did have a friend with me. Strangely enough, though, he didn't look too happy when he saw who it was.

For the first time ever, I saw Jack lost for words, as he gazed up at both of his girlfriends—both of his furious looking girlfriends—and realised that he was handcuffed to a bed with no way of escaping our wrath. He wasn't just facing one woman scorned—he was facing two. He started to wriggle and tug at the bed post, trying to get away, and finally found a few words—really rubbish, predictable, pathetic ones along the lines of 'Wait, wait, I can explain!'

Vogue didn't give him the chance to explain anything. She covered the distance between the door and the bed in two long strides, and was on top of him, grinning with way too much relish.

'Now,' she said, stroking his face in a scary parody of affection, 'we can play this two ways. You can scream and wriggle and fight, and I'll cut your balls off. No. Don't argue. You know what my temper is like, Jack—you know I'll do it. Jess and I have discussed this, and we'll back each other up—we'll say you wanted to play some kind of perverted sex game that went horribly and tragically wrong. I have no idea how long it'll take you to bleed to death, because we won't be in that much of a rush to call the paramedics...and even if you do survive, you'll be living the rest of your life without your bollocks. How does that sound?'

Jack had paled to the point where he resembled Casper the Ghost, and his lower lip was trembling as he tried to find words. I was actually a little worried about Vogue at that point, I have to admit—we had, in fact, never discussed our evil plan for a pretend sex-game-gone-wrong, although it wasn't a bad idea. It was certainly working on Jack, whose crotch was looking a lot less happy than it had been a few minutes earlier.

'Erm...' he mumbled, eyes never leaving Vogue's determined face. 'What's option number two?'

'You apologise, nicely, to both of us. You promise to never, ever do anything like this again to any other woman. And you guarantee that this little exchange of views will have no effect at all on our careers. At some point, when we want something from you, we get it—no questions asked. Simply because you owe us, you cheating fuck.'

'Yes!' he snapped, quickly, desperately. 'I agree! Yes!'

'And,' I added, getting our bag of goodies out of the wardrobe, 'you take part in a little photoshoot with us, Jack...you know how important image is, right?'

Half an hour later, Jack was fleeing the building with his tail well and truly between his legs, and Vogue and I were sitting, laughing our heads off on the sofa, wine bottle open, flicking happily through the picture collection on my phone:

Jack in a stylish feather boa and corset combo. Jack in a long blonde wig with clip-on hoop earrings. Jack in full make-up, complete with my Scarlet Harlot lipstick. Jack in a very fetching pair of white stilettos that we'd picked up at a shop that specialised in clothes for the gentleman who was in touch with his feminine side. Jack in intimate oral contact with one of the battery-operated products that had been sent in the same package as the handcuffs.

Finally, just for kicks, one with both of us, posing either side of him, pointing at his now less-than-impressive manhood and giggling. That was extra mean—it was completely understandable, under the circumstances, that he'd retracted in on himself like a baby turtle—but it was funny. And anything that made us laugh at this particular time in our lives was more than welcome. We were both in pain—but taking some control back had made us feel better. The wine probably helped as well.

At about two in the morning, when we'd given up on Jack and were watching ancient episodes of *Gossip Girl* on cable, instead, we checked the download charts.

'Midnight'—by Vogue, featuring Jessika—has charted at number one.

Chapter 33

I don't think I'd ever been so cold in my entire life. It was Christmas Day, and I was dressed in a short Santa suit, prancing around outside the London Eye. It wasn't a porno-level-short Santa suit, but it was small enough to make me wish I was wearing leggings instead of fake tan and furry Ugg boots.

I'd been there since about seven a.m., sheltering in the Portakabins and warming my hands around paper cups of hot chocolate, waiting for the actual broadcast—which would use up about four minutes of my life.

I'd been in hair and make-up, I'd rehearsed my lines—although it wasn't actually that challenging to say, 'Happy Christmas, everyone!'—and I'd filmed various clips that would be inserted through the live feed. We'd done trips in the capsules, taking in the amazing views and ooh-ing and aah-ing appropriately. The views were amazing—I just preferred the ones from the Liverpool equivalent.

Now we were preparing for a big group scene at the end, where everyone would make their Christmas wishes then all sing 'Have Yourself a Merry Little Christmas', with live reindeers in the foreground.

The live reindeers were not only live, they seemed to have had a curry the night before, and one of the poor TV staff—probably an intern—had to keep rushing forward with a shovel to clear up the less-than-festive remains.

Everyone—apart from us lot, the shivering 'stars' being filmed—was dressed up in jeans and sweaters and gilets and bobble hats and gloves, rushing around with cameras and clipboards and microphones, looking busy and important and most of all warm.

'Hey, kiddo,' said Vogue, sidling up to me, dressed in a similar outfit and looking just as chilly, 'welcome to the exciting world of the outside broadcast. This is glamorous, isn't it?'

'Yeah?' I said, teeth chattering. 'Compared to what? Cleaning a sewer?'

'All part of the job, babe,' she replied, laughing. 'And it's good PR. Your smiling little face broadcast live on Christmas Day. What are you doing later?'

'Oh,' I said, 'the usual: eating, drinking, being merry.'

In reality, I was trying not to think too hard about what the rest of my day held. I'd spent the morning with some of the most famous faces in the UK, as well as the arse-challenged reindeers. But the afternoon? Well, it looked like I'd be spending that alone. I couldn't think about it right then, or I'd burst into tears, and the whole make-up thing would be ruined. I didn't want to be broadcast live to the nation looking like a saddo.

She looked at me with a cynical sideways glance, and added: 'Do you want to come to mine? My mum and dad's, anyway? There's always enough food to feed an army.'

For a moment I was tempted—but I shook my head, and said thanks but no thanks. I was feeling a lot more miserable than I'd thought I would about being away from my family, and spending time with someone else's might just push me over the edge. I was probably better off going back to the flat and wallowing in private.

Luckily, I couldn't start my wallowing just then, as the countdown to live broadcast started—and enforced happiness was the order of the day. I wasn't feeling the Christmas spirit— but I hoped I was faking it well enough to not be a party pooper for the millions of people who might be watching. Including my own parents, I thought, wondering if they had the TV on while they all slouched around the living room waiting for the turkey to cook. And if they did, would they be proud of me, or would they boo and hiss as if I was a pantomime villain?

I did the rest of the broadcast on auto pilot, and then got hijacked for a few more interviews. Patty wasn't there—I'd heard a vicious rumour that not only did she have a family of her own, but that she was with them in Newcastle. *Newcastle.* After all the stick she gave me for my Scouse accent, it turned out she was a Geordie who'd had a few elocution lessons.

Even without her, though, I think I did okay. The whole thing with Neale had kind of helped—as Vogue said, I needed to learn to always think before I spoke. That came in especially handy when I was asked my opinion of that year's Christmas number one—the song that had knocked me and Vogue off the top spot. It was called the Parsnip Rap, and came with its own party dance, performed by two grown men dressed in life-sized vegetable suits. My real opinion ran something

along the lines of 'what a load of shite', but I managed instead
to give a big grin, do a few of the dance moves, and say how
much I loved it.

After that particular ordeal was over, I gave Vogue a hug,
and climbed into the car Starmaker had sent for me. I drove
home in silence, but remembered to hand the chauffeur a big
tip as I got out at the flat. I didn't need to—he'd told me he
was on triple time—but what can I say? I'm the daughter of
a cabbie, and tips had paid for all my dance lessons as a kid.

By the time I made it back to the flat I was ready to sleep
for a million years—not just because I was tired, but because
I was bordering on the depressed, I think.

I'd woken up alone on Christmas morning for the first time
ever. I had the bathroom to myself—no Luke lurking in the
background to prank me. I didn't have to help Mum peel the
mountain of veg she had ready in the kitchen. Nobody was
throwing sprouts at my head. I didn't need to shout everything
at sonic boom volume so my almost-deaf nan could hear me. I
didn't have to put up with Dad wearing his hideous Christmas
jumper, complete with wobbling antlers on his bald head. I
didn't have to put up with anything—it was so peaceful I could
have been in a morgue.

I wandered through to the bedroom, thinking I'd probably
just crawl under the duvet and wake up once it was all over.
My folks had left a message on my phone earlier, all shouting
'Merry Christmas' to me, all sounding as loud and raucous
as ever—but somehow, I couldn't bring myself to call them
back. Maybe it was pride; I'd made the decision to stay in
London for Christmas. I'd made the decision to reject them.

I'd chosen my career over them—and now I had to accept the consequences, just as my mum had said.

Perhaps they'd think I was a snotty cow for not calling. And perhaps I was—but I didn't have it in me. I didn't have the energy to try and reconnect with them, and wasn't even sure I wanted to. Every time we spoke, I seemed to get told off, and I was too fed up to deal with the risk of that happening again.

I sat down in front of the dresser mirror, thinking I should take off my make-up. Thinking, as I stared at my pantomime-dame-level slap and spray-bouffed hair extensions, that I should take everything off. Just get rid of it all, even if it was just for a day.

I started with the make-up, brutally scrubbing the seventeen layers off with wipes and lotion, leaving my skin red and blotchy. Then came the eyelashes, which not only hurt like buggery as I didn't do it properly, but also took a few chunks of my real lashes with them.

There wasn't much I could do about the acrylic nails without hurting myself or faffing around for hours with hot water and varnish remover, but I did at least take off the bright red polish they'd painted on me this morning.

Hair extensions were next—and at least I only had clip-ons. One by one I removed them, piling them on the surface until it looked like a Golden Retriever had shed its coat. I half expected them to move, come alive like a Gremlin and bite me on the nose.

By the time I'd finished de-glamorising myself I looked like a totally different person. I realised that under the layers, my skin was dry and pale. My eyelashes were now stubby. My real hair looked flat and dull without its extra boost. Without all the lining and sculpting and definition, my face was…normal. Not hideous, just normal. Only slightly worse than the way I used to look, back in the days when I was Jessy. When I could leave the house without hiding under all of this—when I didn't always need to look perfect, to be photo-ready, to shine and sparkle even when I felt like I was dying inside.

I looked at the pile of discarded hair, cotton wool, spidery lashes and soiled baby wipes scattered across the dressing table. I'd shed my skin, like a snake—and I wasn't quite sure what lay underneath any more.

It was Christmas Day. I'd snubbed my family in Liverpool and wanted more than anything to call them back. The man I'd thought I'd loved had turned out to be a cheat who now did everything he could to avoid being near me. Neale still wasn't returning my calls.

It was Christmas Day, and I was completely alone. I wasn't sure who I was any more. I supposed I was becoming Jessika—and I really wasn't sure I liked her.

I swept everything off the dresser and into the bin, even the hair extensions. I was starting to see how silly I was being. I had a number one single; I finally had what I wanted. I should get over myself and call my mum back.

I picked up the phone and dialled but it just went through to voicemail.

I was rooting through my drawers for a suitable onesie, still thinking that sleep was the best option, when I heard my phone beeping to tell me that a message had landed. I hoped it was my family.

I pulled the phone out of my bag and stared at the screen, wondering if I should do an 'au naturel' Jess selfie and scare them all to death.

I realised then that the message wasn't from my parents. It was from Daniel.

'Merry Christmas, Jessy,' it said. 'Hope you're having a good one.'

Three kisses and a winky smiley.

On impulse, I hit the Call button, thinking I'd get voice-mail. Instead, I got the man himself. I could hear music in the background, something loud and fast and bass-y.

'Sorry—are you at a party?' I asked, immediately regretting the fact that I'd called. Daniel might be back in my life—but we weren't teenagers any more. We didn't live next door to each other, we didn't have sleepovers, and I shouldn't expect him to be my own personal counsellor every time I felt a bit gloomy.

'Nah,' he said, 'I'm in the car on hands-free. That's one of my client's tracks in the background—I'm not quite happy with it yet. I stayed at my mum and dad's last night and I'm on my way home—the B&B's full, so they're cracking on with Christmas lunch for their guests. Where are you? You okay? We saw you on telly—Mum almost wet herself, she was so excited! She ran round telling everyone who was staying there that she knew you.'

I smiled at the thought—at least I'd cheered someone up by staying in London.

'I can't believe you're on the motorway on Christmas Day, Daniel. Shouldn't you be opening presents and getting drunk on Baileys?'

'I like the motorway on Christmas Day. It's completely empty, so I get to drive too fast, listen to rap, and pretend I'm straight outta Compton. And Baileys is a girl's drink.'

'You love Baileys.'

'I know. I was just trying to be macho. As soon as I get home I'll be cracking open a bottle. What about you—any glamorous showbiz parties to attend?'

'No,' I said, after a pause. 'No showbiz parties. No family lunch. Not even a bottle of Baileys. I'm all by myself, as the old song goes.'

He didn't reply and for a moment I thought we'd been cut off.

'Well,' he said eventually, the music suddenly gone, 'If you want to, you can come over. See the studio. Meet my cat. Say hello to Ruby. Share my Baileys.'

'I would,' I said, pathetically grateful for the offer, 'but I'm in London. And you're in…where the hell are you anyway?'

'In Sussex. The South Downs to be precise. It's only about two hours from there, you know…if you were interested. I could send you directions. Do you have a car? Or are you too drunk to drive already?'

'Cheeky bastard!' I snapped, grinning even as I said it. 'I'm not drunk! I don't have a car, either, but I do know a very nice driver who works for Starmaker. And, as luck would have it, I gave him a massive tip about an hour ago.'

Chapter 34

By the time I'd met the cat (Kylie) and said hello to the cow (Ruby) and helped him collect eggs from the chicken coop (all the chickens were named after members of Girls Aloud), it had gone completely dark. And by that, I mean really, really dark—not city dark, but countryside dark. The farmhouse was set in its own land, tucked away in rolling hills, miles from what I thought of as civilisation. There were more stars shining in that velvety black sky than I'd ever seen in my life. It was beautiful, and incredibly quiet. I could see why he preferred it to packed clubs in London.

After doing the chores and having a look around Daniel's impressive-to-the-max recording studio we settled down inside, wrapped in blankets and lounging on the sofa together in front of a wood burning stove. I'd called at a corner shop on the way there and bought the very best set of festive gifts I could find—more Baileys, a giant box of Roses, a set of clothes pegs, and a bottle of Brut aftershave. It was what you might call an eclectic mix—but it was better than nothing.

We were both drinking the Baileys, and both eating the

chocolate, but I left the Brut all to Daniel. He doused it on liberally before we sat down, and was now stinking the room out.

'Is it wrong,' I said, wrinkling my nostrils, 'that I'm starting to find that smell attractive? It should remind me of my uncles or something, but it's actually kind of…sexy.'

'That's because I'm wearing it,' he said, giving me a comedy wink that made me laugh out loud. Really, he was such a dick. But he was an adorable dick—especially in his own home. He was wearing a battered, faded old pair of Levis, and an equally well-washed black T-shirt that was snug enough to show off his buff new physique. His feet were bare, which just felt especially intimate, and his blond hair was freshly showered and flopping in a touchable, silky mass across his forehead. Plus, he smelled of Brut.

I, on the other hand, was probably looking the worst I'd looked for years—and certainly since Daniel had come back into my life. Every time he'd seen me, I'd been 'done'—and now I was the total opposite. I was completely undone, in many different ways.

'I'm sorry I look like the elephant woman,' I blurted out, as soon as the thought crossed my mind. I'd turned up on his doorstep in leggings and a baggy jumper that reached my knees, carrying a bag that only contained clean knickers and a onesie. Compared to my usual image, I looked like a refugee seeking asylum in his countryside kitchen.

'Erm…you don't?' he said, frowning at me. 'You just look like the real you. You look beautiful, just like you always do. So give over—you don't need all the crap to look good, Jess.

At least not with me. I've held your hair out of your face while you were sick, remember.'

I smiled at him, feeling tears well up in my eyes at his comments. He was so, so…perfect. Always had been, always would be. I didn't know quite what I'd done to deserve a friend like him—or if that was even all he was these days. When I looked at Daniel now, I didn't just see a friend. I saw a fit, healthy, drop-dead gorgeous, grown-up *man*. But a grown-up man who still seemed to 'get' me in exactly the same way his teenaged self had. I'd sat next to him on a sofa drinking many times before—but this time, it felt different. At least it did to me—I had no idea what he was thinking.

'Yeah. You were always good at that, and I took terrible advantage of you, Daniel. I'm a bit worried I still do, if I'm honest—turning up like this, interrupting your life, bringing all my drama.'

'Yes, but you brought Baileys and Brut as well as drama, Jess, so I forgive you. What's up anyway? If you don't want to talk about it, we don't have to. We can just sit here and chat and drink and maybe later, I can hold your hair back while you're sick. But I can tell there's something wrong—what is it?'

'I think,' I said, unable to stop the tears from finally spilling, 'that, actually, everything is wrong. My family can't stand me. My best friend Neale blames me for ruining his life. My boyfriend was cheating on me. And… I just don't know who I am any more, Daniel. It's all just so…fucked up!'

'Come here,' he said simply, gesturing to his side. I did as I was told, and scooched over. He nestled me into his chest, took my legs and placed them over his lap, wrapped his arm around me, and rested his chin on my head. I was completely cocooned in Daniel, and it felt good. It felt safe.

'Now,' he added, once I'd snuggled in and he'd thrown the blanket over us both. 'Tell me everything. And let me know if the Brut fumes are about to give you a blackout.'

'I might get snot on your T-shirt,' I said, sniffing the fabric and finding that everything smelled just perfect. The mix of Brut and Daniel and whatever he used for his laundry was a marvellous blend of sex and security.

'I have more T-shirts. Now spill.'

So I did—tears, snot, and all. I told him about the breakdown of relations with my family, some of which he'd witnessed himself. I told him about missing my nan's birthday, and cancelling Christmas, and not spending any time with them when they visited, and about me never phoning them. About how guilty I felt about getting angry at them because I was stressed and tired, about how I always felt pressurised, and as if I'd let them down, and as though they were constantly disappointed in me instead of proud of me.

I told him about Neale, and how close we'd become, and how great he was, and how we'd helped each other through our crazy early days at Starmaker—how we'd been friends when I was just an intern, and even more so once I made it. And about how I'd accidentally outed him in the national media, and even though I hadn't meant to, I'd completely cocked up his domestic life.

I told him how tired I was. How all the interviews and appearances and shows had drained the life out of me. How the thought of even singing any more felt exhausting—even if

I could ever find a song I wanted to record and release. I told him how I had my own intern, Tilly, who I barely even knew, who organised my whole life for me, and that I'd actually thrown a pen at her head a few days ago; I'd been in the offices signing a stack of photos to be sent out to fans, and the pen had run out. So, just like Patty before me, I'd taken out my petty frustrations on an innocent bystander.

And then, in between the sobs, I told him about my love life. At first I was hesitant, just saying 'my boyfriend', or 'the guy'—until he interrupted me mid-sentence.

'Jess. It's all right. I'm not an idiot—I know it's Jack Duncan. You've always had terrible taste in men—I've known that since you snogged Gareth Murphy at the Christmas disco when we were fourteen. So tell me the whole story, and don't worry—what happens in Sussex, stays in Sussex.'

'Isn't that supposed to be Vegas?' I bleated, embarrassed beyond belief that I was so predictable.

'No. That saying was invented in the South Downs. Not a lot of people know that. Now, go on—finish your story. You'll feel better once you're entirely drained of tears, and you *will* run out eventually, honest.'

So I did. I explained how Jack's charm had sucked me in. I explained how gullible I'd been, and how I'd unwittingly played a part in hurting Vogue, someone who'd been nothing but kind to me. I told him how it had all but destroyed my confidence, and made me wonder if I was even capable of finding a man who genuinely cared about me. How I'd been so lonely ever since. That I'd barely seen him since our show-down, and felt nervous every time I walked into Starmaker, in case that was the day he decided to get rid of me—I was no Vogue. He could axe me whenever he wanted. So as well as the heartache, I was walking on eggshells worrying about everything else as well.

And finally—not realising how much it had bothered me until I said it out loud—I told him how I'd walked out of Yusuf's flat all that time ago, and never even bothered going back to explain, or to thank him for looking after me so well.

By the time I'd finished, I was a damp heap of emotion, and was sobbing openly into Daniel's now very soggy T-shirt. It didn't seem to bother him—he was a man of steel, in fact, and just kept holding me, stroking my hair, and gently kissing the top of my head to comfort me. Eventually, as he'd predicted, I simply ran out of tears.

I peeled my face away from his top, barely able to see straight through my swollen, puffy eyelids, and gazed at him.

'So,' I said, grimacing and wiping my snotty nose on my sleeve. 'Still think I look beautiful?'

He laughed, and held my wet face between his hands.

'Always, Jessy. Always. Now, do you want my advice, or did you just need to get all of that out of your system?'

'I want your advice,' I replied, sniffling. 'You're probably the one person in existence who understands both my old world and my new one. And now, you're definitely the only person who knows all my deep, dark secrets.'

'You mean the fact that you're an ugly crier?'

'Shut up!' I said, mock-punching him in the bicep and realising it hurt me more than it hurt him. He was a man of steel in more ways than one these days.

'Okay, okay… I think, Jessy that you already know what you need to do. You know what you've done wrong—and now it's up to you to fix it. Your family love you—they always will. You just need to go and see them, give them some of your time, let them know they still matter to you. You've always been a family girl at heart—and if you cut them out of your life you'll wither up and die. That simple. With Neale? Well, I don't know Neale—but if he's your friend, he'll forgive you. You just have to make him see how sorry you are. I've worked with so many people in this industry who've made terrible mistakes in the media—it happens. You've learned from it. Hopefully, he'll be able to see that you mean it.

'Your career…well, I have some thoughts on that, Jess. We spoke a few days ago about me writing for you and since then, well, I have been. Once you'd put the idea in my head, it wouldn't go away. I have material. Good material. Stuff that's right for you. *But*—I won't come to Starmaker. I don't think its right for you, and it's definitely not right for me. I never liked Jack Duncan and, after what you've just told me, I feel like driving to London and beating the crap out of him.'

'You can't,' I said, settling back into my cuddle position, 'you've had too much Baileys.'

'I know. But there will be other opportunities. Maybe I'll deck him at the Brits. So, you need to think about your future—do you really want to follow this road? All you're doing is being touted around as a person who's famous for being famous! Do you want your whole career to be a few crappy singles you don't even like, a semi-successful album,

and then a stint on some reality-TV show when it all starts
to go tits up?

'You were always serious about your music—even at college, you could take control of that stage, and make everyone
pay attention. You've always been a star—Jack Duncan didn't
create you, he just noticed you. You have one of the best voices
I've ever heard, even after the last few years working with pros
from all over the world. You're special, Jessy—and I think if
you follow the path Starmaker has you on, you'll lose that. I
think the Jessy I know and love will be dead and buried—and
Jessika with a K will be the only one left standing.'

I'd been listening to every word he said, honest I had, and
it all made perfect sense. But I'd also been a bit distracted by
the fact that my hand had somehow found its way beneath
that black T-shirt of his. It wasn't intentional—it just kind of
drifted, seeking contact and comfort, and before I knew it, my
fingers were resting on his bare skin. Skin that was covering
ridges of muscle that he definitely didn't have when we were
seventeen.

And then, in the middle of all of his brilliant advice and
suggestions that I knew were right, came that one phrase—one
that maybe he didn't even know he'd said.

'The Jessy you know and *love*?' I asked, looking up at him.

He froze still for a moment, the gentle stroking movements
in my hair stopping and his vivid blue gaze meeting mine
head on.

I knew I looked awful. Like something from a horror film.
And I knew I'd had a bad day, and too much to drink, and,
by own admission, had been making some rotten decisions

lately. But suddenly, this felt right—the spark that I'd sensed between me and Daniel was starting to ignite into something a lot brighter. We both knew it, and I hoped that this time, we weren't going to ignore it.

'Yes,' he said, a gentle smile tugging at the corners of his lips. 'I love you, Jess. I always have. And I've been waiting to do this for way too long…'

He tangled his fingers into the hair at the back of my head, pulling my face slowly, steadily, towards his. He paused for a moment before our lips met, and I nodded slightly. Yes. This was what I wanted—what I'd wanted ever since Daniel had walked back into my life. What I wanted more than anything just then.

He nodded back, and kissed me.

It was one of those kisses that starts off slow, and gentle, and soft—both of us taking our time, letting the feeling sweep us away, stepping into unknown territory and enjoying every second of it. Savouring it, relishing it, surrendering to it. I could feel his fingers in my hair, on my neck, stroking my cheeks, bringing everything he touched to life. Even his warm breath against my skin felt sexy.

It was…wonderful. The best first kiss I'd ever had—and a sure sign of terrific things to come. I knew then, as our tongues touched, as our breathing deepened, as we both sighed with arousal, that every time I'd looked at Daniel and felt attracted to him, I'd been right. That this was right. He wasn't just my friend—he was way more than that. And as our kiss became more intense, more desperate and urgent, my body was letting me know that it wanted more. Much more.

The fingers that were already underneath his T-shirt started to explore further, and I heard Daniel sigh as I stroked his flesh, all the time maintaining the passionate momentum of that kiss.

Without even breaking lip contact, he picked me up, then lay me back down on the sofa, his own body following until he was stretched out on top of me—long, lean, and gloriously hard in all kinds of ways.

He finally broke away from my mouth and moved his attention to my neck, my ear lobes, my throat; pulling the fabric of my sweater away so he could drop soft, sensual kisses on my bared shoulders, and the sensitive skin of my collar bone.

I really, really wanted to be able to see his body, as well as touch it, and started to tug at the hem of his T-shirt, trying to pull it up and off over his head.

'You have too many clothes on…' I muttered, smiling as he sat up, still straddling me, and shrugged out of his top. He was, to put it bluntly, magnificent—all lean muscle and flat lines and smooth skin, his perfectly cut torso disappearing off into Levi's that I'd previously admired, but that now seemed to be getting in the way of what we both wanted to happen next.

In one of those comedic shuffling around moves that romance novels never prepare you for when you read about sex as a teenager; I managed to pull my baggy sweater off as well, getting my arm caught at a funny angle and losing all sense of dignity when it stuck around the top of my head. Daniel, grinning, finally tore it away, and looked down at me in my bra—not even my best one, it has to be said—as though he'd never seen anything quite so fascinating before in his whole life.

The way he looked at me—my face, my eyes, my breasts,

my eyes again—made me feel like a goddess. It wasn't just
lust—I'd seen that from men before—it was amazement. It
was desire; it was reverence. It was love.

I blinked my eyes, slowly, and realised that I'd managed
to dredge up a few more tears, just when I thought the well
had run dry.

'Don't worry,' I said, when he noticed and started to look
concerned. 'I'm not sad. I'm just…surprised. And excited.
And turned on. And…it's been a mad day. Would you like to
take those jeans off? You look a bit—uncomfortable.'

He smiled and glanced ruefully at the action-packed denim
straining at the seams. He climbed off me, and I waited for
him to unbutton them.

*

Just as he was reaching the good part—pulling them down
over his angular hips—his phone started to ring. And ring. And
ring. At first he did the logical thing and ignored it, letting it
skitter around on the table. But as soon as it stopped, it started
again—and it went on and on and on.

'Aaaagh!' he said. 'It'll be my mum—I forgot to let her
know I was home, and she'll be convinced I've been killed in
some freak motorway accident. She won't stop calling until
she knows I'm all right…'

I nodded, and bit back a smile. Frustrating as the interrup-
tion was, I got it—mums were just like that. He did a funny
hopping jump over to the table—disabled by a combination of
his jeans being half down, and having what looked like some
serious problems in the boxer department.

He grabbed up the phone, spoke incredibly quickly to his mum, and switched it off. I expected him to hop straight back over to me and continue where we left off.

But he didn't. He looked at me, and smiled, and then just stood there, bare-chested and glorious, running his hands through his hair until he left ruffles. He sighed, blew out a long, frustrated breath, and scooped his T-shirt up from the floor.

'I think that's what you call saved by the bell,' he said, still keeping his distance. He started to fasten his jeans back up as I looked on in confusion.

'What do you mean?' I asked, caught completely unawares and feeling my own frustrations take hold. I'd enjoyed having Daniel on top of me. I'd enjoyed touching his skin, and feeling his lips against mine, and I'd wanted more. I thought he had—but instead, he was backing off just as we seemed to reach the point of no return.

'Don't you…don't you fancy me?' I said, feeling suddenly humiliated. 'Did I do something wrong?'

'No!' he said, firmly, sitting down next to me and covering me with the blanket, tucking me in gently until I was completely wrapped up. 'Don't ever think that—I have *never* fancied anyone more than I fancy you! Even when you think you look like the elephant woman, even when you've been crying so much your baldy eyelashes are glued together, you're still the most beautiful, gorgeous, and sexy creature on the planet. I'm sure you noticed I wasn't exactly bored during that, Jessy—and at least a few of my body parts are regretting ending it.'

'Mine too. So. Why? What's wrong?'

He reached down, and gently tucked a few stray strands of hair behind my ear. I kissed his hand on the way, and he grinned at me.

'Don't do that. I'm only flesh and blood—and I can only hold off for so long.'

'I'm not sure I want you to hold off—I'd quite like you to hold on.'

'I know,' he said, sitting himself out of reach at the far end of the sofa and tickling my toes instead. He knew I was really ticklish, and it was hard to feel sexy when you were laughing so hard you can't breathe.

'Okay,' I said, sitting up myself, and putting my sweater back on. 'I get it. Fun time's over. But I'm still waiting for a reason. You've not signed up to some kind of chastity thing since I saw you last, have you?'

'Hardly,' he smirked. 'And I've not been living like a monk, waiting for you to come back into my life, Jess, pleased as I am that you did. I want this—I want it badly. But I also want it to be right. There's too much in your life that *isn't* right at the moment. We've spent ages talking about the things that aren't right, including the fact that you're still screwed up over Jack. I think, before we start this thing between us, that you have to fix some of those things.

'I want us to be together. I think we've always had something special, and I want to find out just how special—but this isn't the time to begin. I know what I want, a hundred per cent—and I know, right now, you think you want the same. But that, if you'll forgive me for saying so, is lust speaking.

That's not enough. Before this can work you need to sort yourself out, Jessy. I'll help you any way I can.'

I raised an eyebrow at him, and he laughed. I could think of at least one way he could help me.

'Any way but that. Look, does that make sense? Any of it?'

'Annoyingly,' I replied, pouring us both another glass of Baileys. 'It does. I don't want it to, but yes, it makes sense. So. I'm going to have another drink. I'm going to sleep it off. And tomorrow, I'm going to start sorting it all out.'

Chapter 35

I started with the easier ones.

Well, not easier—just more geographically convenient. The London-based items on Jessy's Giant List of Things to Sort Out. This was a list I'd compiled—mentally—while sitting at Daniel's big, scarred pine kitchen table on Boxing Day, as he cooked me an omelette made from Girls Aloud's eggs.

I'd eventually passed out on the sofa halfway through watching *Die Hard* the night before, and when I woke up I was in bed in Daniel's spare room. He'd taken off my leggings, but left me in my long jumper and pants, and there was a bottle of water and a pack of paracetamol on the table next to me.

My very first thought, once I'd woken up, stretched, and relocated my brain, was that I wished I wasn't in Daniel's spare bed. I wished I was in his bed, with him—even if it was just for a cuddle. A cuddle, I now suspected, that could definitely develop into something more, and I was feeling remarkably frisky for a hungover chick who'd recently had her heart broken.

Maybe, I thought, rolling over and hugging the pillow instead, that told me everything I needed to know about my relationship with Jack. If I could wake up days later dreaming about sex with another man, how real could it have all been? It had felt real. The love had felt real, and the pain had certainly felt real. But perhaps—perhaps—I'd been more infatuated than in love? I now realised that I didn't even really know Jack Duncan. I'd never met his parents, or heard him talk about his childhood, or seen embarrassing photos of him as a little boy.

I didn't know what he'd been like at school, or what he wanted to be when he grew up, or where he'd gone to university, even though I knew he had. I'd never met any of his friends, or talked about his ex-girlfriends, or seen what he put in his trolley when he went to the supermarket. Apart from meeting his horrendous niece the summer before, I knew nothing about him—it was as though the Jack Duncan I knew had sprung from the womb, fully formed, as a Starmaker record executive.

He'd been charming and sexy and he'd played me absolutely perfectly—he'd actually made me work for it, which made our relationship even more exciting. Looking back, I felt sick at exactly how naive and trusting I'd been. I'd mistaken a casual fling for something much more. Even one night of *not* having sex with Daniel had shown me that.

Now, I could see things a lot more clearly—even if my eyes were still swollen from crying.

Daniel drove me all the way back to London, and we parted ways outside my flat with a long, lingering kiss that left me breathless, desperate for more, and utterly convinced that I needed to get on with that mental list. If my own conscience hadn't been driving me, sexual frustration would have been.

I took the rest of the day to let myself decompress and think about what I was doing, and what I wanted to do. My life had been completely mental for so long now—I'd not had a minute to sit still, take stock, and think. I'd been bouncing all over the shop like a pinball in a machine, ricocheting from one set of circumstances to another. In my desperation to become a star, to be a success, I'd lost sight of what really mattered—and it was time to figure at least some of that out.

I started the day after by visiting Yusuf. I found him where he usually was—behind his counter wearing a hairnet and a stripy apron—and stayed for a good half an hour, eating my free kebab and signing a poster of me he had Sellotaped up on the tiled walls of the shop. He now had a new tenant, he told me—but he wasn't anywhere near as pretty as me, and played loud dance music at all hours of night and day, and if I ever wanted to come back, he'd let me have the flat again.

I didn't really want the flat again; nostalgic as I felt, I could still remember the damp and the cramped bathroom all too well. He settled for a hug and the promise that I'd stay in touch, and I left.

My next stop was more difficult. I caught a cab from Kentish Town to Clapham, where Neale had a tiny ground-floor flat that looked out onto the Common. On the way, I called at a florist's shop and bought him an enormous, totally over-the-top bouquet of flowers. He might end up lobbing them at my head, but a girl could only try.

As I stood on the steps, waiting for him to answer, shivering in the icy breeze, part of me was hoping that he might not be in. Even though it was a Monday, and usually his day off, the cowardly lion section of my mind was wishing for him to be at work so I could run away from it all.

Typically, I had no such luck. Neale opened the door, wearing a red-and-black kimono that yet again made me wonder how on earth his parents hadn't known the truth about him. He took one look at me, my face peeking out from behind the flamboyant lilies and black orchids, and said, 'My God. Did you steal that flower arrangement from Elton John's house?'

'Yeah,' I replied, nervously. 'I had to mug David Furnish to get it. Can I come in, please, Neale?'

He waited for a few moments, his arms crossed over his chest, chewing his lip and staring at me. Eventually, he turned around abruptly and walked back into his flat. I followed quickly, just in case he changed his mind and slammed the door in my face.

'Erm…where do you want these?' I asked, gesturing at the flowers.

'I don't know. My bouquet room is being refurbished at the moment. Just put them down in the corner there. What do you want, Jess?'

'I want to apologise,' I said simply. 'I messed up. I didn't think before I spoke, and what I did was unforgivable—well, hopefully not completely unforgivable. I just wanted to say how sorry I am, even if you never want to talk to me again. And to tell you I've learned my lesson—I promise I have. I'll always think before I speak from now on, at least to the media—I probably can't promise it all the time, you know what I'm like.

'You've been such a good friend to me, Neale, and I don't

want to lose you. I'm gutted that I hurt you. I never intended
to, I was just a naive idiot. And I'll do anything to make it up
to you, if you will just give me the chance.'

He looked undecided for a moment, and I wasn't sure if
he was going to kick me out or not. Then he pushed his little
glasses back up on his nose in a gesture I was so familiar
with, and said, 'I'm making coffee, with brandy and squirty
cream. Are you in?'

'I'm in,' I said, more relieved than I could ever have
imagined.

Chapter 36

The next thing I had to fix was a lot more complicated. In fact, it took several days of scheming, several secret meetings between me and Vogue, and a call with Daniel where we all spoke over each other on speaker phone.

Ultimately, we came up with a plan. It was ambitious and risky and brave, and if we pulled it off, it would change our lives—mainly mine and Vogue's, admittedly, but Daniel was right behind us. I think he genuinely believed in what we were doing, but he also probably wanted to stick it to Jack in a way that he knew would probably hurt him a lot more than a punch in the chops would hurt him.

We'd checked with Heidi that Jack was at the office and not in one of his many 'meetings'—which both of us now assumed could very likely mean shagging someone else—before we turned up. We didn't have an appointment, but we did have killer outfits and a lot of righteous justification, which was just as good.

The look on his face as we walked into his office together was absolutely priceless—a combination of terror and a vain attempt to seem professional and in control. He gestured at the seats in front of his desk, instead of inviting us to sit on the casual sofas in the break-out area—obviously, he felt a bit safer with a block of wood and steel between him and us. As Vogue had threatened to remove his testicles the last time we were all together, I can't say that I blamed him.

'How can I help you?' he asked, pushing some paper around on his desk, checking his phone, tapping his fingers and generally looking like he had ants in his pants. It was so strange, how I'd once found him irresistible; now, when I looked at him, I saw how handsome he was, but it did nothing for me.

'I'm leaving,' said Vogue, simply. 'And I'm taking Jessika with me.'

He stared at her for a moment, frowning. Clearly, what she was saying did not compute. His hands finally stopped fidgeting and he gave us both his full attention. I'd seen this face before—this was Serious Starmaker Jack. This was business—and possibly even more important than his testicles.

'You can't,' he replied. 'You're both under contract.'

'I think,' I said, stepping in and loving every second of it, 'that you'll find I'm not. Legal never drew one up for me, and, as you told me, I didn't really need a manager because I could trust you with everything, nobody ever chased it up.'

'But we've been paying you…' he spluttered, completely and ironically outraged at my apparent lack of loyalty.

'For services rendered,' I said sweetly, giving him a wink. 'I've worked hard for Starmaker. I've done everything you asked—I was on the single, the video, did all the promo, all the appearances. Plus, you know, I was sleeping with you as well, in case you'd forgotten. I'm not sure if that counts, but I'd be happy to discuss it with HR and accounting if you need me to.'

Jack narrowed his eyes and glared at me. I had him, and he knew it. I felt Vogue stifle a laugh in the chair next to me, and silently high fived her under the table.

She was hurting a lot more than I was at Jack's betrayal—it had been going on for so much longer for her, and she'd sacrificed so much more than I had. I knew she was still in pain—but she was taking the direct approach to recovery. The Girl Power approach.

'And you, Paulette?' he asked, turning his gaze to her. He even managed to look sad. 'You want to leave me too?'

'Oh, yeah,' she said. 'More than you can possibly imagine. And I *am* under contract—but my lawyer is going to talk to your lawyer, and we're going to sort it all out as quickly and amicably as possible, aren't we Jack? Because you promised you'd make things easy for us. And because you owe me. And because…we still have the photos. It's a liberal business—nobody would really care if you were a secret S&M trannie. Apart from you, that is.'

He nodded, taking it all in, and leaning back in his chair. He looked at us both for a few more seconds, obviously turning everything over in his scheming little mind, wondering how he could get out of this mess.

Presumably, he didn't come up with anything—and the next words out of his mouth were: 'Fine. Now both of you, get out of here. Leave the building, and don't come back.'

We stood up, and Vogue gave him a jaunty salute before

we walked out of the office, out of Starmaker, and into our brand new world.

The world where In Vogue Records was about to be born, with a completely fresh approach to music, performing, and talent. The world where In Vogue Records would work with cutting-edge producer and songwriter, Wellsy. The world where In Vogue Records would, within a month, make its very first signing—the incredibly grateful, incredibly excited, Jessika.

Chapter 37

'What did you say, love?' my nan asked, peering at me over her bifocals, her little face wrinkled up like a pickled walnut.

'I said,' I repeated for the third time, 'I'm SORRY I MISSED YOUR BIRTHDAY!'

'Oh, that's all right, girl,' she answered, settling back into her wheelchair. 'I've got plenty more in me, don't you worry. I'm planning quite a do for my ninetieth.'

I leaned down and kissed the skin of her papery cheek, and tucked her tartan blanket more firmly around her skinny legs. She really was great, my nan.

She was also very much enjoying herself, being out and about, and getting lots of fuss made of her in the auditorium of my old college. I suspected she'd had a couple of paper cups of sherry, and she had a death grip on her plate of sandwiches, gnarled old knuckles holding on for dear life.

My mum was sitting next to her, at the end of a row that also contained my dad, Luke, and Becky, who was taking up two seats and glaring at anyone who dared ask her to move up.

It was the first week in January and I'd been home for three days. Three days of apologising and explaining and listening. Which wasn't as bad as it sounds—the listening part, especially. Once I was out of my London bubble, away from the insane pressures of Starmaker, away from my infatuation with Jack and my obsession with chasing fame at the cost of all else, life made much more sense.

I'd sat in our living room, nursing mug after mug of tea, talking things through with my family. Listening to how worried they'd been—about my schedule, about my lifestyle, about my weight loss, about the types of people I'd been mixing with.

Everything I'd mistaken for an attempt to control me, as judging me, was nothing of the sort—it was worry for me, worry that they didn't know quite how to deal with. And I'd thrown their concern back in their faces, time after time, eventually almost cutting myself off from them completely— the lack of phone calls, not coming home for Nan or for Christmas, snubbing them when they'd come all the way to London and were making every effort to spend time with me. Fobbing them off on Tilly. Storming out on the single launch. Even hanging up on my mum on the phone, which still made me cringe.

'You see, you daft cow,' Becky had said, throwing a cushion at my head. I batted it away before it made contact—years of experience. 'You were getting a cob on with us, and it was just because everyone loves you so much.'

'I know,' I replied, chucking the cushion back at her, but gently, as she was a baby mama the size of Jabba the Hut.

'I'm really sorry,' I said, to all of them. Apart from Luke—
he'd got fed up with the girl family drama after about half an
hour and was playing *Call of Duty* in his bedroom instead.

'It's hard to describe,' I continued. 'The way everything
changed. It wasn't just the fame, it was the time before it—
when I was an intern, as well. I was so embarrassed at how
badly everything was going. I felt humiliated by the fact that
I felt like I was failing, letting you all down when you'd
believed in me. When you came down to visit, Becky, and
it was all so crap—I was obviously nothing there, and Patty
was, well…'

'Patty was a bitch to both of us,' Becky finished for me.
'I can't believe you're thinking of asking that woman to join
you and Vogue at the new label.'

'She's excellent at her job,' I said, grinning. 'And we've
made it part of the deal that she has to use her real accent. She's
a Geordie. Anyway… I was low. So once things started to pick
up, once it all started to happen, I kind of lost my balance I
suppose. I was so desperate for it all to work out. I had all
these ideas and plans—and I wanted to pay your mortgage
off, Mum and Dad, and make life easier for you.'

'Oh, love,' said my dad, squeezing me into a giant Bald
Eagle-sized hug. 'You daft mare. We paid our mortgage off
about five years ago!'

'What!' I spluttered. 'Why do you both still work so hard
then?'

'We like work, Jessy,' answered Mum, smiling gently at me.
'It's just part of who we are. Neither of us is ready to retire just
yet but believe me, when we do, we have a few bob tucked

away so we can afford the odd cruise or a hip replacement. We're your parents—it's our job to look after you, not the other way round. At least until we're as old as Nan, and you lot can be on wheelchair duty.'

I shook my head in amazement. I'd been such an idiot. I mean, I hadn't been chasing fame just for them—I wanted it myself, badly. I still did. I still wanted to sing in front of packed crowds, and record music that affected people's lives, and be able to use any talent I had to live a full, rich life. But at least part of my motivation had always been them—and I'd been self-obsessed and arrogant enough to think that if I made it I'd be able to swoop in like the big hero, and solve all their problems. I was starting to realise, the more we talked, that the main problem they'd had recently was *me*.

'I'm so sorry,' I said again, shaking my head. 'I've been a tit. I hope you can forgive me.'

'Course we can,' said Becky, grimacing as she lumbered to her feet. 'You're our Jessy whether you want to be or not. You're stuck with us. Now, I'm off for my hundredth pee of the day. Is Daniel coming to this thing tomorrow night?'

She'd paused in the doorway, waiting for my answer.

'I don't know,' I admitted, feeling my heart sink a few inches. 'I suppose we'll see.'

To be fair to Daniel, I'd organised this event all by myself— no Tilly, no Patty—at the very last minute. A special appearance at the college, where I'd sing a few songs, talk about my time there and how it had started me out on this path, and answer questions. I'd donated some prizes for a big raffle—signed pictures, merchandise, some autographed albums that Vogue had given me—and all the funds were going to the college's Performing Arts department.

I suppose it was part of my attempt to make up for being such an idiot—getting back to my roots and all. I'd even called Ruby and invited her. I think she was more embarrassed about the story in the papers than I had been, plus she'd broken up with Keith, which had to be a good thing.

I wanted Daniel to be there—he was part of my past, and I desperately hoped he'd be a permanent part of my future—but all he'd said was he'd try and make it. It was short notice, and he was busy being an internationally renowned music producer. Our relationship was still completely undefined, and neither of us had made any promises. I knew I had no right to expect him to come—just a whole lot of hope.

*

And now we were here, and my nan was half cut, and the place was absolutely packed and completely buzzing. As the head teacher introduced me, and I walked up into the stage, I felt more nervous than I had at my own single launch, or on a live TV broadcast on Christmas Day. I felt nervous because this was home—this was where the heart was, and this was what mattered.

I didn't have Neale with me—he was serving out his notice with Starmaker, and would be coming with me and Vogue as well—and had done my own hair and make-up. There were no backing dancers. No clever lighting. No dry ice. It was just me, and some video from my end-of-term show from all those years ago. Just me, a microphone, and my voice—and that would have to be enough.

In the end I really shouldn't have worried. The reception was mental—like those scenes on *The X Factor* when the contestants go home in the last week. There was screaming and shouting and so much applause I thought the roof might come in, and then I'd have to do another concert to raise funds to replace it. I was asked questions I expected, and questions I didn't, and I was as honest as I could possibly be. At the end, after doing 'Midnight', I sang the final song from Daniel's school show—the one where our triumphant cheerleader heroine saves the day, and saves the planet.

By the time I finished, the place was in uproar. It was so strange, standing there, listening to the applause and the cheers, all those years later. I was older, and wiser, and there was a whole ocean of experience under the bridge—but in some ways, I felt exactly the same. Blinded by the dazzling glow of the lights, deafened by the response, sweating from the effort. Gazing out at those bopping blobs and knowing I'd entertained them, knowing they were cheering for me. It still felt worth it—especially with my family back in my life, waving and shouting with the best of them.

Eventually, after several minutes of insanity, the curtains closed, just as they had done back when I was a teenager. I could hear the head teacher out front, urging everyone to get more raffle tickets and get their refreshments and to believe in their dreams (in that order), and smiled. I'd done it—and it had felt better than any of my other appearances so far.

I glanced around, taking in the familiar surroundings—the

wooden floorboards and the faded red velvet curtains and the clunky lighting suspended from the ceiling. The clutter in the wings, the electrical wires held down with duct tape, the random props from previous shows stacked in the corners. The same smell of sweat and dust and organised chaos.

'It's hardly changed at all, has it?' said a voice from the shadows. A voice I knew. A voice I loved.

'No,' I said, waiting for him to emerge from his traditional hiding place backstage. 'Unlike us.'

Daniel walked forward, tall and broad and lean, hair perfectly clean and not a spot in sight, unlike his seventeen-year-old self. He'd definitely changed—and not just in the way he looked. He was still private; he still protected himself from what he perceived as showbiz insanity. His farmhouse was now his version of hiding in the sound booth back when we were teenagers. But these days, he did it because he wanted to, not because he was shy—he was confident enough, successful enough, to survive in that world. He just chose not to, and I had to respect that. He'd always been better at seeing through bullshit than I was.

And me? Had I changed that much? God, yes. Beyond recognition. I'd been on a heck of a journey, as they always say on reality TV shows. And now I was hoping, as Daniel approached me, that this particular stretch of the journey was about to have a happy ending.

He closed the distance between us, and I reached out to hold both his hands. He was smiling down at me, and the look on his face gave me more of an adrenalin rush than a number one single and playing Wembley combined. It was that very special look he had—the one that made me feel so treasured, so cherished, so very, very wanted.

He stroked the side of my face, and I leaned into his palm, kissing it gently with my lips. He was here. He was holding me.

It was real.

'I'm glad you came,' I said, looking up to meet his eyes, thrilled at what I saw there. 'I wasn't sure if you'd be able to come.'

'And miss this?' he replied, tugging me closer so our hips touched. 'The famous Jessika, reprising her very best role? That cheerleader song is still awesome.'

'I still have the outfit somewhere at my mum and dad's, you know.'

'Really? Maybe we'll have to crack that open sometime. Although I might turn into a hormonal, crush-ridden teenager again, and be too tongue-tied to tell you what I need to tell you.'

'What's that?' I asked, wrapping my arms around his waist so tightly I thought I might never let go. 'And before you answer that question, I have sorted things out. I've untied the knots in my brain, and I know what I want now.'

'And what do you want, Little Miss Sorted?'

'I want you,' I answered simply.

'That,' said Daniel, 'is very lucky. Because I need to tell you that I love you. That I've always loved you. That I want you so badly it's borderline embarrassing. And that I was hoping you felt the same way. I always knew you'd be a star, Jess—but I could only ever hope that you'd be mine.'

He traced his fingers around my jaw, and turned my face up to his, before leaning down for the kind of kiss that any girl—cheerleader, fake Disney Princess, intern, or pop star—would quite happily die for.

Epilogue

We were all crammed into one tiny room at the maternity hospital, breaking all the visitor rules, making way too much noise, and generally being a nuisance.

Me and my mum were perched on the edge of Becky's bed, and the menfolk—Dad, Luke, and Daniel—stood around the edges, all holding cigars that only my dad would enjoy.

Becky herself was propped up on pillows, looking grey and drawn and exhausted, and somehow managing to appear vibrantly happy at the same time. Both the exhaustion and the happiness probably had a lot to do with the tiny bundle of humanity currently curled up on her lap—Oliver Sean Philip, who had entered the world five hours earlier, at the ridiculously healthy weight of ten pounds nine ounces.

His bright red face was so chubby his eyes disappeared in the folds of his flesh, and he had a shock of eye-piercingly red hair tufting from the top of his big, round head.

'He looks like a fat matchstick,' said Luke, peering at him cautiously. He'd been traumatised by the fact that Becky had her boobs out when we first arrived, and was playing it safe now.

'Thanks, shithead,' said Becky, obviously wishing she could move, but too sore and too laden down to manage. She raised one eyebrow at me, and I got up and gave Luke a slap round the head on her behalf, hard enough to make him yelp.

'How are you feeling, love?' asked my mum, stroking the baby's head and gazing at him in absolute wonder. Dad had burst into tears the moment he'd walked into the room, and now Mum looked like she might follow suit. Becoming a grandparent, it seemed, had been a very emotional experience for them.

'I'm all right,' she replied, giving her a little smile. 'Just knackered. Happy, but knackered, you know?'

'I do,' my mum said. 'That's the way it stays for the next twenty years, hon.'

I reached out to touch Ollie—he was bound to end up as Ollie, or even Ol, as everyone in Liverpool has their name abbreviated—and his tiny, super-soft fingers wrapped around one of mine. I felt tears well up in my eyes, and decided that becoming an aunty was a very emotional experience too.

I glanced up to look at Daniel, and he gave me one of those gentle half-smiles that always made me feel weak at the knees, even when I was sitting down. One of those smiles that said he knew me, inside out and back to front and upside down, and he loved me anyway. One of those smiles that said he knew exactly what I needed, emotionally and physically, and that he'd always be there to provide it. One of those smiles that made me feel like the luckiest woman in the world, and also made me wonder what it would be like to have one of these tiny, gooey little baby creatures of my own one day.

One of the nurses bustled into the room and cast a quick glance around at the assembled Malone and Co. masses. There were only supposed to be two visitors at a time—there were signs all over the place; we'd just chosen to ignore them—and I suspected she was about to tell us off.

Instead, her eyes drifted to me, and widened slightly in a way that told me she'd recognised me—and not as Ollie's aunty.

'Hi,' she said, 'you're Jessika, aren't you? My daughter is obsessed with you! It made her day when she saw you on telly at Christmas, knowing you were from round here.'

She picked up Becky's chart and checked it over, while I uttered my thanks. Sincere ones, as well—that was a nice thing to hear. After taking Becky's blood pressure and cooing a little over the baby, she turned back to me.

'I know you're here with your family,' she said, 'and I completely understand if you say no. But we have a lot of young mums in here, and a lot of kids visiting their new baby brothers and sisters—is there any way you could take a few minutes to visit some of the other rooms? Honestly, it'd be brilliant—they'd be so made up to meet Jessika on the day their babies were born!'

I grinned at her, and cast a glance around the crowded room. At my haggard-yet-radiant sister and the ginger genius attracting all the attention; at my mum, who looked so proud of all of us; at my dad, who I suspected was itching to get outside and start on that cigar. At Luke, who seemed to have grown a foot since I was last home and was, predictably enough, on his phone texting someone. And finally, at Daniel. At the tall, gorgeous, totally yummy, utterly supportive, majestically talented man that I'd somehow been lucky enough to get a second chance with.

Life as I knew it really couldn't be much better.

'I'd be happy to,' I said to the nurse. 'But please—don't call me Jessika. I'm just Jessy.'

Jessy was good enough for my family. Jessy was good enough for Daniel. And finally, I knew, Jessy was good enough for me.